AN UNWILLING BRIDE

"My father . . . the duke is masterminding all this," explained Lucien. "He wants you to be fully accepted by Society."

"But *I* do not want that, Lord Arden. Why don't we elope here and now and live as social outcasts?"

"Because *I* do not want that."

"And what you want will always come first, I suppose?"

He turned sharply to her. "I give you fair warning, Miss Armitage. If you persist in snapping like a spoiled brat, I am likely to treat you like one."

"If there's a spoiled brat here, it is not I, my lord." She turned, quite unaware of how the moonlight gave her rather ordinary face the purity of a della Robbia angel.

She saw him suck in a breath, then walk slowly towards her, smiling. "Perhaps, Miss Armitage, I can seduce you into willingness."

"You would assuredly fail, my lord."

She only got out a squeak before she was in his arms and his mouth covered hers . . .

An Unwilling Bride

Jo Beverley

ZEBRA BOOKS
Kensington Publishing Corp.
http://www.zebrabooks.com

ZEBRA BOOKS are published by

Kensington Publishing Corp.
850 Third Avenue
New York, NY 10022

All Kensington titles, imprints, and distributed lines are available at special quantity discounts for bulk purchases for sales
promotions, premiums, fund raising, educational, or institu-
tional use.

Special book excerpts or customized printings can also be created to fit specific needs. For details, write or phone the office
of the Kensington Special Sales Manager: Kensington Publishing Corp., 850 Third Avenue, New York, NY 10022, Attn: Special Sales Department, Phone: 1-800-221-2647.

Zebra and the Z logo Reg. U.S. Pat. & TM Off.

First Printing: February, 1992
Second Printing: December, 2000
10 9 8 7 6 5 4 3 2

Printed in the United States of America

Chapter One

"Hell and damnation."

The words were muttered rather than shouted but were sufficiently shocking to cause Gerald Westall, secretary to William de Vaux, Duke of Belcraven, to look over at his employer. The duke sat behind his massive, carved desk attending to the day's correspondence. His spectacles, only ever used for reading, were perched on his long straight nose as he reread the missive which had caused the exclamation.

Mr. Westall, a long, thin gentleman who gave the impression of being stretched—like a figure in an el Greco painting—pretended to return to his own work, but his mind was all on the duke. Had those words been a sign of shock? Or anger? No, he thought. Amazement. The young man waited impatiently for his assistance to be sought so that he would learn the cause of it all.

He was to be disappointed. The duke put down the letter and rose to walk over to one of the long windows which overlooked Belcraven Park, seat of the family for three hundred years. Fifteen years ago, to celebrate the new century, hundreds of acres surrounding the great house had been brilliantly landscaped in the picturesque style by Humphry Repton. Four years ago, as part of the grand celebrations which had marked the majority of the heir to Belcraven, the Marquess of Arden, the lake had been enlarged. At the same time it had been further improved by the addition of an island, complete with a Grecian temple from which fireworks had been exploded. It was all very beautiful, but it was familiar, and Mr. Westall's employer was not in the habit of studying his estate.

There was little to be learned from the duke's posture. He stood straight with little trace of his fifty-odd years in his lean body. His unremarkable features as usual told no secrets. The Duke of Belcraven was, in his secretary's opinion, a cold fish.

As the duke's thoughtful silence continued, Mr. Westall grew concerned. If disaster had overtaken the house of de Vaux, would he fall along with the rest?

But that was ridiculous. The duke was one of the richest men in England, and Gerald Westall was in the best position to know his employer was not given to chancy investments or gambling. Nor was his beautiful duchess.

His son, though?

Mr. Westall was not taken by Lucien Philippe de Vaux, Marquess of Arden, a Corinthian Buck who had been born in silk, as the saying goes, and feared nothing and nobody. On his rare visits to the Park, the marquess ignored Westall's existence and treated his father with a formal courtesy which was as good as an insult. The secretary pondered the strange fact that fathers and sons of high degree seemed unable to rub along. Look at the king and the Regent—before the king went mad, that is. Perhaps it was because the heir was forced to wait on the father's death for his own real life to begin, and the father was all too aware of that fact.

For once, Mr. Westall was pleased he had his own way to make in the world.

But then again, he thought, looking at the duke's cool features, it must be hard to develop fondness for a man so lacking any kind of warmth. The marquess was warm enough with his mother, who had a very sweet nature. Very close they were. Well, Arden was known to be a devil with the ladies.

The duke turned at last.

"Mr. Westall, be so good as to send a message to the duchess to request a few moments of her time."

The secretary could find no clue in his face or voice. In fact, thought Mr. Westall as he passed on the instruction to the footman stationed outside the door, a stranger would have assumed that no matter of significance troubled the duke. And yet it clearly was not so. For him to visit the duchess at this time of day was a dramatic variation of routine. The mysterious letter must be to do with their son.

The dashing marquess had probably broken his neck in one of his madcap stunts and then where would they all be? The nearest relative was a second cousin. The house of de Vaux had passed the title from father to son for two hundred years without interruption. The marquess would be no loss, but the end of such a fine tradition was worth regretting.

When the footman returned to say the duchess was available at the duke's convenience and the duke went off to break the sad news to his wife, Mr. Westall was already checking the amount of mourning stationery in his desk.

The duke was admitted to his wife's airy apartments by her dresser who then discreetly disappeared. The duchess was sitting, needlework in hand, by the light of French doors which led to a balcony. The February air was still too chill for the doors to be open, but bright sunlight spilled in to give the illusion of a later season, and daffodils and hyacinth bloomed in pots to scent the air.

The duke admired the fact that, unlike so many women of her age, his wife did not avoid clear light, and he acknowledged she had no need to. Her face announced her fifty-two years and all the smiles and tears they had contained, but that did not detract from her beauty. Silver was steadily muting her bright gold curls, but her eyes were the same clear blue and her lips were still softly curved. He was taken back to the first time he had seen her, sitting in the garden of her parents' chateau . . .

"Good morning, Belcraven," she said in her soft voice, which still retained a trace of the French which had been her childhood tongue. "You wished to speak to me?" Her expression, as always these days, was gently courteous.

He wondered if there was any chance this miracle might

mend things, but then he put such wistful thoughts away and
walked forward to hand her the letter.

"Yes, madam. Read this, if you please."

The duchess adjusted the delicate gold-rimmed pince-nez
she too was obliged to wear for fine work and concentrated
on the letter. The duke watched her reaction carefully but saw
no shock or pain, only mild surprise. When she finished she
looked up at him with a smile.

"How very silly of her not to have applied to you before,
Belcraven. What do you wish to do? I would be happy to have
the girl here. She is your daughter, and I have missed having
daughters around since Joanne was married."

The duke walked away from his wife's calm gaze and took
again to perusing his estate. How foolish of him to expect his
wife's outrage at this proof of his past infidelity, he thought.
How foolish of him to want it. Yet, he longed for something
sharp to finally break the icy shell that had encased his marriage for over twenty years.

"No," he said at last, "I do not want to bring my bastard
daughter here, madam. I intend to arrange a marriage between
her and Arden." He turned back to see his wife's reaction.

She lost the delicate color in her cheeks and seemed to age
before his eyes. "Arden? But he will not do it, Belcraven. Only
last week he wrote to say he was screwing up the resolution
to offer for the Swinnamer girl."

The duke's nostrils flared in anger. "And why did you not
tell me of this? Am I not allowed to take interest in my heir,
even if he is no son of mine?"

The duchess's pale hand rose in instinctive defense against
his accusation and then fell as she lowered her head. "No
matter what I say of Lucien, good or bad, you make a quarrel
of it. I only sought to keep the peace."

"Well," he said sharply, "you had better hope he has not
committed himself to the chit, or there'll be no peace ever
again."

Then he sighed and his face softened into weariness. He
walked over to sit in the chair facing hers. "Do you not see,
Yolande? This is the chance to put everything right, to correct

our old mistakes. If your son marries my daughter the line can continue unbroken."

The duchess's hands were clasped tightly as she looked at him. "But these are people, William. *People.* Lucien has already given his heart. How do you know this girl, this Elizabeth Armitage, has not done so, too? How do you know," she asked desperately, "that she is your daughter at all?"

He looked away from her pleading eyes. "I will have enquiries made, but I believe it. Mary Armitage was extremely honest, if rather stupid. I think that was what drew me to her when we met by chance. After—"

He had begun to turn back to her and so caught the tautness in the duchess as she prepared for the old recriminations. He broke off what he had been thoughtlessly about to say.

"She was virtuous and honest," he continued awkwardly. He was, after all, a man discussing with his wife an act of adultery. "But she also had a kind heart. I was hurt by all that had occurred and she responded to my pain. The act wounded her, though. Wounded her soul. She would take no gift, however small . . ." He rubbed his temples fretfully. "I wish she had come to me for help when she found there was to be a child, but it is typical of her that she did not. She perhaps thought to spare me an encumbrance, but more likely she wanted to put the whole relationship behind her."

The duke took the letter from his wife's fingers and looked down at the wavering handwriting of the woman who had once, so briefly, been his mistress. "Her husband was a naval officer at sea at the time we met. Mary would not have been able to pass the child off as his. She must have been able to conceal the pregnancy from her friends and family. That must be why she enlisted the help of this friend who has raised the girl."

"And on her deathbed," said the duchess softly, "she realized her contributions to her daughter's upbringing would cease and asked you to undertake that duty. A conscientious woman, but as you say, a little stupid. If the girl is your daughter, she will perhaps resemble you. What then, William?"

"I am not the type to be so strongly resembled," said the duke dryly and the duchess had to agree. His hair was dark brown and straight, a little thin now and dusted with gray; his features and build were even and without any remarkable point; his eyes were blue-gray. Even if the girl was his image, it would scarcely be noticed.

With little hope, she tried again to dissuade him. "William, this will not work. What will the world say if our son marries a nobody?"

He smiled bitterly. "One thing about *your* son, madam"—the duchess caught her breath at the pronoun—"is that no one will be surprised at anything he does."

"And if he refuses?" she asked bleakly.

The duke sat even straighter and resolve hardened his features. "Then I will disinherit him of all but the entailed property."

"No, William. You cannot!"

The vast part of the family fortune was not entailed to the oldest son. The duchess knew that without it Lucien would never be able to maintain the great houses, the multitude of servants and dependents, the state expected of a duke.

"I can and I will." The duke rose to his feet. "I inherited a faultless bloodline and I will pass it on. If Arden does not understand this obligation, then he is unworthy of his position."

The duchess rose to her feet in alarm. "You will tell him?"

The duke raised his chin. "Of course I will tell him."

Tears glimmered in her eyes. It was the first time in years the duke had seen her cry. He turned suddenly away. "I have no choice, Yolande," he said softly.

"How he will hate us."

"You should have thought of that," the duke said coldly, "before you took Guy de St. Briac to your bed." With that he left the room.

The duchess groped for her chair and collapsed into it. Fumbling, she found her handkerchief to stem her tears. Indeed, if she had been gifted with foresight, she would have avoided St. Briac like the plague.

Guy de St. Briac had been her first love though, so gay, so charming, in the prerevolutionary gardens and ballrooms of

France. Quite ineligible of course, but a heart-stealer all the same. When the duke—then the Marquess of Arden himself—had offered for her hand, Yolande de Ferrand had responded to her family's urging and accepted him. She had not been in love with him, for he was not dashing or handsome and his manner was reserved, but she had been happy with her parents' choice. She had come, quite soon, to love him in a mild sort of way; she had happily borne him four children, two of them healthy boys, William and John. Throughout those contented early years in England she had never given St. Briac a thought.

But then, as France began to disintegrate, she had met St. Briac again. . . . Ah, he had been so distraught by what was happening to their homeland; she scarcely less so by the shadows gathering over the golden world of her youth. He had *needed* her so and she had still nurtured a trace of her girlhood dreams. William's absence in Scotland shooting grouse had provided opportunity.

It had only been the once, for Guy had been en route to a new life in the Americas. Only once. And it had served to show her that her feelings for her husband were not mild at all. She had thought for a while that her sin had been a blessing and had waited impatiently for William's return to express her newfound passion for him.

If only he had not broken his leg, then perhaps he need never have known. She would not have been sure herself. By the time they could share a bed again, however, she had been forced to confess to him her action and the consequences.

He had been so kind, she remembered as she swallowed back a new flood of tears. Hurt, but kind, and moved by her declaration of the deepest kind of love. He had accepted the unborn child as others had in such a position. It was not as if the child, if a boy, would be his heir . . .

Then there had been that dreadful accident. A nurse grown careless, two naughty boys playing with a boat, the three-year-old slavishly following the five-year-old.

Drowned. Both gone.

The tears were flowing again now as she remembered that tragedy, so much greater than the death of those two darling children. It had been the death of her marriage and all happiness.

She had been in her seventh month and had prayed that in her grief she would lose the baby. When that did not happen, she had prayed throughout her labor that she would bear a daughter. To no avail.

She had wondered what she would feel when she held such a misbegotten child, but she had found only the most overwhelming love. Perhaps it was the recent tragedy, perhaps the estrangement between herself and the duke. She was certain the bond she formed instantly with her last and most beautiful baby was nothing to do with St. Briac, though the duke may not have believed that.

She had suckled him herself, the only one of her children to have taken milk from her breasts, and wished desperately that she had felt this closeness with the others. She had resolved to suckle any future children, but there had been none. From that day on the duke had never come to her bed again.

The duchess shook her head as the old ache trembled inside her. She had thought age would have solved at least this problem. Every time she saw William, however, her love swelled up inside her. Even the sound of his voice could cause her heart to race. At least he had not put her aside, though the awesome formality he had built into their lives was a monstrous barrier. One day, she told herself, his presence a few hours of every day would be enough.

One day.

She forced herself to stop that line of thought.

The duke cast no doubt on the child's parentage, but he would not give him the family names. The babe had been christened Lucien Philippe Louis after her father, her uncle and the King of France. It had been considered a touching gesture of support for the embattled French aristocracy.

She remembered how everyone had commented on God's kindness to so quickly replace what they had lost. She remembered William stonily accepting all the muted congratulations.

They had been so young. She had been twenty-seven, the

duke only thirty-one. Perhaps that was why they had been unable to handle the ruin of their lives.

Once the fuss was over, he had fled to Hartwell, the lovely small house in Surrey in which they had lived before he acceded to the title. There he had apparently sought comfort in the arms of an "honest" woman.

The duchess sighed. It was far too late to feel pain at that betrayal. Quite ridiculous too. Was the result, this Elizabeth Armitage, a blessing or a curse?

What William had hit upon *was* a solution, she supposed, but at what cost? Lucien would know what she had done. It would drive a greater wedge between him and his father. It would tie two people together in a marriage without love.

She must at least warn him.

She hurried over to her elegant escritoire and wrote a hasty explanation to her beloved son: to prepare him, to ask him to agree if at all possible, to beg his forgiveness. She rang the silver bell and a footman entered.

"I wish this note to go to the marquess in London," she said. Then, as the man turned to leave she added, "Has the duke sent a letter also, do you know?"

"I believe the duke is leaving for London at this minute, Your Grace."

The duchess turned to the window. The leafless trees and clear sunlight showed her the picture perfectly. A crested coach drawn by the six fastest horses in the stables was bowling down the driveway. She sighed.

"I do not think my letter is necessary after all," she said and took it back. When the man had withdrawn she tore it into pieces and threw it into the fire.

What would be, would be. The past twenty-five years, years without her husband's love and without hope of it, had taught her a certain resignation.

Chapter Two

That night found Lucien Philippe de Vaux, Marquess of Arden, riding a stolen horse hell-for-leather through the dark and
rain-washed streets of London. Only superb skill and strength
controlled the excited beast on the slippery cobbles. When the
drivers of startled teams cursed, he laughed, white teeth gleaming in the gaslights. When a costermonger yelled, "Bloody
nobs!" and pelted him with some of the less choice of his
wares, he caught one of the apples and shied it back to accu-
rately knock off the man's felt hat.

He reined the horse in at the Drury Lane Theater and summoned a hovering urchin. "Guard the horse and there's a
guinea for you," he called as he sprinted off towards the side
door. The main doors were already locked for the night.

The barefoot street Arab clutched onto the reins of the tired
horse as if they were his hope of heaven, as perhaps they were.

The marquess's banging on the theater door, executed as it
was with a brick he had picked up in the side alley, soon
brought the grumbling caretaker.

"Wot the 'ell ye want?" he snarled through a chink in the
door.

The marquess held up a glittering guinea and the door
opened wide.

The man grabbed the coin. "Everyone's gorn," he said. "If
it's Madam Blanche you're looking for she's off with the Mad
Marquess."

At the visitor's laugh he blinked and held his lantern a little higher. It illuminated clear-cut features and brilliant blue eyes. The fact that the marquess's distinctive gold hair was a sodden brown did not disguise him. "Beggin' yer pardon, milord. No offense."

"None taken," said the marquess blithely as he pushed past. "The White Dove of Drury Lane has left her favorite handkerchief in her room. I come as her humble servant to retrieve it. With that he sped off down the dingy corridor.

The caretaker shook his head. "Mad. Mad, the lot of 'em." He bit the guinea as a matter of habit, though he knew Arden wouldn't offer false coin.

In a few moments the young man ran nimbly back down the corridor and out into the rain, which was surely ruining a small fortune in elegant tailoring. He took the reins of the horse and pulled out another guinea. Then he hesitated, glancing down at the urchin.

"I'd be surprised if you're more than twelve," he said thoughtfully. "You'll have trouble splitting this."

It was not a problem bothering the boy, whose wide eyes were fixed on the gold.

The marquess grinned. "Don't worry. I'm not going to chouse you. How would you like to ride back with me, and I'll fix you up right and tight?"

The boy took a step back. "On the 'orse, guv?"

"Of course on the 'orse," said the marquess, leaping onto the back of the big bay. "Well?"

The boy hesitated, and the marquess impatiently said, "Make up your mind."

The boy held up his arms, and the marquess hoisted his scrawny weight behind him. "Hold tight!" he called and kicked the horse into a gallop again.

The streets were a little quieter as the theater crowd and the hawkers who catered to them had gone home. There were enough people abroad, however, to keep the ride lively and to call up comments from the marquess's nervous passenger. "Gawd's struth." "Watch it, Guv!" and—when the driver of a gig was so startled he steered his horse onto the pavement— "Wha' a slowtop."

The steaming, frothing horse was reined up at a grand mansion in a square in Mayfair far from the urchin's usual beat. The nob slipped off the horse and called back, "Watch the nag a minute!" as he raced up the wide steps. As a bell in a nearby church began to chime the hour, huge double doors at the top were flung open to greet him, spilling glittering light down the wet stone steps.

A delicate vision in white—white from her loose silver hair to a flowing lace gown to white slippers—flung out her arms and cried, "You did it! You did it! I knew you could." The marquess gathered her up and swung her around as she squealed at how wet he was.

As his debtor went into the house, the street Arab heard him laugh and say, "To the devil with your gown. I prefer you without one anyway. Where's Dare?" The big doors closed on the light.

The boy, who went by the name of Sparrow, or Sparra more like, shivered in the chilly damp. "Scummered for sure," he muttered. "Left perched on the back of a soddin' horse. Thank Gawd the beast's too shagged to move." It was a long way down to the ground.

After a while, though, when the horse showed signs of coming back to life, the boy chose the lesser of the evils. Grasping the pommel, he slid down, falling flat in a puddle when he landed. The horse looked around in mild affront.

" 'S'alright fer yous," Sparra muttered as he rubbed at the slimy mud on his already wet and dirty rags. "Sooner nor later summen'll rub yer darn, give yer a feed. They cares for their 'orses, does this lot. I should've grabbed the bloody goldfinch."

He looked the horse over to see if there was anything worth nicking.

Just at that moment thick fingers yanked at his grubby collar, and he was hauled around to face a burly giant of a man. "What are you doing with my horse, you devil's spawn?"

"I—I—" Sparra was half-throttled and scared out of his wits. He kicked and wriggled, but the man's hand was like a vice.

"I'll teach you to take a gentleman's mount, you wretched cur," snarled the man, and swung his riding crop down on Sparra's body.

"Ow! Please, guv . . . Aah!" The crop whistled and cut again and again.

A cool voice broke in. "I hardly think this is the place to correct an erring servant, sir."

The man stopped the beating but held on tight to his captive. "And who the devil are you, sir? And what business is it of yours what I do?"

The newcomer had obviously just arrived in a handsome traveling chariot. Everything about him spoke of top quality, Sparra decided with a beggar's unerring eye. Not just his perfectly cut caped greatcoat and his gleaming boots, his elegant beaver and tan gloves, but the way he stood and the softness of his voice.

A powdered footman stood behind him shielding him from the elements with a large black umbrella.

"I am the Duke of Belcraven, sir," the newcomer said, "and this is my house which you are disturbing with your brawl."

Sparra wished he could see the bully's face at that. He also wished the man would loosen his grip, instead of making it tighter. Then he could get out of here—fast. He wanted nothing to do with dukes, and horse-stealing got you knocked down for a crop.

"I beg pardon, Your Grace," said the man in a strained voice. "I was taking retribution on this wretch for having ridden off on my horse, which I left quietly hereabouts."

The duke raised an eyeglass and studied the horse, a large beast as would be necessary for such a large rider. Then he looked at the culprit.

"If he truly rode that horse into such a state," he said coolly, "I suggest you spare him the beating and promptly hire him as a jockey."

Sparra imagined a lifetime of being forced to ride enormous horses and tried to choke out an objection. The hand on his collar jerked him into silence.

At that moment, the doors of the great house opened again and a clear voice said, "What the hell—? Release the boy!"

Then, in a different tone, drained of all emotion. "Your Grace. I did not expect you."

The duke turned his eyeglass to look up the stairs, carpeted again in slick golden light. There Sparra's debtor stood against a backdrop of servants and gentlemen, with one petite lady in white beside him. The lady swiftly melted back out of sight. After a breathless moment, the duke let his quizzing glass fall and mounted the steps towards his heir, meticulously followed by his umbrella bearer.

"Evidently," he said icily. "If that is your fracas, Arden, kindly remove it from the doorstep."

He then entered his mansion and accepted the ministrations of his servants, forced to switch abruptly from the lighthearted demeanor suitable for the marquess and his friends, to the proper decorum demanded by the duke. The guests discreetly absented themselves from the hall but within minutes singing could be heard from the music room. It was not a particularly respectable song.

As the duke was divested of his damp outer clothing he merely said, "I will retire to my suite with a light supper. Arden, I wish to see you tomorrow after breakfast."

"Yes, sir," said the marquess impassively.

Followed by his valet, the duke ascended the great curving staircase.

The marquess watched his father for a moment, then looked out at the frozen, rain-soaked tableau, where the urchin was still clutched by the dumbfounded horse owner. With a shrug, he accepted the need to ruin another set of clothes and walked out into the rain as easily as if it were perfect weather.

"You will release this boy immediately," he said coldly.

"Oh will I?" sneered the man, misled perhaps by the marquess's dampened finery and the way he had been given orders by the duke. "Well, cockerel, this boy deserves a whipping and he'll get it, and no duke's lackey says otherwise."

"Lay a stroke on the boy and I'll take you apart," said the marquess calmly. *"I stole your horse."*

The man released Sparra, but before the boy could flee he was caught in a grasp just as strong.

"Don't run away," was all the young nob said, but Sparra obeyed. He wasn't sure if it was fear, exhaustion, or just a trust engendered by that voice, but he did as he was told. He witnessed a grand mill.

The "young guv" was tall and strong and probably sparred with Jackson, but the "big guv" was a lot heavier and had some science, too. Once he landed a sweeping right which sent the younger man sprawling, but he was up on his feet in a moment and retaliated with a hard fist to the fat stomach.

By this time half a dozen young sprigs were out in the rain cheering on their friend, and a couple of passersby were giving advice, too. Sparra had never seen such a bunch of drowned swells. It'd be a grand day for the tailors tomorrow, he thought. He hoped the young guv didn't get so bashed up he forgot the dibs.

No danger of that. It became obvious the young man had just been sparring. Despite the hard blows swung at him, he had only been touched that once. Now he began to show his skill, and in a few moves he destroyed the bigger man's guard and landed him an annihilating left hook which laid him out cold.

Sparra's debtor surveyed his opponent and rubbed wincingly at his knuckles. "Repellent specimen. I would happily have paid for the use of his horse." He fished out a few guineas. "Here, someone put that in his pocket."

His friends showed every sign of sweeping him back into the house, but he pulled away. "Where's the lad?"

A glimmer of hope in his breast, Sparra came forward, and the swell studied him. Not ungently he lifted Sparra's tattered shirt and grimaced at the welts there.

"It's nuthin' much, guv," Sparra told him.

"Nevertheless, I owe you something extra for being my whipping boy, don't I? Do you have a home to go to?"

This was a question Sparra had to consider. He had a place in an alley with some other ragamuffins. "I 'as a place t'sleep," he muttered.

"What I mean is, do you have a family who would be missing you?"

"Nah, guv. Me mam died."

"Then spend the night with the grooms in the mews. I'll see you get a good meal and some warm clothing, and tomorrow we'll talk. I really am rather stretched at the moment."

"Aye," said the boy sympathetically, responding to the easy manner of the other. "That duke. He yer gaffer?"

"My master?" The swell gave a twisted smile. "Yes, I suppose he is. Marleigh!" he called out, and the butler stuck his head out the door.

"Your lordship?"

"Send one of the grooms to collect this child. What's your name, boy?"

"Sparra, yer lordship," said the urchin, much awed. "Beggin' yer pardon if'n I bin rude, yer lordship."

"Don't start to toad-eat, little bird," said the swell as he turned away "It's the one thing I will not stand for."

Then he ran up the steps again, followed by his herd of friends. The big doors shut again on the light.

Sparra wondered whether to make himself scarce, forget about the goldfinch. Dukes, lords—such types didn't shine right for kids from Figger's Lane.

Before he could decide, a sturdy boy some years his senior came up the basement stairs.

"You the one as is to be taken in?" he asked with great superiority.

"Yus," muttered Sparra.

The older boy looked him over, then his face relaxed a bit. "Never know what's next with Arden. Don't look so nervous, lad. It's a good house, even when the duke's here and we have to watch it. Come on then."

As they went down the stairs towards the warm lights of the kitchen, Sparra asked, "If this is the duke's 'ouse, 'ow come the young'un can bring me in?"

" 'Cause he's his son. One day this'll all be his anyway. That's not to say he won't catch it for creating such a stir in the street. The duke's the only one Arden looks out for."

Even at this late hour Belcraven House was ready for unexpected guests, both above and below stairs. As the French chef whipped together a hasty gourmet meal for the duke, he served up a bowl of soup and a slab of bread covered with thick butter to Sparra, though Sparra was forced to sit on the floor in the scullery to eat it. After one horrified glance, the chef had banished the ragamuffin boy from the kitchen.

Sparra didn't much care. This was as close to heaven as he could remember. As he slurped up the rich soup with whole chunks of meat in it, he wondered if there was anything he could do to save his benefactor from tomorrow's reckoning. He was still pondering this when he rolled himself in two dry blankets and settled down in a cozy corner of the stables. He was soon asleep, comfortable and well-fed for the first time since his mother died.

The next morning the marquess awoke with a sense of resignation instead of his usual zest for life. Whatever his father's reason for this unannounced visit to Town it augured poorly for himself. As his valet shaved him, Arden wondered why he could never get along with his father. He admired him tremendously, but whenever they were together they were like flint and steel. The slightest tinder and a conflagration would result.

It was damnable luck that the duke had turned up during a scene. Lord Darius Debenham—commonly called Dare—had laid a monkey that the marquess couldn't make it to Drury Lane and back with Blanche's handkerchief before midnight. The marquess never refused a bet. That blasted man's horse had been none the worse for the experience. Probably never had a good run before.

That reminded him.

"Hughes, how's that boy?" he asked, as he began to arrange a black cravat around his high collar. It should suit the mood of the day.

"He seems very happy with his situation, milord," said the valet. "In fact, if I may be so bold, it would be harsh to return him to his previous existence after showing him a taste of a reasonable life."

The marquess lowered his neck carefully to produce the correct creases for a Mathematical. "The devil you say. What the hell am I supposed to do with him?"

"I'm sure some position could be found, milord. The staff find him quite bearable, given his upbringing. Didn't complain much at having a bath, said please and thank you, and asked what he could do to help."

"A regular little gentleman, in fact. Oh well, I'll think about it after I've seen my father."

The marquess was eased into his dark blue jacket and stood before the mirror to consider the effect. "Think it'll turn my father up sweet?" he asked Hughes dryly.

"Any father would be proud of such a son," said Hughes and indeed, he thought, it was true.

The marquess had his father's height—over six feet but with more muscle than the duke. Not a heavy man but broad in the shoulders and with the strong legs of a bruising rider. And of course he had his mother's looks in a masculine way—the fine lines of the bones and a curve on his mouth a girl would envy. He had the duchess's golden curls, too.

The marquess was a delight to dress. His fawn pantaloons showed off his legs a treat and the blue superfine jacket was creaseless across his straight shoulders. The ivory silk waistcoat and three fobs was just the right touch. Yes, the duke would find nothing at which to cavil.

Whatever Hughes's opinion, the marquess found no approval on the duke's face when he presented himself in his father's study. The duke and the duchess kept separate suites in the house, and these rooms were always prepared for their occasional visits. The rest of the house was given over to their son's use.

The duke was seated in a wing chair by the fireplace.

"Good morning, sir," said the marquess, trying to read his father. He did not presume to take a seat.

The duke looked his son up and down, and though the marquess knew he was perfectly turned out, he was made to feel grubby.

"You will please explain what was happening when I arrived last night, Arden."

The marquess did his best. His racing feat was not admired.

"Is the actress your mistress?"

"Yes, sir."

"Do not bring her, or her successors, to this house again."

The marquess stiffened, but it was in acknowledgement of the justice of the reprimand. "Very well. I apologize, sir."

The duke inclined his head slightly. "And the boy?"

"He appears to have found favor with the servants, sir. I thought to find him a place."

The duke inclined his head again. "I understand you still owe him a guinea. I am sure you honor your debts."

The marquess marveled that the duke always seemed to know what was going on. There was, however, the slightest possible lightening of his father's expression. "Of course, sir."

The disciplinary part of the interview was apparently over. The marquess felt the tension seep out of him. Whatever had brought the duke to London so unexpectedly was obviously not to be laid at his door.

"Sit down, Arden. I have something to discuss with you."

As the marquess took the opposing wing chair he detected something in his father's voice which led him to another concern. "I hope *Maman* is well," he said.

"Completely."

Despite the reassuring reply, the duke's untypical uneasiness worried the marquess considerably. He felt an alarming need to fiddle with his cravat or cross and uncross his legs. This elegant room, with its rich gold brocade curtains and Chinese carpet, held no particularly unpleasant memories, but the duke carried the atmosphere with him. Wherever their meetings took place Lucien de Vaux felt as if he were back in his father's formidable study at Belcraven Park quivering under a caustic tongue-lashing or stoically listening as his tutor was instructed as to the number of strokes his latest escapade warranted.

He had always preferred the latter. The system had been

quite clear to him from an early age. Beatings were rarely harsh and were reserved for the kind of mischief common to boys. The sting carried the message that he had done something of which his father disapproved but which did not seriously distress him.

A dressing down by his father was an indication that he had fallen below the standards of the de Vaux, that his father was ashamed of his son and heir. Arden had frequently wept.

Why did this occasion recall those painful times when it was clear the duke was not angry?

Eventually the duke broke the silence. "There is no way to dress this up with ribbons and bows, Arden, but I'm not sure in which order the news will be easiest." He fixed his heir with a direct look. "I have to tell you that you are not my son."

The shock was total. "You are *disinheriting* me? For God's sake, why?"

"No!" said the duke. "The very opposite. I have known since your birth that you are not my son."

Icy shock was replaced by hot fury, and the marquess shot to his feet. "You slander my mother!"

"Don't be ridiculous," said the duke wearily. "I am as tender of the duchess's reputation as you. Ask her if you wish. It is the truth. The briefest indiscretion with a childhood sweetheart . . ."

The marquess saw the old pain in his father—no, not his father. . . .

The world shifted around him, and he grasped the back of the chair by which he stood. His heart was thundering in his chest. It seemed an effort to breath. Surely grown men did not faint . . .

He heard the duke as if over a vast chasm. "It happened when I was in Scotland after grouse. I broke my leg. There was no question of my having fathered you."

His father would not lie. His father . . . this man sitting rigidly before him, had always been truthful, if cold. So much, so much was explained. The marquess felt as if his heart had been ripped out of his body. It was a draining effort, but he focused on essentials. "Why did you acknowledge me?"

The duke shrugged, not looking at him at all. "There were two sons already. It happens in every family now and then, and I loved your mother deeply. She would never willingly have parted with a child." He flicked a glance at his heir and then looked away quickly, paler still. "Then there was the accident and she was near her time. We could have pretended the child had died, I suppose. I have wondered . . . but it would have destroyed her." He sighed heavily. "She clung to you as to none of her other babes. It was not a time of rational thinking."

The marquess felt things begin to settle, to settle into a new and darker world. He looked down and saw his hands were bone white where they gripped the chair. He was quite unable to relax them. "What you are saying," he said, seeking in coldness a mask for the fury of hurt burning within him, "is that you have since wished me out of existence."

He looked up. The duke met his eyes firmly, but there was a whiteness about his mouth. "I have wished, and still wish, the de Vaux bloodline to continue unbroken."

It seemed the most difficult thing he had ever done in his life, but the marquess drew himself up and assumed the grand manner to which he had been so carefully raised. "I understand you, I think, sir. Do you wish me to shoot myself perhaps? Or shall I just flee to the New World under an assumed name? I fail to see how that will gain you a de Vaux heir, though. Or is *Maman* . . . ?" He broke off in incredulity.

"Of course she's too old, Arden," said the duke sharply. "Stop emoting. I do not wish to disinherit you or dispose of you. I just wish to God you were my son." The duke stopped on that admission. After a moment he said, "Now, however, I wish you to marry my daughter."

The marquess gave up and collapsed into his chair. "That idiot last night must have hit me harder than I thought," he muttered. Or perhaps it was just shock which made his head float apart from his body, his thoughts seem like wisps of mist. One thought could be grasped, however. He had been reprieved, after a fashion. Like a man sentenced to hang who finds he is merely to be flogged.

The duke rose and poured two glasses of brandy. He thrust one into the marquess's hand and sat once more. "Drink that and pay attention, Arden."

The fiery liquid flowed down and drove the mist from his brain. The pain of reality returned, but the marquess forced his body to come to order, and prepared to try to make sense of things.

"After your birth, Arden, I was under considerable strain. . . . I myself formed a liaison and, unbeknownst to me, a child resulted. I received news of the girl's existence this morning. She has the de Vaux blood, though no one, now her mother is dead, knows of it except us. If you marry her, the line continues."

Stupidly, the marquess could only think that his father had betrayed his exquisite mother. "I have a better idea," he said bitterly. "Make *her* your heir."

The duke's voice was as chilly as a dash of cold water. "You are being nonsensical again. Are you refusing to do this?"

In his pain, with his devastated pride, the marquess longed to do just that, to throw the whole business in the duke's face and tell him to go to hell and take his bastard with him. But the pride of the de Vaux was in him, no matter how little it seemed he deserved it, and he struggled for an icy control to match the duke's.

"Do we know anything at all of this girl?" he drawled.

"Her age. She is just turned twenty-four, nearly a year younger than you."

"Firmly on the shelf, in other words," observed the marquess coolly. "She's doubtless an antidote."

"Is that your primary consideration?"

"It seems natural enough to wish to share one's life with a woman one finds congenial," remarked the marquess flippantly. "Where does my bride live?"

"In Cheltenham. She is a teacher at a ladies seminary run by a Miss Mallory, who is an old friend of the girl's mother."

"A blue stocking antidote. Oh well," said the marquess with

an assumption of callous indifference, "we must hope that, unlike Prinny, I can do my duty."

"Even the prince begot a daughter," the duke pointed out.

"But that, as we know, is of no use to us." The marquess could endure this discussion no longer. He did not know. whether he was likely to strike his father—the duke—or fall weeping at his feet, but neither was desirable. He rose to his feet with control but did not meet the other man's eyes. "Is there more to be discussed? I have engagements."

"I am having enquiries made about the girl. I only traveled down with urgency because your mother said you might offer for the Swinnamer girl."

A pretty china doll who he had begun to think would do as well as any other for marriage. "I assure you I have given up the notion entirely," said the marquess carelessly, then realized he was shredding a tassel on the chair by which he stood.

"Are you claiming a broken heart?" asked the duke. "What then of Mistress Blanche?"

The marquess crushed the tassel in his fist. "Men have these arrangements," he said bitterly and looked up to meet the duke's eyes. "Surely you are aware of it, My Lord Duke."

With that he turned on his heel and escaped.

The duke sighed and rubbed a hand over his eyes. He had never expected the interview to be pleasant. He was sorry, though, for the pain he had caused the boy. He had spoken the truth when he said he wished the marquess was his own son. He would have been proud.

He was wild, yes, a touch of St. Briac the duke did not appreciate, but nothing had ever besmirched his honor, and he had a keen brain. The duke had no qualms about passing the tremendous burdens of the Duchy of Belcraven over to Lucien one day.

If only, he thought—and not for the first time—he had never known. How happy they could all have been.

The dull ache of the long separation from Yolande was a chronic pain, but what else could he have done? He could not risk getting another son, for then the temptation to do just as Lucien had suggested—get rid of him in some way—would have been overwhelming. Yolande would never have stood for that, but he could never have let his rightful heir take second place to a usurper.

He sighed and hoped for the first time that Elizabeth Armitage turned out to be of a quality to compensate Arden in some way for all of this.

The marquess walked down the wide, curving staircase of his house—to which he apparently had no right—took his cane, his beaver, and his gloves from a footman, and passed through the doors into the May sunshine. His long-limbed strides took him along the streets, but he really had no idea where to go.

To stay in the house would be unbearable. To go to a club insupportable—he did not wish to meet any of his friends.

No, that wasn't quite true. He wished Nicholas Delaney and his wife Eleanor were here in Town. He could talk to them. But they were in Somerset enjoying each other and their new baby. He was tempted to flee to their house as he had fled once before . . . but that had merely been in flight from Phoebe Swinnamer's matchmaking mama, not from the total destruction of his life, of his very self.

Poor Phoebe. She believed her beauty entitled her to the prize of the Marriage Mart. Would she ever realize how close she had come to achieving her ambition?

He had dodged Phoebe, but he couldn't dodge this new trap. As he apparently had no right at all to his rank and privilege, the least he could do was pay for it through sacrifice.

Eventually he found his aimless strides had brought him to a quiet street of small houses. He sighed with relief.

Blanche.

She wouldn't expect him at this hour and so he used the knocker. He didn't believe Blanche would play him false by taking another lover, but if she had, he didn't want to know—he didn't need any more shocks today. He was admitted by her startled maid and in a moment the White Dove was with him.

"Lucien, love," she said, her carefully trained voice still having a slight northern burr. "What brings you here so early?" Despite the question she was already in his arms and studying him. "Are you in trouble, my dear?"

The marquess looked down at her perfect heart-shaped face and her amazing silvery hair, for she was prematurely gray and had turned it to her trademark, and sighed. "I just need a friend, Blanche."

Smiling, she led him to a sofa. "You have one. How can I help?" She brushed golden curls off his forehead with gentle fingers. "Is it your father? Is he very cross? I told you you shouldn't have taken me there."

"You were right." He captured her hand and kissed it. "Will you mind?"

"Don't be daft," she said with a cheeky smile and the accent of her native Manchester. "I've no silly expectations, Lucien. You treat me with respect and that's all I ask. Is that the problem then?"

He lay back and sighed. "No. No, it isn't, sweetheart. But I can't tell you what is. I just need peace and quiet to think something through."

"And you're a bit tight for empty rooms at home," she said understandingly, gaining the laugh she sought, even if it was strained.

He drew her into a friendly hug. "I should have married you," he said, and she chuckled at the joke.

"Lummox. Is that it?" she asked. "Has the Swinnamer girl turned you down?"

"No. Stop asking questions."

She obediently lapsed into silence and rested in his comfortable embrace. She knew there were times when just to have someone nearby was a comfort, and she would give him any comfort she could. In a very real way she loved Lucien de Vaux, but she was three years older than him in age and a century older in experience. She knew better than to let her heart rule her head. The marquess paid her well and she gave what he paid for and more. One day it would end and that was how it should be.

With Blanche soft and perfumed in his arms, Lucien passed

the brief interview with his father—no, the duke—through his mind again and again. Could he not have softened it in some way? It was not news amenable to softening.

So much now clicked into place, such as the formality of his parents' lives despite suggestions of deep feeling. Had his father never forgiven his mother? His words had been gentle this morning and yet the evidence was that they had been estranged for over twenty years. Lucien had always hoped it was just an appearance of formality and that in private they behaved otherwise.

He did not know how he was to face either of them again.

He understood at last the duke's attitude toward himself, why he had never been able to gain the warmth, the approval he sought. His father had chastised or commended him as appropriate but always in the impersonal manner of a guardian. He supposed, given the situation, the duke had been very good to him.

And now he must repay that goodness. It was his duty to make this marriage—though it would feel incestuous and be a mismatched union of the highest order—and produce the male heirs to ensure the line. Then perhaps, he thought bleakly, he could shoot himself.

Blanche was beginning to feel stiff. She stirred a little. "Would you like some wine, Lucien? Or tea?"

He sat up with her and kissed her lightly. "Wine, please. And perhaps some food? I skipped breakfast."

His manner was much like his normal high spirits and yet she could see the strain behind it and ached for him.

"Of course, love," she twinkled. "After all, you pay the grocer."

He grinned. "So I do. And also the jeweler. When I've fortified myself, I'm going to go and buy you more diamonds. Unless I can tempt you to sapphires?"

"And ruin my act?" she protested. "The day the White Dove wears any color I'll be over and done with. I saw some pretty hair pins in the Burlington Arcade."

"Consider them yours," he said. "You are a treasure, Blanche. You would make a man a wonderful wife."

His mind seemed to be fixed on wives. Blanche gave him a saucy look. "Isn't it nice of me then to spread it around a bit?"

He broke out laughing and it was as close to the carefree marquess as she could hope to get.

Chapter Three

The other party to all this, Miss Beth Armitage, had her mind firmly fixed on international problems by the time the de Vaux family came to her notice. March of 1815 had been made notable by the dreadful news that the Corsican Monster, Napoleon Bonaparte, had left his exile on Elba and returned to France. Now, in April, the news was no better.

Miss Mallory's School for Ladies followed, in a modified form, the educational precepts of Emma Mallory's idol, Mary Wollstonecraft. The girls were taught a wide range of subjects, including Latin and science; they were encouraged to take vigorous daily exercise; and they were obliged to keep informed as to the affairs of the day.

No trouble these days holding the girls' attention with the daily reading of the newspaper. Napoleon Bonaparte had been the scourge of Europe all their lives and now, when they had thought him a matter only for the history books, he was back. Many of the girls had fathers or brothers in the army, or recently sold out. The older girls, at least, understood the implications. The events were discussed with all the enthusiasm a teacher could desire.

At first they had thought Napoleon's return to France the act of an utter madman, but the news worsened day by day. Fat King Louis XVIII had made himself unpopular and the ex-emperor was being greeted with enthusiasm by the French people. The armies sent to oppose him were instead pledging allegiance at such a rate that Napoleon was reputed to have sent the Bourbon king a note saying, "My Good Brother, there is no need to send any more troops. I already have enough."

Louis le Gros had fled the country and Napoleon was once more in the Tuileries.

When, one Tuesday morning, Beth was summoned away from her class of little ones to Miss Mallory's yellow parlor, she could only think of international disasters. Invasion, even.

A good schoolmistress never shows alarm before her pupils. She took time to rearrange the embroidery in Susan Digby's hands for the twentieth time and to reassure sweet little Deborah Crawley-Foster that her papa would not mind a few bloodstains on the first handkerchief she had monogrammed for him. She remembered with a pang that Deborah's father was Colonel Crawley-Foster; Bonaparte's return might mean more than a few spots of blood.

Consumed with impatience she left Clarissa Greystone, the senior girl who had brought the message, to cope with further problems and walked briskly through the school.

It was almost unheard of for Aunt Emma to call her from a class, but Beth began to think she was foolish to imagine political emergencies. Even if Bonaparte were marching on London there was nothing Beth Armitage could do to prevent it. It was more likely some problem with a pupil, perhaps an anxious parent. The only pupil she thought might have a problem, however, was Clarissa Greystone, who had been unusually subdued of late.

Of course the girl had hoped to leave school this year and go to London for the Season. Clarissa had been very unhappy when it became clear that the family fortunes were straitened and her debut would have to be postponed. The tears occasioned by that news had been months ago, however, and it was only in the past fortnight that the girl had seemed withdrawn, ever since a parental visit.

Beth was puzzling over this matter when she arrived at the front hall. This was elegantly appointed with a rich carpet runner on the polished oak floor and gleaming modern furnishings. It was, after all, the first impression given to the parent of a prospective pupil.

Beth stopped before the large mirror hanging over a mahogany half-table and straightened her formal cap, tucking a
stray brown curl back under it. To hold her position in the
school in which she had recently been a pupil she found it
useful to adopt severity.

She stepped back to make sure her gray wool round gown
hung smoothly from the high waistband and that no grubby
or bloody fingers had marred it. Satisfied that Aunt Emma
would have no cause to blush for her, she stepped over to
scratch at the parlor door.

When she entered she decided it *was* a parental matter,
though she did not know the man who had risen upon her
entrance. He was, she supposed, middle-aged, but had none of
the vagueness of that description. He was tall, slim, and elegant, with thinning, well-cut hair touched with silver at the
sides, and very regular features. He was, however, studying
her with more attention than was polite. Beth raised her chin
slightly.

"Your Grace," said Miss Mallory in an odd voice, "allow
me to present Miss Elizabeth Armitage. Miss Armitage, this
is the Duke of Belcraven who wishes to speak with you."

Beth dropped a curtsy but did not attempt to conceal her
astonishment. She had never heard of the Duke of Belcraven
and was sure there had been no daughters of that house in the
school in her time.

The duke was still inclined to stare and with something of
a disapproving frown in it. Beth returned the look. She did
not believe in kowtowing to the aristocracy, particularly if they
were not parents of Miss Mallory's pupils.

The man turned to the older woman. "I wish to speak to
Miss Armitage alone, Miss Mallory."

"That would be most improper, Your Grace," said that lady
with immense dignity. She, too, was not one to grovel before
the idle rich.

"I have no designs on Miss Armitage's virtue, ma'am," he
said dryly. "I merely wish to discuss some private matters.
Whether she shares them with you afterwards will be at her

discretion." The tone was mild, but it was clear the duke was not used to having his wishes questioned.

Miss Mallory gave in. Despite her egalitarian principles, she was a businesswoman, and it was no light matter to offend a duke. "I will leave the decision to Miss Armitage, then," she said at last.

Under two pairs of eyes, Beth was not about to admit to any qualms about being alone with a quite elderly gentleman. Her principles were based on the writings of Mary Wollstone-craft—author of *The Rights of Man* and *The Rights of Woman*. She did not allow her behavior to be circumscribed by useless restrictions on the freedom of women.

"I have no objection," she said calmly, and waited as her "aunt" left the room.

"Please sit down," said the duke as he resumed his own seat. "What I have to say to you, Miss Armitage, will seem incredible and perhaps alarming. I hope you will restrain any tendency to become emotional."

Visions of a Napoleonic invasion flashed into Beth's mind again, for she could imagine nothing else which would be so distressing. But that was to be ridiculous. He was doubtless the sort to think that a woman will throw fits over every little thing. As she sat down—back straight, head high, hands in lap—Beth met his eyes, determined to prove otherwise. "I always restrain any tendency to become emotional," she said clearly.

"Do you?" asked the duke with what appeared to be genuine, if uneasy, fascination.

"Yes, Your Grace. Excessive emotions are tiresome for all concerned, and in a school for young ladies they are all too common."

For some reason this very reasonable point of view seemed to take the duke aback, and he started frowning at her again.

"You did say, Your Grace, that you did not want emotionalism?" Beth queried, not above needling a little.

"Not exactly, my dear," he said mildly. "I requested you to restrain your emotions, but I did not wish you without them altogether."

This conversation seemed to Beth to be a waste of her valuable time. "Well then, Your Grace," she said tartly, "consider them restrained. You are not likely to know the difference."

A smile twitched his lips and to her astonishment he said, "I like you, my dear. More than my . . . my other daughters."

Beth frowned in puzzlement. "Other daughters? You have a daughter here, Your Grace? I was not aware of it."

"You are my daughter."

The words created their own tribute of silence.

After a few heartbeats so noticeable she could have counted them, Beth straightened to look directly at him. She had wondered whether this moment would ever occur. Her tone was icy when she responded. "You do not, I hope, expect me to greet you with filial delight."

He paled. "I never knew of your existence until a few weeks ago, my dear."

Despite her earlier comments, Beth found herself in danger of excessive emotion. Fierce anger was stirring in her, but she struggled to remain cool. "I would prefer that you not use any familiarity or endearment with me, Your Grace.

Beth knew nothing of her mother except that Miss Mallory had once been her friend, but she had firm opinions on men who were careless with their progeny.

"So, you are not prepared to like me," said the duke coolly, relaxing back into his chair and crossing one leg over the other. "As you wish. Do you question the relationship?"

"I must," said Beth equally coolly, though she was rather put out by his acceptance of her hostility. She had expected more attempts at fondness, attempts she would have taken pleasure in spurning. "Though, as you do not seem to be in search of a devoted daughter to minister to your old age, it is difficult to imagine what could make you lay such a claim without cause."

"Precisely," said the duke. "It is a pleasure to deal with a rational woman." His words, which would normally have pleased her, irritated Beth almost beyond bearing.

"If you will read this letter," he continued, "it will provide some evidence. You may then wish to seek further confirmation as to your mother's identity from Miss Mallory."

Beth took the letter reluctantly. She had thought she had long ago come to terms with her irregular origins and accepted the absence of parents. This sudden eruption of them was proving painful.

She read the letter slowly and found emotion again threatening her composure. Bitterness. This was the first thing she had ever touched of her mother's, and the woman was now dead. The tone showed clearly that Mary Armitage had always regarded her daughter as a burden and a duty. There was no affection, no longing in the letter at all.

Beth pretended to read long after the letter was finished, needing time to come to terms with it all. "Even if I am this woman's daughter, Your Grace," she said at last, "how can you be sure you are the father?"

"Because of the woman she was," the duke said gently. "She was virtuous, and if you detect coldness in that letter it is only because you represented a constant reminder of a fall from grace. When we know one another better—"

"I do not wish that!" It was intolerable that this man read her heart like an open book.

The duke carried on. "When we know one another better, you may wish to ask me more of her and I will tell you."

"I repeat," said Beth fiercely, "I want *nothing* to do with you, Your Grace. If you think to acknowledge me and dress me in silk and jewels, be clear there is nothing I want less!"

"I am afraid at least some silk and jewels may be necessary." He smiled slightly, which made Beth inclined to throw a very untypical tantrum.

She rose swiftly to her feet. "You are not *listening* to me."

"On the contrary, Elizabeth, *you* are not listening to me," he said calmly. "Silk and jewels have a place at a wedding and that is what I intend for you."

Beth drew herself up and assumed what she hoped was an annihilating sneer. "Of course you believe that all women seek only a husband. Well, My Lord Duke, I am a follower of Mary

Wollstonecraft, and I believe a woman can and should live free of the shackles of matrimony and male domination."

He reflected none of the outrage she had expected and hoped for. In fact, to her fury, he seemed to find some amusement in her words, though he replied to them seriously enough. "But even she, in the end, married to give respectability to her child. Could you not do the same? I would have thought you aware of the problems inherent in illegitimacy."

Beth could feel herself coloring and hated him for it. Her lively discussions with Miss Mallory and a few other like-minded souls had not prepared her for this confrontation with a worldly and sophisticated man. "Since I do not intend to have children," she said awkwardly, "the matter will not arise."

"But I intend you to have children, Elizabeth, and I am afraid it is necessary that they be born in wedlock."

The conversation had drifted so far beyond any previous experience that Beth was forced to resume her seat and say weakly, "I do not understand you."

"That, I must point out, is because you have not given me sufficient opportunity to explain, choosing instead to indulge in emotionalism."

Beth gasped in outrage.

"If," the duke continued, "you will calmly listen, I am willing to attempt to clarify matters."

Beth resisted an astonishing urge to throw something at him. She had never been inclined to tempestuous behavior. With considerable effort she assumed an air of icy indifference. "Please do so, Your Grace. Presumably you will be the sooner gone. I am afraid you are mad."

"That would be unfortunate, Elizabeth, as such things are often inherited." Beth stiffened, and the duke broke off and raised a hand in a fencing gesture. A sweet smile lightened his face. "I apologize. You seem to have the ability to stir me to goading you. I foresee interesting times. . . . No. Don't poker up again. Listen."

Beth shut her mouth hard on her words. The less she argued the quicker it would be over. He could offer her nothing to tempt her to join the ranks of the decadent, idle rich. Nothing.

"You are, without doubt, my daughter. I have two others who are married with children of their own. I had three sons. The oldest two were drowned many years ago, and the last, my heir, the Marquess of Arden, is not, in fact, mine."

He paused as if to give her the opportunity to comment on the morals of the aristocracy. She was tempted but judged it wiser to maintain her silence.

"The blood of the de Vaux," he continued, "has run pure through seven generations to the best of everyone's knowledge. I am reluctant to break that heritage. Your children would be its continuance."

Beth frowned slightly, "But so are the children of your . . . your other daughters."

"But they cannot inherit the title. I intend you to marry my son, so that his sons will be true heirs."

"But that is incest," she said in horror.

"No. There is no blood tie between you, and no one need ever know that you are my child."

Beth stared at him. "You cannot seriously expect me to agree to this. I understand your motives, though they are based on outmoded aristocratic pride, but they are no concern of mine."

"I acknowledge that," said the duke calmly. "I am afraid I am going to have to be crude. I had hoped you would be sufficiently attracted by the life of wealth and elegance before you to need little persuasion, but I can see that is not so. I admire your principles, Elizabeth, but I cannot allow them to stand in the way of my purpose. I have to say, therefore, that you should not underrate the power of the outmoded aristocracy. Miss Mallory has mortgages on this establishment and they are now in my hands. The amounts are modest and the lady will be able to meet her debts if the school continues to prosper. If, however, unfortunate rumors were to circulate about libertarian principles, moral laxity—"

"That is unfair!" said Beth, shocked. "Our principles are our own and are only disseminated in the school to the mildest degree."

"I know that. I am merely giving you fair warning of the

kinds of weapons I can use to force your compliance. If that one fails I have others. A word from me to the parents of your pupils and Miss Mallory would be ruined. You will do my will, Elizabeth."

Beth was so stunned she was trembling. She had always prided herself that she was free of being any man's chattel. She had rejoiced in her illegitimacy which made her no man's daughter. Now, suddenly, she was under the iron fist with no recourse.

"I am sorry to have to distress you," said the duke, and he appeared sincere. "I admire you and have no desire to break your spirit. But you must do as I say."

"And that is not to break my spirit?" Beth whispered.

"It is one reverse. It is a poor soul that cannot weather one reverse. I demand that you marry my heir, live in his house, and bear his children. I insist on nothing more."

"You merely want my life."

"In one sense, yes. But you may conduct yourself as you please, educate yourself as you please, hold whatever opinions you please."

"And what will your son say to that?"

"He will accept it. In return, I think you will have to grant him the same freedom."

"And what are *his* beliefs?" asked Beth caustically.

"You will have to ask him," replied the duke. "It will give you something to discuss on long lonely evenings. But I suspect they encompass the admiration of a well-turned ankle, the knowledge of fine wines, and an ardent belief in the liberty of the aristocracy to do whatever they damn well please."

It was a thumbnail sketch of the worst type of libertine, the type she had always been happy to despise from afar. "You are marrying me to a monster!"

"Not at all. I am marrying you to the most eligible, the most handsome, the most charming rogue in England."

Beth hid her face in her hands. The man seemed to think she should be *pleased* by what he offered. A debauched fop! "If you have any feeling for me at all," she whispered, "be it fondness or guilt, I beg you not to do this. I am happy here."

"I am truly sorry, my dear," said the duke gently. "I have no choice. Happiness is a transportable quality, you know."

"Not into the debauch you describe," protested Beth, raising her head. She knew there were tears on her face and was willing for once in her life to use this feminine weakness to gain her end.

If the duke was touched by them he did not show it. "If the marquess conducts debauches it will be outside his home, I can assure you of that. I can control him, and I promise you will suffer no insult. You may want to consider that one advantage of being very rich and of the highest estate is to be able to arrange your life to suit yourself. If you set up separate apartments and fill yours with poets, philosophers, and artists, no one will be surprised. Once you are with child you may live apart if you wish. No one will object."

"Not even my husband?"

"Least of all him."

Beth found that the most chilling statement of all. Where in this was Mary Wollstonecraft's ideal of marriage, one based on the highest moral standards, mutual respect, and friendship?

"But I will have to submit to this man," she said faintly, "and bear his children."

The duke nodded. "That is unfortunately true. There is no more impersonal way of achieving the purpose. I have to say, however, though you may find it indelicate, that his expertise in that matter should make it possible to achieve the purpose with as little distress to you as possible."

Expertise? Beth shuddered. Was that to be put in the scale against purity and respect? Beth knew her cheeks were red, but she would not hide them again. "I really have no choice, do I? Are you not ashamed of what you are doing?"

He made no reply, though she thought her words had reached him. She added rather helplessly, "What will Aunt Emma think?"

"I suggest you pretend to be willing. If you tell her of the coercion involved she will be obliged to refuse to accept the sacrifice. I will only find other more formidable weapons."

Feeling bruised, Beth rose unsteadily to her feet. "What do I have to do?"

He rose too and began to pull on his gloves. "I will send Arden down and you can become acquainted. He will, for common knowledge, fall madly in love and sweep you off to his family. After a suitable but short period you will be married."

Beth had felt herself no longer capable of shock but that did stun her. "I am to live in your house? What will your wife think?"

"She will be delighted," he replied. "She misses her daughters. We are all civilized people, and if we are careful this can be managed without hurt to any party."

Beth raised her chin. "Balderdash," she said and marched out to find Aunt Emma.

During the next weeks the whole school was aware of the change in Miss Armitage. Where once she had been noted for her patience and composure, now her nerves were constantly on end, her attention inclined to wander. Beth was not helped by the fact that Aunt Emma saw her swift agreement to the duke's outrageous plan as a sign that she had abandoned the principles they had shared through the years.

If it hadn't been for the daily deterioration in the situation in France, Beth knew she would have been subjected to even more questions and dissuasions. Wryly, she acknowledged she had something for which to thank the Corsican Monster. But even that could not make her feel anything but horror at the news that Napoleon was once more in Paris. He had the audacity to seek peace treaties with the other European nations, to try to have them acknowledge him again as ruler of France. That time was past, however, and for once the nations were holding together in a Grand Alliance.

Beth's satisfaction at that was drowned, however, when she was once again summoned to the parlor. She could have no illusion that the cause was anything except her own private disaster.

It was again Clarissa who came with a message that Miss

Armitage was wanted in the yellow parlor. As Beth wiped suddenly damp palms on her apron the girl said, "Miss Armitage, could I speak to you—"

"Not now, Clarissa," said Beth as she hurried off.

Once more she stopped before the large mirror. Her decorous green-stripe muslin was covered by a voluminous plain white apron, for she had been teaching calligraphy, which always resulted in inky fingers and splatters from poorly mended pens. She decided to leave it on. Her neat fitted cap covered all her hair except a few chestnut curls. Roughly, she attempted to push them out of sight. The cap was decorated with a pretty bow over her left ear, and she pulled her scissors from the case in her pocket and snipped it off.

She was, after all, no beauty, and there was always the chance that if she made herself sufficiently ugly the Marquess of Arden would rebel. He was a man and a rich aristocrat and could not be as far under the duke's control as she.

When she was sure she had done her worst, she walked boldly into the room.

There was no sign of Miss Mallory, just a man. The Marquess of Arden.

Beth felt her confidence seep out through the soles of her slippers. He was not a debauched fop. Instead he was everything she feared in men—tall, strong, and arrogant. She saw the flash of disgust at her appearance before it was hidden under ice-cool manners, and even though she had hoped for it, that further depleted her confidence.

He made a slight bow. "Miss Armitage."

She did her best to compete. She made a slight curtsy, "My Lord Marquess."

They stared at one another for a moment then Beth said, "Please be seated, my lord." She chose a chair for herself, one as far away from him as possible.

How ridiculous it was to imagine herself married to such a man. He was a being from another world.

His features reminded her of pictures of the Greek gods, an impression augmented by the style of his bright curls. His eyes were the clear blue of the summer sky and ridiculously fine for a man. He was head and shoulders taller than she and twice as broad. Growing up tall in a society of women, Beth was always made uneasy by height.

Lucien wondered how anyone would believe he had fallen in love with such a plain Jane. She was not exactly ugly—her features were regular and her figure appeared average under an unbecoming gown and a concealing apron—but there was nothing remarkable about her at all. He sighed. He had no choice.

Beth heard the sigh and tightened her lips. She was not about to attempt polite conversation.

The marquess suddenly stood up again. "Come here."

Beth looked up in surprise. "I beg your pardon?"

"Come here. I want to look at you in the light."

"Go to the devil," said Beth clearly and was pleased to see him blink with surprise. After a moment a smile softened his beautiful mouth.

"We are in a mess, aren't we?"

Beth relaxed a little but hoped it didn't show. "Our predicament is of your family's contrivance, my lord, and the solution is to your family's benefit."

He was studying her cynically. "You see no gain for yourself in this, Miss Armitage?"

"None at all."

He sat again, his mouth retaining a trace of humor. "Is there nothing in life you want which you do not now have?" he asked indulgently in the manner of one used to purchasing anything, including people.

"My freedom," Beth replied. It wiped all humor from his face.

"None of us are ever entirely free," he said quietly. "We must marry, Miss Armitage. There is no avoiding it. But I will be as considerate of you as I can. You have my word on it."

It was, she supposed, an admirable expression of intent, but she saw it as a declaration of dominance. He, the ruler, was promising not to mistreat his vassal.

"I will have more than that," she said, having thought on the subject a great deal since the duke's visit. "I want a handsome settlement of independent income. I will not be dependent on your good will."

He stiffened. "It has already been arranged by my father, Miss Armitage. But, I'm sorry, it only comes into effect after you have borne me two sons."

Beth lowered her head. For all the boldness of her demands she had no leverage, and they both knew it. Moreover, this frank talk of children frightened her. Beth had not been raised in ignorance of the mechanics of procreation. At this moment, she wished she had been.

He stood again and walked over to stare into the fire. "There's no point in this, is there?" he asked bitterly. She hoped for a moment that he was rejecting the whole idea, but he simply turned and said, "Miss Armitage, will you do me the honor of becoming my wife?"

Beth stood, too, and swallowed. She considered a further appeal but knew it would do no good. If the de Vaux family wanted her chopped in pieces and served for dinner there was nothing she could do about it.

"I suppose I must," she said.

He produced a ring from his pocket. He would have put it on her finger, but Beth held out her right hand, palm up and after a moment he dropped the ring into it. It was a large diamond surrounded by emeralds and not new. Probably a family heirloom. She placed it on her ring finger herself. It looked utterly ridiculous there.

"What happens now?" she asked, trying to ignore the shackle. She suddenly realized he might expect a symbolic kiss and looked at him in alarm.

Such a thought had obviously not crossed his mind. "I see no point in delaying matters. Come with me now and I will take you to Belcraven."

"Tomorrow. I must gather my belongings."

"There's no need to bring much," he said with a dismissive glance at her attire. "We will buy you a new wardrobe."

Beth drew herself up. "I prefer my own clothes, thank you, Lord Arden. Your father said I need only marry you, live in your house, and bear your children. He said nothing of allowing you to dress me to suit your fancy."

"As you wish, Miss Armitage," said the marquess through tight lips.

Beth dropped him a straight-backed curtsy.

Insolently, he gave her a full court bow, then walked out of the room.

Chapter Four

The next day, waiting for the marquess to arrive, Beth was prey to a distressing degree of nervousness, not helped by Miss Mallory's poorly concealed anxiety.

"Are you *quite* sure, Beth? Do but consider. Once away from here anything could happen to you."

Beth summoned up a cheerful smile for the woman who had been like a mother. "Please don't fret, Aunt Emma. I have the twenty guineas you gave me in my hidden pocket. If anything goes amiss I will fly back to the nest. And when I have my philosophical salon established in London you must come and visit me and meet Hannah More and Mr. Wilberforce."

"Even that is not worth selling yourself for, Beth. The marquess is not a sympathetic man. I can sense such things. How will you endure it?"

"I think you malign him," said Beth, hugging Miss Mallory. It was not a total falsehood. The marquess might be a man of fashion, but he had been sensitive to all the awkwardness of their situation, and he had not forced any physical attentions or false sentiment upon her.

As the coach drew up, she saw he was showing his sensitivity further by riding alongside the luxurious chariot instead of inside with her.

After waving a last farewell to Miss Mallory and a few of the older pupils, Beth collapsed back against thickly padded silk squabs and rested her feet on an embroidered footstool. A soft woolen blanket lay nearby in case she should be cold and velvet curtains could be drawn to ensure her privacy. She admonished herself not to be swayed by such trifling luxuries, but she could not help feeling the contrast between this and her few other journeys, which had been taken on the public stage.

She leaned out for a last acknowledgment of the farewells and only realized as the coach carried her out of sight that one of the waving senior girls had been Clarissa Greystone, and she had been crying. Beth liked the girl and had talked with her from time to time, but she had not thought Clarissa would be so upset at her departure.

Then she remembered how Clarissa had tried to speak to her the day before. It was too late now, but she wished she had found the time. The girl had been unhappy lately. Perhaps she had a brother in the army, though Beth did not think so.

In truth, Beth told herself sternly, there was no justification for her own self-pity when the shadow of war hung over them all. If Napoleon could not be brought to see reason, many fathers, sons, and brothers would be maimed or dead, which made a luxurious, if loveless, marriage seem a petty tragedy indeed.

She occupied herself for a little while in viewing the scenery. Spring had greened the grass and trees, and they rolled past occasional mats of yellow daffodils and blue harebells. A hare ran twisting and turning crazily across a meadow. In another field lambs frolicked near their mothers.

It was Beth's favorite time of year, but this spring heralded only misery, and though her problem was small in the greater scheme of things, it dominated her thoughts.

It would take most of the day to reach Belcraven Park, so Beth took out Miss Mallory's parting gift to her—*Self-Control, a Novel,* by Mary Brunton. It was supposedly based on the most upright principles. Though Mary Wollstonecraft had despised works of fiction, Miss Mallory thought it wise to permit the older girls to indulge their taste for novels, but only through directed reading. She had asked Beth to send back a report on the book as soon as possible.

By the time they paused to change horses, Laura Montreville

had rejected her dashing suitor for the excellent reason that he had first tried to seduce her before attempting the more subtle lure of marriage.

By the time the next halt was called, the handsome colonel had persuaded Laura to allow him two years in which to prove himself a reformed characters, and Beth was becoming a little impatient with the heroine. If she did not love the man she should give him no reason to hope. If, as it appeared, Laura did love him, it was silliness to demand that he give up all outward show of his feelings for her because of some notion that uncontrolled emotions paved the way to hell.

Mary Wollstonecraft had urged the honest expression of feelings and beliefs, and that meshed very well with Beth's naturally honest temperament.

Beth found herself wondering what Laura would have done in her own situation. She decided the young lady was so lacking in reality and common sense she would have sunk into a decline and died. Now *that* would serve the marquess and his father as they deserved, thought Beth with a grim smile, and ruin their plans into the bargain. Unfortunately, she could not see how it would do her any good at all. She decided she just wasn't the stuff of which heroines were made. She lacked the right kind of sensibility.

Beth conceived a better plan than meekly fading away. The marquess was obviously unhappy with the marriage plan. If she was sufficiently abrasive, unattractive, and unpleasant, surely he would think a lifetime tied to her was too high a price to pay for a pure-blooded heir. It would be no effort at all to be abrasive and unpleasant.

The horses were changed frequently and with lightning efficiency, but when the team was unhitched at Chipping Norton the marquess opened the door.

"We will break the journey here," he said. "You will be glad of a meal, I'm sure." The hours of riding had ruffled his curls and brought a shine to his eyes. His smile was genuinely friendly as he asked, "I hope you are not finding the journey too tiring."

As she descended the steps Beth repressed an urge to respond favorably to this goodwill; she was not normally ungracious, but such good humor would not answer at all. She put an edge on her voice as she said, "How could I, my lord, when everything is of the first stare?"

His smile dimmed. "It is going to be very tiresome, Miss Armitage, if you are to carp at everything that is better than utilitarian." They had reached the door of the inn, and the host was bowing low to usher such exalted guests inside. Beth quailed. She had never been treated so in her life.

Lord Arden, however, appeared oblivious to the man as he added, "And if you will not make any effort to consider my feelings, then I perhaps will see no reason to consider yours."

Shocked back into consideration of her main problem, Beth stared at her husband-to-be.

"Truce?" he asked.

That wasn't what Beth wanted at all. "Am I never to say what I think?"

"It depends, I suppose, if you want me to say what I think."

All too aware of the host, still bobbing and bowing, Beth carried on into the private parlor, pondering the marquess's words. When they were alone she challenged him. "Why would I not wish you to speak your mind? I am not afraid of the truth."

He shrugged off his riding cloak and dropped it over a chair. "Very well," he said coldly. "I find you unattractive and this whole situation abominable. Now, how does that help?"

"Since I already knew that," she shot back, "it hardly changes matters at all." But it did. Beth was foolishly hurt by the very disgust she was seeking. And if the situation was abominable, why was he tolerating it?

He was leaning against the mantel, looking at her as if she were an intrusive stranger—an intrusive, ill-bred stranger. "Except now it is spoken," he said, "and before it was decently hidden. Spoken words assume a life of their own, Miss Armitage, and cannot be unsaid. However, in the cause of sanity I am quite willing to pretend if you will join in the game."

"Pretend what?"

"Contentment.

Beth turned away, her hands pressed together. "I cannot."

There was silence, a chinking, then she heard his boots on the floor as he walked towards her. "Here, Elizabeth." He sounded nothing so much as weary.

She turned and took the wine he offered, sipping cautiously. It was a rare indulgence at Miss Mallory's, and it encouraged her to resist the peace offering it represented. She forced herself to meet his disdainful eyes. "I have not given you permission to use my name, sir.

Chin up, eye meeting eye, Beth said, "I would ask you to remember, Lord Arden, that this matter—which is a minor disturbance to your life—has destroyed mine. I have been taken from my home, my friends, and my employment, and forced into a way of life in which I can expect no pleasure." She put her glass down with a snap. "It will take me a few days longer, I am afraid, to be able to pretend *contentment*."

His eyes sparked dangerously. "I am not generally considered to be repulsive, *Miss Armitage*."

Beth's response was swift and tart. "Nor is a baboon, I'm sure, in its proper milieu."

Any retaliation from the outraged marquess was forestalled by the arrival of servants with their meal. He turned away sharply and went to stand by the far window until the meal was ready. When the innkeeper obsequiously encouraged them to partake of his best, Beth and the marquess approached the table like wary opponents and took seats at the opposite ends. By silent agreement they ate in unbroken silence.

Beth kept her eyes on her plate. Her heart was pounding, and the delicious food formed lumps in her dry mouth. For one moment she had faced leashed fury such as she had only ever imagined. She had feared him, had feared that he might hit her, throttle her even. But she *couldn't* be terrified of him. Not if she was to turn him so totally against her.

It was beyond her at the moment, however, to attempt more taunts, and there were no further words before the journey resumed.

Beth opened her book once more but used it as a blind for thought. Her plan was not as easy as she had thought. Could she provoke him sufficiently to give him an overpowering antipathy to her without driving him to the violence she had sensed? She shuddered. She had never encountered such a man before. There was something about him, something coiled tight, able to be unleashed for good or evil.

Hands clenched painfully tight on *Self-Control,* Beth knew she must not, could not, marry such a man. Despite the duke's assurances, as her husband the marquess would have all right to her body. He would be free to beat her if he wished. If he were to beat her to death he would likely incur only a mild penalty, especially as he would have all the riches and power of his family on his side, and she would have no powerful friends to protest.

But she reminded herself of the maxims of Publius. Fear is to be feared more than death or injury. She could not afford fear.

The duke and the marquess needed her in order to achieve their end, needed her in excellent health for successful child-bearing. That was her protection from extreme violence and, after all, if blows were the price she must pay for making him reject her, she would count it—like the heroes of Athens—a small cost for her freedom.

She smiled wryly. It was perhaps uplifting to think of the brave men of Athens who died for freedom, but she did not fool herself that the next few days were likely to be easy or pleasant.

They changed horses again twice but only in minutes. An hour later, at the next change, the coach halted and the door swung open.

"It is another hour or so to Belcraven, Miss Armitage. Would you like some tea? You could take it in the coach or come into the inn." The marquess was a model of impersonal punctiliousness.

In the same manner, Beth extended a hand to be helped down. "I would like to stretch my legs, I think. Perhaps I could walk a little here."

"Certainly," he said and extended an arm.

Despite her silent debate in the coach, Beth found she did

not want his company at all. He was such a big man and so very cold. "There is no need for you to accompany me, my lord."

"Of course there is," he said, staring into the distance. "It would be most odd if I did not."

Helplessly Beth laid her hand lightly on his sleeve, and they strolled along the road of the small town. She tried to force herself to say something offensive, but his silence was like a wall between them, and her tongue stayed frozen.

After about ten minutes, the marquess said, "Perhaps we should turn back now," and they did so.

At the inn he said, "Would you like some tea?" Beth agreed that she would. He arranged it and left her alone.

When she had finished and made a brief toilette, he escorted her to the coach, mounted his horse, and they were off.

Beth contemplated a lifetime of such arid courtesy and shuddered. A marriage like that would be death in life to her, but it doubtless would only be an inconvenience to him. What was needed, after all, to produce a clutch of children? A few brief, soulless encounters. For the rest of the time he would be able to continue with his present life undisturbed.

Her determination to pursue her plan was reborn and strengthened. To escape this kind of life she would do anything, face any threat.

Not during this journey, however. All too soon the groom on the box made a long blast on his horn and they swept through magnificent, gilded, wrought-iron gates. They were in Belcraven Park. The gatekeeper and his family doffed their caps or dipped a curtsy as appropriate. Beth turned her face away. It was not right that these people pay her homage.

The carriage rolled along the smooth drive between ranks of perfect lime trees. In the meadows to either side, speckled deer raised their heads to watch them pass. She saw a lake with what appeared to be a Grecian temple in the middle. She heard the shriek of peacocks—those useless living ornaments of the rich.

Then the curve of the driveway presented Belcraven. Beth gaped. In the setting sun it was a mountain of golden stone decorated with carvings and crenelations and set with the glimmering jewels of hundreds of windows. It was enormous, the largest building Beth had ever seen, and the most beautiful. This was to be her home?

Impossible.

When the coach stopped beneath the great curving double steps which led up to massive gleaming doors already open, Beth wanted to huddle in the coach. It, after all, was of a scale much more to her liking. The door was soon opened however, and the steps let down. The marquess stood waiting for her.

With trembling fingers she set her bonnet on her head and tied the ribbons, then ventured out. Hand on his arm she climbed the thirty steps (she counted them) and hoped no one could tell how her knees were knocking.

Inside the doors there seemed to be a great many people, all servants. A portly gentleman of awe-inspiring dignity bowed, then divested the marquess of his outerwear. "Welcome home, my lord."

"Thank you, Gorsham. Miss Armitage, this is Gorsham, our Groom of the Chambers."

Beth knew this meant he controlled the running of this enormous establishment, and he certainly looked capable of it. She received a bow all for herself. "Miss Armitage. Welcome to Belcraven."

Poor, speechless Beth was hard pressed not to curtsy but contented herself with a little nod, hoping it to be appropriate.

"How long to dinner, Gorsham?" asked the marquess as he strolled into a massive hall. Beth followed quickly after. For the moment he was her only connection in this place. She rather feared if they were separated, she'd be thrown out like the interloper she was, or wished she was . . .

She looked around in awe.

Spiral marble pillars banded with gold marched ahead over a tiled floor which seemed to stretch to infinity. Marble busts and statues of classical type were set about the chamber, and the walls were hung with ancient banners and weapons. Forcing herself not to gape, Beth looked up over three tiers of ornate balustrades and realized the room went all the way to the roof where there was an octagonal skylight which let in the afternoon sun. The whole of Miss Mallory's school could have fit in this one chamber.

"An hour, my lord," said Gorsham in answer to the marquess's question.

The marquess turned to Beth. "Perhaps you would like to go to your apartments, my dear, and meet my parents when you have refreshed yourself."

Apartments? Beth wanted a hidey-hole and agreed to his suggestion. Gorsham's raised finger brought forward one of a small group of maids standing ready.

"This is Redcliff, Miss Armitage," he said as the middle-aged woman curtsied. "If agreeable, she will show you to your room and act as your maid."

Beth nodded, and when the maid turned to lead the way, she followed. She needn't have bothered with the exercise at their last stop. They walked halfway down the hall and mounted wide stairs railed in gilded wrought iron which took them to the next floor. They then followed one wide carpeted corridor after another, all casually set with valuable sculptures and paintings, and dotted with elegant furnishings. They passed three powdered and liveried footman simply standing. It seemed at least ten minutes before the maid opened a door and stood back to allow an overwhelmed Beth to enter.

"Apartments" had apparently been exact. She was to be housed in a suite of rooms.

This first one was a large sitting room, comfortably appointed with velvet-upholstered chairs, small inlaid tables, and a zebrawood desk. There was a chaise to act as a daybed near which two vaguely Egyptian figures held hanging oil lamps for evening light. There was a fireplace with marble bas-relief decoration and a fire already cheerfully burning there, even though it was mild for late April. Graciously arranged spring flowers were placed on two tables, and their sweet perfume floated through all this elegance.

With some trepidation, Beth stepped onto the beautiful silky carpet of jewel-like blues and yellows and went over to one of the two long windows hung with blue damask curtains. It gave a view from the back of the house down over breathtaking grounds to the River Cherwell.

Beth turned to see the maid waiting by an adjoining door. It proved to lead into a dressing room. Quite modest, she supposed. Only twice as large as her bedroom, her only room, at Miss Mallory's.

This room was paneled in some rich, golden wood but was quite spartan in comparison to the other. The floor was bare apart from three small rugs, and the appointments consisted of two chairs, two large armoires, a washstand, a mirror, and a very large chest. There was a fireplace where yet another fire burned. How very wasteful this all seemed.

The maid must have noticed her frowning consideration, for she opened a panel above the fireplace to show a metal tank. "It's to keep the water warm for a bath, miss. The fires are only let out in the hottest weather. You could bathe now if you wish, miss."

The woman flipped back the lid of the chest to reveal a large bathtub ready and waiting. Beth couldn't resist going over to peer at this marvel—it was even decorated with pictures of fish.

This was the first luxury of the day which tempted Beth. At Miss Mallory's a proper bath was a rare treat requiring much planning, and the thought of just being able to order a bath and have one was delicious. And tempting. She suspected, however, that the maid would want to be part of the process, and she was not ready for that as yet.

Beyond the dressing room was her bedroom. This was as stunning as the sitting room, with another rich carpet upon the floor, yellow silk hangings on the large tester bed and matching curtains at the windows. The walls were covered with panels of Chinese silk, picking up the yellow theme, and the paintings hung upon them were not known to Beth but had all the appearance of being Old Masters.

These rooms were not a hidey-hole, they were a gilded cage.

More than anything in the world at that moment, Beth wanted to be alone, yet she could think of no way to get rid of the maid.

"Has my trunk been brought up?" she asked, hoping the woman would go to find it, but at that moment there was a noise from the dressing room.

"That will be it now, miss," said Redcliff and bustled off but only as far as the next room where she supervised the footmen in the placing of the baggage. Beth had only managed to remove her bonnet before she was back.

Beth tried again. "I think I would like to wash, Redcliff," she said.

"Certainly, miss," replied the maid and disappeared. But again only as far as the dressing room where there was the sound of running water. Beth had forgotten the ever-ready tank.

In a moment the woman was back, indicating that Miss Armitage should join her. Beth obeyed. She was beginning to learn about the tyranny of servants.

Beth felt like a child. She managed to undo the buttons at the front of her long-sleeved spencer herself, but it was the maid who eased it off. It was the maid, too, who undid the three buttons at the back of the bodice of her gown and loosened the laces which tightened the waist. In a moment the gown was off, and Beth was standing in her cambric petticoat. The maid's fingers started again, but Beth balked.

"That will be quite enough," she said, somewhat sharply. "Please unpack for me."

At least that got the woman a pace or two away.

Beth took up the thickly woven cotton square and the soap and began to wash what she could reach. If the maid would only leave she could go farther, but she had never undressed before another person since she was a child and could not bring herself to do so now.

The soap was sweetly perfumed and rich and smooth on her skin. The embroidered towel was soft.

As soon as she was finished she found the maid beside her offering an alabaster pot containing cream. "For your hands, miss."

Beth dipped her fingers in the unguent and smoothed it over

her hands. It, too, was perfumed. Before she was finished she
would smell like a spring garden.

"There is lotion for the face, too, if you would wish it,
miss," said Redcliff.

Beth declined, and the maid turned back to the trunks.
"Which gown would you wish to wear this evening, miss?"

Beth knew she had nothing appropriate for this setting and
steadfastly refused to be concerned. It was a matter of pride,
surely, not to have wasted a fortune on her back.

"There is a fawn peau de soie," she said. "I will wear that."

Then Beth was helped into her wrap and could escape to
the sitting room and a moment's peace. She sat by a window,
looking out at the sun-gilded heavenly estate. As far as her
eye could see there were delightful prospects, and the deer
picked their way across greensward with contented elegance.
It was a fairy-tale setting where surely imperfection and suffering never invaded.

After a moment she lowered her head into her hands. A
human might feel superior to a baboon, but it was still distressing to be forced into its milieu.

What was she going to do, she thought with panic, if her
plan didn't work and the marquess went through with the marriage? She couldn't live in this place. It was impossible.

She took her hands from her face and forced herself to her
feet. Panic would destroy her. Only strength would take her
safely home again. She paced the room and rallied her flagging
spirits. Belcraven was a building, nothing more, and its perfect
grounds were just a stage set created with vast amounts of
money.

The luxury surrounding her was doubtless just an indication
of past and present corruption. After all, most of the aristocracy had gained their high estate by acts of violence or im-
morality in the service of similarly violent and immoral
monarchs.

The duke, the duchess, and the marquess were just people,
and no more worthy of awe than the simplest laborer. In fact,
that laborer doubtless came by his daily bread more honestly.

By the time the maid indicated that the requested gown was ready, Beth had talked herself back into courage.

"Jewels, miss?" asked Redcliff.

"There is a gold locket in my reticule," said Beth, making no attempt at pretense. "It is all I have." Then she thought of her ring and looked down at the gaudy thing. It at least was in keeping with Belcraven, which only proved it had no place on her finger.

The maid found the locket and clasped it around Beth's neck.

Beth considered herself in the long mirror. Both she and Miss Mallory made their own gowns, but once a year they commissioned two formal outfits from the local dressmaker— a heavy one for winter and a light one for summer. This was the latter, and it fitted well and had a few stylish details—pin tucks in the bodice and braid around the hem. The style, however, was simple and modest, and Beth knew it would be eclipsed by anything the duchess might wear. Or other guests.

That thought almost swept her back into panic. She could face the family—this was all their fault, after all—but not strangers who would look and see only a homely, poorly dressed female, not a rebellious spirit.

If she had possessed a stunning, fashionable gown and a jewel box she would have used them then and be damned to egalitarian principles.

The maid went to work on her hair. "What pretty hair you have, miss," said Redcliff as she started to brush through the mass of chestnut curls.

Beth knew it. It was unfortunate hair for a schoolmistress who had to convince pupils and parents on a daily basis that she was of sober disposition. That was why she kept it short and hidden beneath caps.

When the maid was satisfied with her work, Beth said, "You will find a cap to match this gown in a box in the gray trunk." In the mirror she saw the protest tremble on the woman's lips. The maid was too well-trained to voice it, however, and found the cap.

Unfortunately for Beth's intentions, the cap was her prettiest, and this time she could hardly strip it of its decoration—rows of ruched ribbons and two silk roses designed to nestle on her left temple. Moreover, as this cap was designed to fit on the back of her head, it was quite impossible to hide all her glossy curls.

If only, she thought, this outfit were not so becoming. The bland color suited her pale skin, giving it delicacy and bringing out a hint of color in her cheeks and lips. The curls on her forehead softened the smooth oval of her face and those blasted roses drew attention to her eyes, which, while nothing out of the ordinary, were clear and surmounted by smooth dark brows.

She had chosen the outfit to be becoming, though, and succeeded all too well. She went about a little in Cheltenham with her aunt and had no desire to appear an antidote. In fact, she remembered with a rueful smile, when this outfit had been commissioned a few months ago she had entertained mild hopes of the interest of a local curate. He had turned out to be a rather stupid man.

Beth gave up the fruitless contemplation of her appearance. The marquess was doubtless acquainted with all the great beauties of the land. He was hardly likely to be overwhelmed by Beth Armitage in her Sunday Best.

The maid looked at the clock. "It is time for you to go down, miss."

Beth started. "I—I confess I have no idea of how to find 'down,' Redcliff. Or where I am supposed to be."

The maid looked mildly surprised and rang a small silver bell which stood on a table. A footman came smartly into the room.

"Miss Armitage is ready to go down, Thomas," said the maid.

The footman gave a little bow and stepped outside again. Redcliff stood by the door to close it when Beth had left. Beth left.

The footman set off at a stately pace and Beth followed, feeling a little like a lap dog being taken for a walk. The young man was tall and well-built. Beth had heard that sometimes footmen were chosen for their handsome appearance and supposed that to be the case here. Again, they passed other footmen just standing like statues; in their yellow liveries and powdered hair there was no easy way to tell them apart.

She followed her guide along corridors and down a different staircase, just as magnificent as the one she had come up. She could not deny the elegance and beauty of her surroundings, but how ridiculous, she told herself staunchly, to have this enormous building and all these servants for just three people.

They approached gilded double doors with panels painted with climbing roses. Beth's footman and another stationed there swung them open with smooth efficiency so she could sweep into the room without breaking step. I am likely to lose the use of my hands entirely, Beth thought, as she prepared to meet her persecutors.

She had expected to be overwhelmed by personal ostentation to match the house and was prepared to sneer. She found instead that the room she entered was small and not particularly grand, and the family was dressed like any people of good birth and comfortable circumstances.

The duke and the marquess were in elegant day dress, the duchess in a charming but simple blue-striped silk with only a delicate sapphire pendant and earrings for ornamentation. She was a tall, slender lady with the same handsome features as her son. The sweetly curved lips moved into a warm smile as she came forward.

"My dear Miss Armitage, welcome to Belcraven." Her voice carried the delicious flavor of her native France. "Thank you so much for coming." It was a statement quite suitable for the hearing of the footman standing by the wall, but Beth knew it said more. The duchess did not resent her arrival. The woman obviously accepted her husband's plan and there was to be no help from her quarter.

"I found it an opportunity quite impossible to resist, Your Grace," said Beth dryly.

A twinkle of amusement and some disarming sympathy

sparkled in the duchess's blue eyes. "Yes," she said. "The de Vaux men are irresistible, are they not, my dear? Tell me now, am I permitted to call you Elizabeth?"

In the circumstances it was impossible to refuse. Next Beth had to face the duke.

"I echo my dear wife's sentiments, Elizabeth. It is a delight to have you here." He smiled at her benignly as if he had never forced her into this. Beth clenched her teeth on unwise words. Offending the duke would achieve nothing.

Beth was directed to a seat on a sofa where the duchess joined her. The duke sat opposite while the marquess stoked the fireplace, watching Beth sardonically. The footman served wine and the duchess asked Beth about the journey. For half an hour Beth found herself skillfully drawn into conversation and entertained by amusing and relevant anecdotes. It was terribly hard not to like this charming lady with her French accent and warm smile.

The duke played his part in the conversation, and Beth noticed how the duchess even drew the marquess in with charming implacability. No plodding topics here, no awkward silences. Beth could not help but be impressed by their proficiency.

In due course the meal was announced, and the duke offered Beth his arm while the marquess escorted his mother. It was only one short corridor to the dining room, but it was a moment of privacy.

"Now that you have met the marquess, Elizabeth," asked the duke, "are you more reconciled to your fate?"

"I am as reconciled as he, Your Grace."

The duke met her cool look with a touch of surprise. "That is a pity, Miss Armitage. He is a man, and proud. I can rule him, but he does not take it gently."

"I am a woman, and proud, Your Grace," retorted Beth. "I do not take it gently either."

"Very well," he said, irritatingly unimpressed. "But remember, Elizabeth, your rancor is against me and me you cannot hurt."

"I do not seek to hurt anyone, Your Grace," said Beth with a hint of desperation. "I strive merely to keep myself intact."

"This is the family dining room," said the duke, smoothly switching subjects as they entered a large room hung with tapestries. The ceiling was painted with half-naked deities.

The family dining room, thought Beth dryly. The dining table was of a size to comfortably seat eight, but there were three other sections against one wall, and the room would certainly hold a "family" of twenty. The duke and duchess took their places at either end and the marquess and Beth sat facing each other at the sides. Service was *à la Russe* with a footman behind each diner and other servants bringing in dishes and taking away remains. Beth thought it utterly ridiculous.

Seeing clearly how it would be, she took only tiny portions of the many courses and still had trouble towards the end of the meal. She noticed that the marquess ate more heartily, but the duke and duchess also ate little and passed many courses by entirely. What on earth was the point of all this? It was obvious that everyone would have been more suited by a simple meal in privacy.

The proficient conversation recommenced, but now the talk was of the war, exhibiting depth of knowledge of international affairs and considerable shrewdness from all parties. Beth reflected that the servants were gaining a first-class education as they performed their duties, but it was as if it were all a performance put on for an audience.

The marquess and his parents must do this every day of their lives. The thought horrified Beth, and she found her tongue frozen. For a little while she managed to hold her silence but then she was implacably woven in again by easy questions directed her way. Short of the worst kind of ill manners, she had no choice but to play her part.

Despite the superficial ease and graciousness, Beth could feel the room pressing in on her, the words and occasional laughter squeezing at her temples. Soon she was going to say something unpardonable, and she didn't want to. Mere rudeness would not set her free, and she hated to think of the

servants tittering below stairs about that silly little body who
didn't know how to behave in a big house.

Was she to perform this ritual every day for the rest of her
life? She would go mad.

Chapter Five

When the duchess rose to take her back to the small drawing room, Beth felt some relief. Once they were settled with the tea tray before them, the duchess dismissed the servants.

She handed Beth tea in an exquisite Spode cup. "You find this hard, Elizabeth," she said as a simple statement.

"I find it unendurable. Why do you dine in such state?"

The duchess smiled. "It does not seem so to us, I suppose. It is just the family."

"But what of all the servants?"

"I suppose they are family, too. What would you have us do? It is impossible to run this place without an army of servants. Should we pull it down? But it is very beautiful, and the staff loves it as much we do. They feel privileged to share it with us."

"What of the footmen standing idle in the corridors hour after hour?"

The duchess laughed. "When the day comes you need something at the other end of the building or a message sent or someone found, you will be grateful, I assure you, Elizabeth. Actually, I recently suggested an improvement. I wanted to give the men chairs to sit on and books to read as they wait. They were most indignant. They felt it would lower the dignity of the house. But they are not ignorant, you know. One of them told me that he always stations himself in front of a good picture and enjoys the time to study it. We have compromised. They have agreed to be changed upon the hour. They are mostly from families who have served Belcraven for generations."

Beth put down her cup untasted. "Perhaps it is necessary to be born into this life, at whatever level."

The duchess looked at her. "From what little I know of you, Elizabeth, you pride yourself on your education and your ability to handle your life. Why then can you not handle this?"

Beth stiffened under the attack. "I did not say I *could* not. I said, I think, that it is pointless."

The duchess's eyes were kind as she said, "First prove you have the courage to face it, my dear, and then change things if you can."

Before Beth could point out that she wanted nothing to do with it at all, the gentlemen joined them. Though there were no servants present, the analysis of affairs on the Continent continued. Beth wondered whether anything might be achieved by an impassioned comparison of her own oppression and conquest with that of Europe, but guessed that it would not. This was all the duke's plot; the duchess appeared to endorse it; the marquess had agreed.

The marquess, therefore, must be her target. She took to studying him.

He held his own in the discussion, but she sensed tension in him. He was not warm or relaxed with his parents and at times seemed to take a point of view just to oppose the duke. Beth wondered if this was because of the present situation or typical of this family. It would hardly be surprising. The duke was not Arden's father and they all knew it; she was the duke's bastard and they all knew that, too; both she and the marquess were being forced into a distasteful marriage. When Beth considered the tangled relationships within the room she was surprised there was any elegance at all.

· After a little while, music was suggested, and they moved into a charming music room with a domed ceiling painted like the night sky. The duchess played beautifully on a harp and then Beth was persuaded to show her skill on the pianoforte. Next, to her surprise, the marquess took up a silver flute and played a duet with his mother. She would not have thought him a man to bother with music.

He must have noticed her surprise, for when he had finished he came over and said, "I have a poor singing voice. When we were all younger, my mother organized many musical evenings and insisted I do my part." His manner was pleasant. In no way was it loverlike, but then there was no reason here to act.

"You play very well," she said honestly.

"I enjoy it, but it's not a talent I advertise. It's not in fashion these days for young men such as I." There was even a touch of humor in that. "The French doors open onto the east terrace. Would you care to walk a little in the fresh air? The evening is quite warm."

After a slight hesitation, Beth agreed. For a moment she had begun to thaw, to react to his easy manner, and that would be fatal. The duke and duchess, the house and the servants, created such a solid fabric of decorum that it would take a cruder spirit than Beth's to rip it in public. She needed to be private with him.

"Perhaps you will need a shawl," he said, glancing at her bare arms. She would have sent for one, but the duchess indicated the one she had laid aside and he brought it for her. It was a beautiful Norwich silk which had doubtless cost more than Beth's entire annual expenditure on clothes.

As the marquess placed it on her shoulders, his fingers brushed against her nape. Beth shivered. Their eyes met and there was a moment of intimate awareness, a moment which frightened Beth to death.

She had to escape. She could never, never do this thing.

Beth hurried towards the doors, which he opened for her.

There was a three-quarter moon bathing the stone terrace, illuminating the sculpted urns set at regular intervals along the top of the balustrade. Ivy trailed from them and plants were poking up but there were no flowers as yet. The smell of the air was just the freshness of the country, and the sounds, too, were all natural—a few rustlings of small creatures and, once, the hoot of a hunting owl.

The air had a slight chill now the sun was down, but, as he had said, it was warm enough for her to be comfortable. She shivered all the same and drew the shawl closer around her shoulders.

He broke the silence. "It is a very beautiful house. Can you not find some pleasure in living in it?"

"How would you feel, my lord, living in the palace of a Indian maharajah?"

She saw his teeth flash white in a grin. The moon had turned his hair to silver gilt. "I might be interested, at least for a while."

"So might I," said Beth coolly, "if this were a temporary diversion."

He broke a spray of ivy from an urn and twirled it in his long fingers. "I do understand," he said gently. "You have to stay here for a while, however. It shows clearly that you are accepted by my family. My mother will introduce you to the people hereabouts. You may find it easier when we move to London for the wedding—"

"I didn't know we were to be married in London!"

He shrugged. "My father—the duke is masterminding all this. His intentions are good. He wants you to be fully accepted by Society."

He was being so reasonable Beth was almost falling into the trap. She forced herself to fight. "But *I* do not want that, Lord Arden. I have a better idea. Why don't we elope here and now and live as social outcasts?" There. That should shock him.

If so, it was not noticeable. "Because *I* do not want that."

"And what you want will always come first, I suppose?"

He turned sharply to her. "I give you fair warning, Miss Armitage. I have a temper. If you persist in snapping like a spoiled brat, I am likely to treat you like one."

Beth refused to be intimidated. "If there's a spoiled brat here," she retorted with a sweeping gesture of her arm, "it is not I, my lord. I am the poor working girl, remember?"

"You are a spitting cat looking for someone to scratch. Go

scratch the duke and I'll defend you. Don't rake your claws at me."

Beth turned away. This bickering would never serve her purpose. "Your father said much the same thing," she admitted. "But it is you with which I am entangled."

"So it is with me you must negotiate," he said more moderately. "Let us find a middle path. I have no intention of having the world think me a fool. Let them wonder why I've chosen a poor woman of insignificant birth for a wife. I want no suggestion that I am forced to this, or that you are displeasing to my parents, or that you are unsuited to your role."

His wants. His intentions. Simple rebellion fired Beth. Still looking out over the moon-silvered gardens, Beth taunted in response. "Or that *I* am unwilling? How, Lord Arden, do you intend to make me show myself willing?" She turned back to him quite unaware of how the moonlight gave her rather ordinary face the purity of a della Robbia angel.

She saw him suck in a breath, perhaps in anger. Then he walked slowly towards her, smiling. "Perhaps, Miss Armitage, I can seduce you into willingness."

Beth's nerves gave a shock of warning as she saw where her words were leading. Unwisely, she retorted, "You would assuredly fail, my lord."

She only got out a squeak before she was in his arms and his mouth covered hers. His arms imprisoned, so struggle was pointless, but he did not hurt her. One hand cradled her head, making it quite impossible to twist away, and his lips, soft and warm, only pressed enough to stifle protest. Beth was totally helpless. She had always known in theory that men were strong; until this moment she had not realized how strong.

Then his tongue slipped through to touch against her lips. She tried to protest and found it against her teeth, tickling against the inside of her upper lip. A quiver of something passed through her; she was alarmed by a sensation of dizziness. With sudden resolution she parted her teeth, prepared to bite. His mouth pulled back and he laughed.

"Life with you is going to be intriguing," he said, eyes gleaming. "And dangerous."

Beth realized with despair that she had somehow stirred his interest.

Still holding her, he said lightly, "Will I have to search our marriage bed for a stiletto?"

"If you handle me like this, my lord," said Beth fiercely, resuming her struggles and getting nowhere, "there will be no such thing. Let go of me! Being an admirer of Mary Wollstonecraft does not mean I give my favors to any man who grabs me!"

He froze. "Do you know what you are saying?" he asked softly, and Beth realized how he had interpreted her words.

Beth swallowed and pasted a bold smile on her face. "Of course I do." If she could make him believe this she'd be sent back to Miss Mallory's tomorrow. In one piece? she wondered.

One large hand gripped her chin as if to prevent her from turning away. His voice was hoarse. "How many have there been?"

Beth tossed her head saucily. "If you will give me a list of your conquests, my lord, I'll oblige you with a list of mine."

He released her so suddenly she staggered. "God!"

Beth turned and leaned on the balustrade, feeling sick. Could she go through with this? But only a few moments more and she would be on her way home. What could the duke do if his son simply refused? And he would refuse. No man would stand for this.

Her shoulders were caught and she was spun roughly to face him again.

"I don't believe you," he said.

"Why not?" It was an honest question. Beth needed to know why he doubted her if she was to act convincingly.

"You and Miss Mallory run a select ladies' seminary. You could hardly succeed in that with a smirched reputation."

Beth schooled her features to project insolence. "I am discreet, my lord."

It was hard to look bold. The man looked positively murderous. He was searching her face as if reading a book. Beth tried to look as an unrepentant exponent of free-love would. Had not Mary Wollstonecraft's daughter, Mary, recently eloped with Percy Shelley—and him a married man? The marquess need never know that this escapade had horrified both Miss Mallory and Beth.

Suddenly he pushed her hands behind her, took her two slender wrists in one hand, and held them there. Terror shot through her at this bondage, and she twisted wildly. She was shocked to find she could not break that grip.

"Don't struggle," he said coldly, "or I'll have to hurt you."

He wasn't going to hurt her? She'd thought he was going to beat her at the very least. His words might reassure, but his expression did not. Her heart was racing, and it was all she could do not to beg for mercy.

If he wasn't going to hurt her, what was he going to do? She supposed a bolder woman would know. Could he see her pounding heart which seemed to be somewhere up at the back of her throat? She longed to take her words back, but that would be to lose her chance of freedom. She could not stop the trembling, however, which was shaking her whole body.

He pressed his hard body against her, against her legs, her hips, her breasts. . . . It was an intolerable invasion of privacy.

God in Heaven, was he going to rape her?

"Why are you so frightened?" he asked silkily. "You surely know I do not intend to hurt you, my dear."

"I am outraged," Beth forced out. "I am furious!"

His free hand came up and stroked her cheek. Beth flinched. "Why, I wonder? In what way were your other lovers so superior to me?"

Beth saw a weapon and grasped it. "Does your pride smart, my lord? They were men of sensitivity and intelligence, and they were *my own choice.*"

"I'm sorry," he said with a lightness which did not hide the fury in his eyes. "By my code it is not intelligent or sensitive to take the virginity of a lady without marriage, yet one of those paragons must have done that."

"It was *given* my lord," she spat back. "Given. It was not taken, nor was it sold for a few guineas or even a wedding ring!"

He caught his breath in shock. His hand momentarily tight-

ened on her wrists so that she could not stifle a cry of pain.
The pressure immediately lessened, but she could feel in the
air around them the intensity of his control and the peril of
its loss.

What now? Beth knew something else was going to happen.
Something terrible.

His face was a stony mask, but his eyes burned. He watched
her fixedly as his hand slid down the side of her neck to her
shoulder. She quivered. He moved his imprisoning body away
and Beth took a deep breath of relief. Then his hand moved
down to settle cupping her left breast.

Gasping, Beth started once more to struggle. Surely any
woman, no matter how experienced, would struggle when so
handled against her will. It was impossible to break his iron
hold.

Beth remembered her purpose and stilled herself. Victory
was so close, and she must not quail now. What was he watching for? What would betray her ignorance and virtue?

She felt his thumb begin to rub lightly over her breast, over
her nipple. It was a shocking sensation. She closed her eyes
before they betrayed her desperation. Extraordinary things
were happening in her body.

Instinct told her she could improve her impression of boldness by responding, by kissing him perhaps. He would hate a
display of wanton lust. But she simply could not, nor did she
know how to do it right.

Instead she wanted to scream and fight. She wanted to escape. If she screamed, his parents would come and stop this
torment but would that gain her end?

She forced herself to stay as still as her trembling body
would allow as she racked her mind for a way to use this
moment. To use it to give him such disgust of her that he
would never consider marrying her, no matter what his parents
wished. And quickly. She could not endure much more of this
without betraying something . . .

She remembered, long ago, eavesdropping on a conversation
between two of the middle-aged daily maids who cleaned the
school. They had been talking of their husbands and the mar-

riage act, and though Beth had scarcely been able to understand them, the words came back now.

"He's a good enough man, my Jem, and lusty, but he does so like to make a meal of it, and there's times I'd just rather have it done and get me sleep." Now she had a glimmer of what "making a meal out of it" might mean.

Summoning up her courage, and with a prayer to whatever deity looked after poor beleaguered women, Beth opened her eyes and drawled, "Do you always make such a meal of it, my lord? Can't we just get on with it?"

He released her and stepped back. There was in his face all the revulsion for which she could wish.

They stared at each other in silence. His face looked white, but that could be the moonlight. Beth thought not. She wondered if she'd live to make the journey back to Miss Mallory's.

"Are you pregnant?" he asked bluntly.

"Of course not!"

"Can you be so sure?"

Beth clenched her teeth to stop them chattering. "Yes."

He took a visible breath. "Will you give me your word," he said carefully, "not to . . . not to indulge your passions before the wedding. I think there are enough bastards in this affair already."

"Really, my lord—"

"It's a little late for offended delicacy, Miss Armitage. I want your word." His lips tightened with distaste. "If your needs are so great they cannot be controlled, I will, with reluctance, accommodate you before the wedding. Any child you bear will be mine."

"You still wish to marry me?" asked Beth in horror.

"I never wished to marry you, Miss Armitage," he said. "Now I would give a fortune not to have to touch you. But I have no choice, for though I would give a fortune, I will not give up my heritage. My father will leave me only the property without the means to maintain it unless I marry you."

A great chill washed over Beth, and she wondered if she would faint. "So you are helpless, too," she whispered, wondering how she could undo what she had done.

"But not powerless," he said coldly. "I will not acknowledge
bastards, and I will not be cuckolded. I think I am able to
keep you satisfied. I will beat you silly and lock you up with
a keeper if you show any sign of going to another man. Do
you understand me?"

Sick with horror at what she had done, Beth could only
whisper, "Yes."

"Now get out of my sight." He turned away from her.

Beth stared at his back. "My—my lord . . ."

"If you value your skin, Miss Armitage, you will leave."

Beth looked at one tightly clenched fist on the cold stone
balustrade and fled.

If the duke and duchess, sitting quietly reading, noticed anything untoward in Beth's appearance, they did not show it.
When she said she wished to retire after a tiring day, the duchess rang the bell by her hand. One of the footmen came to
escort her back to her rooms while another went to inform
Redcliff she was needed.

Beth would have forestalled that if she had known how, but
she simply endured the woman's ministrations. Then alone in
the dark room she assessed the bleak situation.

The duke had said he could compel his son, but she had
not really understood him. Now her fight for freedom had
backfired disastrously. The marquess had not been insensitive
to the awkwardness of her position and had been disposed to
be kind. She had destroyed that and in a way that would shame
her to her dying day.

How could she even face him tomorrow, never mind attempt
to undo her work and find a basis for marriage between them?

The duchess watched the young woman leave the room.
Miss Armitage had a great deal of control, but it would seem
the time alone with Lucien had not gone well. She waited for
her son to reappear so she could better judge what had occurred. Eventually she realized he was not coming.

"William, I worry about this plan of yours," she said softly.

The duke looked up from his book. "They will deal well enough in time."

"Did you look at her when she passed through this room, William?" she asked. "That poor girl looked bruised."

The duke stiffened. "You think he struck her?"

"No, of course not. Bruised in spirit. But will you care," she asked angrily, "if he beats her as long as she gives him sons?"

"I have assured Elizabeth of her welfare," said the duke, gazing at his wife. "I will not have her hurt."

"So what are you going to do if he mistreats her, William?" she challenged. "Forbid the marriage? You can't do that and still achieve your purpose. Or will you bring them together for occasional matings, carefully guarded like a dangerous stallion and a prize mare?"

"Yolande!"

She leapt to her feet and challenged him. "Tell me. What are you going to do?"

He rose too, color on his cheeks. "A fine opinion you have of your son, madam! From knowledge of the father, no doubt."

"His manners have been learned from you, Belcraven. And his cruelty."

"*You* dare accuse me of cruelty?"

She turned away and ran her hands through her hair.

To the duke she looked like the girl he had married and adored. Her figure was still shapely and in the candlelight her hair looked guinea-gold.

"Yes, cruel," she said softly, still facing away. "I never realized until you proposed this plan just how ruthless you could be. All these years I have thought you suffered," she said, turning to stare at him with tear-filled eyes. "Now I see you were merely obsessed with punishing me."

With that she fled the room. Too fast. Straight on the thought he realized how stupid it was to worry about the servants. Why should they not for once see the family as human beings, not remote demigods without emotions or flaws?

Punishing her? She thought he had been punishing her all these years? All these years of anguish and self-denial . . .

He remembered wanting something sharp to break their crystal prison. Was this what he wanted? To be hated? To see Yolande cry?

Seeking an outlet, the duke's anguish turned to rage and found a focus. It was all Arden's fault. Everything was Arden's fault, and now he could not even manage a simple dynastic marriage with grace.

The duke stalked out onto the terrace to castigate his heir but found the place empty in the cold moonlight. Control slowly returned. The girl had been tired after her journey and nervous in a strange place. If there had been trouble, it had doubtless been over nothing and soon smoothed over.

He returned to the drawing room and extinguished the candles one by one. In the moonlight he saw his wife's book where it had tumbled to the floor, and he picked it up, smoothing the pages. She had looked magnificent in her rage. He remembered those rages when they had been young. He felt remarkably young himself tonight.

Again he clamped control upon himself. Their crystal cage was protection as well as restraint. Like an old lion he did not think he could live without the bars.

The marquess had left the terrace by the steps which led down to the knot garden.

He was marrying a whore. He might as well marry Blanche. Much better, in fact. He liked Blanche, and she had her own impeccable sense of honor. What would the duke say if he told him about Elizabeth Armitage's promiscuity?

He wouldn't care as long as the children were legitimate. No, he wouldn't care as long as they appeared to be legitimate. The marquess only had to give them a name. As long as they were Elizabeth's brats they'd be worthy of the de Vaux inheritance.

He slammed his hand into a tree. It hurt, but he didn't care.

He strode over the rolling parkland, relishing his hate. Who did he hate the most? Elizabeth? No. He despised her, but she was just another puppet like himself. The duke? Oh yes, he could hate the duke, but, legitimate or not, the marquess was a de Vaux with all the pride of the line, and he understood the duke's motives. He, too, wanted his sons to carry on the line.

His mother? Yes, that was the person to hate. Her foolish lust had caused all this. But with the thought came such desolation he could have howled.

Fury and activity burnt away some of his pain, and he began to think as he retraced his steps to the house. Elizabeth Armitage was not unintelligent, and he had no evidence she was crazed with lust. He'd met women like that and Beth showed none of their concupiscence. She could probably control herself, and he would make sure she did. It offended him to think she was impure, but he could make sure it was no worse than that.

Seeking some kind of solace, he wandered towards the stables, his boyhood haunt. Every second he could steal away from his tutor had been spent here or out riding. It was dark and quiet, but the familiar pungent smell of horse and hay was there, and soft rustlings as the beasts moved in their sleep. He wandered around for a while.

He was about to leave when he heard a faint whistling. He followed the sound to a dark corner where a figure sat on a bale of hay, staring at the moon and whistling out of tune.

"What are you doing here?" he asked in a quiet voice.

The figure started and turned. The marquess recognized the boy he had found in London. Sparrow.

"Nothin', milord."

The boy was scared, and that seemed ridiculous. What was there between them except good luck? They were both misbegotten brats. He'd seen the boy only once after that night, given him his guinea in shillings, and arranged for him to become a stable boy.

Now he went and sat beside the lad on the bale. "Don't be afraid. If you want to spend your sleep time staring at the moon, it's no skin off my back. If I know Jarvis, he'll take it out of yours if you're slow in your work tomorrow.

"That he will, milord, but I don't need a lot of sleep mostly, and I like to look at the night and listen. It's different from Lunnon."

"I suppose it is. Do you like it here, then?"

"Yus, I does.

The marquess leaned back and looked at the night sky, too. "Those three stars over there," he said to the boy, "the ones in a straight line. That's Orion."

"That's what?"

"Orion. It's a name given to those particular stars. He was a mighty Greek hunter, but he chose the wrong prey and went after the Pleiades, so Artemis killed him and now he's three stars."

"Lord love us," murmured the boy. "Furriners are a funny lot and no mistake."

The marquess realized his musings were being taken seriously but only laughed. "Let that be a lesson to you, Sparrow, not to cross Greek women. If you can avoid Greeks altogether, it would be as well."

He was on Sparra's ground here, though, and the boy caught the reference to card sharps and other thieves. "That's what me old friend Micky Rafferty used to say. 'Just learn to know a Greek when you see one.' You'd have liked Micky," he said wistfully. "He were transported for slumming." Suddenly he recollected who he was talking to. "Beggin' your pardon, milord."

"Oh, don't start that again, Sparrow," said the marquess wearily. "You know, I really can't keep calling you that. Don't you have a real name?"

"It is me real moniker."

"Well, what was your mother called?"

"Babs, milord."

The marquess looked at the boy. Even in the past few weeks his face had filled out, and in his sturdy clothes he looked quite promising. He deserved a better name than Sparrow.

"I know," he said. "We'll change the bird. How would you like to be called Robin?"

"Dunno. I'm used to Sparra."

"But it's not a name for a young man who's going up in the world, is it? Robin Babson. How's that?"

The boy's eyes seemed to shine like the stars in Orion. "Robin Babson? That'd be me?"

"If you want."

"Yus," said the boy fiercely.

"Good." The marquess rose and yawned. "If you like the country you can stay here."

"Forever?"

"Well, unless you want to go elsewhere when you're trained."

"If—if you don't mind, milord, I'd rather stay with you." The worship in the young voice was unmistakable.

The marquess considered his devotee ruefully. His attention had only been a whimsical kindness, a salve to his own wounded pride, but he couldn't hurt the child. "Work hard while we're here and you can help my groom, Dooley," he said.

"Thanks, milord," said the boy, bouncing up not out of manners but from sheer excitement. "Thanks."

"If you're going to look after my cattle, though, you need your sleep. Go to bed."

"Yus, sir." The boy ran off and then turned. "G'night."

"Good night, Robin," said the marquess softly in the dark.

Chapter Six

Beth was astonished how easy it was for two people to avoid meeting at Belcraven, especially when one seemed set on it. Beth only encountered the marquess at dinner and for the social interaction which followed. Moreover, after that first occasion, it was never just the family.

There was a resident chaplain at Belcraven, the Reverend Augustus Steep, who also served as the family archivist and historian. A Mrs. Sysonby turned up from time to time. She was a distant connection of the duke's who had found herself impoverished in widowhood. She had been taken in as companion to the duchess but as the duchess felt no need of a companion and Mrs. Sysonby was an enthusiastic entomologist, the lady lived independently in her rooms pursuing her hobby, coming and going as she pleased.

The duchess's emigré aunt and uncle, the Comte and Comtesse de Nouilly, inhabited one whole wing along with a crippled daughter and a handful of faithful servants. Occasionally they, too, without the daughter, appeared for dinner.

Mr. Westall, the duke's secretary, and Mr. Holden, his steward, were entitled to dine with the family and did so from time to time, though the steward had his own family in a house on the estate, and Mr. Westall ate frequently at the vicarage where the interest, Beth gathered, was the vicar's daughter.

In fact, Beth found Mr. Westall exactly the kind of quiet, studious young man with whom she felt comfortable. She enjoyed his occasional company, but whenever she conversed with him she would look up to see the marquess's eyes on them, hard and suspicious.

Beth wished she could wipe away that suspicion but, even if she found the words, when was there occasion to say them?

During the evenings the marquess did not again attempt to take Beth aside despite hints from the duchess. During the days, he disappeared. The duke maintained a pack of hounds, though he rarely hunted himself, and the marquess was spending some days chasing foxes. Beth gathered most of the rest was spent riding and angling. Anything that took him out of the house.

When they met, his manner was always impeccably courteous and formidably distant. Beth matched his courtesy as best she could and waited for an opportunity to undo the damage, to convince him of her purity. Two attempts to have him segregate himself with her having failed, she was driven to desperate measures and wrote him a note, asking to speak with him privately.

When they met that evening before the meal he said coolly, "I received your note, my dear. Is your need so urgent?"

Understanding him, Beth felt her face go red and snapped, "No."

Afterwards she wondered with despair if she should have invited him to her bed. It might be her only chance to speak to him in private and presumably then he would discover she was a virgin, or had been.

As they hardly ever spoke to each other, surely no one could believe this farce of a betrothal. The duke and duchess, of course, simply smoothed over the surface of things, though Beth was aware of the duchess's concern. The Comte and Comtesse de Nouilly were entirely absorbed by their own bitterness. But the upper servants—Mr. Holden, Mr. Westall, and the Reverend Steep—must have surely found the situation very strange. If so, they were careful to give no sign of it.

All the same Beth had reason to be grateful to Napoleon Bonaparte. Without the increasingly bad situation on the Continent certainly even the clever de Vaux family would some-

times have been short of something to say. Instead, each evening, they plunged with relief into the day's news.

One evening the marquess shocked everyone. "I think it is
every man's duty to oppose the Corsican," he said. "I wish to
offer my services."

The duke and duchess both paled. "Impossible," snapped
the duke.

"It is perfectly possible," replied the marquess, and Beth
knew this was his attempt to escape. Even into death? Or did
he think himself invincible?

"You forget, Arden," said the duke, once more calm and
controlled, "your wedding is set for a few weeks hence. After
that and what is now called the honeymoon, we can discuss
this subject again." The words were accompanied by a warning
look. Beth knew the duke was reminding his heir of the
weapon he held over his head.

For once the marquess broke the pattern of decorum, pushed
back his chair, and left the table. The comte and comtesse
looked blankly astonished.

"Is something amiss?" the comtesse asked.

"No, Tante," said the duchess. "It is merely that Arden has
finished."

The comtesse sniffed. "The manners of the English youth
leave much to be desired." With that she returned to her cake.

For once silence was allowed to take hold of them all. Both
the duke and the duchess were pale. The duke's pallor could
well be simple displeasure; the duchess's was fear.

How many mothers, Beth wondered, were living with fear
as the dark shadow of war crept once more over Europe and
sons decided they must join the fight?

When the duchess looked up and their eyes met, Beth sent
her a look of compassion, and the duchess smiled back. It was
the first moment of true understanding Beth had experienced
since coming to Belcraven. She found it strangely frightening.
Perhaps it was the first tentative feeling of belonging, and that
was what troubled her.

Beth found herself increasingly fond of the duchess's company. The lady was clever, witty, and kind. One day, as they

sat in ladylike occupation embroidering a new frontal for the chapel, the duchess ventured a mild criticism. "Elizabeth, my dear. . . . Our story, for the curious, is that you and Lucien are madly in love. It would help the fabrication if you were to spend more time together."

Beth kept her eyes on her stitches. "I suppose that is true, Your Grace. The marquess, however, shows no inclination to spend time in my company."

"Do you wish that he would spend more time with you?"

Beth looked up. "Not particularly."

The duchess frowned slightly. "Elizabeth, are you perhaps, as they say, cutting off your nose to spite your face? What more could you want in a husband than Lucien? He is handsome. He can be delightfully charming."

"I do not care if my husband be handsome or not, Your Grace," Beth replied, "and if Lord Arden is charming, he has not been so to me. I find him cold and arrogant." But then she had to admit to herself that he had not been so until she had said those terrible things.

"It is not really like him, my dear," said the duchess. "He does not like this situation any more than you. But someone has to give a little. Could you not make the first approach?"

Beth had tried that. She shuddered. "No."

The duchess sighed. "I will speak to Lucien then." If she did so, it had no effect.

Apart from the problem of the marquess, Beth became somewhat reconciled to life at Belcraven. She grew accustomed to the scale of the great house with an ease which surprised her and could soon find her way to all the principle rooms unaided. She could not deny that she obtained enjoyment from the beauty of the spacious chambers, the exquisite moldings and decorations, and the priceless works of art. Who could complain, being able to sit in private contemplation of a Rafael Madonna, a Van Dyke portrait, or a landscape of merry Breughel villagers? Who could be totally unhappy in a marvelously well-stocked library?

This lofty, magnificent room with its two tiers of gilded, glass-fronted shelves became Beth's primary haunt. Here were all the classics and many newer and exciting works. It soon became known that if Miss Armitage were needed, one need look no farther than one of the three deep window embrasures in the library.

Nor did Beth often have to share the room with the Reverend Steep. Though he held the position of librarian, his passionate interest was the muniment room and the family archives. Only if his researches required it did he invade Beth's territory.

She encountered a different invader one day, however. She was sitting curled up on the brown velvet window seat when clipped footsteps caused her to peer around the curtains.

"Good morning, Mr. Westall," she said cheerfully, always pleased to see the pleasant young man.

He turned with an open smile. "And to you, Miss Armitage. I should have known I'd find you here. I don't suppose I can prevail upon you to assist me, can I?"

Beth willingly laid down the entrancing adventures of Sir John Mandeville. "Of course. What is it you require?"

"The duke is interesting himself in a new invention by a Mr. Stephenson. It is a traveling machine, a locomotive which is driven by steam. He believes there is an article on a similar subject by a man called Trevithick, but," he added with a twinkle, "he cannot recollect in what journal it was published."

Beth chuckled in sympathy. "It cannot be so very long ago, though," she said, "for I surely heard of Mr. Trevithick not ten years since."

"Less than that, I believe. Where shall we start?"

Beth thought for a moment. "Well, I haven't seen any purely technical collections here, such as those put out by the Royal Society. Have you?"

"Indeed no. I cannot say the duke has shown much interest in engineering before now. Now, however, he says he is resigned to such engines being the key to the future and is determined to understand them."

"I think either the *Annual Register* or the *Monthly Magazine* then. There are complete collections of both. Which do you choose?"

With a shrug the young man said, "The *Annual Register.*" Then he looked at Beth suspiciously. "Now why are you looking triumphant, Miss Armitage?"

"Why," said Beth saucily, "because the *Monthly Magazine* has an index, sir, while the *Annual Register* has merely a list of contents."

They were both laughing over this when the marquess walked in. His eyes narrowed. If he had hackles, Beth thought, they would have risen. She knew she was blushing guiltily when there was absolutely nothing about which to be guilty.

He nodded coolly at the secretary. "Westall."

Mr. Westall made a more substantial inclination, "My lord." He quickly retreated to the other end of the room to begin his search.

Beth held on to cool composure and just looked a question at her husband-to-be. What could have brought him to seek her out? The answer was the duchess.

"My mother asked me to bring this to you," he said, offering a copy of *Ackerman Repository.* "She has apparently mentioned to you some designs for a wedding gown."

Beth had no enthusiasm for choosing such a gown and took the magazine with limp fingers. "Thank you."

The marquess looked at Mr. Westall, skimming through bound copies of the *Annual Register.* "Perhaps you would like to drive, Miss Armitage?" he said at last.

"No, my lord, I don't think I would," said Beth firmly. Surely he couldn't believe she and Mr. Westall . . .

Of course he could. With frozen features he sat in a heavy library chair and prepared to watch their every move. Though the back of her neck prickled, Beth forced herself to take up the business of helping the secretary. She saw Mr. Westall cast one or two nervous glances in the marquess's direction and wondered if she were being fair to the secretary. He, after all, was an employee here and could be easily dismissed. The one thing of which Beth could be sure was that no one was going to cast her out of Belcraven.

She could not bear to quiver into submissive silence under

the marquess's glare, however, and when she came upon a relevant article she took it over to the secretary.

"See, here is an account of a steam carriage in use in a Yorkshire mine. It could be of interest."

"Indeed it could," he said, taking it. "And here is an article about Trevithick which must be the one the duke had in mind. Thank you, Miss Armitage."

Clutching his volumes, Mr. Westall left, clearly relieved to escape the atmosphere in the room.

Beth turned to look stonily at the marquess. "There," she said, "not a lascivious moment."

He rose with slow arrogance. "I will tell Westall he is not to be here alone with you again."

Beth was so angry it took a moment for her to get words out. She was still spluttering, "You—you—" when he left the room. Ferociously she slammed a glass door shut and a crack shot out from the beveled edge. She looked at it with horror. "Heavens above," she whispered, "what does one of those cost?"

Then she remembered she had no need to fret about such things. Willy-nilly she was one of the family. She walked briskly to the center table and rang the bell there. Promptly, a footmen entered.

"A piece of glass has cracked," she said. "Please inform someone so it may be fixed, Thomas." All the footman were known as Thomas when on duty. It simplified things a great deal.

"Yes, Miss Armitage," said the young man with a slightly startled look and left. Beth realized it was the first time she'd addressed a member of the staff with the crisp arrogance of one born to it. She didn't know if that was progress or defeat.

She knew she still felt embarrassment that the footman might have heard or guessed some of what had happened here but then she shrugged. She had soon come to realize that the only way to endure life at Belcraven was to pretend the servants were wooden dummies.

It occurred to her that she would, in fact, be much happier as a servant at Belcraven rather than one of the family. An upper servant, of course. The housekeeper or at least one of the senior maids. Then she could spend the evenings discussing the strange goings-on among the ducal family and relax and be herself.

It only later dawned on her that she had been given an opportunity to speak to the marquess and clear up the matter of her morals and had thrown it away.

The duchess's maneuvers had failed and so the duke took a hand. During an evening *en famille,* he looked sternly at his heir. "The notice is in the papers, Arden," he said, passing over a copy of the *Gazette.* "It is time to formally introduce your bride to our people here."

"As you will, sir," drawled the marquess in a bored voice, with only the briefest glance at the newspaper. He had been reading a book and kept his finger in his place.

"Don't doubt my will," said the duke coldly. "There is to be a reception for the tenants and a ball for our neighbors. You may expect a great many callers. You and Elizabeth will greet them together and behave appropriately."

Beth could see the marquess tense as he looked over at the duke. She wondered if he would rebel, but he merely repeated in a mechanical voice, "As you will, sir."

The duke's face became tinged with anger, and the duchess hastily intervened. "Even the servants think your behavior peculiar, Lucien. You are supposed to be in love. Besides, how are you and Elizabeth to come to an understanding if you avoid each other?"

The marquess smiled at Beth, a smile that could have frozen the oceans. "I believe Elizabeth and I have come to understand each other very well, *maman.*"

The duchess looked helplessly between the two of them.

"Tomorrow," stated the duke, "you will take Elizabeth on a tour of the house and estate, Arden, and explain it to her."

The two men stared at one another, and Beth saw the duke silently promise retribution if the marquess repeated his abrasive "As you will." The silence stretched beyond bearing.

Then the marquess turned to her, impersonally courteous.

"Of course," he said. "What time will be convenient, Elizabeth?"

"After breakfast, my lord?" said Beth a little squeakily. "Half-past nine?"

He inclined his head and, after a sardonic look at the duke, returned to his book.

Beth looked around the room. The duke was glaring at the marquess as if he would demand something more. The duchess was glancing between her husband and son with concern. The marquess was ostensibly absorbed in his book. Beth found the atmosphere in this family so hard to bear. Was it just this marriage, was it the past infidelities, or had it always been so? She was surprised to find she would like to help them in some way, then put the thought away. She had enough to do to save herself and had no strength to spare.

She quietly excused herself and escaped to her rooms.

In bed she considered the next day, a day to be spent in the marquess's company. Her nerves were already jumping at the thought. But perhaps, she thought, she would find an opportunity to undo the damage her silly words had caused. Then at least they could start afresh and seek to build some basis for an honest marriage out of all this.

Though she had found her way about the dozen or so rooms in family use, the next day Beth realized she had not grasped the scale of the enterprise which was the Duchy of Belcraven. The marquess, on the other hand, knew the great house from cool cellars to dusty attics. Despite his apparent arrogance, he knew of and understood all the servants who maintained the place, and even knew many of their names.

They spoke with the butler, Morrisby; and the senior housemaid, Kelly; the head laundress, Margery Coombs; and one of the stillroom maids, Elspeth.

In addition, there were the many anonymous workers, some clearly startled to find themselves face-to-face with one of the family. There was the clock winder, for example, and two men whose sole task was to pass through the house trimming and replacing candles. There were the carpenters, painters, masons, and roofers who worked constantly to maintain the great house, the home farm, and the myriad of attendant buildings. In addition to the services for the family—the food, the laundry, the housecleaning—all this had to be done as well for the three hundred people who kept the machinery running. There were servants for the servants.

There was a brewery, a bakery, a vast laundry, and a bevy of seamstresses. Soap was made and vinegar, and all the produce of the home farm was cooked, preserved, or used in some manner.

The higher servants—the estate manager, the steward, the groom of the chambers, and the housekeeper—supervised the machine and lived in the state of country gentry.

As he guided her around and explained all this, the marquess was polite, so dauntingly polite that Beth found it impossible to raise a personal subject.

After lunch the tour continued. They progressed through the kitchen gardens and the orchards, the herb gardens and the succession-houses. They passed by the kennels full of hounds and on, by way of the farriery, to the huge stables which housed forty horses and could accommodate a hundred more when there were guests.

Mentally and physically exhausted, Beth called a halt. The marquess obviously loved his home, and she felt he had relaxed a little during the tour. If she was to attempt an explanation it had best be now. She began with simple conversation.

"How do you begin to understand such a place?" she asked him.

He shrugged twirling a piece of straw in his fingers. "I know it as the place where I grew up. I spent my childhood, when I could escape from my tutors, under the grooms' feet, or sticking a finger into a cook's mixing bowl, or wandering with Morrisby through the wine cellar looking at the wine laid down for my coming of age. But as for running it, I only know how to direct the people who run it. That is all you will need to know."

Beth could only hope the day was long distant.

"I never asked you," the marquess said. "Do you ride?"

"No. I never had the opportunity."

"We must get you a habit and I'll teach you. It will give us something to do on our honeymoon."

Beth stared at him in surprise and he stiffened, memory and coolness returning in a second.

"Surely you don't want to spend *every* moment in bed?" he asked unpleasantly. "Even if you do, my dear, you must excuse me. No matter how lusty your previous lovers, I have only the capacity of a normal male. But I forget," he added with a sneer, "you satisfied yourself with plurality, didn't you? That I cannot accept."

Beth turned away to hide her burning cheeks. "I didn't," she muttered.

"I beg your pardon?"

Beth swallowed hard and turned to face him. "I didn't . . . what you said. I haven't . . ."

He didn't thaw a bit. "It's a little late for maidenly modesty, Elizabeth, though I congratulate you on your acting. It relieves my mind. You will have no difficulty in persuading the local people we are in love."

"I am not acting, Lord Arden," said Beth desperately.

He leaned against a stall door and studied her. "Let me understand you. You are now claiming to be what . . . ? Surely not a virgin?"

Beth felt as if she would be sick. "Yes."

"Why?"

Beth shook her head in bewilderment. "Why what?"

"Why lie about it now? The truth will out. I am not likely to be fooled by the bladder of blood hidden in the bedroom to stain the sheets."

Beth took a deep breath. "I am telling you the truth, my lord. I am untouched. I . . . I said what I did that first night in the hope you would end the engagement. I didn't realize you couldn't."

He walked over to her thoughtfully and raised her chin with a finger. Beth knew there were tears in her eyes and hoped they would work for her.

"The trouble with a lie, Elizabeth, is that it poisons truth. How do I know you are telling the truth now?"

"As you said," Beth replied hoarsely. "You will know."

He released her sharply and strode away to stand looking out at the stable yard. "You don't know how strong is the temptation, Miss Armitage, to ravish you here and now. If you spoke the truth before, it is doubtless what you want. If you lied, it is what you deserve. No matter how untouched, no decent woman could have spoken so."

"You choose to define 'decent woman' to suit yourself, my lord," said Beth angrily. "Yes, I believe marriage to be an oppressive institution best avoided by women, but lust is another kind of prison. I would never give myself to a man I did not love and trust, and," she added formidably, "I have not met such a man yet."

He turned then, eyes cold and hard. "And if you meet him after we are married? I meant what I said. I will not be cuckolded."

Beth raised her chin. "I will keep *my* marriage vows if I make them," she said with something of a sneer. "Will you, my lord?"

She was pleased to see him flush, but her sense of victory was short-lived. He stepped closer and smiled unpleasantly. "It all depends," he said with smiling menace, "on how well you serve me, my sweet. Let us hope the men who have handled you have taught you something."

Beth gasped. "No men have handled me!"

He raised his brows. "And yet you stood so coolly as I did? Come now, Elizabeth, let's not stretch credulity too far. I'm willing to believe, with admiration, that you have controlled your swains so as to retain your maidenhead, but that you have never been handled in that manner before? No."

Tears were streaming out of her, and Beth could hardly see. She pressed a hand over her eyes as if to push the weak tears back. "Oh, let me be, my lord. I am sorry, truly sorry, to have said what I did . . ." She shook her head and swallowed. "And now I am punished."

She tried to push past him, but he grabbed her roughly by

the shoulders. "You consider this punishment? You deserve a whipping!"

Beth pulled against his tight hands. "Let me go!"

Someone nearby cleared his throat.

Shocked, Beth and the marquess turned to see Jarvis, the head groom. He looked white and scared to death but he said, "Perhaps I could escort Miss Armitage back to the house, my lord."

The marquess sucked in a sharp breath and his hands tightened on Beth's shoulders so that she gave a choked cry.

"If you want your post, Jarvis, leave now," said the marquess in a voice of ice.

The man said nothing, but stood there.

Beth knew that in a moment the marquess would vent all his frustrated fury on the gallant man. He'd probably kill him. He was also well on the way to destroying the credibility of their betrothal. As it seemed they must go through with it, Beth wanted as little talk as possible. She just hoped she was as good an actress as he thought.

"My lord," she said softly. "Jarvis thinks you mean to hurt me. He doesn't know you would never do such a thing."

She dragged out a smile and raised a shaking hand to touch the marquess's cheek, hoping he would stop looking death at the servant. He turned to her, and she flinched at the flame of fury still burning in his eyes.

"Our lovers' quarrels," she said in a whisper, for it was all she seemed to be able to produce, "must seem real to him. Surely you do not blame him for wanting to protect me?"

Control smoothed the frown from his face and he too smiled, though his eyes still betrayed his feelings. "Of course not, my darling. I can only be pleased you have such champions."

He moved his hands to lay an arm at her waist and hold her close. Very close. Beth had to fight not to pull away from his body. "Don't be concerned, Jarvis," he said calmly. "Both Miss Armitage and I are merely suffering from prenuptial nerves."

The man, visibly relieved, touched his forelock and moved off. Beth let out a long shuddering breath.

"You keep your wits remarkably," said the marquess softly.

"Please let me go," said Beth, pulling away. But his arm was like iron. If anything, he pressed her closer, so that she could feel the hard shape of his chest, his hip, his thigh . . .

"Why?" he asked, grasping her chin and turning her face up toward him. "Don't you think an open demonstration of our fondness would be in order?"

"No!" Beth could imagine nothing worse than to be kissed with hate. She pulled harder. "Let me go!" It was hopeless.

"I have a bargain for you," he said with a smile she distrusted.

Beth stilled. "What is it?"

He ran a finger down her cheek. Beth flinched. His smile became even wider and colder. "I will refrain from forcing my unwelcome attentions on you, sweeting, and from throwing your disgusting exploits in your face, if you will act your part to the full."

"I am," Beth protested.

"I want you to dress properly, assume the appropriate manner for a future marchioness, and give all the appearance of being in love."

Beth shuddered. "You are asking for total submission."

He drew her even closer, turning slightly so that he pressed against her sensitive breasts, and smiled a conqueror's smile. "In return, you are free of my attentions except for polite public performances. That *is* what you want, isn't it, Elizabeth?"

Beth had absolutely no choice. She needed to escape from this situation before it once more ripped out of control. "I agree. Let go of me."

He released her at last. "So be it."

Beth moved quickly to leave the stables, to leave him. His hand fastened around her arm. Beth jerked around like a scalded cat. "Gently, my dear. Our pact begins here. Dry your eyes." He offered a handkerchief and Beth used it to wipe the tears. Dear Lord, what now?

Then he extended his arm and she laid her hand upon it. Sedately, a proper lord and his lady, they walked back to the house.

* * *

Jarvis watched them go. He'd thought he'd lost his place, perhaps his life, for a moment there, but he couldn't stand by and do nothing. He'd perched the marquess on his first pony and taught him nearly all he knew about horses. Arden was a good lad, but he'd always had the devil's own temper when crossed. Back in those days, Jarvis had held the duke's permission to cuff him if he were stupid. He remembered taking his riding crop to the marquess one day when the boy had worked out one of his rages on a horse.

The lad had then run to his father, and the duke had come out to inspect the poor mare. Then he'd ordered Jarvis to give the lad six more strokes there in the stable yard. There'd been no more trouble after that, and the marquess had not held a grudge. Pity there was no one to take a whip to him now, treating a pleasant lady like Miss Armitage so. Lovers' quarrel indeed. Funny kind of love.

There was talk in the servants' hall about those two, though no one could figure out what was going on. Some thought the marquess had given her one in the basket, so to speak, but there wasn't that much hurry about getting them wed. They certainly didn't act like lovebirds, though.

Miss Armitage was a very well-liked lady as far as the staff went—pleasant, ladylike, but with no airs and graces. But hardly the marquess's type. Hardly his type at all.

Jarvis shook his head as he went back to care for his horses. Nags had more sense than people any day.

Chapter Seven

When she separated from the taciturn marquess, Beth took refuge in the library.

He seemed to believe she was a virgin and yet it had not greatly helped matters. She had no idea what he thought she had done. A solid education including the unexpurgated classics had left her, she thought, well informed about men and women and what they did together. The reality, however, was like thinking knowledge of a bathtub adequate preparation for a life at sea.

She had not wished to be kissed in hate. What would it be like if she had to share a marriage bed in that spirit?

Tears threatened again, and again she pressed them back ruthlessly. She would not degenerate into a watering pot. She wished desperately that she had someone in whom to confide, someone to turn to for advice. It could not be Miss Mallory, for she would simply tell her to return home and give up all notion of the marriage. And besides, Beth had to suppose that lady's worldly wisdom to be as flawed as her own.

The duchess was the only married woman available to her, and she could not bring herself to lay the whole sordid mess before the marquess's mother.

Her only choice seemed to be to behave with such impeccable good breeding that the marquess would realize she could not be the kind of monster he imagined.

Who on earth were these men who were supposed to have

handled her? With a choke of laughter Beth thought of her beaux, such as they had been.

Mr. Rutherford, the curate, who had blushed fiercely when forced one day to untangle her skirt from a rose bush; Mr. Grainger, the philosopher, who had once kissed her on the lips then apologized profusely for the presumption and fled; Dr. Carnarvon, who cared for the pupils at Miss Mallory's. The good doctor had hovered about her for a year before saying that he was quite unworthy of her because of his earthy desires. He had then married a sensible widow.

She tried to imagine any of those men treating her as the marquess had done—kissing her with an open mouth, touching her breast. That was not how a man touched a respectable woman. Perhaps she should write to the "men in her life" and ask for character references.

Then an illustration popped into her mind—a picture from one of Miss Mallory's more outré books, one of the ones kept locked from the pupils. It was of Venus and Mars. Venus was lying half-naked in the lap of Mars who had one of his hands on her naked breast.

Good God! Did the marquess think she had done *that?* With Mr. Rutherford? Beth leapt to her feet, her hands pressed to flaming cheeks. How could she ever face him again? Surely such things only occurred in pagan times!

It was at that moment that the duchess walked in. "I knew I would find you here, my dear—" She halted, puzzled to see Beth standing in the middle of the room. "Is anything the matter, Elizabeth?"

Beth knew an outright denial would not be believed and so she said, "Just a little *crise de nerfs,* that's all, Your Grace."

"I hope it was nothing Lucien did," said the duchess, coming closer. Beth knew she had just turned even redder. "He is fundamentally a good man, but he has enough of his father in him to be difficult at times."

Startled at this casual reference to the marquess's parentage, Beth could only say, "Oh."

The duchess smiled her sweet smile which always had a dimming overlay of sadness. "It needn't be a forbidden subject between us. St. Briac was dashing but totally unreliable. He was a mess of fiery emotions, a constant explosion of impulses. I could have married him, you know. He had property, and though a poor prospect for one such as I, was not totally ineligible. He asked for my hand, but I would not marry him. He was too . . . explosive."

So that was where the marquess got his temper. "And yet I am to marry his son," said Beth.

"Lucien is not very like him, I assure you, Elizabeth. He is a lot like me and I, as you can see, am a very practical woman. He also has modeled himself a great deal on the duke, who is everything that St. Briac was not."

Beth had suspected there was a deep love between the duke and duchess, hidden somehow by the formality of their lives. She saw it clearly now as the duchess spoke admiringly of her husband. But why then did they live as they did? She tried to imagine the duke and duchess. . . . Hastily she controlled her mind.

The duchess said again, "But as Lucien has that touch of wildness and a temper, I wondered if he had upset you."

"It is only my situation, Your Grace, which disturbs me. It would be the same with any man." Even as she said it, Beth knew that was not true. The marquess had a particular genius for setting her on edge.

The duchess, the practical woman, shrugged. *"C'est la vie.* And I am afraid I must disturb you more. There will be callers and there is the ball to consider. I am afraid, my dear, if you do not wish to be a quiz, you are going to have to allow us to procure you new clothes. Lucien said you would agree to this."

Beth looked down at her simple yellow round gown. She had thought such gowns ubiquitous and unremarkable.

"Yes, I know," said the duchess with a deprecating smile, "But it looks homemade, my dear. We are not going to try to pretend to anyone that you bring a fortune, but they are bound to wonder why we don't dress you."

"Very well," sighed Beth. She had, after all, given her word to the marquess. "But I must have some say in my clothes."

"But of course," said the duchess happily. "Now come along."

Beth had already discovered that the duchess could move with great speed, and she was almost running as she kept up with the older woman on the way to her rooms. A footman was sent to find the head seamstress.

"Mrs. Butler is well able to make a stylish plain gown and will take your measurements. We will send a muslin toile to London and have a ballgown made for you. In fact," she said with a shrewd glance at Beth, "I think I will send Lucien. It will get him out of the way and give him some light relief. He can execute a number of necessary commissions far better than a servant. We must look at the periodicals."

Another footman was sent off to bring these from the duchess's suite.

"We must do something about jewels, too," said the duchess. "Lucien will buy you some, but there are pieces among the family jewels which you should have." Another footman went hurrying on his way.

In Beth's room they went straight into the dressing room.

"You had best slip out of your gown, my dear," the duchess said briskly. Beth did as she was told and put on her wrap.

"Underclothes," said the duchess, as if making a mental list. "Silk nightdresses." Beth felt her cheeks heat up again. "Do you wish us to buy you a full wardrobe now or would you rather purchase it for yourself when you are married?"

"Does it make any difference?" asked Beth, feeling like someone who has moved one small stone and caused a landslide.

"It depends on where you are to honeymoon and how soon you intend to take up fashionable life."

"I don't know."

"Ask Lucien," said the duchess. Beth was not sure if it was an instruction or another mental note.

By then the summonses were having effect. A tall gaunt woman, followed by a little maid carrying a basket and a selection of swatches, proved to be the seamstress. She swiftly

took measurements of all parts of Beth's body as the duchess
chattered on about types of gowns.

"Round gowns," she said. "Of the simplest lines, I think.
You agree, Elizabeth?" Before Beth had time to respond, she
went on. "Muslin. Let me see. This cream jaconet is lovely,
isn't it? Or this figured lawn . . ."

Beth gave up and allowed the duchess to choose three gowns
to be made quickly—one of figured lawn, one of jaconet muslin sprigged with green, and one of plain cambric. She also
gave orders for the beginning of a trousseau of personal gar-
ments, all to be monogrammed.

The dressmaker left, and Beth resumed her maligned homemade gown. She was immediately drawn over to look through
the fashion magazines with the duchess. She was prepared to
protest if she thought the choices unsuitable, but otherwise she
was resigned to letting the duchess make them. What did she
know of such silly matters?

In a moment, it seemed, six grand, and surely expensive,
outfits had been selected to be ordered from London. "And a
habit," said the duchess firmly. "And boots."

Next, the beleaguered Beth had a small fortune of jewelry
spread casually on the table before her—silver, gold, diamonds,
rubies, emeralds, sapphires, pearls. . . . She could not help her
fingers going out to touch a beautiful diamond bracelet that
shot fire in the light of the sun, and a string of softly glowing
pearls. She pulled her hand back. Truly she was being seduced,
and not with kisses. She resolutely refused to accept anything
except the string of pearls, traditional ornament of a gently
bred young woman, a set of amber baubles which did not look
expensive, and, under pressure, some diamonds. She chose a
delicate parure as being the least overwhelming.

"It is very pretty," said the duchess doubtfully, fingering
the diamonds, "but the stones are small. Will you not take this
one?" she asked, opening a case to show a magnificent set in
which huge diamonds flashed blades of rainbow colors.

Beth shrank away. What had Beth Armitage to do with a
thing like that? "No, Your Grace. Truly. I much prefer the
other."

"Comme vous voudrez, ma chère," the duchess said with her typical Gallic shrug.

Beth could not imagine the hours which must have been worked in the Belcraven sewing rooms, but one of her new gowns, the green sprig, was ready the next day when the first callers came. It was a very simple gown, gathered with draw-strings at the waist and only ornamented by a green silk sash, and yet it was much superior to her own creations. The duchess inspected her and was pleased. She tried to prevent Beth from wearing one of her caps but failed. In some way the caps had become a symbol for Beth and she would not give them up.

The guests proved to be close neighbors, a Lady Frogmorton and her daughters, Lucy and Diane. They were accompanied by a friend, Miss Phoebe Swinnamer, a young lady of quite remarkable beauty. Of which, thought Beth, she was far too aware. Still, she had to admit that it would be hard for the possessor to ignore a perfect oval face, translucent skin, big blue eyes, and thick, glossy, mahogany, waving hair.

There was something disturbing about the young lady, how-ever—about the way she looked at Beth and the marquess, and the way her friends looked at her. It didn't take genius to see that Miss Swinnamer wished to be in Beth's position. It was clear that Lucy Frogmorton also was envious. Beth then sup-posed that most of the young ladies in England shared that feeling.

For the first time she thought how ludicrous it was that fate had delivered this supposed honor to one of the few sane women who did not want it.

Beth was still puzzling over Phoebe Swinnamer when the young lady managed to snatch a seat beside her. Beth realized that the duchess had been delicately attempting to prevent just such an occurrence.

"Do you live in Berkshire, Miss Swinnamer?" Beth asked politely. After years of teaching, jealous young minxes did not frighten her.

"Oh no," said Phoebe with a slight smile which did not

reach her eyes. "My home is in Sussex, but we spend a great deal of time in London."

"Then you must enjoy it. I have rarely visited the capital."

"It is my duty," said Phoebe. "I am my parents' heiress. I must make a good match."

Beth smiled. "I am sure with your beauty and fortune, the choice must be entirely yours, Miss Swinnamer."

There was the slightest stiffening of Phoebe's beautiful features, though it was clear she never let the stronger emotions disturb them. "It is kind of you to say so, Miss Armitage." She looked around. "Belcraven is very beautiful, is it not? I spent the Christmas here."

Beth now understood that Phoebe had been a serious contender for the marquess's hand. Were they in fact disappointed lovers? Selfishly, it had never occurred to her that he might have had to give up a chosen partner to make this match. Beth glanced over at him, but he was relaxed in friendly talk with the Frogmortons and there was nothing to learn.

She looked back and saw Phoebe had noted that look with satisfaction. Beth took hold of her wits. The little cat was out to make trouble. She doubtless had faint hopes of somehow spoiling the present arrangement and reviving her chances. Beth knew there was no possibility of that and had no mind to have her life made more difficult by the girl.

"Personally," she said, "I prefer a quiet family Christmas."

"And where does your family live?" asked Phoebe, probing for a weakness.

"I lived with my aunt in Cheltenham," countered Beth. "Are your parents here with you, Miss Swinnamer?"

"No, my mother has been in Bath while my father was in Melton for the hunting. I'm surprised," she drawled, with a somehow familiar look at the marquess, "Arden has been dragged away from there. He usually spends most of the winter in the Shires."

"The power of love," said Beth sweetly. "I was not in such a mighty hurry to be wed, I assure you, Miss Swinnamer. But the marquess was positively insistent."

Phoebe's charming, shapely nose became decidedly pinched.

Before she could rally, the duchess was there, drawing Beth away. "You must come and talk to Lady Frogmorton, my dear." As soon as they were out of earshot, she said, "I do hope the girl did not offend you, Elizabeth."

"Of course not," Beth said. "I am well used to young misses. But am I correct in thinking there was an attachment between her and the marquess?"

"Oh no, not an attachment," the duchess said quickly. "She did seem to have a great deal to offer, and Lucien considered her—partly at my urging, I confess. I do not think he was ever particularly drawn to her. In fact," she admitted with a rueful twinkle, "he was called away shortly after Christmas on some mysterious urgent business, much to poor Phoebe's annoyance."

Beth shared the amusement, relieved to think her future husband wasn't nursing a broken heart. They had enough trouble without that.

She sat down to gossip with Lady Frogmorton, a kindly woman who said everything that was proper. Beth had been right about the jealousy of the daughters, however. Lucy, in particular, being the elder and sharply pretty, with vivid dark-haired, cherry-lipped looks, eyed Beth with disbelief. Beth supposed she would just have to become accustomed to this reaction.

When Lucien came to join them she was grateful for the way he behaved. There was no crude outward show of fondness, of course, but in the way he stood beside her and the tone of his voice he clearly convinced the visitors that, strange though it was, this mousy and rather old woman had stolen his heart.

Beth recognized, however, that this salve to her pride was bought at cost to her heart. When he acted so proficiently it was all too easy to fall under the spell, to forget this was a pact imposed ruthlessly and supported by threats of violence.

She watched carefully when he exchanged pleasantries with Phoebe Swinnamer. Beth could not hear the words, but his attitude was friendly and brotherly. In as far as she was capable of it, Miss Swinnamer looked cross, and Beth took unkind satisfaction from that. It was unfortunate but human to dislike a young woman who was so set up in her own opinion and who clearly regarded Beth as something lower than an earthworm.

The next day brought the vicar and his wife in the company of Sir George Matlock, the local squire, and Lady Matlock. They, too, Beth thought, looked at her with a trace of puzzlement, but accepted matters, doubtless due to the marquess's excellent acting. They were also, however, inclined to gush. Beth found it strange to be looked up to as a member of the ducal family when she still felt like Beth Armitage the schoolmistress.

She feared it would be much more of the same at the upcoming ball. Beth helped the duchess and Mrs. Sysonby to address the hundred invitations.

"I confess," she remarked as she dipped her pen into the standish again, "this seems a great many invitations for a country ball."

"Oh, but this is a small affair," said the duchess. "As there will be other events in London we are only asking the local people and at least half will have to decline, my dear." She tidied one stack with deft fingers. "Men are still in the Shires hunting. Women are visiting family. Some have already gone up to Town to prepare for the Season. But, even so, they would be affronted if we failed to send an invitation."

This was no relief to Beth. She could still apparently expect over thirty families to come and gawk. She wished she was being sent an invitation, for then she presumably could refuse.

She supposed the marquess, too, wished he could escape the event. He at least escaped to London to execute the duchess's commissions. Before he left he sought out Beth in the library.

"I felt for form's sake I should take a tender farewell of you," he said dryly.

"Consider it taken," she responded in the same manner. She would never show weakness before him again.

That didn't prevent a tremor of nervousness when he walked toward her window seat. He brought to mind a big cat stalking its prey and she was trapped in the deep embrasure. She began to fear he might break his promise and assault her, but he merely removed her book from her lax fingers and glanced at the title.

"Sallust?" he noted in surprise. "You read Latin?"

How typical that he should think it remarkable. "Yes," she said coldly, "I read Latin. It isn't always easy, but it is good exercise for the mind . . ." Her voice trailed off because he had sat beside her and taken her hand. Quite gently. There was no anger on his face, only bemusement.

"I find you impossible to understand, Elizabeth," he said thoughtfully. "You read Latin and refuse a fortune in jewels. And yet you claim to be—"

"I explained that," Beth interrupted angrily, dragging her fingers from his hold.

He shook his head and put the book, open, in her hands again. "Read me a passage and translate it."

With a grunt of anger Beth slammed the book closed. "Putting me to the test again?" she exclaimed. She waved the tome in his face. "Really, my lord. Do you think knowledge of Latin a proof of virtue? What then of the whole of the male aristocracy?"

Disarmingly, he laughed. "Ah, but it's the Greek that does us in."

He gently rescued the book and let it fall open again. He smiled as he read, " 'Ita in maxima fortuna minima licentia est.' I seem to remember at Harrow I didn't believe that high station limited freedom. Perhaps old Gaius Salustius had something after all." He closed the book and placed it on the seat. "Can we possibly, do you think, cry quarter? This is all going to drive me mad. If you are willing to behave like a lady, the least I can do is act the gentleman. I promise never to refer to our unfortunate conversations again."

Beth rose to her feet, partly in a simple need to move away from him. There was something disturbing in his mere proximity, especially when he was in a mellow mood. "That would be an improvement," she responded. "But can you forget them?"

"I can try," he replied. "At least until you give me further reason to doubt you."

An angry retort rose to her lips, but Beth suppressed it. She, too, found it unbearable to live in a state of war. She studied him and decided he was completely honest. "Truce then," she said, holding out her hand.

He took it and kissed her fingers formally. *"Forsan et haec olim meminisse iuvabit.* Truce, Elizabeth."

With that he turned and quietly left. Beth had to work out a translation of his words. Something like, "Someday it may be pleasant to remember this." Why was she disconcerted to discover him well-educated? He had doubtless spent most of his youth declining Latin and translating Cicero. But was she not even to be able to retain a sense of superiority as defense?

With one hand covering the spot on the other where he had placed that soft kiss, Beth dealt with conflicting feelings. For the first time they had met in honesty and reached an agreement. Perhaps there was some hope of building a relationship of respect.

On the other hand she was aware of a dangerous response within herself to his kindness and intelligence. Her anger and disdain had formed a bulwark. Without it she feared the marquess could steal her heart as easily as plucking a flower from a stem, and probably as meaninglessly.

It might perhaps have been safer to continue the war.

More than ever she needed an adviser. She suddenly remembered she had a father. The duke was the originator of all her troubles. Why then should he not bear the burden of them?

But how was it to be accomplished? They met at dinner and for part of the evening but rarely otherwise. Send one of the footmen? With a note or a verbal message? She was tempted to give up, but the project assumed the nature of a challenge, an opportunity to prove to herself that she could cope in the structured world of Belcraven. A little nervously she rang the bell. A footman quickly came in. "Miss Armitage?"

"I wish to speak to the duke, Thomas," said Beth.

"He is usually with his secretary at this time of day, miss. Do you wish me to enquire?"

"Yes, please," said Beth, and when the man had gone she sank down into a chair with relief and a small glow of triumph. It was just a matter of playing the game by the rules.

In a little while she was bowed into the duke's study by Mr. Westall, who discreetly took himself elsewhere.

"Yes, Elizabeth?" asked the duke, removing his spectacles and rubbing the groove they had left in the bridge of his nose.

Now the moment was upon her, Beth was not at all sure what she wished to say. "You are my father," she said at last. "It seemed I might be able to talk to you, but now I am not sure."

His austere features softened slightly. "I would like to think that was true. I have watched and admired your handling of this situation. You may think it would have been easier to avoid this time at Belcraven, Elizabeth, to have lived more quietly before your marriage, but that would have been a cruel type of kindness. You are learning to cope."

"I can cope, I believe, with the pomp. I am not sure I can cope with the marquess."

The duke's lips tightened. "What has he done?"

"Nothing," said Beth hastily. She had no wish to cause further dissension in this unhappy family. "I simply cannot decide how to handle him."

The duke relaxed and smiled a little. "I am afraid you have come to the wrong person for advice on that, my dear. I am not sure how to handle him either. I manage, because I long ago decided what I wanted from him—that he grow up with a well-educated mind, a healthy body, and the manners of a gentleman. I have steered him in that direction with whatever force was necessary at the time. What do *you* want from him?"

Beth raised her hands helplessly and let them fall. "I don't know."

"What do you want from him that you do not currently receive?"

Beth shook her head. These questions did not help. "I am so lonely," she said at last.

He sighed. "Ah, loneliness . . ." He looked at her. "Perhaps what you want from him, my dear, is friendship. The heir to a dukedom is not overly endowed with true friends. If you offer Arden simple companionship, I do not think he would reject it."

Beth had known friendship in her younger years, but in the course of time her friends had left the school to take up different kinds of lives. Beth knew the duke was correct. She did want a friend, and friendship in marriage had always been her ideal. But her rash lies has made such a treasure impossible between herself and the marquess.

To share secret feelings, to listen to anxieties, to know the other person will immediately understand—that all depended on trust.

"I cannot imagine it," she said bleakly.

The duke rose and paced the room. "I am perplexed. I am not blind: I have seen the constraint between the two of you. It seems to me that the marquess could charm any woman, but you are not charmed. It seems to me that two people of sense could find common ground upon which to build and yet you appear to be achieving nothing. Is your future happiness not worth some effort?"

Beth met his look. "We are trying. We keep finding ourselves setting stones in quicksand."

After a frowning study of her, the duke sighed and looked away with a shake of his head. "When we all move to London," he said, "you will make friends of your own. These recent days have not been typical of your future life. As you have seen," he said dryly, "people such as we do not need to live in one another's pockets. Once you are married, there is no need for you and Arden to see much of each other. Or if you do, it will mostly be in company."

Beth knew with a pang this was not what she wanted at all. Then she nervously considered the private moments. "If I could be more at ease with him . . ." She could not finish the sentence.

Perhaps it was her rising color which enabled the duke to read her mind. "You are concerned about the intimacies of marriage, Elizabeth. It is only to be expected. I can merely say this, my dear. I have absolute trust in Arden's ability to handle a marriage bed with courtesy and kindness."

But, despite their truce, would the marquess feel he needed to handle the marriage bed so carefully? And even so, no matter how it was handled, it was going to be a gross invasion by a man who had no desire for the business at all.

Beth looked up at the duke and said, "You are my father." She had not the slightest idea what she intended by it.

"Yes. And I love you, Elizabeth, as I did not expect to when this started." The genuine concern on his face, however, was wiped away. "I will cherish you as best I can," he said in his usual manner, "but I will not give up my plan."

Beth stood and said desperately, "I wish it were all done!"

The duke walked over and took her hand. "It will soon begin, Elizabeth. The ending, of course, is death."

Beth had only looked ahead to the wedding. Now her life stretched before her, intimately entangled with a stranger, watching every word and treading among quicksands. She stared at the duke for a moment, then wrenched her hand from his and ran out of the room.

Catching the interested look in the eye of a footman, she pulled herself together. Oh, how she hated the fishbowl life of Belcraven. She forced herself to walk composedly to her room, where she found her cloak, then slipped out of a side entrance to march mindlessly along the many paths of the grounds.

"Till death us do part." Soon she would have to say those words to the marquess, and it was true. Once there were children they would be entangled forever. Even if she were to flee him, the knowledge of the children would always be there.

There was no going back in life.

Her life had been so unchanging before that she had never realized the simple truth, though she had read it in Lucretius. "Whenever a thing changes and quits its proper limits, this change is at once the death of that which was before."

Quietly in the spring garden, Beth mourned her previous life.

Chapter Eight

Once in town the marquess lost little time in going to Blanche's house. She threw herself into his arms. "Lucien, love!"

He buried his head in her sweet-smelling hair and sighed. "You know why I have come?"

She pulled back and smiled sadly at him. "It's goodbye? I saw the notice of your engagement. Is she worthy of you, love?"

He let her go and said fiercely, "What do you mean by that?"

Blanche went as white as her softly draped gown. "I'm sorry, Lucien. I didn't mean it badly. If you have chosen a bride from nowhere you must love her, and that's all that matters."

He ran a hand through his curls. "We shouldn't even be discussing it."

"Well then," said Blanche lightly, though she was still pale, "let me order tea, and I can tell you all the scandal."

He sat across from her and let her chatter.

Blanche hoped he could not tell how hard it was for her. She had prepared to receive her *congé* ever since she had seen the notice, but she had not been prepared for the shadow in his eyes. What had happened? It clearly was not a love match he was entering, but more than that she could not guess. She ached for him.

When she interrupted her light account of the latest crim-con to refill his cup, he asked abruptly, "How can a man tell if a woman is virtuous, Blanche?"

She looked up, puzzled. "Do you mean, if she's a virgin?"

"No. Just the tenor of her mind."

Blanche shrugged. "I could ask, why should a man care? He could see how easily she was shocked, I suppose."

He laughed without humor, put down his cup, and pulled her up and away from the table. "And are you easily shocked, my winter rose?"

She knew she had colored, which didn't happen often these days. "I think you've shocked me now, Lucien. You said this was goodbye. You're as good as married."

He drew down both the loose sleeves of her gown until her breasts were bare, then gently cupped them in his hands and pushed them up. "That's no impediment to making love to the most beautiful woman in London." He lowered his head to kiss the swell of each.

Blanche was already halfway to passion just from simple memory. "You said 'in England' the last time," she teased softly.

He looked up and smiled, and it was his old smile. "Did I?" He swept her into his arms and headed for the stairs. "Well, that diminution of your sphere must be my tribute to the obligations of matrimony, *ma belle.*" He stopped to pay tribute to each sensitive nipple. "We are in London, aren't we?"

Blanche arched and clutched him. "That or heaven, dear one."

As he laid her on the bed, he held back her hair and let it drift down last to lie all around her like a silvery pillow. "That's all right then," he whispered and lowered his head to kiss her.

Later, he leaned over her and pushed her damp hair off her face. Gently he said, "It is still goodbye, my lovely one."

Blanche stroked his smoothly muscled shoulder. "I know it, love. You're not a man to keep a mistress when newly wed. I hope you never keep one again. I'll miss you, though."

He smiled. "That's soothing to my ego. If you want, you'll have the pick of London to replace me."

"Ah, but there's not many with your beauty," she said honestly and with a cheeky twinkle. "I like to just look at you, you know. Care to come back and pose a few times?"

He laughed and sprang out of bed to strike a noble pose.

"Mmm." She lay watching as he dressed.

When he was ready, he took a flat box from his pocket with a trace of hesitation and came back to sit on the bed. "There's always been more between you and me, Blanche, than payment," he said. "Can you take this gift in friendship, with my gratitude? I never have enough friends."

Blanche had expected a gift, and in a way she had dreaded it. It smacked too much of a baser relationship. She felt tears tickling the back of her eyes at his sensitivity, even though she should have expected it. She opened the box to see a paper which proved to be the deed to the house in which they stood. She glanced at it, but her attention was snared by what was underneath—a glittering rainbow of a necklace, exquisite flowers of emerald green, sapphire blue, ruby red, and topaz yellow.

She gasped then laughed up at him. "Lucien, you gaby. What am I supposed to do with this?"

He grinned. "Save it for your retirement?"

"I'll wear it in private if I'm feeling low." She gave him her sweetest smile. "You will always have a friend in me, my dear, and," she added carefully, "you need never fear I'll try to be more."

She looked down at the necklace for a moment and then back, frowning slightly. "I would like to say something else. About virtuous minds. There's little I don't know about men and women, love, and little I haven't experienced, but you've always treated me as a woman of honor. Virtue is a standard society puts on us, often an unreasonable one. Honor is something within ourselves. Only we can give away our honor."

Moved by her words, he kissed her hands and her lips. "I will always honor you, Blanche."

With that he was gone, and she could let the tears fall as she smiled at the ridiculously gaudy necklace.

* * *

Lucien impulsively stopped by at White's. He was in no mood for his own company and found the Belcraven mansion a bleak place unless filled with guests. He was rewarded by the sight of Con Somerford, Viscount Amleigh. The dark-haired young man was frowning as he read the day's *Times*. When he heard his name, he looked up, and the frown was replaced by a smile. "Good day, Luce."

"It's good to see a friendly face, Con," Lucien said as he took the viscount's hand. "I'd no real hope of meeting anyone I knew. I thought everyone would be in Melton still."

"Was," said the handsome young viscount as he summoned more of the claret he was drinking. "Couldn't keep my mind on foxes with all this going on." He waved the paper. "Anyway, I heard Nicholas was in Town."

That could only be the Honorable Nicholas Delaney, leader of the schoolboy clique to which they had both belonged and which had been revived the year before for more serious business. "Nick's here? Why?"

"Same thing," said Con, indicating the paper. The viscount's gray eyes turned bleak. "There's nothing to do, of course, but he must feel as sick as I do over it after all he did last year." He looked soberly into his wine. "I'm rejoining my regiment."

Lucien felt a chill. "It'll come to that again?"

"Bound to."

"God damn it all, someone should have shot the Corsican." Lucien thought of all the friends who had lost their lives in the long war. Was it all to do again? "I wish to heaven I felt free to fight. Perhaps if I have a son . . ."

Con looked at him quizzically. "I don't think Boney'll wait that long. You're not even married yet."

"As good as," Lucien admitted. "Notice is in the papers. Doubtless in that very one you're reading."

The viscount blinked in astonishment but then raised his glass. "Congratulations! The Swinnamer girl?"

"No," said Lucien, making a snap decision not to reveal the truth to this or any other friend. "You won't know her. Name of Elizabeth Armitage. From Gloucestershire."

"Knocked you for a loop, has she?" remarked the viscount,

clearly not giving the matter much attention. "Even so, old boy, I don't think the question of Napoleon will last ten months or so. It'll be this summer and you'd do best to stay home. It'll be bloody."

"What of you? You have responsibilities now." Con had sold out the year before when he inherited the title.

"I've got two brothers," said Con carelessly. "Dare's offered his services at the Horse Guards, too. I think we're the only two who aren't the sole dependence of their families so we have to do our bit." He meant the only two of the Company of Rogues. He took a swig of claret. "Except Miles, I suppose. But he has some Irish notion about not serving the crown. . . . But look," he said in a brighter manner, "we're invited over to Nicholas's tonight. You must come."

"We?"

"Stephen's in town," Con said in a sonorous tone, "being an important man in the government." Stephen Ball was member for Barham. "And Hal Beaumont's here."

"Hal!" exclaimed Lucien, a grin starting. Hal Beaumont had been his closest friend until their paths had split when Hal joined a line regiment and was posted to the American war. "I haven't heard from him in over a year. Thought he was still in Canada."

"Part of him still is," Con said gently. "He's lost an arm."

"Christ." Lucien stared at his friend numbly. He and Hal had been partners in so many youthful adventures, most of them depending on superb physical condition.

"Cannon exploded. He's come through it well enough. He'll want to see you. Was thinking of going up your way."

Lucien wanted to see Hal, too, but was aware of a reluctance to see him maimed and was instantly ashamed of it. "Tonight at Lauriston Street?" he confirmed briskly. "I'll send round a note, but Nicholas won't mind. Is Eleanor here, too?"

"Of course. And the child. They're on their way to a family gathering at his brother's place. Just came up a bit early to get the latest news."

Lucien buried the shock of Hal's injury under the pleasant prospect of meeting all these friends. He wondered how Nicho-

las Delaney was now, four months after his return to England,
seven months after their last meeting. That had been on the
night when Nicholas had succeeded in gaining the plans of a
plot to liberate Napoleon from Elba and restore him to power
in France.

That success had been at great cost to himself, and in those
days Nicholas had been tense and worn. His efforts had almost
cost him his life, and his marriage, too. And after all the sac-
rifices it had all turned out to be a fraud. Or had it?

Napoleon, after all, was back in France and in power.

The beautiful Madame Bellaire had said in the end that the
supporters of Napoleon had been tricked and that she was
keeping the money for her own use. Had that been yet another
lie? And if so, would Nicholas consider himself to blame in
that he had only got the list of names from the woman and
not relieved her of her ill-gotten gains?

Lucien had had letters from Nicholas which painted a pleasant picture of contentment with rural life, matrimony, and a
new baby, but he'd be pleased to have it confirmed with his
own eyes.

He'd be curious too to see the little Delaney. Arabel must
be four months old. The babe had only been a few days old
when last he'd seen her, and he couldn't say she'd shown promise of beauty back then.

That evening, when he was ushered into the elegant house
at Lauriston Street the first sight to meet his eyes was Eleanor
Delaney—looking finer and happier than she ever had—
dressed in silk and jewels, with her baby in her arms. She
turned and a wide, vivacious smile lit her face. "Lucien!" she
exclaimed as she came over to greet him. "We were so thrilled
to receive your note. And you are due our congratulations."
She reached his side and leaned forward for a kiss. "You must
tell us all about your bride-to-be."

He had to work around a fragrant infant to kiss her cheek,
which was a new experience. He looked down to be trapped
by enormous gold-brown eyes fringed by outrageous lashes.

The child had incredible skin—he would never be able to call a woman's skin petal-soft again—and a sweet, soft mouth.

"Lord above, Eleanor. You can't let that loose on the world. There'll be no male left sane."

Eleanor smiled down in pride. "She is quite pretty, isn't she? But not much hair yet. There's no guarantee she'll be anything out of the ordinary later though. Babies are generally appealing."

"Appealing has nothing to do with it. She's a man-slayer."

Eleanor chuckled with pleasure at this praise. "Here," she said and passed the child over. "Be slain. I just have to have a word with Mrs. Cooke."

"Eleanor!" protested Lucien as the child settled in his arms. "Come back here!"

"Nicholas is in the drawing room," she called as she disappeared.

Lucien looked down at the child. It was disconcerting to be so readily accepted. Arabel was not the slightest bit disturbed by being in strange arms and appeared fascinated by his sapphire cravat pin. Delicate starfish fingers reached aimlessly for it. "Typical woman," grumbled Lucien with a smile. "Fascinated by something glittery. Come on. Let's find Papa."

But as he crossed the hall the thought of a child of his own became for the first time something other than a burdensome duty.

He entered the drawing room to find his host, Nicholas Delaney, talking to some members of the Company: Sir Stephen Ball M.P.; Lord Darius Debenham—third son of the Duke of Yeovil; and the viscount. They all turned and grinned at the sight of him with a baby in his arms.

"Good Lord," said Nicholas, coming forward. "I heard you were engaged to marry, but aren't you a bit beforehand?"

Lucien couldn't help a grin, but he said, "This, if you can't recognize it, is yours."

Nicholas took the babe easily, and Arabel broke out a bright smile and a chortle. "So it is."

Lucien found simple pleasure in seeing how healthy Nicholas appeared—his skin tanned, his gold-flecked brown eyes clear and happy. He'd known from Eleanor's radiant looks that nothing had occurred to tarnish their new-built marriage, but now it was confirmed.

He hadn't realized what a burden of concern he'd carried until it was removed.

The business Nicholas had involved them all in last year had seemed a jape at first, very like the schoolboy plots they had indulged in at Harrow. It had stopped being a joke when Lucien had realized how it was hurting Eleanor to know her husband was so often with another woman; he had become a great admirer of Eleanor Delaney.

It had taken longer for him to realize how playing the lover for Thérèse Bellaire was slowly destroying Nicholas.

He hadn't really understood until the night he'd tried to be noble and distract the predatory Madame's attention to himself. She'd managed merely with a look of her eyes to make him feel raped. When Nicholas finally drew her off, Lucien had been beyond feeling noble and had just felt grateful. The one good thing, he supposed, was that since then he'd been more thoughtful in his dealings with women, knowing how it felt to be so casually defiled.

He remembered with a touch of shame the way he'd handled Elizabeth Armitage, doing in a cruder way what Thérèse Bellaire had done to him. It had been necessary, he'd thought. But if she weren't quite as he thought . . .

"Trouble?" asked Nicholas softly, a smile still on his lips but his eyes serious. Trust Nick to see beyond the surface.

"Some," admitted Lucien.

"We're here for a week," Nicholas said and left it at that. "Come and help yourself to sherry. You'll have gathered we're not standing on ceremony."

The conversation was all of Napoleon. Stephen, a slender blond man with shrewd, heavy-lidded eyes, was concerned with alliances and the balance of power; Dare couldn't quite suppress his excitement; Amleigh was angry with the resolute anger of the professional soldier.

They all turned as Eleanor entered the room with Hal Beaumont at her side.

He looked the same, Lucien thought. Almost. They hadn't met for four years, and heaven knew what Hal had experienced in that time. There were new lines in his face, but his smile still quirked to the right, his dark hair still waved handsomely, and he was even taller and stronger than he had been at twenty-one. Lucien was filled with tremendous joy that his friend was still alive.

"Hal!" Lucien went forward and took his friend's right hand in his own. His eyes went irresistibly to the empty sleeve tucked in between the buttons of his friend's jacket, and he felt a surge of rage at fate. And an awareness of frustrating impotence. This was something neither wealth nor rank could alter.

Hal read his face and shrugged. "There are worse things. The devil of it is, I won't be able to take my turn at bashing Boney." He in turn gave Lucien the once-over. "You look suitably rich and powerful, Luce."

Lucien took refuge in the familiar teasing about his high estate. "Noblesse oblige, old boy. Can't have the higher aristocracy groveling in the gutter."

"Assuredly not. Personally, I think you should wear strawberry leaves around your hat."

"I'm saving that for when I'm duke."

By then everyone else had gathered around, conversation became general, and Lucien had opportunity to try to come to terms with it all. He'd had friends who'd died in the war but none until now who'd been maimed. It was easy to forget the dead, or at least remember them as they had been, but Hal was a living reminder of suffering.

He looked at Amleigh and Debenham and wondered if this evidence of the consequences of war gave them pause. Or whether, as with him, it created a renewed desire to fight—to get revenge but also to assuage his guilt. Guilt he felt because he'd been here in England—getting drunk, dancing at Almack's, making love to Blanche—when that cannon had exploded, when the army surgeons had hacked off what remained of his friend's arm.

Even as he thought all this, he was smiling and adding the

odd quip to the light-hearted conversation. They all knew there was no point in miserying over the matter, and Hal would hate it.

And, of course, the Marquess of Arden couldn't take the easy way out and go off to suffer and die. He had to marry and produce the next generation of great and noble de Vaux.

Which brought everything, as always, back to Elizabeth Armitage—whom he didn't trust but sometimes liked, and who, despite being so damned ordinary, was far too often in his mind.

Eleanor once more had the baby and was playing a silly game which seemed to involve talking nonsense and rubbing noses. It made sense to Arabel, at least, for she was smiling and making happy gurgles which sounded like a language of its own. A nursemaid was hovering ready to take the child away, but Eleanor was clearly in no hurry to part with her child.

Nicholas was being a good host and even taking part in the discussion, but half his mind was clearly on his wife and child, and probably always was. Lucien suspected Nicholas would rather be part of that strange gurgling conversation than discussing the amazing pig-faced woman with Dare. Lucien caught at least two shared glances between Nicholas and Eleanor which spoke of the joy they found in each other's presence, even hinted at more private, familiar, and anticipated delights.

He remembered he had once thought that Eleanor Delaney was the kind of wife he'd like as opposed to Phoebe Swinnamer who seemed to be the kind of wife he was expected to choose. All the candidates for Marchioness of Arden had seemed to be beautiful, well-bred fashion dolls with just brain enough to master polite conversation. Eleanor Delaney had a shrewd brain and a pleasantly natural manner.

Nicholas topped up Lucien's glass and followed his gaze to his wife. "She's still taken," he said lightly but added more seriously, "A newly betrothed man shouldn't be looking at another man's wife quite like that, you know."

It was an opening, deliberately given. Lucien wasn't ready to bare his heart, but he would appreciate any scraps of wisdom. "I was just wondering," he said lightly, "if you ever felt the urge to throttle her."

Nicholas quirked a brow. "Just because she left you holding the baby?"

"Not Eleanor. Elizabeth."

Nicholas looked puzzled for a minute but then smiled. "Ah, your Elizabeth. Want to throttle her, do you? I could suggest," he said with a grin, "that it is in lieu of other forms of intimate contact." He sobered. "But no, I never felt that urge. But then we hardly had a normal courtship and Eleanor is not one to stir the coals. And I . . ." he added, smiling in self-mockery, "I have always prided myself on controlling everything, including my emotions."

Lucien wondered what lay behind the slightly bitter tone. "Whereas I," he responded to pass the moment off, "being a de Vaux, have never felt the slightest need for self-control in my whole life."

Nicholas laughed. "Hardly fair on yourself. So, what does your future marchioness do to stir the coals?"

Lucien found it difficult to express concisely the hundred ways Beth Armitage churned up his emotions, and so he fastened on the most obvious problem. "She's a follower of Mary Wollstonecraft."

Nicholas was raising his glass to his lips. It froze. A spark of incredulous humor lit his eyes, escaping in a full laugh. Wine splashed from the glass. "God Almighty!" he exclaimed when he'd got control of himself. "The whole story. Now."

Everyone else had turned to listen, and Lucien realized he'd gone too far. He shrugged and simply said, "Sorry."

Nicholas sobered and nodded. "Doubtless illegal," he said smoothly. "Can't have things like that with Stephen in the room." Again, he said, "We're here for a week."

Not having heard the first part of the conversation, the others were satisfied with this and conversation became general again. Nicholas made no attempt to pry, and though Lucien was aware of a few thoughtful looks from his host, there was no further reference to his personal life. He really didn't know if he wanted to have a heart-to-heart talk with Nicholas at all. There were too many secrets involved.

When Lucien left in the small hours of the morning it was

with Hal. There was a light drizzle, but their greatcoats and beavers were adequate protection.

"Where're you staying?" Lucien asked.

"The Guard's."

"I could give you a bed at the palace for a couple of nights." They'd always referred to Belcraven House as "the palace." Lucien could remember wonderfully crazy games with Hal which seemed to involve charging along endless corridors and hurtling down flight after flight of stairs. The chance of coming across the duke or actually breaking some precious ornament had given the whole thing a delicious, and real, edge of danger.

Hal had found danger even more real since then.

"Just one bed?" teased Hal as they turned off Bentink Street onto Welbeck. "You're a bit close with your riches, ain't you?"

"As many as you want," said Lucien grandiosely and ran a gloved finger boyishly along a railing to disturb the beaded drops of rain. He felt like a schoolboy again. When they got home he'd maybe try sliding down the banister of the main staircase. "You can have your pick of at least ten, all well-equipped with the best down mattresses. You can push them side by side to give you room to stretch. You can stack the mattresses in a pile until they're soft enough for your pampered skin."

"Like the princess and the pea?" queried Hal with a grin. "I'm far too plebeian for that. Could your blue blood detect a pea through ten mattresses?"

Lucien was snapped back to reality and maturity and all sorts of other unpleasant things. "Probably not," he said briefly. "But I rattle in the palace like one pea in a pod. Come and take up some space."

"Are you saying I'm a rattle, too?" Hal demanded lightly but with concerned and curious eyes. But he went on, "I'd like to. The Guard's is full of fogies. There's too many well-meant commiserations and altogether too much talk of war."

"Come along then. I'll send someone for your things."

They turned into Marlborough Square. When the Season began there would still be lit windows and traffic at this hour, but at this time of year it was quiet. Despite the flambeaux burning in front of each great house, the square was rendered eerie by the gray light and the misting rain. Lucien shuddered. "Come to think of it," he said, "why don't you come back to Belcraven and support me through the coming ordeal? My mother always had a soft spot for you."

"Won't I blight the celebrations?" Hal asked, the first sign he'd shown of awkwardness about his injury.

"Hardly. You'll be a hero."

"Heaven forbid." He looked sideways. "Why is it going to be an ordeal? Anything to do with whatever broke up Nick?"

Lucien wasn't ready to talk, not even to Hal. He made a business of finding the key to the big front doors. "Of course not," he said. He turned the well-oiled lock and let them both into the high, shadowed hall. A lighted lamp stood on a small table but, by his instruction, there was no staff waiting in case he had need of some service. His and Hal's footsteps seemed to echo hollowly on the marble tiles.

He was not used to coming home to a lifeless house. He'd never given such instructions before, and he suspected there were some bewildered hurt feelings below stairs. All Elizabeth Armitage's fault. Without saying a word she'd made him vividly aware of all the servants who were the constant fabric of his life.

He suddenly laughed. "Do you need anything else tonight other than a nightshirt, Hal? I've sent everyone to bed and it seems damned stupid to be knocking them up at this hour. Apart from the fact that I've no idea how to do it other than ringing the fire bell."

"Of course not. I've slept in my clothes in the mud more often than I care to remember. And, yes. I'd be happy to visit Belcraven again. You know your mother is my first and only love. Why don't you ask Con and Dare, too? They're merely waiting for orders."

Which was a very attractive idea, thought Lucien as they went upstairs. Something to do with safety in numbers.

Chapter Nine

For her part, Beth found her days too full for philosophizing. She was set numerous tasks to do with the ball, given advanced etiquette lessons, and taken on drives and shopping expeditions. Three times they went to Oxford for silk stockings and satin slippers, artificial flowers and kid gloves. She had the feeling that much of the activity was designed expressly to keep her busy but, if so, she was grateful. Not only did it allow less time to think, it provided an opportunity to learn. Resigned to the fact that this was to be her life, she observed everything and learned quickly.

She even began to accept the constant presence of servants and not be awkwardly aware of their every action. But she could not make herself unaware of them as people.

When one day she came across a young boy crying in the garden, she stopped in concern. She remembered seeing the lad in the stables. Though he had a sharp face and a broken nose, there was something appealing about his lively features and bright eyes, and she did not like to see him sad.

"What's the matter?" she asked gently.

He looked up, alarmed, then leapt to his feet. "Nothing. ma'am," he said, scrubbing at his damp face.

"Don't run away," Beth said. "You work in the stables, don't you?"

"Yes, ma'am."

"Will you be in trouble for not being there?"

He hung his head. "No, ma'am. They won't expect me back quick after old Jarvis took a whip to me."

Beth could tell from the way he moved that his punishment had not been brutal, but she offered sympathy. "Oh dear," she said. "Did you do something very bad?"

He nodded, head still lowered. He couldn't be very old, Beth thought. Not much over ten. She sat on the ground close to him. "I'm Beth Armitage," she said. "What's your name?"

He looked down at her with a frown as if the question posed a problem. "I'm Robin," he said at last, slightly defiantly. "Robin Babson."

"Well, Robin. Why don't you sit here for a moment and tell me what's been going on. Perhaps we can prevent further punishment."

He sat down and grimaced. "Don't reckon," he said morosely. "Me and old Jarvis don't get on."

"What did you do this time?"

"Let go of an 'orse. Viking. The marquess's big stallion. He's done sommat to his leg."

"Oh dear," said Beth, dismayed. She knew the value Arden placed on that horse. "That does sound rather serious."

"When he comes back he'll kill me," said the boy with a gulp. "That or get rid o' me."

"The marquess?"

The boy nodded, fresh tears breaking out to streak his face.

Beth wished she could promise to intercede on the boy's behalf but didn't think she had sufficient influence in that quarter. Despite their truce, she was not at all sure any words of hers would outweigh damage to Arden's favorite mount.

"How did you come to let the horse go?" she asked.

The boy looked up warily then obviously decided to trust. "He snapped at me. I got scared . . ." In a mumble he added, "I don't like horses. Ruddy great brutes."

Beth stared at him. "You don't—? But then why are you working in the stables, Robin?"

"He put me there."

"Who?"

"Lord Arden. He brought me in and gave me a job in the stables."

Beth had only the faintest notion of what he meant, but one thing was clear. "If you don't like the work the marquess will surely find you something more congenial, Robin. Especially as you are not suited to working with horses. I'll speak to him—"

"No!" exclaimed the boy, eyes wide. "Please, ma'am. Don't do that. He promised I can work with his horses!"

"But you don't like horses," Beth pointed out.

The boy looked away, stubbornly mute, and Beth frowned in bewilderment. "So you don't wish me to speak to the marquess on your behalf?" she said at last.

"No, ma'am." He stood and wiped his face on his sleeve. The effect was to smear rather than clean. "I'm sorry for bothering you, ma'am. Please don't say nothing to him."

Beth was genuinely touched. She suspected that this waif was as much astray at Belcraven as she and, for some reason, as bound. "I won't, Robin," she assured him. "But if you need help you must ask for me and I will do what I can."

"Thank ye kindly, ma'am," he said and ran off.

Beth sighed. Would the marquess really beat the boy again, she wondered, and perhaps more severely? She didn't like to think so, and yet many masters would feel themselves well within their rights. She knew so little of Arden, but she did suspect him to be capable of violence.

And what was she to do about it? She was so unused to violence that she wanted to hide from it, to hide even from the thought of it, but she couldn't live like that.

Beth rose and stiffened her resolution. Despite the awkwardness of her situation she would keep an eye on the matter of Robin Babson. She could not spend the rest of her life turning a blind eye to violence and cruelty, and Lord Arden would have to come to understand that.

The marquess returned on the day of the ball. When he strode into the duchess' boudoir, where she and Beth were taking tea, Beth almost saw him as a stranger. He looked quite unlike the cold, forbidding despot she had built in her mind.

He had taken the time to change, of course, but there was something of the outdoors and exercise still about him. He was relaxed, and the exhilaration of the drive was still in his eyes.

Had he heard about his horse? she wondered. And what had happened to poor Robin? She could not believe he was just come from a scene of violent retribution.

He kissed his mother's cheek and grinned at her. "You are blooming, *Maman*. We should force you to hold grand entertainments more often."

"Silly boy. You are the last of my children to marry. I hope not to do this kind of thing again."

He was still smiling when he turned to Beth, but the warmth became impersonal. "Elizabeth. I hope you are not being run ragged by all this."

If this aloof tone was the best he could do, thought Elizabeth, they were in the suds. "Of course not," she said, assuming a lively manner. "But anyway, this all has the attraction of novelty for me, my lord. I never realized the amount of hard work involved in celebrating a wedding."

"Only the wedding of the heir to a dukedom," he said dryly. Beth thought she detected a genuine dislike of pomp. How strange. More and more Lucien de Vaux was becoming a conundrum she very much wanted to solve.

"So after the wedding we can live quietly?" she queried.

He produced a creditably fond smile, but it covered implacable intent. "I hadn't planned on it, no. We have the pride of the de Vaux to consider, my dear. Will you dislike a life of fashionable entertaining very much?"

The silent message was that her likes and dislikes carried no weight with him at all. Oh God, thought Beth, they were back to their old ways. Quicksands indeed. They never said what they meant and never meant what they said.

She turned away, making a business out of pouring him some tea. "If I do dislike it," she said as she passed him the cup, "you will be sure to hear of it . . . my dear."

After a startled moment he smiled in a genuine manner. "I fear I will . . . my sweet despot." Cap that, his eyes said.

Beth was tempted but didn't know where it would all end. The marquess was not a man to bow out of a conflict. She contented herself with fluttering her lashes and aiming at him a sweet, hopefully simpering, smile. She had the satisfaction of seeing his lips twitch with genuine humor.

Beth noted the duchess watching them with a misty smile and thought, don't build on this too much, Your Grace. We are both learning well to be actors.

"I have brought you some eligible men, *Maman,*" said the marquess. "I hope you don't mind."

"Mind! Of course not, you dear boy. There can never be too many eligible men. Who? And where are they?"

"Amleigh, Debenham, and Beaumont. I've left them in the morning room enjoying more substantial refreshment."

The duchess frowned slightly, though there was a twinkle in her blue eyes. "The last time Lord Darius was here he attempted to build a champagne fountain. And Mr. Beaumont has always caused a great lack of attention among the younger maids."

"Well," said the marquess turning sober, "he will doubtless be a focus of interest again but in a different way. He's lost his left arm."

The duchess mirrored his sobriety. "Oh, the poor man. How is he?"

"Well as always, really. And he manages nearly everything. He don't like to be fussed."

"I'll tell Gorsham," said the duchess. "And I'll go odds it will only increase his attraction among the maids and every other female in the vicinity. I look to you to control your guests, Lucien."

"Of course, *Maman,*" he said with a boyish grin. "I gather you wish this to be a devilish dull affair."

His mother laughed. "Of course I do not. How would anyone believe it was *your* betrothal ball if it went off smoothly, you wretched boy? Go away and look to your friends before they find mischief."

He kissed her cheek again before he left, but Beth only received a slight wave of the hand. She looked up to see the duchess studying her enigmatically. Nothing was said, however, and soon she was sent to her room to prepare for the evening.

Laid out on her bed Beth discovered a beautiful gown, the one the duchess had ordered from London and that the marquess had been sent to collect. Beth had approved the selection without much interest, but the picture in *Ackerman's Repository* had not prepared her for the beauty of the garment.

The ivory figured silk, inset with satin panels edged in pearls, glowed and shimmered in the candlelight. Beth had never even seen such an exquisite gown in her life. When she touched it it rustled and slithered against her fingers in an orchestration of sensuality. Redcliff hovered over the gown with all the pride and protectiveness of a mother with a new baby.

By the gown rested a bouquet of pink and ivory roses packed in damp moss, and a small package.

"What is this, Redcliff?"

" 'Tis from the marquess, I believe, miss," said the woman with a knowing smile.

Beth felt a strange reluctance to open it. It would surely be a gift and perhaps not one she wished to accept. But she had no choice.

It was a fan. With a turn of her wrist Beth flicked it open. It was a work of art. Ivory sticks carved into lace supported fine silk painted in the Chinese style. The pin was gold and the endpieces were overlaid with mother-of-pearl. She turned her hand again and it flowed smoothly, as a good fan should, back into its closed position.

It was an elegant, appropriate, well-thought-of gift. For some reason that disturbed her. What was her husband-to-be? The scholar or the rake, the friend or the man of violence? Perhaps all of these. A man could quote Sallust and still be a brute.

Redcliff wanted her to rest, but Beth preferred to read, a pastime denied her recently. Mrs. Brunton, however, did not suit her mood, and she picked up some volumes of poetry she

had brought from the library. Dipping here and there she came
across Pope's *Rape of the Lock:*

> *Say what strange motive, Goddess! could compel*
> *A well-bred Lord to assault a gentle Belle?*
> *O say what stranger cause, yet unexplored,*
> *Could make a gentle Belle reject a Lord?*

What indeed? thought Beth, on reading these relevant lines.
Most people would think her mad. Most people would not
realize how painful it was to be thrown into such foreign circumstances, no matter how luxurious. On the brink of what
to most young ladies would be a night of triumph, Beth Armitage wanted only to be back in her small, chilly room at
Aunt Emma's preparing a project for the next day's classes.

When Redcliff indicated it was time, she took her bath in
delicately perfumed water. She dried herself and dressed in
light stays, silk stockings, and shift. Then the maid assisted
her into the gown. It was as if it had a life of its own; it flowed
and hissed and demanded only the most graceful, the most
elegant movements.

She had not realized how fine the fabric was. It was true
that over her shift the outfit could not be considered revealing,
and yet it did not hide her figure as she would wish. She had
not realized how low the neckline was, nor how cleverly
shaped to raise and emphasize her breasts. It did not seem at
all proper, but she had to wear it.

She had insisted that a cap be ordered to match, but this
too proved to be a shock. *Cap* was obviously a word open to
interpretation. This was merely a bandeau of matching silk and
pearls upon a stiffened frame. It was trimmed with satin ribbons which formed a love knot at one side.

"Should I dress your hair in a knot behind?" asked the maid.

A knot sounded very decorous, and Beth agreed, but when
it was done Beth knew it had not helped. With her hair drawn
tightly up, her neck appeared more slender, and when the diamond necklace was clasped around it, positively swanlike. Resigned, Beth allowed the maid to assist her into the long kid

gloves and fasten the bracelet over one wrist. Redcliff then clipped the pendant diamonds onto her ears and pinned the brooch in the center of the knot of ribbons on her bandeau.

It only remained to step into her satin slippers and stand before the mirror. Beth knew what she would see. It was Beth Armitage at her prettiest—slender but well-rounded, clear-skinned and glossy-haired. The problem, as she had known, was that she still was no beauty. She did well enough and her hosts would have no cause to blush for her, but this, the best that could be done for her, left her still just a passably pretty young woman. She would rather not appear to have tried.

She was surprised when told the marquess had come to escort her downstairs but accepted her fate with resignation. Tonight was their acting debut.

She had forgotten to wonder what he would look like. Her breath caught at the sight of him in formal black and pure white, his tanned skin and golden hair thrown into brilliance. She felt that little tremor inside which warned her again that she was not immune to his charms.

Why should she wish it when he was to be her husband?

Because it was a matter of pride not to go willingly into slavery.

"How pretty you look," he said in a friendly way.

Nerves abraded, Beth responded sharply, "I could say the same to you, I think. Fine feathers do make fine birds, do they not?"

His eyes flashed, but his smile never faltered. He drew her arm into his and they began their walk.

"Are you suggesting, Miss Armitage, that under this magnificence, I am a mere sparrow?" His tone was still light.

She glanced up at him. "Too small. A rooster, perhaps?"

He met her look and, though he continued to smile, his eyes were chilling rapidly. "You assume I will not take vengeance when you are in all your finery? You could be right. But perhaps I will hold a grudge."

That was too close to the mark. Beth knew she was guilty of holding onto her resentment. "Then we can be a pair of broody hens," she said bitterly, "sitting on our grievances until they hatch into disaster."

She intended it to be a kind of peace offering and perhaps he took it that way for he laughed. "I refuse to be any species of fowl. I prefer to be thought of as a hawk. Noble hunter, sharp of claw."

That was too frightening an image. "I'm sure you do," Beth said tartly, "but I think it is more a case of a magpie, snatching at small glittering things of no particular value."

"And you, my dear," he retorted, good humor fled, "to stretch the analogy a little, are developing into a harpy, all teeth and claws."

Without warning he opened a door and swung her into a room. A bedroom.

Beth looked up at him wide-eyed, fear shivering along her nerves. Why could she not control her clever tongue? Why could she not remember he was quite unlike any man she had ever known?

He was dangerous.

Beth the radical reminded herself she had determined to stand up to the marquess. Beth the cautious whispered that she hadn't reckoned on doing it alone, in a bedroom.

"What are you doing?" she said. It came out rather squeakily.

He was not touching her, but he was standing close, deliberately looming over her. Beth forced herself to not step back. "I am reminding you of our bargain," he said tersely. "Are you going to behave yourself tonight?"

It was the wrong word to use. Beth intended to honor her bargain, but she did not like to be told to behave herself. She raised her chin. "Do you not see me dressed like a peacock," she asked bitterly, "sporting the family jewels?"

"You know that is only the minor part."

Beth sneered. "I am not going to call you a baboon in front of your friends and neighbors, my lord."

His lips tightened. "Not good enough, Elizabeth. The only sane reason for this match is that we are in love. Madly, crazily in love. Good breeding takes away the necessity for us to be demonstrative, thank God." He took a step back, but that was no relief, for he used the space to let his eyes wander dismissively over her.

Beth could feel herself color.

"But," he drawled, "we need a certain something in the eyes, don't you think?"

Beth forced a careless shrug and gave him exactly the same slow dismissive scrutiny. "It will be an effort, my lord, but I will try."

She heard his breath hiss between his teeth. He stepped closer again and placed one finger beneath her chin, forcing her to meet his eyes. "Make sure you do, Elizabeth, or I will take payment for the dishonored debt."

"You do not try at all," she said fiercely, jerking away from his touch. "Can you not see this is no way to make me be as you would wish?"

He moved away and turned to face her, one brow raised. "How then? I have been as kind as I know how and had it thrown in my face. I have offered you kisses and had them rejected. I have left you be and returned to sharp words. At the moment, my dear bride-to-be, I simply want to be sure there will be no scandal from this evening. I am not considering your feelings at all."

"That is blunt," said Beth, shocked by his all-too-accurate analysis.

"You once said you preferred plain speaking. You have it. Behave yourself."

Beth felt a tremor and did not know whether it was fear or anger. "Like most animals, my lord, I do not like the whip." She took a deep breath and fought for composure before this quarrel spun out of control. "If you would stop reminding me you have the upper hand I think I would behave a great deal better." She meant it to be a conciliatory suggestion, but he did not take it that way.

"I see no sign of that," he said implacably. "But if you behave well I will have no reason to wield the whip, will I?"

Beth clenched one fist and drove it into her other palm. She had never felt so close to violence. "But it is always *there!*"

she protested. "I can never for one moment be unaware of your power!"

He shrugged, and she could tell he was genuinely perplexed by her words. "That is the way of the world, Elizabeth. You cannot change it and neither can I. If I promise never to compel you to do anything, that won't alter the fact that I could, and probably with the full force of the law behind me."

He offered a smile and she could tell he was making a genuine effort to be kind. "There's no need for all this heat, my dear. I am not likely to be a demanding husband, and," he added lightly, "pretty women generally find it easy enough to control their men. I know many men who live under the cat's paw."

It was as if a chasm yawned between them, as if they spoke different languages entirely. Anger drained from Beth, leaving only sadness. "You need not fear that, my lord," she said quietly. "I will never try to use feminine wiles to rule you."

With that she turned away toward the door but waited politely for him to open it.

"You will notice," he said as she walked out ahead of him, "that I suppressed the obvious rejoinder."

Beth responded to his light tone with one of her own. "That you would prefer feminine wiles? You are bound for disappointment there, Lord Arden. I have none."

"How fortunate then," he drawled, "that I have wiles enough for two."

It was, she supposed, a gallant attempt on both their parts to restore some kind of harmony, but the evening loomed before them, full of traps and disasters.

They walked along in silence until they were nearly at the open doors of the drawing room. A rumble of conversation escaped the room, lightened by exclamations and laughter. Through the door Beth could see a number of glittering people, and she knew there were many more out of sight. She came to understand his concern about appearances. They were about to go on stage before the cream of the county.

She stopped and turned to him. "I'm sorry if I've been unreasonable, my lord. I no longer seem to know right from wrong, sense from nonsense. When we are struggling to keep afloat in strange waters, we do not always take care of others."

He considered her seriously and again she had the impression that he was at least trying to understand her point of view. He began to reply, then glanced over her shoulder. "We are observed. I am gong to give you a very small kiss, Elizabeth. It will do our reputation as mad romantics a world of good and cut down," he added dryly, "on the required number of languishing looks."

Despite an urge to escape, Beth stood still as he held her by the shoulders and touched his lips to hers. As he said, it was gentle and unalarming, but it was not without effect. It was their first kiss and contained a grain of something of worth—perhaps concern, or even the greater warmth of embryonic friendship. Beth was aware that it was precious and raised one hand to gently touch the side of his handsome face.

He gave her a swift suspicious look. With a sinking heart, she realized he saw the gesture as evidence of boldness. Quicksands indeed.

She was not a blushing schoolgirl, after all. She was mature and confident, with at least book knowledge of men and yet, because of her foolish words, if she relaxed for a second he saw her as wanton. With a sigh, she replaced her hand on his arm and allowed herself to be drawn into the lion's den.

The large, gilded drawing room was hung with huge Gobelin tapestries separated by ornate pilasters. The arms of the de Vaux, repeated again and again in blue, red, and gold marched across the ceiling lit by hundreds of candles in scintillating chandeliers which seemed to spark flashes from ostentatious jewelry and avid eyes. Conversation ceased. To Beth it appeared they were the focus of hundreds of pairs of eyes.

Her hand clutched at the marquess's arm.

The duke and duchess came forward to stand by their side. Then the duke introduced Beth. All these friends and neighbors applauded, but Beth was sure she could see incredulity in some eyes and envy in others. When the guests looked away and recommenced their chatter, Beth knew that now they were talking about her.

She could imagine the words. "Such a dab of a thing." "Nothing special about her at all." "Can't hold a candle to . . ."

Abandoning notions of independence, Beth thanked the heavens that the nature of the occasion made it proper for the marquess to stay by her side, for she might otherwise have given in to panic. As it was she found her nerves jumping from the number of people—and these were only the ones invited to dinner—and the way they looked at her as she and the marquess circled the room talking to first one group then the next.

There were impertinent questions. There were jealous looks from a number of young ladies and their mamas. There was insincere, gushing familiarity. She was amazed and embarrassed by the number of people who tried to toady to her. She was really just Beth Armitage, schoolteacher.

The three young men brought from London seemed to have no problems with the betrothal, however. Beth wondered what the marquess had told them, for these guests must know him well.

Lord Amleigh was a handsome, dark-haired young man with lively gray eyes. He seemed rather intense, almost fiery.

Lord Darius Debenham was sandy haired with blue eyes. He would never be described as handsome, but his lively features were full of attractive good humor. He looked exactly the kind of man who would try to build a champagne fountain.

Mr. Beaumont was rather like the marquess in build and almost matched him in looks in a dark-haired, dark-eyed way. She noted with sympathy his empty sleeve.

The three were talking to two local men—Mr. Pedersby and Sir Vincent Hooke, both ruddy-faced and a little too loud.

It was Mr. Beaumont who stepped forward after the introductions. "Well, Miss Armitage," he said, raising her hand and kissing it with the air of a practiced flirt. "So you are Arden's secret treasure. I can quite see how it is. You are definitely out of the usual way."

Beth glanced up sharply to see if there was innuendo in that comment, but if so it was well-concealed. "Thank you, Mr.

Beaumont," she said. "I have never sought to be one of the herd."

"But you are the very leader of the flock," said Sir Vincent with a silly laugh. "The flock of beauties who have hunted poor Arden down."

Beth glanced to the marquess for help, but he was laughing at some remark by Lord Darius. She gave in to the temptation to vent her irritation on a suitable target. "Flock?" she queried lightly, making play with her fan. "Sheep? But sheep do not hunt. Or starlings? Pray tell me, Sir Vincent. Which birds hunt in flocks?"

"Well . . ." Plump Sir Vincent had turned even redder and was opening and closing his mouth like a fish. "A manner of speaking . . ."

"Perhaps you meant wolves," said Beth kindly in her best schoolmistress manner. "The collective noun, however, is pack. Or lions? A pride?"

She became aware that the marquess, along with everyone else in the group, was listening to her.

"Are we starting a zoo?" he asked mildly. "A pride of lions? Perhaps it should be a pride of dukes."

Beth couldn't help a laugh. "Or marquesses. What about a peep of chickens? We could change that to a peep of maidens."

"A gaggle of geese becomes a gaggle of dowagers," he returned with a grin. "No, that doesn't work too well. I have a better one. A leap of leopards. A leap of libertines."

"Should I perhaps 'peep' at that one?" asked Beth, delighted at this quick-witted and absurd conversation. "And what would you do with a shrewdness of apes, my lord?"

"A shrewdness of schoolteachers," he said triumphantly. "We are neglecting our guests, my dear."

Beth became aware of the five young men watching them with various degrees of astonishment. For a few moments she had forgotten her circumstances and discovered something precious. She could not remember matching her wits like that before and it was a heady delight. She flashed a quick, self-conscious look at the marquess and met a similar one of his own. He, too, had been surprised.

It was Viscount Amleigh who stepped into the silence. "You'd need a very special word, Miss Armitage, to describe the hunting beasts of Almack's."

Beth smiled at the handsome young man who had doubtless been pursued there with great determination. "A militia of mamas?" she offered.

"A desperation of debutantes," was the marquess's dry contribution. "I think we should stop, Elizabeth, or we'll get an unconquerable reputation for bookishness." He turned to his friends. "I didn't bring you three here to enjoy yourselves, you know. You're supposed to be lessening the desperation of some of the local debutantes. You, too, Pedersby, Sir Vincent."

The men good-humoredly took their marching orders and went off to pay addresses to the young ladies sitting quietly with their parents.

Still relaxed from that exchange of wit, Beth grew careless. "Do you regret your bachelorhood, my lord?"

He looked down at her coolly. "What has that to say to anything? I do not blame you for our situation." There was a slight emphasis on the pronouns.

Forgetting where they were, Beth felt anger boil in her again. "Well—"

She gasped as her elbow was taken in a vicelike grip and pain shot up her arm. She found herself in a chair.

"You are unwell, Elizabeth?" asked the marquess kindly.

The duchess hurried over. "Is something the matter, my dears?"

Beth shook her head, hiding her shock. "Not at all," she said. "I felt a sudden pain," she glanced up at the cool eyes of her betrothed, ". . . from my ankle. I sprained it last year and it sometimes betrays me."

"I hope it will not prevent you from dancing, Elizabeth," said the duchess.

Beth stood. "Oh no, Your Grace. It was the marquess's excessive concern," she said, "that forced me to sit in the first place."

She flashed a look at him and realized they were back into conflict again. At that moment the meal was announced and, as it was a betrothal event, Beth had to place her hand on his arm and lead the procession to the formal dining room.

"What a remarkable liar you are," he said with cool admiration.

"Yes, aren't I?" replied Beth, too angered by that moment of brutal dominance to choose her words.

They went ten steps in silence and she could not resist the urge to look over at him.

His lips were tight and his eyes cool. "Yes, it was unwise, wasn't it? If you fight me, Elizabeth, you will lose and be hurt into the bargain. You can hardly expect me to be concerned about your sensibilities."

"What happened to our truce?" she asked with quiet intensity.

"It holds as long as you behave yourself."

Beth bit back angry words and faced forward again. Her situation, she thought bitterly, reminded her of a forlorn hope, when soldiers facing defeat without chance of survival, charged bravely, foolhardily, at the enemy. She could be compliant and enslaved, or she could fight and be defeated.

She could at least die with honor. A flaming row was out of the question and so, as they took their seats, she took up more subtle weapons. "I promise," she said sweetly, "to be exactly the kind of bride you deserve, oh noble one."

The marquess, after a brief startled moment, assumed a similar loverlike manner, raised her hand, and placed a warm and lingering kiss upon it. A ripple of laughter and sentimental looks greeted this action and set the tone for the meal.

" 'Use every man after his desert,' " he murmured, " 'and who should escape whipping?' "

Beth raised her brows. "I do not recollect any member of the peerage being tickled at the cart's tail recently. And yet," she continued amiably, "doesn't the Bible say, 'Whatsoever a man soweth, so shall he reap'?"

"But I'm a lily of the field," he countered. "I neither sow nor reap."

"Aha!" she exclaimed. "You've mixed your verses, my lord. The lilies of the field toil not, neither do they spin. It's the fowls of the air who do not sow and reap. I thought," she queried gently, "you did not wish to be considered any species of fowl."

"Very clever," he said with a smile which acknowledged her victory. But then his smile became a triumphant grin and Beth waited warily. "And so you reduce me to a cock? Unwary lady . . ."

Even Beth was aware of the rude meaning to which he alluded, and she turned pink. But she knew as well that there was a warm stirring inside her at his words and the almost sultry look in his eyes. She fought it.

"Every cock is proud on its own dungheap," she shot back in an attempt to drag the contest back into safer waters.

Mirth glittered in his bright blue eyes. "As in upstanding?" he asked.

The contest had passed out of Beth's control and beyond her true understanding, but she knew she had to retreat. She grabbed the first quotation that came to mind. "Small things make base men proud," she declared and directed her attention firmly to the soup which had somehow arrived before her.

She found it difficult to swallow the first spoonful. There was something dangerous emanating from her left.

She slanted a wary glance in his direction. He was in control and his face was politely amiable but outrage glittered in his eyes. Beth ran the words back through her mind, seeking the unintentional offense. Oh, heavens. Base. That was it. He thought it was a reference to his birth.

"I am sorry," she said, trying to sound sincere while keeping her tone and manner light for the sake of those nearby. "I didn't mean . . . I didn't mean anything . . . personal, my lord."

Her words appeared to anger him more. "So you do realize what you were implying," he commented in the same light tone but through tight teeth. "You must tell me your opinion of my endowments when you have more *personal* experience."

Beth hadn't the slightest notion what he meant but took the only wise course and addressed her soup.

By the time six types of fish were being offered Beth had

nerve enough to direct an innocuous comment to him and he was restored enough to answer it. Knowing silence would be cause for comment they began to converse and even slowly returned to playful flirtation. But now it was a careful, wary business, despite their smiles.

The marquess threw insincere flattery at Beth and Beth reciprocated. Gradually, despite their discord, Beth went from satisfaction in holding her own to pleasure in matching wits. But she was careful—as careful as a person can be when walking over ground set with invisible traps.

She thought she saw genuine amusement in the marquess' eyes now and then, but it wasn't the unguarded warmth of their earlier exchange. At one point when she capped his praise of her eyes with a positive laudation of his, he murmured, "It would be more ladylike just to simper, my dear."

Beth, by now outside three glasses of wine, simply opened her eyes wide and said, "Really?"

He bowed his head and laughed. They received yet more indulgent looks. Beth thought his humor was genuine. But then he had been draining his wine glasses with regularity, too.

The whole company was relaxed by good food and wine, and when the speeches started, wit, both coarse and fine, began to fly. The Regent was toasted and all the royal family. The soldiers and sailors received their due.

Then the duke rose. "My friends. This is a joyous occasion indeed for us, and we are pleased to share it with you today. It is not often a family is so fortunate as to welcome within it a bride who is so like a daughter."

Beth could feel her eyes open wide and resisted with difficulty the temptation to look at the marquess with alarm. He laid a hand over hers in what would look like fondness but was, she hoped, reassurance. If not, it was control.

"The duchess and I had wondered when Arden would choose a bride. So many young men these days seem to find no need for one, to their great loss. We would have been happy to welcome any young woman who found favor in his eyes, but thank him sincerely for choosing our dear Elizabeth."

Everyone joined in the toast and then the marquess rose

to reply. "Some young men," he said with pointed looks at his friends, "do indeed seem to think a bride a low priority in life. I can assure them they are wrong. Does Euripides not say, 'Man's best possession is a sympathetic wife'?" Beth stiffened at the word *possession,* knowing it had been deliberately employed, but she maintained her smile. "Euripides was right. I have already found my life enlivened by my bride-to-be, and I look forward with confidence to yet greater delight."

The words were without offense and yet something in the delivery caused titters and guffaws. Beth knew she was turning pink, and it was one part embarrassment to three parts anger. Why did society ordain that the men make all the speeches? She would delight in an opportunity to land some clever shots of her own.

"The heir to a great house," he continued, "cannot choose the single life, but I felt no urgency to seek a bride. You can see then that Elizabeth caught me quite unawares. We make no secret of the fact that she brings no fortune or proud bloodlines to this match, and I am pleased by this. For how can anyone doubt that we are joined by the strongest *compulsion . . .*"

The emphasis he placed on the word sent a shiver down Beth's spine. It seemed an age before he added, "Love."

She looked up and their eyes clashed. "There is something inexpressibly charming in falling in love," he added blithely. "I recommend it to all you lonely bachelors."

Beth looked down at her plate, wondering how many would recognize that quotation from Molière, which went on to say that the whole pleasure of love lies in the fact that love is soon over. But at least she and the marquess need not fear the loss of something they did not have. She realized she was missing some of his speech, but if that was the style of it she did not regret it.

"I ask you," said the marquess in conclusion, "to drink again to Elizabeth. And to families. And to love."

Everyone did this resoundingly, and Beth could detect no ambivalence in the smiling faces. Perhaps people heard what they expected to hear. Or perhaps, as Shakespeare had it, "All the world's a stage, and all the men and women merely players . . ."

Chapter Ten

There was no lingering after the dinner, for more guests were arriving for the ball and now was the time for the formal reception line. Beth felt very like an actor moving onto the next scene of a play.

She stood between the duke and the marquess and touched hands with what seemed to be hundreds of people. Again there were the astonished looks, the speculation, and the envy. She could swear she saw a few matrons look closely at her waistline.

It was a relief when the dancing began, for then she could escape this scrutiny, but when the marquess led her out for the opening minuet it was, in a sense, the first time they had been out of the earshot of others since their *sotto voce* discussion at the table. She braced herself for a hostile comment, no matter how sweetly uttered. It did not come.

"You look nervous," he said. "Have you forgotten the steps?"

"My dear sir," she retorted, "I was raised in a girl's school. I have been watching, learning, and teaching dancing all my life. I could perform a minuet in my sleep."

"Ah," he said with a mischievous glitter, "but have you ever performed it with a man?"

They were taking their place among the four couples who were to open the ball with the formal minuet, facing toward the duke and duchess at the head of the room. "Assuredly," said Beth. "I frequently gave demonstrations with Monsieur de Lo, our dancing master."

"The minuet *à deux?*" he queried.

"Occasionally," Beth replied, mistrusting his tone.

"That is generally held to be the cause of so many susceptible young ladies falling in love with their dancing masters. All that staring into one another's eyes."

"I assure you—" Beth's protest was cut off by the opening chords of the music. Along with the other dancers she made obeisance to the duke and duchess. Even as she pointed her right toe and sank slowly down on her left leg and rose she was aware of the elegance of the marquess' bow. A spirit of competitiveness stirred in her. He was well-trained in the courtly art, but she was, after all, a professional.

They turned to face each other. She watched him carefully. When, as she expected, he performed a deeply elaborate full bow, she sank into as deep a court curtsy as her skirt would allow, her eyes correctly on his at all times. Then she rose slowly with smooth control. She did not place her hand in his outstretched one until the last moment to make it clear to all that she needed no assistance in rising.

A ripple of applause ran around the room.

He smiled and a slight inclination of the head gave her the victory. Then he took both her hands and raised them for a kiss while still maintaining the eye contact. Beth began to see what he meant. A minuet *à deux*, constantly gazing into the partner's eyes, could easily turn a young girl's head. How fortunate that she was not a young girl and that they were dancing in a set of eight.

The music proper began and Beth could look away as she and the other ladies moved into the center using the slow and graceful minuet step then joined hands to circle. The ladies circled to the right as the gentlemen circled to the left.

Having been so recently a teacher Beth couldn't help assessing performances. She could not recollect the name of one young lady, but she and Miss Frogmorton performed well but with a little more of the bounce of a country dance than the glide which was necessary. Phoebe Swinnamer was the fourth

lady and she glided like a swan. She was, however, inclined
to pose for effect every now and then and thus break the flow.

The ladies broke the circle to join their partners again, left
hand to right, continuing the circling for one more step so as
to smoothly link both hands and circle each other, eye to eye.

"Monsieur de Lo was a very good teacher," the marquess
complimented her.

"As was your master, my lord," said Beth kindly. "Though
you could perhaps point your foot a little more."

He raised a brow. "Are you perhaps accusing me of not
being high enough in the instep, my dear?"

Beth hit her lip to stifle a giggle. They let one hand drop
and flowed into the next movement deliberately holding eye
contact as long as possible. Phoebe Swinnamer looked sour
and almost missed a step.

Beth had to admit that her teaching experience and her demonstrations with Monsieur de Lo had not alerted her to the
potential for flirtation in the stately dance. No, not flirtation.
Seduction.

Lady and gentleman moved around each other but never far
apart and ever aware. They came together, intensely linked by
hands and eyes, the slow movements allowing skilled dancers
who did not need to think of their steps to linger upon one
another like a slow kiss.

Caught by her extraordinary thoughts Beth stared up at the
marquess as she slowly circled him. It was the look in his eyes
which was causing all these ideas.

"We will do a minuet *à deux* at our wedding ball, Elizabeth."

"No," Beth said instinctively.

"But yes. It is the custom!"

The dance separated them again. It seemed very like their
life together: brief moments of contact always moving into
division. A minuet *à deux* would be an appropriate beginning
to their marriage, and it was ridiculous to fear it. It would
merely be a prelude to the greater trials of their life together.

After the minuet the dancing became general and much less
formal. Beth danced a country set with the duke. After that,

she passed from one partner to the next, glad to be lost in the dancing instead of pilloried for idle curiosity. The young eligibles had been dragooned by the duchess into doing their duty by the wallflowers, so Beth found herself dancing mainly with the older men, which suited her very well.

Only one gave her a problem. Lord Deveril. He was sallow and bony but with a kind of brutish strength in his jaw and hands. He also smelt. Not particularly unwashed—there were a number of people present who had obviously not taken up the fashion for cleanliness—but stale and slightly decayed. It could have mainly been his teeth, for when he smiled, which was rarely, they could be seen to be rotten.

"You must consider yourself a lucky young lady," he sneered at one point. "Not many plain Janes without a fortune find themselves so favored."

His manner was so unpleasant that Beth felt free to retort sharply. "On the contrary, my lord. The marquess is the fortunate one. Not many young bucks find themselves a woman of sense."

He showed his rotten teeth. "Now what would they want with such a thing? What good are brains in bed?"

Faced with this appalling ill-breeding Beth would normally have walked away, but she didn't want to create a scene, and this dreadful man was a guest. "I must ask you not to speak to me of such things, Lord Deveril," she said coldly.

"Good gracious. But you claimed to be a woman of sense. Surely you know the purpose of marriage? It is stated explicitly in the service."

Beth took refuge in silence, praying for the dance to end. It did at least move into a pattern which prevented conversation for a while.

But inevitably she found herself back with her partner.

"We are having such beautiful weather, are we not?" she said determinedly before he could pick his own topic.

"A perfect spring," he agreed. "Seeing the birds in their nests turns all our minds to matrimony. After all, I have no legal heir, not even a distant cousin. Like the marquess, I have obeyed the call of duty and selected my own satin pillow for the long cold nights."

Beth punished him with silence and heard with relief the music die.

As he led her from the floor Lord Deveril said, "Speaking of birds, my little pigeon, you should ask the marquess about the doves at Drury Lane."

Beth had not the slightest intention of asking the marquess anything at that man's instigation, but she sought him out from a simple desire for protection. She felt as if she had brushed up against something noxious.

His raised finger brought her a glass of champagne, and she drank deeply from it for refreshment and choked. "I think I would do better with lemonade, my lord."

"If you're going to quaff it like that, I should think so. You look hot. Why don't we walk on the terrace?"

She looked at him suspiciously, but he smiled. "Don't worry. We won't be alone. There are a number of couples out there in the cool. Come."

It was refreshing, and he had told the truth. They were not alone though there was space enough for a kind of privacy.

"Are you enjoying your first ball?" he asked. He seemed to be genuinely friendly. With the memory of that brief moment of pleasure during the kiss and their occasional accord during their battles of wits, Beth began to hope.

"It is pleasant enough," she said. "Except for Lord Deveril."

He frowned. "A man like that shouldn't even be here. Lady Gorgros brought him and it was decided not to create a fuss by throwing him out. Why did you agree to dance with him?"

Beth remembered it was Lady Gorgros who had presented the viscount to her. "I accepted anyone who asked," she admitted. Then she shrugged. "They all seemed respectable."

She saw him stiffen and fix his interest on her. "And was he not respectable? Am I to call him out?"

He was completely serious. "Don't be ridiculous," she retorted. "Of all the stupidities of fashionable life, the worst is the habit of men fighting each other over trifles."

Ice settled. "Of course," he said. "You would consider your

honor a trifle. How then did he offend you? Call Mary Wollstonecraft a doxy?"

Beth opened her mouth to blister him, but it was impossible
with others close by. Beth discovered she had a crashing headache and closed her eyes.

"Elizabeth?"

"Just leave me alone."

"Are you unwell?"

"I have a headache," she bit out.

"Come then and we'll find *Maman*. She will take care of
you. Perhaps you should retire."

Beth opened her eyes. There seemed to be genuine concern
in his voice. More material for her conundrum. "I can't do
that. What will people think?"

"That you have danced too hard and perhaps drunk a little
too much. Come along." He put a hand gently on her back to
urge her forward, but she resisted.

"Collapsing before dinner, retiring early. People will think
our marriage a necessity."

He turned to her with close attention. "And is it?"

Beth wished the earth would swallow her. Why, oh why, had
she been betrayed into those unforgivable words on this very
terrace? "You know it is," she muttered.

"And you know what I mean. Are you with child?"

"No, of course I'm not," she said sharply. "You said you
would never raise that ridiculous conversation again."

"Because if you were," he continued, "that would be cause
to break off this engagement. Even my father wouldn't insist
on it."

Beth forced herself to look at him. "I am afraid I cannot
offer that escape route. And though it would suit you, my lord,
it would be a poor sort of freedom for me, with a bastard in
tow."

She could almost see the strain as he forced his mouth into
a smile. "We are becoming heated, Elizabeth. Remember, we
are the two turtledoves."

As they made their way back to the ballroom, Beth said,

simply from the desire to hurt, "Doves of Drury Lane, perhaps?"

She was amazed to see him color up, but at that moment her next partner came to claim her. She smiled through her headache and cast a languishing look back at her betrothed.

Once she was away from him her headache began to fade. Another poor indicator for their future.

Eventually it was the supper waltz, for which the marquess was her partner. Beth joined him with some trepidation, wondering if he would pick up their quarrel. She was also concerned about her ability to maintain her high standard of dancing. The daring waltz had not been taught at Miss Mallory's.

But all went well. He did not refer to their earlier conversation, and Beth found her recent lessons to be adequate when reinforced by an excellent partner.

Beth found the risqué dance something of a disappointment. Certainly to be with the same partner for the whole dance was strange and could lead to intimacy, but at such close quarters it was also possible to stare over one another's shoulders and address scarcely any conversation at all, as they proved.

When they sat down to the meal they were at a large table, and Beth found she had Mr. Beaumont on her other side. She liked this man very much, for he was of easy address and had a wry sense of humor and, of course, she felt sorry for him because of his injury. Though he was as tall and strong as the marquess Beth never felt intimidated by him, perhaps because of the softer lines of his sun-darkened face or the warmth of his dark brown eyes.

She was less pleased to have Phoebe Swinnamer at the table, for she always felt the young lady would like to skewer her with the nearest sharp implement. The beauty's supper partner was Lord Darius. Beth could only hope the son of a duke would assuage the beauty's vanity though she feared the fact that Lord Darius was not the heir would weigh heavily with the girl, who had thought she had such a one in her grasp.

Beth turned to Mr. Beaumont. "Have you been a friend of the marquess for a long time, Mr. Beaumont?"

"Since Harrow, Miss Armitage," he said with a smile. "And I can reveal things about his school days he wouldn't want known."

Beth could tell from his manner he was not going to offend her, but the marquess overheard and broke in. "What are you up to, Hal?"

"Why, Luce, I think it only fair to tell your bride-to-be your terrible secret."

"Not the cow," said the marquess in alarm, causing Beth's eyebrows to rise.

"Of course not," said Mr. Beaumont, straight-faced.

"The bells?" queried the marquess anxiously.

"The merest peccadillo," replied his friend with a dismissive gesture. "In fact, I think you're still rather proud of that one."

Beth turned and saw the marquess grin as he said, "I am indeed. It took a great deal of ingenuity to cross all the wires on the servants' bells at school. Mind, it wasn't such a good idea to try it here."

Mr. Beaumont hooted with laughter. "You didn't!"

"I did," said the marquess ruefully. "I had to sort it all out again and then my father—" perhaps only Beth caught the little catch in his voice before he continued, "made me run useless errands for him all over this place to teach me not to cause the servants unnecessary work."

"How extraordinary," drawled Miss Swinnamer. "What does it matter to a servant whether they are called correctly or not? They can always make themselves useful."

"Well then," said Lord Darius dryly, "look at it from the point of view of the guest who rings for breakfast and doesn't receive it because the servant thinks the bell rang in quite another chamber."

"Oh, I see," said the young lady with a warm smile at her partner. Obviously a duke's son in the hand was worth something. "Of course, my lord, that would be most annoying."

"Doubtless gets the servant a fine jawing."

"Well, of course, Lord Darius," said the young lady blandly. "They would be fortunate not to be dismissed."

Lord Darius looked at her. "When it was all the fault of some prankster?"

"My mama," stated Miss Swinnamer, "says servants cannot be allowed to make excuses for poor performance or they will be forever shirking." She looked around and perhaps detected disapproval in the group. "The mischief-maker, of course, deserves a sound whipping."

"My dear Phoebe," drawled the marquess, "are you expressing a desire to whip me?"

Poor Phoebe had clearly lost track of the origins of the conversation. She merely gaped while others hid smiles with greater or lesser success.

Beth decided to intervene. "As I understand it," she said, "the offense has already been adequately punished. I approve of the duke's disciplinary measures. It is my belief that corporal punishment rarely achieves anything except to brutalize."

The marquess looked at Lord Darius and Mr. Beaumont. "I think she's calling us brutes," he said. He glanced sideways at Beth. "Probably baboons."

"Baboons?" they queried in unison.

Beth could feel the color in her face, but she frowned severely at the marquess. "Lord Arden is funning. I merely point out that children learn right from wrong more clearly if their fault is explained to them than if they are hit."

The marquess grinned. "Did I neglect to mention the whipping? But the explanation was very thorough, too. I think we're going to fight over the raising of our children, my dear."

The mere thought of children was enough to have Beth turn to Mr. Beaumont in search of a safer topic. "I think I will need ammunition. What was the dreadful secret you were going to impart, sir?"

The man smiled. "Why, the one he has kept hidden most carefully," he said. "Though I am not sure how you will find a way to use it, I am sure if anyone can it will be you." He cast a mock-wary glance at his friend, who was sharing a joke with Lord Darius, then lowered his voice to a conspiratorial whisper. "He was brilliant," he murmured. "Quite the best student in our form.

After a startled moment, Beth chuckled. "I admit, I had begun to suspect. . . . But why keep it secret?"

"Good God, ma'am, you can't be serious! Be known as a scholar? It was just a temporary lapse of judgment due to inexperience. By the time we went on to Cambridge he was wiser and managed to survive his years there without drawing attention to himself."

Beth was about to protest this insanity, but she saw there was a strong element of truth in it and shook her head. "And you, Mr. Beaumont? Were you an intellectual prodigy?"

"Not at all," he assured her earnestly, yet with a twinkle of amusement. "Straight down the middle. Give you my word, Miss Armitage."

"And what have you done with your middling abilities, Mr. Beaumont?" Beth queried, knowing this man was no dullard.

"A very ordinary time in the army, Miss Armitage."

"And that's a lie," said the marquess, entering the conversation again; Beth suspected he'd been monitoring it. "Reached the rank of major, though he chooses not to use it now. Mentioned in dispatches so often the Horse Guards were tired of hearing his name—"

"Weren't we all?" broke in Mr. Beaumont hastily. "Have to be dashed unlucky in a war not to be noticed now and then."

"Let this be a lesson to you, Hal," said the marquess, and Beth knew he was referring to the spilling of secrets, not the war.

"Point taken," said Mr. Beaumont. "But I don't think Miss Armitage will take it amiss that you like to use your brain."

The marquess looked at Beth thoughtfully. "I wonder. Being very clever herself, she might have thought to outsmart me now and then."

Beth colored at this piece of perception. "I still do expect that," she said saucily. "Now and then."

"A challenge!" said Mr. Beaumont. "I wouldn't care to lay odds on the winner either."

"I would," said Miss Swinnamer complacently with a malicious glance at Beth. "Mama says a lady never wins by besting a gentleman in anything."

"Well, Miss Swinnamer," said Beth politely. "I am sure it is a pleasure to us all to know you will never cause your Mama any anxiety in that regard."

The marquess choked on a mouthful of wine. The beauty was still puzzling over the strange remark when the marquess and Beth left the table.

"When I think I was close to offering for her, I shudder," he said, still fighting laughter.

"Why were you going to offer for someone with whom you have so little in common?"

He shrugged. "It was my duty to marry, and I didn't seem to be the type to fall in love. Phoebe Swinnamer is the sort of girl I was supposed to marry—well-born, well-dowered, beautiful and . . . perfectly amiable."

"Because she has been trained to be," said Beth pointedly, knowing that in that list of qualities she scored a round nothing.

He smiled at her and shook his head. "Not one of your failings, as we are both aware."

"I am perfectly amiable," retorted Beth, "unless I am given reason not to be."

"You are a shrew," said the marquess, amusement still softening his face. "Don't fly into alt about it. I'm coming to like it well enough." With that he handed her over to her next partner, leaving Beth not a little off balance.

Eventually, at four in the morning, the affair was over and Beth could seek her bed. As she slipped between the sheets exhausted, she wandered through memories of the evening, confused by it all. Moments of affinity, moments of strife.

As the maid walked toward the door, Beth asked, "Do you know anything about doves of Drury Lane, Redcliff?"

"No, miss. I've only been to London the once and never visited a theater. I suppose they have them in cages, for decoration like."

"Yes. But it's all very strange," said Beth as she drifted off to sleep.

Redcliff happened to mention this strange conversation the next morning at the upper servant's breakfast. She was surprised when Hughes, the marquess's very proper valet, took her aside afterwards.

"If I were you, Miss Redcliff," he said. "I would dissuade Miss Armitage from speaking of doves of Drury Lane."

"Why, Mr. Hughes?"

The man pursed his lips. "Let us just say that the White Dove of Drury Lane is a particular favorite of the marquess'. If you see what I mean."

The maid flushed. "I do indeed. Oh, the poor dear! And who would put such a thing into her head?"

"Exactly what I was wondering. And so will his lordship if it comes to his ears."

Lucien, however, had forgotten Beth's comment. He was more concerned with other matters, and before he collapsed into bed he sat down and scribbled a note to Nicholas Delaney.

Dear Nicholas,
   Deveril turned up at my betrothal ball. I thought he'd fled with Madame, but he must have straightened things out with the authorities. Thought you should know. He's just as nasty as ever.
                                                          L de V

He arranged for it to be dispatched to Grattingley, home of Nicholas's twin brother, Lord Stainbridge.

He didn't know why the intrusion of Lord Deveril made him so uneasy, other than the man was evil with very low and nasty tastes. It was a natural instinct not to want such a specimen within miles of one's home, but there was more to it than that.

Deveril had been entwined with Thérèse Bellaire in her plot to trick Napoleonic sympathizers out of their money. Lucien had gained the impression that Deveril also had had something to do with Eleanor Delaney in the days when she'd been living with her loathsome worm of a brother. There was certainly no love lost between Nicholas and Deveril.

They had all assumed Lord Deveril had fled with Thérèse Bellaire to enjoy their ill-gotten gains and their shared taste for depravity. His reemergence raised worrying questions.

Chapter Eleven

Beth rose the next morning feeling wrung out. Her head throbbed, her mouth tasted sour, and the negative aspects of the previous evening sat solidly at the front of her mind.

Why could she not act a prim and proper innocent? Perhaps she should take lessons from Miss Swinnamer's mama. Why could the marquess not see that a fighting spirit and a little worldly wisdom did not make her a trollop?

She remembered what he had said about her being a shrew. He couldn't really like a shrew. He couldn't like someone he didn't trust, and he had shown on the terrace that he didn't trust her at all.

She sighed bitterly. It seemed to be as he had said. Words once spoken had a life of their own. They could not be unsaid. Every time Beth and the marquess were on edge, that dreadful evening on the terrace came back to haunt them.

On top of her misery at this was her anger that he made no claim to purity of any kind and yet felt free to castigate her for some vague form of misdoing. She knew he was behaving according to his code, but the temptation to lash out at him was tremendous.

And then, of course, she would be called a shrew.

The duchess sent for Beth to share a late breakfast in her suite, and she felt obliged to go. Some toast and coffee made her feel better, but the duchess's cheerful chatter was hard to respond to.

"I was pleased to see you and Lucien so at ease," the duchess said. "His few days in Town did him good, as I knew they would. He's more himself and that should make it easier for you, my dear. And there isn't much more of this falderol to endure. We have a week of festivities here, culminating in the reception for all the local people, and then we will remove to London. Then it will be only two weeks to your wedding."

Two weeks. Buttered toast turned to sawdust in Beth's mouth. She had known the date set for the event, but now it loomed frighteningly close. "It is all rather rushed," she protested. "It will cause talk."

"Yes, but the duke wants it done," said the duchess apologetically. "And your first child will be born after the nine months, so the speculation will end then."

Beth swallowed, and the duchess looked at her with shrewd eyes. "My dear, do you know about marriage? I feel I stand in the place of a mother to you."

"I know all about marriage," said Beth hastily and then saw the shock in the duchess's eyes. "I mean, I have read widely."

"What extraordinary books you must come across," the duchess remarked. "But even so it is easy to be . . . confused on such a subject. My older daughter, Maria, thought that the act of sleeping in a bed with a man caused babies. By the time I talked to her, she had already convinced Graviston that they should have separate bedrooms because she snored. She thought her troubles were over."

Beth was aghast. "How could you force her into such a distasteful marriage?"

"Distasteful?" said the duchess. "Oh no, it was a love match. But Maria felt, being but eighteen, that she did not want children just yet. Having heard that 'sleeping together' caused babies," the duchess explained with a twinkle, "she thought she could have Graviston's kisses and all they promised without consequences."

Beth desperately wanted to ask whether she could have the babies without the kisses and all they promised, but she lowered her eyes.

The duchess looked at the young woman thoughtfully. "Do

you know, Elizabeth, I think I will you give you my little talk anyway. Books can be so unreliable."

And she did so.

Beth listened, wide-eyed. So that was what "making a meal of it" meant.

In the end, rosy-cheeked and with the picture of Venus and Mars in her mind, Beth protested, "But surely all this . . . this playing around is not necessary?"

"Not necessary, no," said the duchess calmly. "But if I thought Lucien would neglect such courtesies I would be very cross with him. Leaving aside any question of your pleasure, they are necessary for your comfort."

Beth remembered a thumb cold-bloodedly rubbing against her nipple and the effect it had achieved, and raised her hands to her heated cheeks. "Oh, I would much rather not!"

The duchess came over and gathered her into her arms. "Oh my dear, I am sorry to have distressed you. As I said, my daughters' matches were love matches, and though they were a little nervous, they did not go to their marriage beds afraid. I can see how it is different for you and Lucien, thrown together as you are."

She patted Beth's shoulder and her tone lightened. "But count your blessings, Elizabeth. He is a very handsome man, well-trained in courtesy. You must find him a little bit appealing, yes?"

Beth shook her head. It was not so much a denial as a gesture of despair at his undoubted physical appeal which she did not welcome at all.

The duchess sighed. "Then I would ask you to think that it is much the same for him." When Beth looked at her in surprise she explained, "Certainly he is not a virgin, but he must come to you without love. If he is sharp at times, remember his nerves are stretched, too."

Beth wished she could bring herself to tell the duchess what she had done and seek her counsel, but it would shock her so. It was impossible.

After that explicit description of the intimacies of marriage, it was also impossible to face the man with whom she would be doing these things. Beth took to her bed, claiming a sick headache.

Over the next days Beth dutifully appeared at public functions and stood by Lord Arden's side as they listened to deputations from this place and that, all expressing the warmest best wishes for the future. All these speeches also mentioned their wish for the speedy production of an heir to Belcraven. As the horrible Lord Deveril had said, the purpose of marriage was quite clear to all.

Beth could only think of the means of getting that heir.

After one of these events, her husband-to-be waylaid her before she could escape back to her apartments. "You are doing wonders for my reputation," he said with a smile, tucking her hand in the crook of his arm. "All these worthy souls know an admirable woman when they see one. They are not used to thinking me to have such sense."

He was trying to be kind, but Beth's nerves were sensitized beyond bearing and she tried to pull away.

He would not release her. "Walk with me," he said, still kindly, but implacably.

Beth had little choice but to stroll with him toward the yew walk.

"You must not be afraid of me, Elizabeth," he said bluntly.

"Is that a command?" she asked. She had intended it to be light, but it came out deadly serious. She looked anxiously up at him. It was as if she had lost the connection between her will and her words.

He was frowning slightly, but with puzzlement, not anger. "What has happened to you recently, Elizabeth? You're like a whip-shy horse. Has someone done or said something to upset you?"

"No," said Beth quickly, too quickly. The last thing she wanted to talk about was the duchess's explanation of the marriage act. To move the conversation on she asked, "What would you do with a whip-shy horse?"

"Feed it to the hounds?"

"What!" Then she saw the teasing light in his eyes.

"I'm sorry," he said. "Of course I'd try to repair the damage first." He stopped and turned to face her, putting a hand up to cradle the side of her face.

Beth flinched and tried to pull away. He tightened his hold. "For God's sake, stop that! What's the matter with you?"

The matter was that every intimacy made her think of Venus and Mars. She had no notion of how to deal with it graciously and was terrified of where it might lead. "I don't like to be handled," she said stiffly, his hand a burning brand against the side of her neck.

"Why not?"

Beth stared at him. "Surely it is normal—"

"No, not particularly. You're intelligent enough to know we have to learn to be comfortable with one another, and yet you're making no effort—"

"I'm sorry it's such an effort," Beth snapped.

He sucked in his breath with irritation but took his hand away. "Is it because of how I touched you that night?" he asked.

Beth swallowed. "Yes." It was a lie. It hadn't helped, for it had given vivid force to the duchess's talk, but it wasn't the main problem.

He actually looked uncomfortable, almost guilty. "I'm sorry for it then. At the time it seemed necessary, but it was not good of me, regardless of your . . ." He took a careful breath. "I won't do that again, Elizabeth. You have my word."

Beth was aware of a mixture of hope and disappointment. "You won't touch me there again?"

"You know that's not what I mean."

He seemed to be once again implying she had vast knowledge of men. "All I know, my lord," she snapped, "is that you had better keep your hands to yourself until I am legally obliged to endure your loathsome maulings!" With that Beth stalked away, ignoring the muttered curse behind her, nerves twitching for fear of attack.

He let her go, however, and over the next few days Beth was allowed to hide away between events without his interference.

Then one day she found herself carelessly alone in a carriage with the marquess as they returned from a visit to the village school. They had gone with the duke and duchess, but the marquess' parents had accepted an invitation to take tea with the vicar. It was only as she realized the consequences that Beth thought it might have been a deliberate maneuver.

The marquess lounged back—if he was feeling any irritation of the nerves it wasn't obvious, thought Beth waspishly—and looked at the gift the children had presented to them. It was a carefully polished board with a design made of brass nails. It had the de Vaux coat of arms and the initials E and L. "Do you have any idea what we are supposed to do with that?" he asked lazily.

"Hang it over the door, perhaps?" she suggested, knowing full well the de Vaux arms were carved in granite over the main door of Belcraven.

"Or over our bed?"

Beth couldn't help a start.

"There you go again," he said. "We are going to have to deal with this one of these days, you know."

Beth could feel her color flare. She glanced nervously at the coachman and groom. "I am naturally nervous," she muttered.

"Or worried about what I will discover."

Beth stared at him. Was that what he thought? "You promised never to mention that again."

He met her eyes. "I apologize then. But your reactions argue a very strange state of mind. I am bound to be suspicious."

Beth looked again at the servants. Did he know they couldn't hear such a soft-voiced conversation, or did he just, with de Vaux arrogance, not care? She couldn't let his insinuations go unchallenged. "You might suspect," she hissed, "that I am suffering from normal maidenly modesty."

"I might," he said with dry lack of conviction.

"You are a loathsome man!" she snapped and was sure she saw the groom twitch. Well, she doubted they were fooling the Belcraven servants.

"Along with my loathsome maulings," he drawled, still relaxed. But she could see the anger in him.

The rest of the journey passed in total silence.

When he handed her down from the carriage by the porte-cochere, Beth stalked away, eager to escape. He caught up and gripped her arm. "Slowly," he said. "Remember our agreement."

Beth glanced at the coach, just pulling away. "If you think we fool them, you are more stupid than I imagined."

"But you have never imagined me stupid, Elizabeth. The servants observe a great deal, but that is no reason to behave outrageously. You promised to act the part in public."

Beth turned on him. For once, rare blessing there was no servant in sight. *"You* promised to believe me an honest woman."

"Not quite. I promised to act as if you were. And am I supposed to believe you to be a naive little widgeon? A woman who reads the classics."

"There is surely some ground between an empty-headed idiot and a brazen hussy!"

"No man's land," he commented thoughtfully. "Is that what you are claiming still?"

"I am no man's," Beth stated, confused.

"You are mine."

"I am not. I am my own woman and always will be."

A spark lit in his eyes and his hands came around her throat. She froze. "What—"

"I have this urge to throttle you," he said in a strange, contemplative voice. "I wonder if Nicholas is right?"

Beth gaped at him. He'd run mad. When she swallowed nervously she could feel the tightness of his thumbs across the front of her throat. Just a little tighter and she would be in mortal danger. Where, for heaven's sake, were the ubiquitous servants?

Then his thumbs slid up until they rested on the soft underside of her jaw, making small circles against her jawbone, bringing a sweet, melting sensation she couldn't fight, though she tried. He lowered his head.

"Don't," she pleaded, but he ignored her.

His lips were firm and warm and gentle, but Beth was

frightened. She tried to twist away, but his hands trapped her. She felt the moistness of his mouth on hers and the invasion of a teasing tongue. She moaned a protest but at the same time she could feel that melting sensation weaving through her, softening her bones.

His lips left hers slowly and she felt their absence. He ran a thumb across her trembling lips. "Perhaps Nicholas is right," he said. "But I apologize again. I have no wish to frighten you and, as you said recently, there's no need for my loathsome maulings yet, is there? Ah, Thomas . . ."

Beth jerked around to see a footman standing stonily nearby. How long had he been there?

"Perhaps you would escort Miss Armitage to her apartments," the marquess said. He looked down at Beth. "A new compact?" he offered.

Beth swallowed. That kiss had not been loathsome at all. The fact that he remembered her comment, though, told her she might actually have hurt him. The duchess had perhaps been right about the state of his nerves.

"Very well," she said. "A new compact."

She followed the footman but looked back. The marquess was still watching her, frowning. Was he angry? Or was he, in fact, as anxious and unsure as she?

Lucien saw his betrothed's anxious, puzzled backwards glance. She had reason to be bemused, but she was enough to make a man fit for Bedlam. She defied him and challenged him, and his every instinct clamored to overpower her, to make her call him master.

He could bully her, he could force her, but he was equally sure he could seduce her if he really tried.

The ridiculous thing was that he suspected he could do nothing. The thought of hurting Elizabeth, even in such a minor way as stealing an unwilling kiss, was repugnant.

He *had* wanted to throttle her, but it had been a need to mark her, to make her notice him and not some phantasm she carried in her overeducated head. He'd found in kissing her the same need. He wanted to seduce her, to ravish her, to drive all her clever, caustic thoughts out of her head until she was subject to him, needing him.

He'd never felt this way about a woman before, and he wasn't at all sure it was healthy.

As a result of these thoughts he took a leaf out of his betrothed's book and went to ground, in his case in the billiard room, aimlessly potting balls.

Hal Beaumont found him there. "Blue-devilled?"

Lucien looked up. "Weddings are hell."

Hal laughed. "You should have eloped."

"Elizabeth said that once. Perhaps I should pay more attention to her suggestions."

"Perhaps you should. She seems to be a woman of sense."

Lucien dropped his cue on the baize. "Not at the moment, she doesn't."

"I can't say either of you are showing to advantage. You can tell me to go to the devil, Luce, but I have to ask. What's going on?"

"Go to the devil," said Lucien amiably.

Hal shrugged. "As you will. I've been halfway to hell and back as it is." He must have seen something on the marquess' face, for he grimaced. "I apologize. Nasty kind of emotional pressure to exert." He sighed. "It's just that a brush with death changes things. I hate to see people making stupid mistakes. I wouldn't like to see you in an arid marriage."

"I don't much want to be in one," said Lucien grimly. He looked around. The billiard table had been set up in a wide gallery which still boasted massed ranks of medieval armaments on the walls. "Come on. It must be this room that's depressing us both. If one of those hooks gives way we'll be sliced to ribbons. Let's find more convivial surroundings."

Hal's strong right hand stopped him. "Why, Luce? If it's all been a mistake there must be a way out. I can't believe Miss Armitage is desperate to hold you to this marriage."

It went against all sense of right to lie to Hal. Lucien tried to give him part of the truth. "It's an arranged marriage. Elizabeth is my parent's choice."

Hal seemed to read a great deal from the words. After a moment he released his grip. "Then make a go of it. She's a warm woman of intelligence and humor. I think you suit very well."

"Like a Bedlamite and a straitjacket," snapped Lucien and escaped. Hal, being a man of sense, let him go.

The next day was the reception for all the local people. The gentry and other local worthies were entertained in the ballroom with wine, fine dishes, and Mozart. The lesser tenants and local residents were in the meadow where various large carcasses were roasting, jugs of ale never seemed to empty, and a band played for dancing.

Beth paraded around both locations on the marquess' arm. She exchanged pleasantries with the doctor, the lawyer, and the prosperous farmers. She made stilted conversation with the wives of small holders and farm laborers. It wasn't that she felt above them but that they were so clearly in awe. Couldn't they see that despite her new finery, she was just like them?

The simple fact was that all these people gained pleasure from a few words from the future duchess when they would have thought nothing of a day spent with Beth Armitage, schoolmistress. It was a preposterous situation and yet Beth couldn't deny them that pleasure when this celebration was clearly a red-letter day in lives of endless, tedious drudgery.

She did enjoy the children, for they were more natural with her. She sat down at one point with a group of little ones to teach them a finger song.

The marquess stood by watching. When she finally escaped he said, "You do that very well."

"It is my profession."

"Not anymore, I'm afraid."

Beth didn't argue. "I'm less at ease with their parents. I feel so awkward, as if I'm acting in a play. 'Enter future duchess, stage right.' I have never been very good at that sort of thing."

"Nonsense. They love you. You don't just speak to them.

You listen. You make it seem as if you are, for a moment, one of them."

Beth looked at him. "But I am one of them."

He was arrested. After a pensive moment he shook his head. "Not anymore, I'm afraid." There was a trace of apology in it.

"I know," said Beth with a sigh. "But at least I can remember." She looked around the meadow full of people—chattering, dancing, eating, drinking. "Can you imagine," she demanded, "what it feels like to be one of these people? To worry about food for the table, a roof over your head, medicine for a sick child?"

"No," he retorted. "But if necessary I will put food on their table and a roof over their head, and send a doctor for their child. Who has the greater worry in the end?"

Before Beth could make a response he looked behind her. "Here's someone of the same lowly order as yourself. I'll leave you to wallow in your righteousness."

Beth abruptly found herself abandoned to the company of Mr. Beaumont, feeling very much as if she had been scolded, and possibly with justice. More than that she felt she might have hurt him again. It was time she started thinking of sensibilities other than her own. The marquess was arrogantly sure of his high place in the order of things, but he also took his responsibilities very seriously.

She wished he hadn't gone, so she could try to make amends, but for now all she could do was to continue to act her part. She chattered to Mr. Beaumont, trying to look like an ecstatic bride to be.

"Do you know, Miss Armitage," he said as they strolled back toward the house, "I wish you would not feel such a need to perform."

"What?"

"There's no need," he said gently. "Lucien has told me all about it."

Beth's eyes opened wide. *"All* about it?"

Mr. Beaumont studied her shrewdly. "Well no. He did not

say quite why you had been chosen to be his bride, merely that it was his parents' wish."

"And it surprises you to find the chosen one so plain and ordinary?" Beth asked waspishly.

"Begging for compliments, Miss Armitage?" he teased. "You know you are neither."

Beth looked at him in surprise. "On the contrary. My mirror tells me daily that I am no beauty. And I set no store in compliments, Mr. Beaumont."

"Perhaps you do not see yourself in animation," he said with a smile. "It is true your features are quite ordinary, but they become lively when you talk and you have what are called 'speaking eyes.' They shine with the light of your quick mind."

Beth could feel herself turning pink. "Please, Mr. Beaumont, you must not say such things to me. And they are quite untrue."

"Do you mean Lucien has not told you this?" he said with surprise. "I'd thought him more adroit. In fact," he added with a light of humor glinting in his eyes, "he's a devil of a flirt. But if he is going to leave the field to others . . ."

They had arrived at the rose garden close by the house. It was now full of the better quality of guest who were strolling about and admiring the flowers, but Beth and Mr. Beaumont were some distance from the nearest people. He stole an early rosebud from a bed and brushed it softly against her cheek. He leaned closer, and she felt his warm breath against her ear as he murmured, "Tell you what, Miss Armitage. I think you're wasted on him. Let's elope."

Beth choked with laughter. "You are quite outrageous, sir!" She was free of the tangled nervousness she felt with the marquess and was quite enjoying herself.

He smiled appreciatively. "Yes, I know. I'm the devil of a flirt, too. Shall we?"

Despite his declaration as a flirt there was a touch of honesty in the question which startled her. "Why are you saying such things when you know I cannot?"

He smiled still, but there was a wistfulness there. "I know a treasure when I see one, Miss Armitage. I would like a wife, you know, but what do I see around me? The Phoebe Swinnamers and the Lucy Frogmortons. You are a different type entirely."

There was no doubting his honesty, no matter how absurd it all seemed, and Beth was at a loss. "I know that, Mr. Beaumont, but . . ."

"But I have startled you." All humor was gone, and he met her eyes honestly. "When I first mentioned an elopement, Miss Armitage, it was a mere pleasantry. It is becoming more solid and desirable second by second. It will not do and I apologize."

He looked down at the creamy rosebud in his hand. "I am going to leave and you will not see me again before your wedding day. After that it will be as if this conversation never took place, as it never should. But before that, Miss Armitage," he said as he looked up again and held out the rose, "if it should seem wise to you, you may remind me of it."

Numbly, Beth took the flower and watched as he walked away. In truth, if there had been any way out of her predicament, she might have been tempted by Mr. Beaumont's offer, for he was a much more comfortable man than her betrothed. She could rub along with him without quicksands and violence.

Then she looked across the garden and saw Lucien de Vaux laughing with one of the tenants. The sun gilded his bright hair and he was relaxed and graceful. The air seemed suddenly thinner, and Beth knew that any place on earth other than this beautiful setting for a beautiful man would be bleak for her.

Beth moved quickly to join another adoring group.

In a little while the marquess was again by her side introducing her to yet more people to whom the Duchy of Belcraven was everything. She could do her part now almost by rote and had time to study the marquess' performance with these people.

He did take his job seriously.

He was surprisingly amenable. He knew most of the people by name and could often make flattering reference to some past encounter. He clearly understood the farmers' land and the major concerns of the professional men's occupations. He knew, too, that the women's lives were not of idleness and made mention of egg money, dairy work, and concerns over children.

He could flirt gently with the wives of all ages without giving offense—Beth remembered Mr. Beaumont saying he was a devil of a flirt and knew it to be true. It made her bitter that he never used his skill on her. Then she had to admit that he had tried once or twice and now doubtless expected to have a poker wrapped around his head did he do anything so foolish again.

Beth was interested to note that he could depress pretension firmly but subtly so that the offender realized his or her mistake without public shaming. Much though she hated the necessity Beth thought she should study his technique.

She was surprised, though, by it all. Lucien de Vaux was good at his trade. He would, in time, make an excellent duke.

"And why are you frowning?" he asked as they moved on again, leaving the local corn factor and the ironmonger content. "Am I offending your radical sympathies again?"

"Tiredness, I'm afraid," Beth said in as conciliatory a tone as she could muster. "And I think I need to apologize. You do take your responsibilities seriously, don't you?"

"Of course." She thought he was pleased by her words. "It's a strange business, though. I am in training for a job I hope will be a very long time coming, and in the meantime I often have too much time on my hands."

"Would the duke not let you share in the running of the duchy?"

He looked at her skeptically. "The two of us in harness?"

Beth had completely forgotten the problem of his birth. "I think one needs to train for this kind of thing," she said. "It will be years, if ever, before I feel I belong in the role of duchess."

"You will get used to it in time. Now, however, I think you should go and rest. The event is all but over. Tomorrow we leave for London and there, I gather, you are supposed to cram a Season into a fortnight. You will need every scrap of stamina."

And that was the way it was. The next day they all set off for Town with three coaches. Beth traveled with the duchess in her chariot, the one which had brought her from Cheltenham, while servants were conveyed in the other two. The duke drove himself in a curricle while the marquess rode Viking, the horse with which the boy had been careless.

Beth was guiltily aware that she had forgotten about Robin Babson. The large black stallion showed no sign of injury and was restive and difficult to handle, even for the marquess. It was unfair to even think of a child trying to control such an animal.

When they stopped for refreshments, Beth looked over the many servants but saw no sign of the boy. *Had* the marquess beaten him half to death? Dismissed him? She had to know.

As they took a turn around a small orchard next to the inn she raised the subject. "I met a young boy in the Belcraven stables. He said he worked with your horses, but I do not see him here."

"You must mean Robin. He's a troublesome scamp." It was an indulgent comment but didn't explain the boy's absence.

"Where is he?"

"He and Dooley are bringing my bays to Town by easy stages. Why?" The last word held a note of suspicion.

"I took a liking to the boy," Beth explained. "I gather he'd been in hot water for something to do with Viking. Is the horse all right?"

"Yes, but Jarvis thought he might have thrown a splint and dusted the lad's jacket for him." He looked down at her with a frown. "I hope he didn't come running to you to complain."

"Oh no," she assured him. "The subject came up quite by accident." After a moment she added, "He did seem worried you'd thrash him again when you found out."

"I might well have done," he replied casually, "if the damage had been serious. He's inclined to be careless and that horse cost me eight hundred guineas."

"For a horse!" Beth exclaimed.

"Yes," he replied with asperity, "for a horse. And if you give me prosy lecture on the extravagance of the aristocracy I'll doubtless thrash you, Elizabeth."

Beth wasn't at all sure he was joking.

Chapter Twelve

Back in the safety of the carriage Beth could at least be reassured that he wasn't a cruel master to his servants no matter how he was going to behave to his wife. She really thought he ought to know that Robin was afraid of horses, but she had given her word to the boy. She decided she would try to sort out this minor problem. It would take her mind off her own predicament.

When they reached London, however, it soon drove thoughts of Robin out of her head. It was a whole new world.

She had only twice been to London, and though she and Aunt Emma had visited the Royal Academy exhibition at Somerset House and strolled by the Queen's Palace, she had never ventured within the more select areas of Mayfair. Her previous experiences had given her the impression that London was universally noisy and dirty, but she discovered there were islands of peace and beauty for those who could afford them.

Marlborough Square was surrounded by about twenty fine mansions, some fronted by courtyards set apart by wrought-iron barriers, and others with magnificent steps leading up to great, gleaming doorways. The center of the square was a fine garden around a fountain. Trees were in fresh leaf and flowers bloomed.

The carriage drew up before a large double-fronted house. The arms blazoned proudly above the door confirmed that this was Belcraven House. The doors swung open and an army of servants trooped out to take care of the family. Of whom Beth was now supposedly one.

She felt as if she had been politely escorted from one prison to another.

Once in the house in Marlborough Square Beth never had a moment to herself, and she certainly never set eyes on Robin Babson. She was taken on an exhausting round of shopping, had endless fittings for clothes, and was dragged to one social affair after another every evening. The Season was scarcely begun and yet there did not seem to be a shortage of gatherings at which the Belcraven heir and his bride could be displayed.

It was usually three or four in the morning before Beth rolled into bed, but she was not afforded the luxury of rising at noon like the rest of Society. She was up in the morning for extra lessons in court etiquette and the correct handling of social inferiors. It was strongly impressed upon her by the duchess that soon everyone short of royalty would be her social inferior and any mistakes in her interactions with them would be disastrous.

Beth felt a rebellious desire to sit down with the housemaid and discuss the position of woman in modern society, but she knew the maid would be as distressed by this as the duchess.

After luncheon, the cycle began again with morning visits, salons, a drive in the park, an opulent dinner, the theater, a soirée, a ball or a rout. Everyone stared at her; people said the same boring things over and over. Even interesting events such as the maneuvers of Napoleon and the defeat of Murat by the Austrians were gossiped to death with so little insight as to be tedious. Beth felt she never wanted to attend another social event for the rest of her life.

The marquess was nearly always by her side, but they were never alone. This meant there was no opportunity to grow closer but at least they could not quarrel. As a consequence, he ceased to be a person to fear and even at times became her support. He was surefooted in this quagmire and could be depended upon to rescue her if she faltered, if only for the sake of the damned pride of the de Vaux. He could even at times be depended on for a little intelligent conversation though it was clearly unfashionable to be too serious, even about the prospect of war.

Beth constantly hoped to encounter a friend, for Miss Mallory's had catered to some of the higher families and Beth had made friends with some of the girls of her own age. The friendships had lapsed as their lives had settled into different patterns—Beth's into study and teaching and her friends' into social life, marriage, and motherhood—but she had every faith that some of them could be revived now she had entered her friends' world. She never encountered any, however, and could not always remember married names or even their place of residence.

Nor was she successful at making new friends. In this artificial environment where she felt as much an object of curiosity as a freak, there was little basis for true understanding.

Beth was sure at least some of her troubles could be laid at Phoebe Swinnamer's door. The beauty and her mother had come up to Town, and Phoebe was affecting an air of hurt restraint as if she'd actually been jilted. Heaven knew what stories the girl was telling, but if the marquess stopped to say good evening to her it was as if the whole room held its breath to listen. The one time when he was somehow inveigled into standing up with her, other dancers were tripping over each other as they attempted to watch his every expression.

If they saw anything, they saw the marquess throw Beth a look of mock despair which made her want to laugh. Their situation was not comfortable, but Beth was relieved to see that he was not enamored of another. She remembered he had expressed horror at the thought of marrying such a vain widgeon. Poor Phoebe.

It was not so amusing however when she found herself in conversation with the girl, aware of nearby ears stretched to catch every word.

"How tiresome for you, Miss Armitage, to have your wedding rushed so," the girl drawled. "I would have—" Phoebe broke off and lowered her lashes. She would doubtless have blushed had it been within her control. "I *will*," she corrected sweetly, "insist on plenty of time to make all proper arrangements."

This was clearly a rehearsed speech. Beth lost all sympathy for the little cat. "Will you?" she said. "I am sure your husband will be pleased to know that your desire for show and ceremony outweighs your desire to be his wife."

The beauty stared glassily but rallied. "I merely meant, Miss Armitage, that I would wish the wedding to be done properly."

"How kind," countered Beth with a smile. "I'm sure the duchess would appreciate your advice. Pray go and tell her in what ways you think the wedding will fall short."

Phoebe had lost her script and was close to losing her composure, which in her case meant that the flawless perfection of her features was slightly troubled by emotion. "La!" she said with a little laugh. "How you do take me up. I declare it must be exhausting to converse with one so clever as you. You cannot help but be aware, Miss Armitage, that it is usual in our circles for there to be a longer period between the betrothal and the wedding."

The "our" clearly did not encompass Beth. Beth was framing an annihilating and yet permissible reply when she became aware of the marquess beside her. "Alas Miss Swinnamer, *you* must surely know," he said with razor-edged meaning, "that I disdain to do the usual. I'm sure one day, when some man falls into the snare of your beauty, he will rush you to the altar just as I am rushing Elizabeth."

This masterly speech scored so many points that some titters were heard. Mrs. Swinnamer, who had been hovering nearby, swept down to shepherd her daughter away. The mother looked flustered and angry, but Phoebe wore only the slightest frown. She glanced back once, exquisitely puzzled, and it occurred to Beth that the girl had never considered until that moment that the marquess was not truly smitten by her beauty.

"I confess, I feel sorry for the poor fool," she said to him as they moved away from their audience toward a refreshment room.

"Don't," he said firmly. "She's like a honey trap—to be avoided at all times."

"If you had avoided her," Beth pointed out, "we would not be subjected to such sugared ambushes."

He steered her to a seat in a relatively quiet corner. "Would you like wine? Or they have negus and orgeat."

"Negus, please.

He signed to a hovering footman and commanded it. "If you have any complaint," he said, "you must make it to my mother. She was the one throwing the beautiful Phoebe at my head."

"She believed her a suitable wife for you?" asked Beth, puzzled. She'd thought the duchess more astute.

"She thought her a *possible* wife," he corrected, "and was nobly willing to do her best." The footman arrived, and the marquess passed Beth her chilled drink. "It was all my fault, I confess. Phoebe was making a dead set at me and I was falling into the trap. Not of her beauty," he said, "but of her lacquered gloss. I developed an obsessive desire to disturb it. It could have proved fatal if I hadn't come to my senses enough to flee her orbit entirely."

It was one of the relaxed times when he talked to her as if she were just another human being, and perhaps one he liked.

She sipped her drink and said, "I'm sure even Phoebe must wake up with her hair disordered and sheet marks on her cheek."

"Do you think so?" he queried lazily. "That was one of my almost fatal questions. Whether she could preserve the perfect finish throughout a wedding night."

Beth froze. The negus went the wrong way, and she spluttered and choked. He rescued her glass before the contents spilled over her green silk gown. Beth finally gasped a breath.

"Are you all right?" he asked. "I didn't think it was quite that funny."

Beth rose to her feet. "I'm perfectly recovered," she said, with another little cough which gave her the lie. "I think I have a partner waiting."

He placed her glass on a table and caught her up, staying her with a hand on her arm. "I claim precedence," he said. "What's the matter?" He studied her features for a moment then said, "Ah, the dreadful prospect of the marriage bed. More maidenly modesty?" The familiar bitter edge was back in his voice.

"That is surely not unreasonable?"

"It's damned inconvenient," he said, and she could tell the use of the word *damned* was deliberate. "You will have to make up your mind, sweeting, whether you wish to be treated as a delicate bloom, to be protected from all crudity, even the need—especially the need—to think. Or whether you wish to be treated as an equal."

"As an equal," said Beth instantly. "But that surely does not disallow a little maidenly modesty, my lord. Does a man not suffer some qualms before a new event? A duel, for example?"

He took her at her word. "I'm a virgin," he said. "In the matter of duels, that is. Is that how you regard our wedding night? Pistols at twenty paces?" The mischievous twinkle she was coming to know too well entered his eyes. "Wrestling would be nearer the mark," he murmured. "Or a sword fight."

Beth could feel herself color but knew she had no right to complain. She'd asked for this. "I hope," she said, "that peace, not combat, will mark our marriage bed."

He was serious again. "If you are as honest as you claim to be, Elizabeth, blood will mark our marriage bed. Blood is not usually a product of peace."

If she had been pink before, Beth knew now she must be pale. His words were perfectly true and yet there was a hint of violence, and a reminder of his lingering doubts.

He sighed and took her hand. "I'm sorry. I'm not very good at this. I have been trained to treat women one way, and you are asking for something different. No matter how much of a sturdy plant you wish to be, I think it would be wiser for me to treat you as a delicate bloom for a little while yet. You may be made of steel, but my nerves aren't up to the strain."

He led her into the ballroom where a county dance was in progress which could easily be joined. He wove them adroitly into the pattern.

"For a little while yet . . ." Until their wedding night was over, her composure ruthlessly reduced to wild lust, her blood spilt, his doubts finally satisfied.

Beth fixed a bright smile and surrendered to the mindlessness of the dance.

From then on he treated her with a warm courtesy which at the same time was chillingly impersonal. Beth missed the brief moments of relaxed conversation but was willing enough to sacrifice them to avoid the quicksands.

Phoebe Swinnamer, too, seemed to have been routed and had all her attention fixed on the young Earl of Bolton who appeared to be as much of a cold stick as herself.

This was some relief, but Beth still had the endless daily round of entertainments at which she was always under curious scrutiny and must always appear to be a lover on the verge of marriage—in the most polite and decorous way, of course.

The marquess occasionally escaped to a club or time with his friends, but Beth had no such relief. One night, to everyone's amazement, she burst into tears as they were about to leave for the theater. Simply because he was closest, she found herself in the marquess' arms.

He settled her on a sofa and kept an arm about her. *"Maman, this has got to stop,"* he said.

The duke and duchess shared a glance.

"Miss Armitage isn't used to this way of life," said the marquess. "It's a strain on me, but it must be far worse for her, surrounded always by strangers. It is less than a week to the wedding. Let her rest. Everyone will understand."

"If she appears to be sickly . . ." said the duchess doubtfully.

"Is it any better for her to collapse in public than for her to miss a few events?"

By this time Beth had pulled herself together. "Please," she said, quite touched by the marquess' concern. "I am recovered now."

"No, you're not," he said roughly. "You're as white as a sheet and have black shadows under your eyes." With a touch of humor he added, "You're doing nothing for my reputation as a lover, you know. Go to bed and we'll tell the world you have a cold. Anyone can catch a cold."

Beth took out her tiny lacy handkerchief and blew her nose. "I sound as if I have one," she sniffed.

"Exactly," he said, providing a much larger and more practical one. "Tomorrow you can receive some callers, sniff a lot, and retreat again. If you rouge your nose a little to give it verisimilitude, it should gain you at least two days of peace and quiet."

Beth couldn't help it; she chuckled. "What a master of deceit you are, my lord," she said. She felt the temperature immediately drop.

"Aren't we all?" he replied coolly and rang the bell. Once she was safely in the custody of her maid, the marquess, the duke, and the duchess took their leave.

Beth was left lying miserably on her bed wondering how every moment of harmony and kindness was soured. Was there any hope for them at all?

His plan did gain her the respite she needed, however. Beth spent two peaceful days in her room, reading and resting. By the time she was "recovered" there were only two more days before the wedding and the duchess used that fact as a reason to curtail their social activities.

This did not leave Beth with time on her hands, for she was expected to assist the duchess in supervising arrangements and had final fittings for her wedding gown. Also, a bewildering number of relatives began to arrive in Town and all paid calls. The only good point was that the marquess exempted himself from these occasions, saying blithely that he'd known all the old frumps from the cradle and had no need to be introduced. Beth was convinced that even if absence did not make her heart grow fonder, it provided fewer occasions for discord.

What that had to offer for the rest of their lives, she didn't like to think at all.

* * *

Beth's resting period also liberated Lucien. Once his bride-to-be was excused from the endless round of socialization there was not much point in his attending. He was not short of entertainment, for the Company of Rogues had assembled to bid farewell to Con and Dare, who were off to join Wellington's army on the very day of the wedding. The focus of the Company, as always, was the Delaney house in Lauriston Street. Nicholas and Eleanor had returned there after their family visit to Grattingley, and it was always open house for their friends.

Lucien spent most of his evenings there.

Three days before the wedding, Eleanor was bold enough to venture a saucy query. "Shouldn't you perhaps stay home with Elizabeth, My Lord Marquess?"

"Like Godric and Godgifu, sitting by the hearth?" he replied. "She's resting, and anyway, it would be no fit pattern for our elevated future."

Eleanor frowned slightly at his tone and he repented of the bitterness. But before he could say anything she summoned Nicholas. "Who were Godric and Godgifu?" she demanded.

He looked intrigued but said, "King Henry I and his wife Matilda. A somewhat sneering reference by the Normans to their domestic happiness and their attempts to Anglicize their court." He looked over at Lucien and added, "She refuses to buy an encyclopedia and just drags me around everywhere."

"I suppose a husband should be of some use," Lucien said and grimaced as he again heard bitterness ring through.

"Just consider," said Eleanor to Nicholas, smoothing over the moment, "if Miss Fitcham had been the kind of schoolmistress to actually teach her pupils something, I doubtless would have no use for you at all."

"Do you think not?" he said lazily.

Eleanor colored and rose to her feet. "If you are going to be bold, I'm escaping while I can." She turned and fired a parting shot at Lucien. "If it was good enough for the king of England, My Lord Marquess, I cannot see how it is beneath you."

"Broadsided, by God," said Lucien with a laugh and gave

her the victory. He turned to Nicholas. "How do you live with a sharp-witted woman?"

"In constant delight. She is also warm-hearted. Is Elizabeth cold?"

This was the attack direct. "I don't know," Lucien said at last.

"Luce," said Nicholas, "you are rich, handsome, and the most skillful, the most outrageous, flirt in England. You even had Eleanor bedazzled in front of my very nose. How can you not know if your bride is warm or cold?"

Lucien realized he'd never flirted with Elizabeth Armitage. Assaulted her, yes, threatened and berated her. But flirted with her? No. It was not a matter he could discuss, even with Nicholas. "How can I not know?" he repeated lightly. "Because she's a cactus and I'm an inflated bag of pride and consequence, and I'm afraid to get close enough to find out."

Nicholas's lips twitched. "There goes the de Vaux succession, I gather."

"Oh," said Lucien, "there'll have to be an heir for de Vaux even if it leaves me limp and useless . . ." Hearing his own words he burst out laughing.

"Perfectly natural," agreed Nicholas with a grin, "if only in the temporary sense. Don't I recall you saying once that your minions inflate your consequence with a foot pump every day? I'm gaining a whole new insight into the bed manners of the great."

"Have some reverence," Lucien chided, still fighting laughter. "Not that I've not always wondered about my parents . . ."

"Don't we all."

Thought of his parents—of his father who was not his father—effectively sobered Lucien. "Do you ever feel grateful," he asked, "not to have the responsibility of carrying on a line?"

"As my brother is disinclined to marry, I probably have that duty. I don't find it unbearable," Nicholas said with a grin, "but then I'm not all puffed up with pride." He burst out laughing. "You know, I'll never be able to hear that phrase again without lurid imaginings." He shook his head. "Eleanor renders me limp with satisfying regularity but leaves her spines at the bedroom door."

"Eleanor has no spines."

Eleanor's devoted husband hooted with mirth. "Has she not, indeed! You got to know her when circumstances had her somewhat subdued. I tell her it's no wonder she was whipped so often as a child. The remarkable thing is that it had so little effect."

"How do you keep her in line, then?"

Nicholas grew serious in a way his friends had reason to know. "In what line?"

It was a challenge and Lucien reacted by stiffening. "Within the line of appropriate behavior."

Nicholas's warm brown eyes became remarkably cold. "I've never stayed within that line myself. Why should I try to impose it on anyone else?"

"She's your wife, damn it."

Nicholas shook his head. "She's Eleanor. I never wanted to become the guardian of another adult human being and God was good and granted me a wife able to accept freedom. Are you going to try to keep Elizabeth 'in line'?"

Lucien knew he was already trying to do that. But what else could he do when heaven only knew what the woman would do if he let her loose? Wear rags. Hobnob with the servants. Preach revolution. Give her body to any Tom, Dick, or Harry? He realized he didn't really care about the rest, just that. Even though she'd preserved her virginity—or so she said—what was to restrain her once that was gone? Mary Wollstonecraft's daughter was a prime example of where her mother's teaching led.

"Elizabeth is no Eleanor," Lucien said.

"No. I gather she's better educated."

"Crammed full of the Wollstonecraft's immoral teaching."

"Have you read it?"

"No."

"Come on," said Nicholas and rose to lead the way out of the room. Lucien was in the hall before it occurred to him that there wasn't one damn reason in the world why he should follow at Nicholas Delaney's bidding. Except that he was Nicholas Delaney.

They went into the library. Nicholas lit a lamp and took two books from the well-filled shelves, finding them with ease. Mary Wollstonecraft's *A Vindication of the Rights of Man* and *A Vindication of the Rights of Woman.*

Nicholas touched the second. "Every man should read that, if only to understand. I think in your case you should read it carefully."

Even Nicholas could stir Lucien's anger. "I am supposed to convert to the cause of radical feminism?"

Nicholas smiled. "The earth would crumble at the shock. No, but at least you would speak the same language."

"It would be better if Elizabeth learned to speak mine. What do you think of Mary Godwin's elopement with Percy Shelley?" Lucien challenged. "He leaves a wife and two children behind. And takes his mistress's friend along for variety."

"I think," said Nicholas seriously, "if I had met Eleanor when I was married to another . . . But I'm not sure that applies here. I think all of them—wife, mistress, mistress's friend, and the poet himself—are quite mad." He shrugged. "I refuse to think of such strange poetical antics. I'm trying very hard to unload the world from my shoulders. It's not very fair to Eleanor to expect her to carry my weight and all that, too."

Lucien was pleased enough to have Nicholas change the subject. "And Napoleon?" he asked, to keep the talk drifting the right way.

"The same."

"And Deveril?"

At that name, Nicholas nodded. "I have a score to settle with him," he admitted quietly, looking every bit as dangerous as he could be. "But I won't pursue it. There's no good to be done. It would merely be revenge."

"Revenge can be sweet."

"I have never found it so."

"What about all our antics at Harrow?" Lucien put down the books in his hand.

"They weren't revenge. They were boyish stratagems."

Nicholas picked the books up and returned them to Lucien's hand.

Lucien met his friend's eyes for a tense moment but then gave in. He made sure, however, that the talk stayed off his business. "I was astonished to see Deveril in England," he said. "I thought he fled with Thérèse Bellaire?"

"Thérèse would deny anything so gauche as flight," Nicholas pointed out as he extinguished the lamp. "But yes," he said as they left the room, "Deveril was with us. An extremely unpleasant traveling companion." A flicker of something passed over his face which made Lucien wonder about that strange journey when Madame Bellaire had kidnapped Nicholas. He had been kept with them for many days, then put on board another ship headed for the Cape Colony. It had taken him nearly four months to get home, during which time many people had feared him dead.

"If he's back," Nicholas continued, "she must have dismissed him. After all, he was never her lover."

They were alone in the hall. Lucien hazarded a question, for he had a morbid curiosity about the cold-hearted courtesan. "What exactly was he to her?"

Nicholas shrugged. "Someone who shared some of her tastes. Slimy things tend to huddle together. He has a crude, but vigorous imagination." He went on smoothly before Lucien could think of a comment or further question. "Being a greedy man, he was also very interested in her scheme. He traveled with us to be sure of getting his share of the money."

"He must have succeeded," said Lucien. "He was never poor but word is he's come back filthy rich—the emphasis as always being on the filthy. That's why he's got his toe back into Society. Money will always open doors."

Nicholas looked at him alertly. "Rich? There wasn't that much money, and Thérèse intended most of it for her own use."

"Perhaps he's just putting on a show. But he's taken a house in Grosvenor Square. He's driving some damned fine cattle— topped my price for Millham's bays and it irks me to see him out with them. He's a hard-handed driver. Rumor has it he's looking for a wife, and not an heiress. More a question of buying something to his taste."

Nicholas grimaced. "That any parent would sell their child to such as he. . . . But I wonder, Luce, where all his money comes from. I wonder, in fact, whether he didn't manage to beat Thérèse at her own game."

"Cheated the Madame out of her lucre?" asked Lucien with a grin. "You may say revenge isn't sweet, but I could relish that."

"Justice, not revenge," said Nicholas with a matching grin. *"Fiat justicia et pereat mundus.* It's not complete, though. I don't see why Deveril should enjoy the ill-gotten gains."

"Nor do I, by God. What shall we do about it?"

Nicholas looked at him. "Nothing for the moment. He'll keep. You are getting married, which takes a certain amount of concentrated effort. As I found out to my cost. You also have some reading to do."

Lucien looked at the books. "You expect these to make a difference. I think I understand Elizabeth perfectly. I just don't approve."

"And I took you for a man of sense. We never understand another human being and to think we do is the most dangerous illusion of all." Nicholas was completely serious and when that happened it was wise for all to pay attention. "I wish," he said thoughtfully, "we'd come back sooner and had an opportunity to meet your Elizabeth. I suspect she could use a friend or two."

Lucien was guiltily aware that he'd never considered his betrothed's lack of friends. "I could bring her over one day."

"If you wish, of course. But it's only three days to the Wedding of the Season, and she'll doubtless appreciate peace and quiet rather than more strangers. Bring her around after your honeymoon. I think, in view of this Deveril business, we will stay here for a few more weeks."

They walked towards the drawing-room door, but there Nicholas stopped with his hand on the knob. "Giving advice is rarely a good idea, Luce, but I can't resist. No matter what problems there are between you and Elizabeth, the marriage bed is no place for them." He looked up. "Fight if you have to, but in bed just love her. And if you can't do that yet, wait until you can."

Chapter Thirteen

The wedding was to be held in the ballroom of Belcraven House and on her wedding eve Beth found herself drawn there. The large room with its gilded pillars and arched ceiling was illuminated by only a cold touch of moonlight which reduced its magnificence to shades of silver and gray. The flowers were already in place—in huge urns, on trellises, and hanging on the walls. The moist perfume weighted the air and made it hard to breathe.

She was for once quite alone. The servants had finished their work here and were in their beds, resting before the long hard day they would have tomorrow.

In the pale light, the room looked rather like a chapel, but Beth was glad she was not to be married in a church. There was nothing spiritual about this enforced joining. Though it was sugared by civilized behavior, it was as brutal as the calculated abductions of ages past, where the affections of the woman mattered not a whit, only her fortune.

"And my fortune is just my misbegotten blood," she murmured. "Wealth beyond measure to the de Vaux."

She had to admit that the marquess had mostly been kind and considerate in recent weeks, particularly so during the past few days. She could even confess that she was not immune to his charms. He was a beautiful man and viewed only as an *objet d'art* there was pleasure to be found. He was intelligent and, after his own fashion, sensitive. She could have enjoyed his company if they weren't in this terrible situation.

After all, she would never have known his company if it weren't for this terrible situation. With a caught breath Beth realized that even if she were given the chance she might not be able to find satisfaction any more in her old life. Without him.

He had the power to move her. The formal touch of his hand was often more than a touch; the sense of his body nearby could catch her breath; a look in his eyes could set her skin to tingling.

Perhaps this more than anything caused her to face her marriage with dread. By this time tomorrow she would be totally in his power, in the grip of these wanton sensations. And yet he felt nothing.

She wrapped her arms around herself as she shivered. She desperately wished the duchess had left her in misty ignorance of where the marquess's power over her might lead. She remembered that horrible encounter on the terrace at Belcraven and the way he had been able to set fire to her body while his expression stayed cold as ice. Now she was constantly assailed by the vision of him cold-bloodedly manipulating her into some frantic state, a state she knew was just a few touches away . . .

The duchess walked into the room carrying a branch of candles. Leaping flames picked out the red walls and the gilding and made them dance. The room became gay instead of mysterious.

"Is something the matter, Elizabeth?"

"No," said Beth, unable to fabricate an explanation for her presence here in the dark.

The duchess put down the candles and came over to take Beth in her arms. "Oh, my poor child. Please do not be afraid. Truly, there is nothing of which to be afraid in Lucien."

"Nothing?" Beth queried, pulling herself out of the comforting embrace. "Nothing? After tomorrow he could beat me half to death and no one would care!"

"What?" exclaimed the duchess. "Has he ever struck you Elizabeth? If he has I will flog him myself!"

"No," said Beth hastily, for the duchess was truly enraged. She swallowed the response that he'd twice threatened to.

"Thank God," said the duchess and calmed. "There is something of violence in Lucien, I will admit, but there is in most men. Let us be honest, Elizabeth, we are glad of it when we want them to defend us or fight for our country as so many of them will have to do very soon. Lucien is a gentleman, however, and can control himself. You must not fear him. If he ever hurts you, you must tell me, and I promise he will regret it bitterly."

There was some reassurance to be found in this, but Beth was surprised to find she was ambivalent. She pinned down her reluctance to accept help and realized she preferred the battle between the marquess and herself to be an honest fight, just the two of them. How strange.

"Now tell me," asked the duchess. "Why are you smiling like that?"

"I really don't know, Your Grace," said Beth. "It is all so ridiculous, though. I never wanted any of this." She shook her head. "I think I had best go to bed and rest."

The duchess watched Elizabeth walk away and sighed. She had observed her son and his bride-to-be and was perplexed. At times they acted well and at others they ignored one another. Sometimes, if they had the opportunity to talk, they appeared to rub along together marvelously; she had been pleased to see her intelligent son using his brains instead of sinking to the inanities of most of his fashionable friends. At other times, however, they almost seemed to hate each other and now, it would appear, Elizabeth was afraid of him.

She thought of speaking to Lucien, but Marleigh informed her he was out with his friends. As usual. She went instead in search of the duke and found him in the library.

He stood courteously until she had taken a seat opposite him, but he watched her warily. The duchess realized she had never sought him out like this before, and following the thought, she had a revelation. Their whole life since Lucien's birth seemed now to have been distorted beyond reason. She forgot that she had come to talk of the marriage.

"Why?" she asked softly. "Why have we done this to ourselves?" She saw him almost flinch under the question. "William, why have we let such small mistakes ruin our lives?"

"Small?" he asked sharply. "Having an heir who is not my son is not a small matter to me."

She almost fled back behind the barriers of formality but steeled herself. "It happens, though. The whole world knows Melbourne's heir is Lord Egremont's, and there are other families in the same predicament. Do they all fall apart as we have done?"

He stood sharply. "We have not fallen apart. I have treated you with respect. I have treated Arden as my own son in every way."

"In every way?" she queried.

He turned back, and her heart caught at the feeling in his eyes. "I love him, Yolande. How many times have I longed for ignorance? He can infuriate me," he said with a slight smile, "but all offspring do that at times. At his best I could never wish for a finer son."

"Why then can you not forgive me?" she cried.

He came quickly over and fell to one knee by her chair. "Forgive you? I forgave you the moment you told me, Yolande. Have I reproached you?"

She felt quite strange. Was she really over fifty years old? She was flustered like a girl again. She reached out to touch his hair, first with her fingers, then with the whole of her hand as she caressed him. "No, my dear," she said softly, "you never reproached me. But you could not bear to touch me."

He captured her hand and pressed a burning kiss into her palm. "I have ached for you, Yolande, with a greater pain than I could ever have imagined. Sleepless nights. Dreams of you so real I would wake in horror, thinking I had been with you . . ."

"Horror?" she asked, clenching her hands on his. *"Horror?"*

You will hate me for this," he said softly, but he raised his head to meet her eyes. "If I had given you another son, Yolande, I believe I would have killed Arden."

Her grip relaxed, but she did not loose his hand. "William, you could never have done that."

He pulled away from her, rose, and went to stand across the room. "Perhaps not," he said in a hard voice, "but I would certainly have arranged his disappearance. The dukedom belongs to a de Vaux. Ironically, I think Lucien could understand that, even if you cannot."

The duchess could feel the smile on her face and the tears in her eyes. She rose lightly and went to him. She wrapped her arms around him. "Well, it is certainly not a matter which need bother us anymore, my love."

His arms had come around her with a life of their own, and he looked dazed. "Yolande? After what I said?"

"Perhaps you would have done as you say. We will never know now." She reached up gently to touch his cheek. "I, too, have ached," she said unsteadily. Her fingers traced softly over his lips. "You called him Lucien."

The duke captured her wandering fingers and imprisoned them in his own. "I what?"

"You have never ever called him Lucien. It has always been Arden, even when he was a baby. Thank God for Elizabeth." She was beyond subterfuge and the simplest of words escaped her. "Love me, William."

His eyes darkened. "Yolande. It's been so long."

Fires kept banked for over twenty years were burning in her. "Have you forgotten how?" she teased. "Don't worry. I remember."

"Oh God," he groaned. "So do I." With that his lips came down on hers, and it was as if the years between evaporated and they were still young. Her hands slipped under his jacket and felt the same fine lines of his back. Her tongue tasted the special, wonderful taste of him. Her body easily found the well-remembered contours and fitted itself to them.

His lips left hers and traced down her neck. To come against the ruffled collar of her gown. "Since when," he growled, "did you take to wearing high-necked gowns?"

"Since I was forty," she laughed, giddy with delight. "Allow me a moment with my maid and I can correct it.

His hand slid down over the front of her sensible dimity gown and took possession of her breast. "I can play maid," he said huskily. "My memory is recovering remarkably quickly. I remember undressing you many a time, my golden treasure."

He turned her quickly and began to unfasten all the little buttons down her back, tracing kisses after his fingers.

The duchess came to her senses. *"Here,* William? We cannot."

"Here. Now," he said roughly. His fingers stopped their work and he gripped her, pulling her against his body. "Am I dreaming, Yolande? I can't bear it if I'm dreaming."

She tilted her head back. "No, my love. You aren't dreaming unless I'm dreaming, too. And I make you a promise, if this is a dream, I'm coming to your bed as soon as I awake."

He buried his head in her curls and laughed. "No man deserves to be this happy." His hands traveled up and his fingers brushed softly over her breasts. She trembled at the power of a wave of giddy lust.

"William!" she gasped.

"Yes. But I must be growing old," he said as he continued the delicate torment. "Bed does sound like an attractive notion. As I remember, making love on the floor can be deuced uncomfortable."

Reluctantly, the duchess agreed though she didn't know if her legs could support her to the upper floor, and she did not want to part from him. She was terrified this moment would evaporate. But she pulled free of his hands and said, "It will take me only a few moments to be ready."

He pulled her back into his arms. "I go with you," he said. He traced her face with unsteady fingers then kissed her hungrily. Then pulled back.

"Thomas!" he shouted and a footman popped into the room. "Go tell my valet and the duchess's maid they will not be required."

"Yes, Your Grace," said the footman, but his eyes bulged at the sight of his disheveled master and mistress entwined together.

As the footman left on his errand, the duchess chuckled and hid her face in the duke's shoulder. "What will they think?"

"Who cares?" He placed his hands beneath her breasts and pushed their fullness up, then slowly and deliberately he lowered his lips first to one nipple then the other. As they swelled beneath the cloth he brought his teeth to bear gently so that the duchess moaned and clutched at him.

"I told you my memory was returning," he said with a grin "Let's to bed, *reine de mon coeur.*

The marquess returned to Marlborough Square rather early. Tonight had been the farewell party for Con and Dare, but it had also turned into a farewell to his days of bachelor freedom.

It had been pleasant enough, but he'd begun to find the bawdy jokes of his friends tiresome and their advice inappropriate to his bedding of Elizabeth Armitage. He'd noticed Nicholas twice turn the conversation when it became too crude, which he wouldn't have bothered to do in other circumstances.

In the end, though, Lucien had slipped away and walked home to clear his head. It would not be a bad idea anyway to have all his wits about him tomorrow.

It had only occurred to him this evening that he'd never tried to bed a woman without the positive desire to do so. Sometimes it had been only a momentary lust; at other times, as with Blanche, it had been something much deeper, but the desire had always been strong.

Did he desire Elizabeth Armitage? Not particularly. He admired her spirit and her wit; when animated she became quite pretty, but she stirred no ardent feelings in him, apart from the times she'd roused his temper.

The one time he'd kissed her there'd been something, but he had ended it without regret, except the regret that he had forced on her a kiss she did not want. What if she resisted consummation? He doubted he could bring himself to force her.

Even if she was acquiescent there was no guarantee that he

would feel desire. It was going to be damned embarrassing if he couldn't perform.

He entered the house. "Everyone abed, Thomas?" he inquired of the night footman.

"Yes, m'lord. The duke and duchess retired not long ago, m'lord."

The marquess went up the stairs feeling mildly surprised that the footman had volunteered that extra sentence. He then became aware it had been said in a strange voice. He looked back at the young man in his livery and powdered hair. The footman was sitting in the chair provided at night, upright and alert. Impersonal, as a good servant should be.

He was not to know that the young man was still stunned by the sight of those rarefied beings, the Duke and Duchess of Belcraven, making their way, disheveled and laughing, up the stairs, arms wrapped around each other. At their age, too.

The marquess thought of going to speak to his mother as she was presumably still awake. He felt strangely restless and in need of something. At the duchess's door, however, he heard faint voices and didn't knock.

The maid? No, a man's voice. The marquess did not particularly want to see the duke. As he turned away, however, he thought he heard a faint shriek. He turned quickly back, but the sound was followed by laughter.

He stood looking at the mahogany panels with perplexity. If he didn't know better, he'd think there was a private orgy going on in there.

His mother and whom, was the disturbing question. A strange thought that was all the fault of Elizabeth Armitage and her dubious, radical morals.

He went quickly to the duke's suite which was around the corner. A knock on the door brought no one, so he opened it. In the three rooms there was no sign of the duke. His bed was turned down, his nightshirt laid out, his washing water cooling and unused.

The marquess walked slowly back past his mother's rooms and unashamedly listened again. The sounds were faint but quite unmistakable. A smile broadened to a grin. Thank God he'd been wrong all these years. In some quite illogical way, he felt the evidence of his parents'—he hesitated a moment over the word in his mind and then let it lie—his parents' intimacy gave hope for his own marriage.

He was soon deep and dreamlessly asleep while elsewhere in the big house the duke and duchess scarcely slept the whole night long.

Beth felt like a doll the next day, her wedding day. She was moved and placed by others. As she was supposed not to see her bridegroom before the evening wedding, she was confined to her rooms. She felt some slight disgruntlement that he doubtless was free to go where he wished, but in fact the arrangement suited her well enough. She was in a fine state of nerves and was sure she would disgrace herself in public.

The duchess spent some time with her in the morning and seemed to be in quite extraordinary spirits, despite looking tired and even yawning once. Beth also received a flying visit from one of the marquess's sisters, Lady Graviston. The former Lady Maria was petite and very smart but not of an analytical nature. She appeared to accept her brother's choice of bride without question, said all the right things, then talked for twenty minutes about her three lively children. She then kissed Beth's cheek and announced she must be off if she were to look her best for the wedding.

The marquess' other sister, Lady Joanne Cuthbert-Harby had previously sent a polite note of regret as she was "expecting an interesting event" at any moment. It would be her fifth child. All this evidence of fecundity did little to soothe Beth's nerves.

The duke visited her. He, too, seemed to be in marvelous spirits but then he was seeing the fruition of his plans. He brought with him the marquess' bride gift, a splendid diamond parure, far grander than the one she had rejected. It included a tiara with diamond drops which swayed and twinkled in the light. Beth tried to balk at the tiara but was soon persuaded it was appropriate to her position. She found, faced with the awareness of the night to come, she had no heart for minor battles.

Even Miss Mallory, when she arrived, was little comfort. There was such a vast gulf between them now, made greater by deception, that Beth found her time with the lady more trial than support.

"I have to confess," said Miss Mallory, as she sipped her tea, "that it is delightful to travel in such comfort. So kind of the duke to send a carriage just for me. And this house is very beautiful."

"You must come to visit Belcraven Park sometime, Aunt Emma," said Beth, not without a touch of dryness.

Miss Mallory did not seem to notice. "I have heard it is famous. You look very fine, Beth." She showed her principles had not been totally undermined by wealth, however. "Are you happy, Beth? There is still time to change your mind if you have doubts."

Doubts, thought Beth. Doubts was a mild word for it. For her aunt's sake, however, she smiled and lied. "Very happy. The marquess and I get along remarkably."

"Well, I am relieved. Though I could understand the duke's predicament, I did not like his solution, and I was very surprised you so quickly agreed. I was afraid you had been swayed by worldly considerations, and perhaps," she added in a whisper, though they were quite alone, *"lust."*

Beth could feel herself go red. "Certainly not!"

"Of course, of course," said Miss Mallory, quite pink herself. "You saw in the marquess the finer feelings. You are wiser than I. How unfair it is that when we see a handsome man or a beautiful woman, we are inclined to think them shallow or thoughtless."

Beth could not face more discussion of her marriage. "How is the school? I do miss it," she said, then added quickly, "even though I am so happy here."

"And everyone misses you, my dear. I have had such a time finding a replacement. The applicants are either quite silly or too harsh. I believe I have one now who will do, however. Little else has changed, except that Clarissa Greystone has left at last."

"Really? How came that about?"

"Her family's fortunes took a turn for the better. She should be here in London now, making her curtsy. After all the fuss she made, the silly girl seemed quite tearful to be leaving us." The lady rose to her feet. "Well, I suppose I must find the way to my room and prepare for all this grandeur. I could hardly believe it when the duchess said the Regent is to give you away!"

"Is it not incredible?" agreed Beth, though in truth, she had long since grown numb to surprises, and would probably not even blink if a dragon were to invade the room and gobble up Miss Mallory whole.

The older lady's eyes twinkled. "I tell myself it gives me a family connection to royalty. I hope to heavens the duke's arrangements for your fictitious background hold up though, Beth, or there will be a dreadful scandal now royalty is involved."

"Arrangements?" queried Beth.

"Did you not know?" said the woman. "I suppose they thought you had enough on your plate."

She sat down again and leaned close. "You could not be admitted to be Mary Armitage's daughter, Beth, because she had five other children and a wide family, none of whom has ever heard of you. A check of your birthdate would show you to be illegitimate. Fortunately, Denis Armitage—Mary's husband—had a scapegrace brother who wandered all over the place, living on his wits. An utterly hopeless case. This Arthur Armitage married a curate's daughter in Lincolnshire and then deserted her. The duke has apparently had all the records fixed so that the wife—what was her name? Marianna—gave birth to a baby. Mary, so the story goes, placed her niece in my care and paid for your raising."

"And what happened to my 'parents'?" queried Beth, not altogether pleased at this new genesis.

"Marianna Armitage died of fever when you were less than two. Arthur fell into the Wash when drunk and drowned. About ten years ago, I believe. It should all hold up."

"Do you know, Aunt Emma," said Beth quietly, "I wonder

if I will ever become accustomed to making life fit my wishes,
as they do."

"They?"

"We," Beth corrected, forcing a smile. "The rich. The highest levels of Society. Go and pretty yourself up, Aunt Emma.
The Prince will doubtless want to shake your hand."

Miss Mallory took alarm at this and hurried away.

Beth sat quietly contemplating a tasteful arrangement of del-
phiniums. What she had long suspected was true. There was
only one person in the world she could meet with on terms
of equality and honesty these days. The marquess.

It should be an excellent basis for marriage, but in fact she
felt dreadfully alone.

In time, like a child, Beth was bathed, dried, and perfumed.
Her hair was trimmed and arranged so as to display the tiara
to the greatest advantage. She was then dressed in white satin,
with an overdress of Valenciennes gathered into scallops all
around the hem and flowing into a train at the back. She was
festooned with the diamonds around her neck and her wrists,
a brooch between her breasts, and drops trembling like tears
from her earlobes. The beautiful tiara held a filmy veil on her
curls.

When she looked at herself she found the usual magic had
worked. Like all brides, she was beautiful. She even looked
worthy of the heir to a dukedom. She wished she felt anything
like she looked.

She was escorted downstairs by the duchess and a cluster
of bridesmaids of good family—young women she scarcely
knew at all. She made her curtsy to the Regent and received
his fulsome compliments with admirable calm.

To orchestral music she walked into the crowded ballroom
beside the gargantuan figure. She felt scarcely a twinge of
nerves. Dread of the coming night numbed her to all other
problems.

Because of the Regent all the guests paid homage as they
passed, a dizzying, jewel-encrusted wave rippling the length
of the room toward the marquess. And he looked far too magnificent for little Beth Armitage to handle.

His wedding attire was almost as fine as hers. His knee breeches were of white satin and his jacket of cream-gold brocade. His buttons were diamonds set in gold, and a magnificent blue diamond shot fire from among the folds of his cravat. But he was perhaps more brilliant than his adornment. His hair was spun gold in the thousand candles, and his eyes were sapphires. He took her hand from the Prince and kissed it. The warmth lingered there throughout the ceremony.

Beth said her vows firmly, as did the marquess. She wondered if at times the beautiful words threatened to choke him as they did her. It seemed almost sacrilegious what they were doing, and yet she knew marriages based on practicality rather than love were not uncommon.

"With my body I thee worship . . ." That wasn't what he intended to do with his body at all, and everyone here knew it. She hoped the horrible Lord Deveril was not here to point out again the reality behind the glitter.

Another reception line, and now—extraordinarily—she was "my lady." The Marchioness of Arden. It all seemed laughably unlikely. When she had touched hands, it seemed, with the whole world, there was a moment's respite before the toasts and the dancing. The marquess summoned two glasses of champagne and drank his as if he needed it. Beth did the same. She was wise enough by now not to gulp it, but she was surprised by how soon the glass was empty.

When another waiter stopped nearby, she replaced her empty glass and took a full one. The marquess looked at her in surprise, then took another glass himself and raised it. "To marriage," he said.

Beth raised her glass and threw a challenge. "To equality."

He sighed. As she drank down that glass, too, he said, "I hope you ate."

"I had a tray in my room," said Beth with perfect honesty. She neglected to tell him she'd hardly been able to force down a scrap. She took the indirect warning, however, and resisted the temptation to take another glass. She could already feel some effect from the wine, and though it was pleasant, she didn't want to overdo things. She imagined the new marchioness falling flat on her face and giggled.

She heard the marquess give a faint groan. He took her hand. "Come along. We're supposed to be at the head of the room for the toasts."

He led her there in the old style, hand in hand, and the crowd parted before them like the Red Sea. There were further murmured congratulations and the usual wedding asides— "lovely bride," "so handsome," "so fortunate" "must have cost a fortune."

"What do you think must have cost a fortune?" she asked him quietly. "My dress or your jacket?"

"Your diamonds," he said.

"Did they?" she queried, glancing at her glittering bracelet "Perhaps I should give them to the poor."

He didn't react. "I'd only have to buy you another set and another and another until we were in the back slums ourselves."

She glanced at him and saw he was, in a sense, serious. The pride of the de Vaux demanded that the ladies be festooned with a fortune in gems. "I wonder," she mused, "how many diamond parures stand between us and poverty?"

"If you put it to the test we will find out. And I'm glad," he said with a smile, "that you finally feel one of the family."

Beth felt a chill at how easily that "us" had slipped out. And yet it was ridiculous to keep fighting against reality.

They had arrived at the dais which had seats for the Regent, the duke and duchess, and themselves. They took their places as the loyal toasts were made, which meant Beth consumed yet more champagne. When the toasts were to herself she did not drink but found herself increasingly lighthearted.

By the time the music started for their minuet à deux she was not at all nervous.

As the first bars played she and the marquess executed full court obeisance to the Regent. Then they turned to face each other. As she curtsied to her new husband Beth remembered his warning about this dance and thought it strange. It was certainly interesting to be performing before hundreds of people but it was, after all, just a dance.

It was not, after all, just a dance.

Beth had forgotten the intensity of focus of the minuet *à deux*. Monsieur de Lo had been able to stare into her eyes throughout a performance without disturbing her in the least; now she found the need to maintain eye contact with the marquess made her heart race.

The stately movements had them circling one another, shifting and changing, eddying like leaves on restless water, touching only to spin away again. And always, his blue eyes speaking secrets into hers. Her breathing became shallow, her nerves were sensitized so that even the swirl of her silk skirts against her skin sent shivers through her. When they came together, when his fingers took warm grasp of hers, it was as if they bonded; when they parted it was as if something whole had been torn apart.

Beth didn't know this world. It frightened her.

At last it was over. She could curtsy then look away. But he held her hand after she rose and placed a warm, even heated, kiss on her skin. Beth felt almost as if he would ravish her then and there. Her face burned; thoughts of the wedding night surged back to obsess her.

Her next partner was the duke which gave her an opportunity to regain her external composure. A further glass of champagne seemed to help drive back her inner demons. She danced with the Duke of Devonshire and the Duke of York. In fact, she thought, it was quite beneath her dignity now to dance with anyone lower than a duke, except a marquess, she supposed. This made her giggle, and the Duke of York pinched her cheek approvingly. She drank more champagne and found she could partner her husband again without a care in the world.

Next she came down in the world with a bump. The marquess presented her to her next partner, a mere commoner.

"Mr. Nicholas Delaney," the marquess said, "and his wife, Eleanor. Two of my closest friends."

Two? thought Beth suspiciously, viewing the handsome

woman. But something magical between Nicholas and Eleanor Delaney defused suspicion. Even when the marquess led Mrs. Delaney away to join a set, laughing at something she had said, Beth could not feel jealous.

Though Nicholas Delaney was not as handsome as the marquess, she could see how a woman could love him. His rather unruly dusky gold hair and his lean, tanned cheeks might be unfashionable, but they were remarkably attractive. There was also a disarming warmth in his sherry brown eyes.

As he led her onto the floor, he said, "I consider this quite barbarous, you know."

Beth looked at him in alarm. Had the marquess told him the basis for this marriage?

His brow quirked at her alarm. "Such a performance over a marriage," he explained. "Eleanor and I were married very quietly. I'm afraid after all this you'll need your honeymoon more as a repairing lease than a holiday."

A holiday? Beth had never thought of that impending nightmare, the honeymoon—when the marquess would finally have her in his solitary power—as any kind of pleasure. She realized she had no idea whether they were to stay here or go back to Belcraven. Surely the latter. "It will be pleasant to be in the country," she said.

"Yes. Eleanor and I intend to spend most of our time at our place in Somerset."

In another time and place Beth felt as if she could have had a real conversation with this man, but at the moment all she seemed able to produce were banalities. "We were at Belcraven until recently."

He laughed. "Red Oaks certainly isn't anything like Belcraven. That isn't the country. It's a town within walls."

Beth was startled into a chuckle. "You have it exactly. I would much rather live in a small house."

"So much easier to manage. When you return to Town you must come and visit us. We have a small house in Lauriston Street." He grinned at her. "We're *very* informal."

She grinned back. "That sounds wonderful."

He must have a magic touch. He had broken through her

constraint and for a moment she felt normal, ordinary, sane. But then they were caught up in the vigorous country dance and there was little further opportunity for discussion.

Afterwards, when he rejoined his wife, Nicholas Delaney said, "We should have befriended her sooner."

"Why?" asked Eleanor.

"She's terrified and feels very alone."

Eleanor looked at the bride who was standing with her husband and his parents, smiling and appearing reasonably happy. But she didn't doubt Nicholas's judgment; he had a gift for it. "Do you know what's going on?" she asked.

"No, but it's . . . treacherous. I think you, of all women, could have helped Elizabeth. But it's too late now."

"You think they should never have married."

She said it as a statement, but he shook his head. "I think they'll suit marvelously well if they give themselves a chance." He smiled at his wife and raised her hand for a kiss. "We know better than most how easy it is to dice with a chance of heaven. And nearly lose."

She smiled at him, wishing as she always did that they were alone. They needed no one else, except Arabel. "Can't you say something to Lucien?" she asked.

"I have, though I didn't understand how serious it is. There's nothing more to be done now. He's as keyed up as she is."

Eleanor looked at the handsome marquess. He, too, looked merely the proud and happy groom but here, because she knew him, she could see the artifice as well as Nicholas. The sparking brilliance that made him look like a glittering gem was his response to tension and trouble. And it was dangerous. She looked her concern at her husband, an infinitely fascinating man but one who had never terrified her.

He shook his head. "He's beyond a soothing lecture. We can only hope his natural kindness wins out over his arrogant bloody-mindedness. And, I suppose, that he's read the books I gave him."

A waltz struck up and he led her toward the floor. "Books?" Eleanor queried in amazement. "Lucien?"

He tutted. "I do have a few volumes other than erotic texts."

"Of use to a man on his wedding night?" she queried naughtily.

They took their position for the waltz. "If you remember our wedding night," he said, "you will admit that a manual of clever moves would have been irrelevant."

Eleanor knew what he meant. Frightened by a series of strange events and by dim memories of a drugged rape, what she had needed, and found, was sensitivity and kindness.

"Are there books to teach magic of the heart?" she asked.

The music started and they began the twirling dance. "The Bible?" he suggested with a slight smile. "The Koran. The Veda. The Abhidhamma Pitaka. The Bhagavad-Gita . . ."

"You are trying to make me feel my ignorance," she said without rancor. "But I can at least guess that they are all books of religion. Are you saying you gave these to Lucien?"

"I wish I had thought of it," he said with a laugh. "In fact, I gave him Mary Wollstonecraft."

"You expect them to spend tonight debating the rights of women?" she asked skeptically.

"I think it would be a very good thing," he replied. "But having a mind above this prurient interest in other people's beds . . ." He drew her slowly closer, until they were joined together in a way that was quite improper. Fortunately by then he had also migrated them out of the room into a quiet corridor.

Eleanor was ready for his lips when he kissed her. She could feel the familiar aching melting, the longing for home, for Nicholas. She clung to him. "I'm trying to imagine," she whispered when the kiss ended, "what it would have been like if it had been like this on our wedding night. This hunger. And the knowledge that it would soon be satisfied to the full."

One sensitive finger played knowingly at the base of her skull, sending a shudder through her. "I wonder if a welding night is ever like that," he said. "A knowledgeable wedding night seems to be a contradiction in terms." He sighed. "As I said to Elizabeth, this is a barbarous affair. I think it's time to leave. I have no wish to watch the victims led to the sacrificial stone."

"I will be pleased to be home. I would be pleased to be returning to Somerset." It was a strong hint.

As they descended the grand staircase he said, "So would I. But I think we have to look into this matter of Deveril. I may have forsworn petty revenge, but I don't like seeing him at such high water. I'd rather see him in the mud."

"So would I," she said, remembering the horrible man who had tried to buy her, then ruin her into marriage. "But he's a dangerous man, Nicholas."

"So am I," said Nicholas Delaney calmly.

Chapter Fourteen

Beth saw the Delaneys leave and felt strangely as if she'd lost her only allies. True to his promise, Mr. Beaumont was not here. Lord Darius and Viscount Amleigh were apparently already on their way to Belgium to take part in the ever-more-likely war. She supposed Aunt Emma was somewhere about, but she didn't think that lady would be able to help.

No one would be able to help.

Beth took wine whenever it was presented and found it drew a comforting mist between herself and reality.

All too soon, however, it was time for her and the marquess to retire for the night. The duke and duchess, the bridesmaids, and a number of the marquess's friends all formed a procession to escort them to the bedchamber.

His bedchamber.

Beth had never considered before how public an announcement of their intended activity this would be. The picture of Mars and Venus loomed monstrous in her mind, and she desperately wished to run and hide from all the knowing looks, all the sniggering laughter. What an extraordinarily vulgar business a wedding was.

Then she found herself alone with him. The alcoholic veil fell away leaving her chilled with nerves and slightly sick. She simply stood and looked at him. So large, so strong . . .

After a moment he sighed. "Are you as terrified as you look or is this more acting?"

"Yes," she whispered. "I mean, terrified."

He poured her a glass of rich red wine. "Here," he said as he passed it over. "This should help." He took one for himself, drank it down, and poured another.

Beth supposed it might. She'd like the misty comfort back again, but her hands began to shake and the wine splashed a deep red stain down her beautiful white gown. She dropped the glass and began to cry.

She was swept up into his arms. She struggled frantically as he carried her to the bed and laid her on the silken cover.

"Be still, my dear," he said softly as he took his hands away. "I'm not going to rape you."

He sat beside her on the bed. "You really are an innocent, aren't you, Elizabeth?"

Beth nodded.

"You're a damn fool," he said almost angrily. Then he extended a finger to wipe away one of her tears. "What have we done to that spirited Miss Armitage I brought away from Cheltenham?"

Beth attempted a smile. "Turned her into a marchioness?"

He reached out and gently disentangled the tiara from her hair, tossing it carelessly on the bedside table. "So much for aristocratic grandeur. You know, my dear, it occurs to me that the duke has had it all his own way so far. We are married. He has no more say as to how we conduct our lives. I think you need a long period of repair before we progress to parenthood."

No Mars and Venus, thought Beth hopefully. "Will you not mind?" she asked.

"No," he said gently, "I will not mind." He sounded relieved. Perversely, Beth was a little hurt.

"But where will you sleep?" she asked.

"With you tonight. We don't want to cause talk. A man can sleep with a woman without anything intimate occurring." He collapsed down beside her on the bed, one arm over his eyes. "God. I've drunk too much."

His manner was so easy, so natural, all Beth's fears melted away and she giggled. "I think I have, too. The champagne made me feel so carefree." She found giggling suited her mood entirely and couldn't stop.

"And what do you find so amusing, Elizabeth?" he asked, rolling onto his side and grinning in sympathy.

"Beth," said Beth as she tried to control her laughter.

"Beth?"

At last she succeeded and turned her head to look at him. "My name is Beth," she said clearly.

"Why the deuce didn't you say so before?"

Beth shrugged. "It was a symbol."

He smiled. His blue eyes danced in the candlelight. "And now you've told me. Is that a symbol?"

"I suppose it is," said Beth, finding it difficult to focus or keep her eyes open. "Friends?"

"Friends," he said with a soft laugh and rolled her over to get at the buttons on the back of her gown. "I've done this for many a friend before now."

Beth was surprised at how little she cared that he undressed her—her body seemed a long, long way from her head. When she found herself slipped naked between the sheets, however, she giggled again. "How improper."

"Not at all," he said cheerfully. "No one would expect you to retain your nightgown anyway. If you want to give the servants a thrill, I could tear it a little."

"But it was so expensive."

"A curiosity of servants and a frugality of Armitages," he said, and at that moment it seemed profound. "Go to sleep, my sweet marchioness."

With that he left the room. Beth found his advice sound and let oblivion claim her.

The marquess took the wine with him to his dressing room, and he downed another glass as soon as he got there. Perhaps he should get thoroughly drunk; it was said to remove the ability to perform, though he had never experienced that himself. Having promised his wife a platonic marriage, the process of undressing her had made him feel very unplatonic indeed. What a surprisingly lovely body she had—Creamy white skin, firm, full breasts, long, shapely legs, and the pertest round rump he'd ever wanted to kiss and squeeze in his life . . .

He drank another glass of wine.

And she was an innocent. He supposed he'd known it for a while now, but she was unlike the women he was accustomed to—either worldly wise and experienced, or naive virgins. She was quick-witted and intelligent and had the ability to think for herself. He would never have sought out those qualities in a wife, but now they appealed to him strongly.

Reading the Wollstonecraft woman's books had given him insight, too. He didn't agree with all she wrote, but there was enough sense there to interest him. He was looking forward to an opportunity to discuss some of the questions raised.

He sighed. They'd probably have plenty of time for academic discussion. He'd rather be extending the education of his blue-stocking bride in other directions, but she was not ready yet. She was a wounded bird, his Beth.

He almost drank off another glass of wine but desisted. It would not be advisable to be found fully dressed and flat out on the floor in the morning. He stripped off and climbed into bed with his wife, keeping well away from the soft, warm, perfumed body so close nearby.

When Beth awoke in the morning she slowly became aware of something different. She was naked. She never slept naked. Some hazy memories of the night before came to her.

She opened her eyes a crack and looked sideways.

She was alone in the bed.

She remembered the night before. She had been *inebriated*. On the go. Jug-shot. She felt herself blush at the thought that it might have been obvious to all the guests.

And the marquess had undressed her. She remembered that. And he hadn't . . .

Beth sat up abruptly, saw the marquess sitting in a chair watching her, and, with a gasp, slid back down under the covers. He was dressed in a marvelous blue damask banjan robe and his hair was engagingly unkempt.

"Good morning, my lady," he said with a warm smile.

"Good morning," Beth replied, watching him warily.

He frowned slightly. "Don't look so scared, Beth," he said. "I want my spirited radical back."

Beth felt some of her courage return. "It's hard to be bold when naked under the sheets, my lord."

His blue eyes twinkled with mirth. "Is it? I hadn't noticed that before."

Beth felt her face grow hot but couldn't help smile back. "You are a very wicked man."

"The only sort worth having." He came over to the bed with her heavy satin wrap in his hand and let it slither slowly down onto the covers. "I sent your maid away." He studied her a moment. Beth wondered if he were going to slide down on top of her as the wrap had slid, and cover her. . . . But he moved away. "I'm going to order breakfast for us in your boudoir. What would you like?"

"Eggs," said Beth, realizing she was hungry.

He grinned. "I'm pleased to see we're compatible in drink at least. I never have hangovers either." With that he left the room.

Beth lost no time in scrambling out of bed and into both her nightgown and wrap. It was, in fact, a more concealing ensemble than her wedding gown, tossed carelessly on the floor and quite ruined by the wine stain, but she still felt undressed. She slipped cautiously through into her dressing room but found it deserted. She sat to brush her tangled curls and wished for a cap to give her courage.

What a wedding. She had got drunk, had hysterics, and been stripped naked by a man. She found herself wishing he'd done "it" while she was so drunk. Now she must wait daily for him to consummate the marriage.

When, under the compulsion of a lifetime's training, she went back to tidy the bed she gasped with shock. There was a bloodstain on the sheet. But her body felt no different. Could he have done it without her having the slightest awareness?

He walked in. "Breakfast is here—What is it?" Then he saw the sheets. "Don't worry. That's not your blood. I just didn't want to start talk, our marriage being a trifle hasty. I gave myself a small cut with my razor and decorated the sheets."

"You think of everything, my lord," said Beth, somehow offended that he should have arranged matters so competently while she had gone to pieces.

A certain restraint settled on him. "You would rather, I am sure, be tied for life to an inefficient bungler of noble heart and great mind. You are, however, compelled to make do with me."

"Nobody is questioning your nobility," said Beth smartly. And then stopped, horrified.

He politely stood back so she could precede him through the door. "We had best ignore that comment, I think."

Beth was pleased to do so. Quicksands again. Would it ever change?

They walked in silence through her dressing room and bedroom to the luxurious boudoir where a table had been laid with linen and china. Beth helped herself to perfect eggs and also took some sausages and bacon from another platter. Her nerves had been so overwrought in recent days she had eaten little. The present moment was not perhaps the most comfortable of her life, but like most feared events, it was easier to handle when arrived at.

Considering the traps to be found in the most innocent conversation she was happy to follow his example and eat in silence. When her hunger was satisfied, though, the silence began to weigh on her.

She fidgeted with the new, unaccustomed wedding ring. "For how long, my lord, do we live here in seclusion?"

He looked at her thoughtfully. "Until, I think, you call me Lucien."

Beth met his eyes. "You really must learn not to challenge me, Lord Arden. We are likely to become the hermits of Marlborough Square."

"You refuse to use my given name?"

"Under those terms, yes."

He studied her then turned on his most glittering smile.

"Please, my dear Beth," he said softly, "will you call me Lucien?"

"Yes, Lucien, I will," replied Beth in her best schoolmistress's voice, hoping it disguised the way her pulse had speeded under his attentions.

The marquess set his elbows on the table and rested his shapely chin on his hands. His blue eyes were bright and mischievous. "Is that the key to your heart, my blushing rose? Please, my perfumed paradise, my angel of delight, come sit on my lap and kiss me."

Beth eyed him warily and tried to deny the turmoil his words stirred in her. "No."

He sighed and leaned back in his chair. "It was worth a try. I think I'll wait for you to seduce me, my dear."

"In that case there are unlikely to be heirs to the glory of the de Vaux."

"We shall see." He rose and stretched. "Now, having solved the name problem, it is time for us to leave and spend a few days at Hartwell."

"Hartwell?"

"Don't worry. It's not Louis *le Désiré's* miniature Versailles in Buckinghamshire. It's my country estate in Surrey. Just a small place, a cottage ornée. Only a handful of servants. We can relax in bucolic isolation."

"And after that?" asked Beth.

"After that we really should return for the remainder of the Season. We need to establish your place in Society, but I promise not to run you ragged as my mother did."

"You most certainly will not," said Beth also rising. "Please stop treating me like a child, my . . . Lucien. I will arrange my own social life."

"To a point. Be fair, Beth. You still need some guidance on managing in Society."

Beth didn't feel fair, but she was forced to agree. "Very well. And now, my lord . . . *Lucien, my darling,*" she corrected, causing a laugh, "I must summon Redcliff. Unless you intend to be my maid today as well."

Her unwary tongue had betrayed her again, and Beth saw

the glitter in his eyes with alarm. He came over and began to
unfasten the pearl clusters down the front of the wrap, his
attention completely focussed on his task. Beth looked at his
handsome face blankly and wondered what she should do,
what she wanted to do.

He slid his hands beneath the satin and pushed the wrap off
her shoulders. His hands were hot against her skin. The garment slithered into a snowy pool on the carpet, and Beth was
intensely grateful she had put on the nightgown. It still provided a decent covering.

His fingers rose to the three buttons which fastened it to
the scooped and filled neckline. Beth's hand came up to stop
him.

He looked up, amused eyes challenging her.

"A maid would never leave my wrap lying on the floor,"
she said hastily.

"Whatever made you think I was a maid?" he asked. In a
single movement, he swept her hands behind her and trapped
them. Just like that terrible night and yet so different. Beth
might be nervous and uncertain, but she felt no fear.

He placed a soft kiss on the tip of her nose and Beth jerked
back, wriggling in his grasp. "Let go of me! You said you'd
wait for me to seduce you."

He released her hands but wrapped his arms around her so
she was still helpless. "Ah, but do you know what seduction
is?" he asked. "You've made a prodigious start, I'll grant you.
Provocative remarks are a wonderful beginning . . ."

"I did not—" Her protests were stopped with a kiss.

When he raised his lips Beth tried again, "I—" and was
stopped again.

The next time he raised his lips she wisely remained silent.
She doubted her ability to be coherent in any case. Her whole
body seemed to be vibrating with an energy she had never
experienced before, an energy which burnt away thought like
the sun burning away a morning mist.

". . . but you have to know what to do next," he completed.
"Also," he added softly, "you have to know you want the
prize." He lowered his head for another kiss.

This time he did not merely seal her lips. This time he gently teased them open and she felt his tongue upon hers for the first time. She moaned, but whether it was protest or delight she could not have said. Nothing in any book had prepared her for this.

She could feel the heat of his hands through the thin silk, one between her shoulder blades, one lower, in the small of her back, rubbing in small circles which pressed her against his body. The rough texture of his damask robe fretted her skin through the fine silk, and her nipples, ah, her nipples had developed a life of their own. She inhaled the aroma of soap and something more—something warm, spicy, and dangerous.

The scent of a man.

Instinct drove her to open her mouth to further invasion. She felt fingers trace up to thread through her curls, sending shivers down her spine to weave with the magic of his other hand. A fever spread throughout her body. She surrendered utterly, her hands clutching at his robe.

Eventually his mouth released hers. She shuddered and rested her swimming head on his shoulder, feeling his hand stroke over her hair.

"Beth?" he asked softly.

Chapter Fifteen

A part of Beth's body reacted to the question like a child offered sugar plums, but her mind balked. If he had carried her to the bed then and taken her, she would not have resisted, but she could not, at that moment, consent. She was too overwhelmed by the strangeness of it all. Having regained a degree of sanity she was afraid to return to that wild disintegration.

She shook her head against his shoulder.

He sighed and released her. But then he slipped his fingers to twine with hers and pulled her into her bedroom. Beth could feel the thudding of her heart as he studied her. A part of her still wanted him to persuade her.

But in the end he let her go. "Ring for your maid. We'll speak to the duke and duchess and set off. Don't dally."

With that he left for his own rooms and Beth collapsed down on a bench, not at all sure she was grateful for his restraint.

An hour later, armored in a new walking dress of sage green crepe, Beth rejoined her husband. He was safely conventional in blue and buff and that moment of uninhibited passion seemed like a fevered dream. Together they went to find the duke and duchess.

The duchess kissed Beth on the cheek. "How smart you look, my dear. I understand Lucien is wafting you off to Hartwell. The duke and I spent part of our honeymoon there."

Beth noticed the duchess flash a look at the duke and saw

that austere gentleman smile. For some reason she felt embarrassed, as if she had witnessed an intimacy.

The duke also gave Beth a kiss. "Welcome to the de Vaux family," he said with a degree of complacency which Beth longed to disturb. He obviously thought his stratagem was working perfectly. Beth was sourly pleased he would have to wait longer than nine months for his pure-blooded grandchildren.

In fact, she was surprised at how vinegary she felt. The worst was over and she had not been subjected to intimate assault. It appeared that the marquess was willing to wait until she was ready to consummate the marriage. They were going off to some peace and quiet in a small house in the country. She should be feeling sweet, not sour.

She determined to be sweet, not sour.

As soon as she was in the luxurious chariot, this time with the marquess beside her, she set herself to be pleasant. The weather certainly contributed to good humor, for the late spring countryside was at its very best.

"Tell me more about this estate, Hartwell," she said.

He was lounged at his ease and showed no sign of amorousness, thank heavens. "As I said, it's a cottage ornée. Quite pretty, I think, with charming rustic gardens." His lips twitched into a grin. "Deceptive simplicity sums it up, actually. It takes a great deal of work and money to preserve its bucolic charms, but it's charming all the same. There's a stream at the end of the garden and an orchard and a dovecot."

"Should I have brought my silk and lace shepherdess outfit?" Beth teased.

"Like Marie Antoinette at the Petit Trianon? Definitely not. But the real charm of Hartwell is that we may wear exactly what we wish." He reached up and unknotted his cravat, unwound it, and tossed it onto the opposite seat. *"Voila!* Freedom."

Beth undid the strings of her high straw bonnet, pulled it off, and tossed it to lie over his neckcloth.

His eyes sparkled and he undid the buttons of his shirt.

Beth eyed him warily. "This is not a competition I am willing to engage in, my lord."

He smiled. "Lucien—or I'll strip naked here and now."

"Lucien," Beth said hurriedly.

"Lucien, my darling?" he suggested.

"Just Lucien," she replied. "I call your bluff. You would not strip naked here."

"You really must learn not to challenge me, my lady," he said softly, echoing the words she had used earlier. But then he laughed. "I'll not take you up now. You did, after all, fulfill my condition. And I want no forced endearments."

Beth looked down for a moment to gather her thoughts. "I want to thank you," she said. "You are being very kind."

"You needn't sound so damned surprised." When she looked up in alarm she saw he was mostly teasing. "I'm not a candidate for sainthood," he said. "Love, sex, marital duties," he grimaced at the term, "call it what you will. It should at least be pleasant for both parties. I refuse to settle for less. We have the rest of our lives."

"Not quite that if I am to bear the heir to Belcraven," Beth pointed out, amazed that she was having this calm discussion on such a subject.

He flashed her a look of exasperation. "If you continue to be such a pedant," he said, "the rest of your life is likely to be a very short period of time."

Beth frowned at him. "You are constantly threatening me with violence."

"Oh, come now," he drawled. "There must have been a moment or two when I was less than bloodthirsty."

"Now who's being the pedant?"

"What's good for the goose . . ." he said.

"That," she retorted, "sounds remarkably like another challenge."

He didn't deny it. " 'What dire offense from amorous causes springs, / What mighty contests rise from trivial things?' "

"Pope. *Rape of the Lock,*" she said promptly. "Trivial," she mused, then offered, " 'Women are systematically degraded by receiving the trivial attentions which men think it manly to pay to the sex, when, in fact, men are insultingly supporting their own superiority.' "

"Must be the divine Mary," he sighed, but there was still humor in his eyes. He thought for a moment then countered with, " 'Friendship does not admit of assumptions of superiority.' "

Beth frowned. "I don't think I know that. It sounds like an excellent sentiment, though, and one Mary Wollstonecraft would have endorsed."

"I confess, I don't know where it comes from either. I think it was something Nicholas Delaney once quoted to me." He took her hand. "Last night we pledged friendship, Beth. Can I hope it still holds?"

She was alarmingly sensitive to his slightest touch but struggled not to show it. "We seem destined to squabble. It's a strange kind of friendship."

"The only kind," he said with a grin. "I don't have a friend whose eye I've not blacked."

"Violence again," she protested, but lightly.

He laughed. "I promise never to black your eye."

"Not even if I top your best quotation?"

"Not even then."

"Very well." Beth grinned at him. " 'Friendship is a disinterested commerce between equals; love, an abject intercourse between tyrants and slaves.' Oliver Goldsmith."

With a shake of his head he gave her the victory. His thumb rubbed absently against the back of her hand and he considered his words. "Would it make any difference, I wonder, who was the tyrant, who the slave?"

"Not to me. I have no desire to be either."

He kissed her hand and let it go. "Then we must work at friendship. I don't suppose," he said dryly, "it will be particularly easy. *Idem velle atque idem nolle, ea demum firma amicitia est.*"

"You fear our tastes are too different?" she said. "How then do you suppose we recognize each other's quotations? And I do like your friends."

"That gives me hope," he said with a grin. "You obviously have a taste for rogues."

They arrived at Hartwell in excellent humor and it proved to be as unalarming as he had promised. It was a small house of two stories boasting only four modest bedrooms. It sat comfortably in pleasant gardens bordered along one edge by a stream. Beyond the walls the rest of the marquess' estate was given over to farming. The staff proved to be only five, and Beth felt she could manage that well enough.

She was relieved to find that she and the marquess were to have separate bedrooms but was aware that there was no lock on the linking door and that she could not use one if there were. She had been coerced into this marriage, but she had agreed, agreed to a marriage in full. To be acting a farce over it at this point would be ridiculous.

Beth was disconcerted by her mental confusion about the intimacies of marriage, for she had always considered herself a practical woman. Despite their new harmony, any thought of the marquess and the marriage bed plunged her into a morass of fascination and fear. She hated the turmoil of it. She would much rather postpone the whole business until she could approach it in a calm and rational way.

But would he wait? Despite his strange words about waiting for her to seduce him, about waiting for pleasure, she did not expect much patience from such a man. Would his resolve last even the day? And would she perhaps not be better to get it over with?

There was no amorousness in his manner as he took her on a tour of the house, the gardens, and the outbuildings. In the stables they once more discussed riding lessons but this time without heat. She was touched to discover he had carefully selected a horse for her and had it sent to Hartwell to await them. The dappled gelding which carried the feminine name, Stella, seemed quiet and had a friendly look in its eye.

At six o'clock they ate a well-prepared but simple meal in the small dining room. The maid brought in all the dishes, including the cold desserts, and then left them to serve themselves. Beth felt it was the first normal meal she'd eaten since leaving Cheltenham but thought it wiser not to say so. Wiser not to raise any kind of controversy.

They talked mainly of poetry, contrasting Ben Jonson's statement that a good poet is made as much as born with Socrates's statement that poets work not by wisdom but by inspiration and an almost magical gift. Beth was surprised at how much she had to stretch her mind to hold her own. Hal Beaumont had obviously been telling the truth about the marquess' intellectual abilities. Beth was rather alarmed. She had once anticipated facing a fribble on this marital battlefield.

When they eventually called truce they settled for a less demanding activity—a few hands of casino. Then Beth played the piano for him, though she knew her performance to be competent rather than gifted.

It was superficially the most commonplace of evenings, but Beth's nerves were stretched like the strings of the instrument she played.

Eventually, unable to bear the situation any longer, she announced her intention of going to bed. He rose. She looked at him in alarm. He merely opened the door for her, kissed her fingers, and bid her good night.

She desperately wanted to ask what his intentions were but dared not. Redcliff prepared her for bed and left. Beth lay awake listening for movement next door, for the turning of the knob. She didn't know whether she would greet her husband's appearance with alarm or relief, but as the clock ticked the minutes away she began to think it would be relief. She couldn't bear much more of this tension . . .

The Marchioness of Arden drifted into sleep; she woke the next morning still an unsullied virgin. She told herself firmly it was exactly what she wanted and a sure way to foil the duke's plans.

They stayed ten days at Hartwell and the first day was the pattern for the rest. Every morning they rode, and Lucien proved to be a surprisingly patient and understanding teacher. Beth made progress but paid for it with aches and bruises. He taught her piquet and won a small fortune from her. She beat him at draughts every time. They sat in pleasurable silence reading books from the small but excellent library; later they indulged in fiery discussion of their reading, welcoming the sharing of ideas and insights but also seeking to gain points in the ongoing competition of their lives.

As they strolled in the garden or walked briskly across the fields, they discussed the international situation and the danger of Napoleon defeating the allies gathered against him and re-commencing his attempt to rule the world. Lucien was sure he would be defeated and clearly longed to be with his friends who were preparing for that fight.

One day he even quoted the words Shakespeare put in the mouth of Henry V. " 'And gentlemen in England now abed/ Shall think themselves accursed they were not here, / And hold their manhoods cheap whiles any speaks / That fought with us—' " He broke off. "The where and when are yet to be decided. I doubt it will hold off until Saint Crispin's day, however."

If it would have served any purpose Beth would have laid down on the grass and told him to take her and be off to fight. But there was no guarantee that one act would achieve the end, nor that their first child would be the necessary son. Nor, she supposed, that it would live. The burden of privilege demanded that he stay as safe as possible and breed on her until the line was safe.

As Nicholas Delaney had said, it was all barbarous.

Apart from that outburst he avoided high emotion and most personal or controversial topics, though they did, tentatively, share some of their views on the liberty of the individual and theories of government. Beth was surprised to find him liberal for his class, though she was still tempted at times to blast him for arrogant shortsightedness.

He touched her only in the way a gentleman would touch any lady—to hand her over an obstacle, lift her down from her horse, or offer an arm when walking. Sometimes, though,

Beth would catch him watching her, and the expression in his eyes would send shivers through her.

On June 15th, their last day at Hartwell, a lazy, sunny afternoon, they sat reading on the grassy bank of the stream. Lucien was in comfortable country clothes. His pantaloons were loose fitting, his jacket casual, and he had left off his cravat in favor of a knotted neckerchief. A straw hat shaded his eyes. Beth herself was in the lightest and simplest of her muslins with a wide villager hat to protect her from the sun.

Birdsong surrounded them and the busy clamor of the insects. Occasional soft splashes announced the presence of feeding fish.

"Perhaps you should do some angling here, Lucien," Beth said lazily. "You could catch our supper."

He looked up from his book with a grin. "Not unless you want to feast on gudgeon and chub, a nibble per fish. There's little in this stream worth catching."

"Could you not stock it?"

"I believe my father tried. It's not a good stream for sport fish. For one thing it almost dries up in a drought . . ."

They were interrupted by the demanding quacks of a family of ducks which paddled busily around the bend, mother in front and ducklings in an orderly line behind, all except one which straggled, lagging absentmindedly then putting on a mad dash to catch up.

Beth chuckled as she reached for the bag of oats she had brought to feed them. "I do believe, our little sluggard is of a poetical disposition," she said to Lucien as he came forward to join her at the edge of the stream. "He is clearly so taken by the beauties of the scenery that he forgets to paddle."

"We'll have to name him Wordsworth then," said Lucien, watching his wife as she scattered the food widely on the water.

Despite her bonnets, the sun had brought out a few freckles on her nose which he found charming. Here in the country, living quietly, she had begun to relax and show him her spirit, her wit, and her humor. He was rapidly becoming entranced. If he'd considered the matter he would have said days spent in country walks and evenings with just one person, reading and discussing ideas, would soon pall. Now, however, he was reluctant to return to London and the social round.

There was something magical about Beth, he thought. On first acquaintance she seemed ordinary, and yet many things—the tilt of her head when she was curious, the twitch of her mouth when she was amused, the way her eyes lit up when she laughed—all transformed her into a spellbinder. It was a fragile magic, however easily banished when she was unhappy. He was desperately afraid of destroying it forever. Watching her now as she talked nonsense to little "Wordsworth" and scolded his mother for snatching food from her infant's beak, he longed to take her in his arms here on the sunny, grassy bank, and teach her the wonders of love.

Beth looked up and caught him studying her. Her eyes questioned him.

"I was just standing guard," he said lightly, "in case your enthusiasm pitched you into the water."

Beth hastily looked back at the ducks. It had happened before, this awareness. A perfectly ordinary moment would be broken by turbulent thoughts, disturbing sensations. Did he feel any of it, or was it just her own anxious mind?

He crouched down beside her so his breath warmed her cheek as he said, "Perhaps I should teach you to swim. There's a place near Belcraven which is deep enough and safe."

Beth felt her heart speed. She couldn't imagine going into water with him, perhaps being held by him there, their clothes pressed damply to their bodies. Or would he bathe naked as men were said to do? Her mouth dried and she knew her face was red. She kept her head down and concentrated on the ducks. "I don't think I would care for that, Lucien.

"Tut-tut," he murmured and brushed a curl back from her heated cheek. "Doesn't Shakespeare say, 'True nobility is exempt from fear.'? A marchioness should be afraid of nothing."

Beth rose quickly to her feet and faced him, dusting the last few oats from her hands. "He also says, I recollect, 'Sweet mercy is nobility's true badge?' I pray you, Lord Arden," she said with mock appeal, "of your mercy spare me the water."

He laughed as he rose gracefully to his feet. He touched

her nose gently with one finger. "Will you always have a quotation to cap each of mine? You've spent too much time buried in books, my lady."

"Apparently an excellent training for marriage, my lord."

"Only to me, I suspect." He collapsed down again on the grass near their books. "Come and sit by me, Beth."

Before, they had been sitting feet apart, but it was not unusual for them to sit closer. Now, however, she sensed some significance in his request. She was very aware that today was their last day here.

Heart racing, but hoping she was outwardly composed, Beth did as he asked. As soon as she was settled on the rug on the grass, he tossed his hat aside and slid over to lay his head in her lap. "Read to me," he said and closed his eyes.

The weight of him across her thighs was like a brand. Beth's mouth was so dry she doubted she could articulate at all. But she was able to study him, laid out there before her in all his strength and beauty like an offering on an altar. Her fingers itched to work through the golden curls that fell over his smooth forehead, to trace down his straight nose to the elegant curve of his firm lips.

His blue eyes opened and spoke a challenge. "No?"

"Of course," she said hastily, not sure why it was so important to deny the effect he was having on her, the effect he surely *knew* he was having on her.

She picked up the new volume by Mr. Coleridge with unsteady fingers and began to read, " 'In Xanadu did Kubla Khan / A stately pleasure dome decree . . .' "

Though a strange work, it seemed innocent enough, or had seemed innocent enough on first reading. Now, with her husband's body stretched by her, his handsome head nestled against her abdomen, the poem took on new meaning. Her voice trembled slightly as she read, " 'As if this earth in fast thick pants were breathing . . .' "

It was the last lines which struck her most, however:

Weave a circle round him thrice,
And close your eyes with holy dread,

For he on honeydew hath fed,
And drunk the milk of Paradise.

Without opening his eyes he commented, "An adequate description of the pampered aristocracy, though not what poor Samuel means, I think. Are your eyes suitably closed, my houri?"

"No," she admitted, for she was feasting on his beauty.

" 'Beware! Beware!' " he quoted from an earlier line. His eyes flicked open and held hers. " 'For thou art with me here upon the banks / Of this fair river; thou my dearest friend . . .' "

Captured by his gaze, Beth licked her lips. "I don't recognize that."

He curled smoothly to his feet, leaving a chill where he had been. "Wordsworth, of course, though I don't remember which poem." He gave her a hand and pulled her up. Beth wanted to ask if she was his friend, if she was only his friend. Another line of Wordsworth had sprung disconcertingly into her mind and echoed there: " 'Strange fits of passion have I known . . .' "

He retained her hand and quoted teasingly, " 'A perfect woman, nobly plann'd. To warn, to comfort, and command . . .' "

It sounded like the description of a mother or even a governess. "I'm not sure I wish to be that kind of woman," Beth protested.

"No? I thought it would be the Wollstonecraft ideal. You may like the next two lines better. 'And yet a Spirit still and bright / With something of an angel light? It's time to return to the house, I think, my angel."

He turned away and gathered up their books and the rug, leaving Beth itchily dissatisfied.

As they walked back she admitted this friendship, this virtue, this talk of spirits and angels, which would surely have delighted Laura Montreville to ecstasy, frustrated her. Why? Because her thoughts were constantly on more earthy matters. How long could they go on like this, like Wordsworth and his

devoted sister, Dorothy? For despite their strange family connection, brother and sister they most certainly were not. Would
he really wait for her to make the first move? It was so unfair.
She had no notion what to do.

That night, their last night at Hartwell, Beth suggested a
walk in the moonlight. It was a perfect June evening and the
full moon sailed beneficently over them. Again it turned his
springy curls to silver gilt and Beth remembered that time at
Belcraven and that casual thumb on her nipple. She shuddered,
but this time it was not with fear or disgust.

"Are you cold?" he asked with concern.

"No, of course not. Someone walked over my grave, I suppose."

They were in the laburnum walk, and the long yellow blos-
soms were all about them, filling the air with their perfume.
Beth sighed.

"Will you be so sorry to return to Town?" he asked.

"I will, a little. This simple life is more to my taste, but I
know we must."

"When the Season's over we can return here if you wish."

"What would you normally have done?"

He shrugged. "Brighton for a while. Some time at Belcraven. Visiting friends."

"Do you miss your friends?" asked Beth curiously.

He smiled, teeth white in the moonlight. "I have a new
friend."

She had to speak of it, but she turned away. "Do you not
mind?" she asked.

"Having a friend?"

"Having only a friend."

He turned her with gentle hands. "Do I appear to be driven
crazy with frustration?" he asked. "I'm able to enjoy a
woman's company without demanding more."

Beth raised her hands helplessly and let them drop. "I know
nothing."

He took her chin gently and raised her head so he could
study her face. "I don't mean to tease you, Beth. If you want
me, you have only to say."

She stared up at him, trying to read his secret thoughts in his features. "I don't know."

No flicker of regret or frustration marked him. He smiled and dropped a butterfly kiss on her lips. "When you do, you have only to tell me." He then drew her hand through his arm, and they turned back to the house.

As they reached the French doors through which they had left, it became unbearable to Beth that they simply go off to their separate rooms as they had every other night. She said suddenly, "Kiss me, Lucien."

He stopped and looked down at her, a smile tugging at his lips, warmth growing in his eyes. "Like a manservant with a maid? Well, why not?"

He placed his hands on her shoulders and slid them, soft as warm velvet, up her neck to cradle her head. Beth closed her eyes to savor his touch and felt his thumbs rub, gently rough, against the line of her jaw as he stepped closer and his body brushed against hers.

"Hold me, Beth." he whispered.

She put her arms around him and, driven by some unsuspected need, pulled him hungrily close. His hands released her and his arms came around as tightly so they were fused, as it seemed, into one.

He tilted her head and set his lips to hers and that touch became a point of light burning in the dark behind her eyes. The whole of him—his arms, his body, his spirit, and his mind—seemed to whirl about her and that point of contact.

When his lips slowly left hers she was still spinning and whirling. His mouth trailed softly, moistly down her neck. She let her head fall back and he explored the front of her throat. Then his hands came up along her ribs to cup her breasts.

A shuddering response swept through her. Her wanton body recognized it with delight, but her mind flinched in alarm. She felt like a person who has prayed for gentle rain and received a raging torrent.

The French doors were pushed open and knocked against them.

They broke apart and turned sharply to see the horrified

face of the butler. "My lord. My lady. I beg your pardon!" The red-faced man fled. Beth and Lucien looked at one another and burst into laughter. Beth could feel her face burning, though. She had never been so embarrassed in her life. She hastily readjusted her disarranged bodice.

"He probably thought it *was* the footman with the maid in the shrubbery," Lucien chuckled. "Well, it establishes our reputation as romantics." He looked at her, still smiling but thoughtful. She could see the passion in his eyes and yet he was once more in control of himself, and she was glad of it. Someone had to be in control in these wild waters, or they would surely drown.

For all that, she wanted to be in his arms again.

He made no move in that direction and merely held the door for her to pass through, then locked it after them.

They went through the parlor to the small hall. He picked up the lamp set ready for them there and carried it as they walked up the stairs. The lamp formed a globe of light in the dark of the quiet house, as if they lived inside their own magic circle, alone.

Though they walked apart, Beth was aware of him as if they touched. Surely he would come into her bedroom now and complete the swirling madness they had started with that kiss.

Did she want it? Oh, she didn't know. It terrified her and yet drew her . . . One thing she knew, she wanted it done. They couldn't live on this knife edge much longer. Surely once it was done they could relax and be comfortable again.

He entered her bedroom but only to put the lamp down on a table there. He turned to look at her and Beth fretted over what she should do.

"You look terrified again," he said.

Beth tried to protest, but her voice formed an unconvincing choke out of her denial.

"It is doubtless very foolish of me," he said with a whimsical smile, "but when I love you first, my angel, I want my wife to be that fiery termagant who called me a baboon."

She watched helplessly as he strolled towards the door.

He turned and cocked an eyebrow. "I could be seduced out of that, if you wished to try."

At that moment, deeply stirred by the teasing humor in his blue eyes and driven by strange forces within, Beth would have made the attempt if she had any notion of what to do. While she was struggling to think of a provocative remark, he quietly left.

Collapsing sadly on her bed, Beth had to admit he was right. On their wedding night he had called her a wounded bird and though this time at Hartwell had been a time of healing, she still felt bruised in her spirit. She did not fear him anymore, but she didn't have in her the spirit to call a marquess a baboon. If that was the Beth he wanted, it would take a little while yet.

She could not bear to disappoint him.

Chapter Sixteen

Lucien chose to ride back alongside the chariot. Despite the way their superficial friendship had grown, it was just like the first journey they had made and the rift was almost as great. During their journey from Cheltenham Beth had read *Self-Control,* but she no longer had any taste for Laura Montreville. What had that arid search for unimpeachable virtue to do with this . . . this roaring passion? Instead she spent the hours in serious thought.

There was something very precious almost within grasp. She thought it might be that ideal, friendship within marriage. She had imagined, however, that it would be separate from more earthy passions and might even be jeopardized by them. Now she saw it was quite the opposite. The incompleteness of their marriage formed a barrier to their true harmony.

She must apply herself to that and not let any trivial qualms on her part, or on his, interfere. She laughed at the folly of it all. After years of warning girls to avoid lustful men, it seemed to her ridiculous that she couldn't quite manage to get her husband into her bed.

The duke and duchess welcomed them back to Belcraven House. Beth thought she detected concerned scrutiny, particularly from the duchess, but Lucien's parents were both too courteous to be blatant about it, and there was enough natural ease between herself and Lucien to reassure.

Once in her bedchamber, Beth considered the unlocked doors between her and her husband. Only her dressing room lay between their bedchambers. Not a great distance and yet seeming very far. It should not be so terribly hard to just walk through those doors tonight and say, "Make love to me, Lucien."

It was quite beyond her. She must look for a more subtle approach than that. What a shame there weren't books of instruction on seduction.

A knock on her dressing room door made her start. At her nod Redcliff went to open it. Beth's heart was pounding even as she acknowledged that it was highly unlikely that he be coming to seduce her in the middle of the afternoon.

He had changed from his dusty riding clothes into formal Town wear—pantaloons, Hessians, dark jacket, and, for the first time in ten days, a high cravat. "Imprisoned again," he remarked when her eyes noted it. "I don't know why women complain about the dictates of fashion. At least no one expects you to strangle yourself and wear all this lot on a hot day."

"How true. But no one expects you to go around in a thin layer of silk in the middle of January."

"We should turn eccentric and develop a new style of rational dress. I wonder what it should be."

Beth considered this. "I see no reason why men should not have summerwear made out of fine cotton with a low, open neck as ladies have. Already the loose Cossack trousers are becoming fashionable, and they look very comfortable."

"Look dashed silly if you ask me. . . . But the ladies could have their winter ball gowns made of wool and velvet and incorporating a cape and hood, ready for the draughtiest situation."

"I shall design one today. But perhaps," she suggested naughtily, "it would be simpler if women took to trousers for the winter and men to skirts for the summer."

He burst out laughing. "It would look extremely odd at Almack's."

Beth raised her brows. "I can't interest you, milord, in a charming togalike garment in figured muslin, perhaps with your armorial bearings embroidered around the hem?"

"In the hottest days of summer you could probably interest

me in it very much, but it would never wash. How would we ride?"

"The Romans managed, as did the men of the early Middle Ages. Your noble de Vaux forbearers who came over at the conquest were undoubtedly wearing skirts. And look at the Scots who have retained the tradition."

He threw up one hand. "Enough. I surrender. In fact, I'm going to retreat while I'm still able. Do you have everything here to your satisfaction?"

"Yes, of course. You're going out?"

"Just for a little while." He sobered. "According to the duke a meeting between Napoleon and the allies is expected any day. May even be going on now, though we have no news. I want to see what's being said."

Beth felt a chill at the thought that even now, at this apparently peaceful moment, the fate of Europe might be in the balance. Somewhere in Belgium cannons could be roaring and men falling dead. Perhaps men they knew.

"Yes, please go and see what you can discover."

He dropped a kiss on her cheek then was gone.

Beth thought of vibrant Viscount Amleigh and lighthearted Darius Debenham and said a prayer for their safety, for the safety of all. What nonsense that was. How could there be safety in war? Despite the prayers said in the churches every Sunday, she didn't see how God could have any part to play in war.

How strange that even if the battle raged now they would not hear word of it for days, and it would be even longer before there was definite information about casualties.

There was nothing to do but address herself to her own life.

She supposed wistfully that Lucien would soon meet up with friends and acquaintances. She had none of the former and very few of the latter. As soon as the notice of their return to Town appeared she supposed she would have callers, but they would only be curious strangers, and she was tired of that artificial way of life.

She remembered Eleanor Delaney. She had liked the look of the woman and been drawn, in the most respectable way, to her husband. She wondered if they were still in Town, for she had been invited to visit them. As they were his friends, perhaps Lucien would take her there.

Beth found, however, that she would be hard pressed to find the time for informal visits. The duchess invited herself to take tea in Beth's boudoir and soon asked whether Beth felt able to undertake a full social life again. When Beth reluctantly said she was, the duchess outlined an overwhelming schedule.

"There is so little time left," she explained with an apologetic smile, "and we must establish you. After all, if you are *enceinte* you will be out of circulation for quite some time."

Beth felt her color flare at the impossibility of this, but the duchess interpreted it as becoming modesty. "It is not impossible," she said cheerfully, "and you must be presented while you still have a trim waist. Have you seen the gown?"

"No, ma'am," Beth said numbly.

"We did speak of it," the duchess said, "but trying to talk to a bride just before her wedding . . ." She threw up her hands in a typically Gallic gesture. "We agreed to have Joanna's court dress remodeled for you, remember? It is all ridiculous anyway, for one never has any occasion to wear the things again. Come, we have put it in the next room out of the way."

Redcliff opened the doors as they passed through Beth's boudoir and into an adjoining unused bedroom. A small mountain stood there swathed in mull muslin. Redcliff whipped off the covering to reveal the most fanciful, beautiful, ridiculous gown Beth had ever seen.

The bodice was fitted to the waist in the old style and the skirt spread for feet all around. The fabric was a delicate figured blue silk overlayed with festooned blond and embroidered with sprays of seed pearls.

"And Lucien and I were taking about rational dress," Beth said faintly.

"Were you?" the duchess asked in surprise. "There is nothing rational in the business of court, my dear. Lucien hates going there."

"Why?" Beth asked.

"Wigs."

"Wigs?"

"Everything is in the old style. The gentlemen have to wear powder, and as few of them have the hair for a queue anymore, that means wigs." The duchess gestured for Redcliff to cover the gown. "You will have to rehearse with it on."

"But why must I be presented?" Beth asked. "I am hardly a young girl making her curtsy and I have no interest in such matters."

"That has nothing to do with it, Elizabeth," said the duchess sternly. "At any major change in our lives the sovereign must be informed. It is not for nothing that Lucien and Belcraven are formally addressed by the sovereign as 'Our right trusty and entirely beloved cousin.' "

Despite her egalitarian principles, Beth was overwhelmed by the notion that the monarch was assumed to be interested in her affairs. She was also honest enough to admit that being presented at the Queen's drawing room would be exciting, but it would also be terrifying. "I haven't the slightest idea of what to do," she said.

"Oh it is simple enough," said the duchess casually as they returned to Beth's boudoir. "A formal curtsy—and you are very adept at the court curtsy—a few words if you are favored . . ." She was already considering other matters and looking at the pile of invitations she had brought with her. "We will go to Almack's and Lady Bessington's ball," she said as she sifted through the stack. "Some of these are for you in the expectation of your return." She passed them over. "You may recognize some acquaintances I do not."

"I doubt it," said Beth, but she looked. "No, there is no one who is of significance. I did hope to meet a friend or two from Miss Mallory's, but that has not been the case. I will go to the events you select."

"If you could give me the names of any friends, Elizabeth, I could have enquiries made. They may not be moving in our circle and yet be quite acceptable."

Beth gave the duchess the names of five girls, women now, but without much hope. Two she knew to have married military men and were unlikely to be in London. Of the other three, only one, Isabel Creighton, had married a title and Beth had not heard from her in years.

The duchess then decreed that Beth should have some time to herself before dinner. For the evening, a visit was planned to the Drury Lane Theater.

The duchess wanted Beth to lie down and rest, but she chose instead to sit in her private boudoir and continue her reading of *Self-Control*. She had, after all, promised Aunt Emma a critical evaluation, and she was so out of patience with the book she wanted to be rid of it.

The sentiments expressed there were impossible to reconcile with the reality of her situation. Once, from a state of ignorance, she would have found Laura's search for a man of unblemished perfection quite understandable. Now she doubted such a paragon could exist, and if he did she suspected he would turn out to be hard to live with. It would be such an effort to live up to his standards. Moreover, having taken the first tentative steps into the world of passion, Beth distrusted this "controlled" assessment of candidates for matrimony.

Beth was guiltily aware that Mary Wollstonecraft had thought passion a poor basis for marriage, but surely there had to be something in it of the heart as well as the head.

Beth considered the intimate details of Mary Wollstonecraft's life, which had always been tactfully glossed over by Aunt Emma. Mary Wollstonecraft had, after all, lived for many years with her lover, Gilbert Imlay, and borne him a child. She had tried to commit suicide when the relationship began to fail. Not much of self-control there.

Laura, Beth thought sourly, would doubtless have been delighted to be described as, "A perfect woman, nobly plann'd / To warn, to comfort, and command." Beth had considered that quotation again and again and was beginning to wonder if it hadn't been a subtle insult, or at least a complaint. Lucien doubtless wanted a paragon for wife as little as she wanted one for husband.

She was doggedly reading, disliking Laura more and more with every page, when Marleigh announced a visitor. "A young lady, your ladyship, unaccompanied but respectable. Miss Clarissa Greystone."

"Clarissa!" said Beth, delighted. "How wonderful. Please bring her up." Clarissa could not really be said to be a friend, having been a pupil and six years Beth's junior, but she was a serious-minded young woman and pleasant company, better than Laura Montreville.

When she came in, however, there was something brittle and forced in the girl's manner. She was dressed in an expensive cambric gown with a fashionable bonnet on her head, all evidence that the family finances must have improved, but she did not look happy.

"Clarissa," said Beth. "How nice to see you. So you have your Season after all."

"Yes," said Clarissa in a quiet voice.

Beth ordered a tea tray and seated her guest.

"Are you enjoying yourself?" she asked.

Clarissa waited until the door closed behind Marleigh and then fell to her knees by Beth's chair. "No! Oh dear Miss Armitage—I mean, your ladyship. Oh please help me!"

Beth pulled the girl to her feet. "Whatever is the matter Clarissa?"

"I . . . I am being forced to marry."

Beth pushed the girl onto a lounge and sat beside her. "Marriage is the lot of most women, my dear," she said reasonably. "You see that even I have come to it."

"But you have married the Marquess of Arden," wailed Clarissa, "and I am to marry Lord Deveril!"

"Deveril!" exclaimed Beth in horror.

Clarissa sunk her head in her hands. "I see you know him. Miss—Your ladyship, I cannot! Not to save us all from the Fleet I cannot!" She suddenly fumbled in her reticule and pulled out a sheet of paper. "He gave me this."

Beth unfolded it to read the heavy black script. It was a list of rules for Deveril's wife, stressing total compliance and spelling out the punishments for transgression, mostly physical. It sounded like the rules for the sternest house of correction.

Beth was stunned. "I quite see how you feel . . . I hear Marleigh. Try to compose yourself, my dear."

The entrance of the butler, followed by a maid with a cake stand, gave Beth time to collect her wits. What a pickle. But she would never abandon this child. She had suffered the distress of a forced marriage but, she admitted, to a man who had much to recommend him. To be forced to wed such as Lord Deveril!

It roused personal feelings. On the one hand, she was grateful that her fate had been kinder. On the other she recognized that the duke would still have forced the match if his son had been an imbecile or another Deveril.

She poured some tea and sweetened it heavily. "Come, Clarissa, drink this and we will talk."

The girl sipped the drink and then put it down, choosing instead to wring her hands. "My parents have no trace of mercy. I have begged them! But my father. . . . He gambles. We have nothing left and there are my two brothers. . . . My mother says it is a daughter's duty."

"It is no daughter's duty to marry Lord Deveril," said Beth firmly. "If you must marry, surely a better match can be found." But even as she spoke Beth knew it was not so. A dowry was needed for a good match. Only such as Lord Deveril would pay to gain a bride. It was not as if Clarissa were a beauty. She had a rather long face and a wide mouth and unruly gingery hair. It was true that she had a lively personality and, at the moment, had youth on her side, but she was not the type to drive a man to forget the advantages of a handsome dowry.

"Is the marriage imminent?" Beth asked.

Clarissa shook her head. "The engagement is to be announced next week, but the wedding will be in September."

Beth took the girl's hands. "I *will* help you, Clarissa. I do not know yet what can be done, but I will find a way."

Clarissa smiled mistily. "Oh, your ladyship!"

"And I think in view of that you must call me Beth. We are, after all, conspirators."

Clarissa relaxed as if a great burden had been lifted. By the time the girl left, Beth felt as if the burden had been shifted to her own shoulders. Clarissa had such faith in her and yet Beth had no idea how to change her situation.

Clarissa had left Lord Deveril's set of rules on her chair and Beth picked them up. A rereading stiffened her resolution. Clarissa's distress was justified; no woman of integrity could stand by and allow what was little more than a lifetime of legalized rape and slavery. Beth may not have been able to fight against her own situation, but she could fight for Clarissa. She thoughtfully placed the sheet of paper between the pages of her book.

This also reminded her of Robin Babson. She had been so entangled in her own predicament that she had not given the boy a thought for weeks. She rang for Redcliff and together they made their way to the area behind the square where all the big houses kept their horses and carriages. There was only accommodation for about ten horses and three carriages in the Belcraven mews. Quite modest by de Vaux standards, thought Beth wryly.

Just the tax on horses and carriages paid by the Belcraven estates would bankrupt most people.

She told herself firmly to stop thinking in such a vinegarish way and went to pay respects to her horse, which had just arrived up from Hartwell. Goodness knew when she'd find time to ride Stella again.

All the time, Beth was alert for any sign of Robin.

Then he came out of a stall with a bucket in his hand. He looked in good health and was whistling.

"Robin," said Beth.

He turned curiously, then put down his bucket and touched his forelock. "Milady."

Beth went over to him, aware of Redcliff's disapproval. "I wasn't sure you'd remember me," she said.

"Course I do," he said cockily. "Watched yer leaving after the wedding, didn't I? Right fine do that was."

Beth was surprised. "Are you saying you were at the wedding?"

He goggled. "Not likely! No, ma'am. We had a right bangup

feast the day after. All the staff. It were bloody marvelous. Beggin' your pardon, milady." He wasn't the slightest bit repentant for his language. Lucien was right. He was a scamp.

Beth was content. There was clearly no tragedy here. At that moment a man came into the yard. Beth thought he was the head groom. He said nothing but clearly disapproved. "You had best be on with your work then, Robin," she said.

The boy cast a cheeky look at his boss and winked. "Right enough. All the best, ma'am."

"Thank you, Robin."

He went whistling on his way and Beth returned to the house with one burden eased. That did not help the problem of Clarissa, however, and further consideration of that situation was not reassuring. Clarissa's parents were unlikely to give up their plan unless another way out of their predicament could be found. That meant, Beth supposed, money or a better and equally generous husband. Beth was in no position to find either. She supposed the marquess might be, but would he sympathize with Clarissa's predicament? The duke or duchess? Even if they saw the wickedness of the projected match she doubted they would interfere between a daughter and her parents. It was surely against the law. By the time Beth prepared for dinner, she was no further ahead in her search for a solution to Clarissa's problems.

Lucien returned home with no definite news of Napoleon's whereabouts. The fact that Bonaparte had imposed an embargo on the French ports, preventing goods, people, and news from leaving the country, suggested the worst. All those in the know seemed to think the confrontation would be any day. Prices on 'Change were fluctuating madly with each rumor.

But for all that, life must go on, and the Season was in its final lighthearted weeks. Even the news from Brussels was as much of balls and receptions as it was of war. Beth found it extraordinary.

That evening they attended the Drury Lane Theater to see *Othello*. It was the first time Beth had visited this theater and she looked around for caged birds but found none. Perhaps Lord Deveril's words had been meaningless.

The great Kean was playing Iago with truly menacing cunning. The actress playing the part of Desdemona was an ethereal vision with soft white hair rippling loose down her back, her gown of floating white and silver scattered with twinkling stars. A few lines had even been added to the play to refer to this whiteness, contrasting it with the Moor's black.

Beth had always thought Desdemona an interesting part, her plight that of a woman maligned and stripped of her reputation. For the first time she saw similarities to her own situation except that she had destroyed her reputation herself, and she and her husband had managed to sort it all out. She shivered slightly when she thought of the end of the play, Othello strangling his wife in a jealous rage. It was fortunate that she and Lucien were more sensible—and yes, self-controlled—than the characters on the stage.

Beth admired the interpretation of the actress, however. She brought intelligence and dignity to the part. Beth consulted her program to see that the actress was Mrs. Blanche Hardcastle. In brackets after her name it said, "The White Dove of Drury Lane." A chill crept down her spine. Without moving, Beth slid a glance at her husband. He was absorbed by the performance but nothing on his face betrayed personal involvement. Had Lord Deveril's words had meaning?

Then Desdemona floated into a dance, executed with marvelous fluidity of movement and classic elegance. Beth looked at her husband again and the chill seemed to eat into her bones. The smile on his face could only be called doting. Was this, in fact, where he had disappeared this afternoon with such alacrity, not in search of news? Of which he had significantly found so little.

Beth looked back at the exquisite creature on the stage. She couldn't blame any man for loving such beauty. How could Lucien's interest in Beth Armitage be more than dutiful when the White Dove was waiting for him? Marital duty. The phrase he had used. Though once Beth would not have cared, now to be taken in the marriage bed out of *duty* was unbearable.

Had his considerate reasons for not consummating the marriage been merely a polite fabrication to disguise his unwillingness? After all, on that last night her willingness must have been clear, and they had both known he could overcome her fears if he tried . . .

The pain Beth felt was so deep she was surprised he could not sense it. But why should she expect him to be sensitive to her hidden hurts when his true love moved fluidly on the stage before him?

How cloying he must have found her, thought Beth, when he wanted only to return to his true friends and his true love. If there had been any way, Beth would have fled, never to face her husband again.

The horror passed, as such things are inclined to. By the time of the first intermission Beth was able to discuss the performance in a rational way and even compliment the leading actors. She listened closely to every word her husband spoke, but he said nothing exceptionable about the White Dove.

Then it was back to watching the lady once again and trying unsuccessfully to block all awareness of Lucien's warm reaction to the performance. Beth was pleased with herself. She behaved throughout the evening with calm good breeding, steadfastly ignoring the cold, hard lump of pain which had taken up residence in her heart.

When they returned to Marlborough Square they took supper. The duke and duchess retired, leaving Beth alone with her husband. She looked up to see him thoughtfully studying her, and she had a moment's paralyzing horror that Lucien might choose this night, of all nights, to demand his right to her bed.

"You look tired," he said. "We should never have gone out on our first night back. You mustn't let us bully you, Beth. If you don't want to dance this mad caper then say so."

"The duchess says I must be established. And presented."

He grimaced. "I suppose so. But that doesn't demand constant socializing. *Maman* is a creature of extremes. She either lives very quietly at Belcraven or descends on Town like a hurricane, unable to leave any moment untouched. You don't have to play the game by her rules."

"I have to do something," Beth said and then regretted what might sound like a plea for his company.

"There are any number of more stimulating events. I'll see what lectures are scheduled at the institutes. If you like, I'll introduce you to Fanny Ball. She's the sister of a friend of mine and a regular blue stocking."

For some reason this did not attract Beth. Was she so changed? "I don't know," she said, then added impulsively, "I would like to visit the Delaneys."

He smiled. "A wonderful idea. Tomorrow afternoon?"

"Will they be at home?" Beth asked, meaning in the formal sense.

"There's no point in any of that with Eleanor and Nicholas," he said carelessly. "If they're out we'll do something else and visit them another time. Go look over the Royal Academy, perhaps. You may want to buy a picture or two. If you're for bed," he added cheerfully, "I think I'll pop out."

And I know where, thought Beth bitterly.

Her choice appeared to be between dragging him to his *marital duties* or waving him off to his mistress. With a very tight smile she did the latter and marched up to her lonely room.

For his part, Lucien went to his club and had a miserable time. He was depressed by those who took the military situation seriously and irritated by those who carried on as if there weren't a battle in the wind at all. All the time he was wondering what would have happened if he'd given in to his baser instincts and carried Beth up to her bed and seduced all her fears away.

Chapter Seventeen

The next day Beth had to admit that regardless of the way
he spent his nights, her husband was doing his duty during
the day. He presented himself after lunch to escort her to the
Delaneys and also provided her with a neatly written list of
the more interesting intellectual events taking place in Town
over the next few weeks.

Hannah More was scheduled to talk, and Maria Edgeworth.
There was a presentation on the sculpture of the Renaissance
and a lecture on the migration patterns of birds. As an indication that such events were not beyond the bounds of the
haut ton there was a musical and literary entertainment under
the patronage of the Marchioness of Salisbury and the Count-
ess of Jersey.

"Perhaps I should set up as a patroness of the arts," she
said.

"If you wish."

Beth searched his face for any change, for any hint that he
had spent a night of passion with his mistress. There was none.

"If you don't object," he said as they left her room, "we
could walk to Lauriston Street. It's not far and it's a pleasant
day."

Beth was happy to agree but found it difficult to strike up
a conversation. The obvious topic was the play the night before
and she wouldn't touch that with a barge pole.

"No more news of a battle," she said in the end. It was an

idiotic thing to say as the word would be all over Town in minutes when it arrived.

"Mad rumors. The news we're getting is four or five days old. Someone was spreading word that the allies are routed. Another that Napoleon is shot by his own men. Both are denied by the War Office."

"Is it possible it won't come to battle?"

"Not unless someone does shoot the Corsican. It seems mad that one man's overweening ambition can cause such destruction. So many lives . . ." He broke off and they walked a way in silence. "We have this group of friends," he said at last. "We were all at Harrow together. Nicholas, Con, Francis, Hal, Dare. . . . There were twelve of us. Only ten are still alive. Hal's lost his arm—Damn the Corsican."

"Surely it isn't all Napoleon's fault," Beth pointed out. "Hal lost his arm in the Americas, and that war can't be laid at Bonaparte's door. Men, after all, don't seem to need much excuse for war."

He flashed her an irritated look but then gave a brief laugh and said, "Oh no. I'm not going to be entangled in a topic like that just now. I'm pleased you want to get to know the Delaneys," he said. "I think you'll like Eleanor, though she's not bookish. If you're wise you won't tangle in a battle of wits with Nicholas."

"He's a genius?" Beth queried skeptically.

"I don't know what he is. He never went up to university. Took this mad fit to travel then went to some strange places. Any meaningful conversation with him travels equally unpredictable roads. I once saw him reduce a parson to incoherence. I'm not actually sure," he said thoughtfully, "that he's a Christian."

"Good heavens."

Lucien looked at her in mock astonishment. "Have I shocked you? Drag your mind out of narrow, conformist paths, my dear."

Beth *was* shocked. She and Aunt Emma had questioned many things but never Christianity. She and Lucien had arrived at a neat, narrow house which at least did not look pagan.

"What is he, then?" asked Beth nervously.

Lucien just grinned and applied the door knocker.

An immensely proper butler answered the door and smiled. "Welcome, my lord. They are at home." Beth was somewhat reassured. This was not a house of disrepute.

"Good," said Lucien. "My dear, this is Hollygirt. Hollygirt, make known my wife, Lady Arden."

The butler bowed. "Honored to make your acquaintance, your ladyship."

It soon became clear formality at number eight, Lauriston Street, stopped with the butler. Lucien swept Beth along and into a large drawing room which had more the look of the senior girls' parlor at Miss Mallory's, except that most of the occupants were male.

Nicholas Delaney was sitting on the floor with two young men—one an amazingly handsome russet-haired specimen and one snub-nosed ginger—apparently playing with a large toy soldier. Another man, a fine-boned blond, was sitting at a table by the window writing. Hal Beaumont, Eleanor Delaney, and a noticeably pregnant young lady were sitting in a group being amused by a beautiful, amiable baby. A darkly poetic man was playing the piano. He looked up as they entered and swung into a creditable version of a fanfare of trumpets.

Everyone looked up and in an instant Beth was caught up in a whirlwind of welcomes, introductions, and questions. It was like a large and very strange family.

She was snared by Eleanor and cut out of the group. "You'll never remember who's who," said Eleanor, "so pay no attention. Come and meet Arabel instead. She has more manners than anyone else here."

Beth found herself on a sofa beside Hal Beaumont, meeting him for the first time since that extraordinary conversation in the rose garden. He smiled at her without constraint. "You're looking well, Elizabeth. I was sorry not to be at the wedding. Problems at my estate."

That had been his excuse. Beth saw he was keeping to his word; now she was married there was no hint of the warmth he had expressed just that once. "We missed you," she said and added, "I have to tell you that I prefer to be called Beth."

He looked intrigued but said, "Beth, then."

"And I'm Amy Lavering," said the girl holding the baby. "And this is Arabel. I hold her a lot in the hope she can teach my little one some decorum. My husband's Peter, the handsome one on the floor."

Beth looked over. Peter Lavering certainly was handsome but since Lucien had now joined that group, Beth felt she could debate the singular. She let it pass. "What are they doing?" she asked.

Eleanor explained. "Miles Cavanagh—he's the gingery one—brought that thing as a gift for Arabel. Entirely unsuitable for a girl, but Nicholas, of course, said there was no reason Arabel shouldn't grow up to be a soldier—horrid man. It doesn't work. Instead of marching it hurtles like the mail. It shot right off the table and broke its musket, so now it's restricted to the floor."

Someone released the switch and the rosy-cheeked grenadier shot forward about three feet and fell on its nose. Its feet gave a few pathetic little twitches. Arabel's attention was caught, and she gave a squeal and stretched for it.

Her father leapt to his feet and came to sweep her up. "No, no, little plum. Learn to resist wounded soldiers. They've been the ruin of many a fair maid." He grinned at Hal with no awkwardness about the injury at all, then smiled over the child's head at Beth. "Welcome. What form of insanity does your heart crave? Here we satisfy all."

Beth was a second too late to stop the betraying flicker of her eyes towards Lucien, and she saw it register on Nicholas Delaney though his expression never altered. "I don't know," she said hastily. "I think I like sanity."

He promptly popped the baby on her lap. "Talk to Arabel. She's the only sane one here."

Beth had never held a baby before. The youngest girls at Miss Mallory's had been seven. The baby at least was a professional and settled happily against her chest mouthing one of her own knuckles.

Beth looked at Eleanor. "What a lovely child."

For a moment Eleanor looked very serious. "Yes. We receive precious gifts from strange places." But then she smiled. "She's due for a feeding and her nap. If you'd care to come upstairs we could all take tea in civilized peace while I feed her."

Though the notion was startling, Beth agreed, as did Amy.

Eleanor took the baby and carried her over to her father who kissed her softly on the lips. "Sleep well, Plumkin." Arabel gave him a smile but turned straight back to her mother with a serious look. Clearly the demands of her stomach were beginning to wear down her manners.

Beth wondered if such a sweet nature was the cause of the devotion everyone showed the child or the result. She had no experience of family life, but she'd never imagined a father as warmly loving as Nicholas Delaney.

Her eyes sought Lucien's. He smiled. "Go and learn how it's done. I want a child just as charming and well-behaved as Arabel."

Beth raised her brows. "I thought you wanted an heir for Belcraven."

"No," he said, "that's my father. I want a string of little Arabels. Then," he added mischievously, "an heir for Belcraven."

Considering her virginity, Beth was finding this discussion in front of a roomful of strangers rather challenging. "What a shame," she said tartly, "men cannot carry and birth the children. We could share the load." There was a burst of laughter, and Beth took the chance to escape and catch up with Eleanor and Amy.

"Good for you," said Eleanor. "Men sometimes talk as if producing babies is as easy as making a loaf of bread. Ah, Hollygirt," she said as the butler appeared. "We'll have tea in my boudoir and then perhaps you could see what the gentlemen want."

Beth spent an enjoyable hour drinking tea and chattering. The conversation was mostly of pregnancy and babies, but she didn't mind. Presumably she would come to that one day though at the moment she didn't quite see how. She wished she had the nerve to ask these two friendly and clearly happily married ladies for advice on husband management, most specifically how to make him want to seek her bed, but she didn't dare.

When it was time to leave Eleanor Delaney drew Beth in for a warm hug. "I'm so glad you came. You must come again. It isn't normally quite so chaotic. Everyone is gathering in Town hoping to hear first news of the battle. Peter has a brother with the 42nd, and there's four of the Company over there. For some reason," she said with a smile, "they all gather here."

"It's . . . it's a very happy house."

"Yes," said Eleanor "it is. But it's happiness that's been worked for."

That was all she said and yet it was a message of sorts.

When the ladies left the room, Nicholas Delaney said, "Your attention, gentleman." The six men turned to look at him.

"Eleanor doesn't much care for talk of Deveril. Doesn't much care for me to be dabbling my fingers in mischief again, but we can't let such a man get away with anything."

There was a chorus of quiet agreement.

"I've looked into the situation. It's clear he has a lot more money this year than last. I have to assume that he somehow relieved Thérèse Bellaire of most of her swindled fortune, which warms my heart, but I can't say I care to see him prosper. For one thing, he's the sort of man who'll use money for evil."

"How are we going to get it off him?" asked the pianist, Lord Middlethorpe.

"I don't know, Francis. As far as I can tell he's not keeping it in any bank, nor has he made investments. My guess is he has it in gold in chests in his house."

Hal Beaumont grinned. "We're going to crack the ken?"

Nicholas Delaney frowned. "We are not. We are all respectable men here and besides, we have a member of parliament present."

The fine-boned blond turned back to his papers. "I'm deaf as a post," he said.

"So?" asked Hal.

"So," said Nicholas, "the first thing Deveril did on returning to England was to hire a squad of bullyboys. They guard him and the house pretty well. It's tempting to break in and steal the lot, but it would suit him to catch me in the act and haul me before the courts. I'm looking for a more subtle way to rearrange his fortune."

"I hear rumors," said Lord Middlethorpe, "that he's looking to use some of his money to buy a bride."

"All the more reason," said Nicholas Delaney, "to render him penniless. His tastes are too foul for even the street drabs of Saint Giles."

Stephen Ball, M.P., recovered the use of his ears. "He was implicated in the death of that girl a few months back. Body was found in the river. She'd been badly used. Just up from the country, as fresh and innocent as a lamb. Nothing ever came of the enquiries, though. No real evidence."

"Or carefully used money," said Lucien angrily. "God but the man's a nasty specimen."

"We'll sort him out," said Nicholas. "There's no hurry."

He wound up the soldier. With a whir the grenadier began to march, head turning first left then right. Everyone let out a cheer. Then, with a loud and ominous twang, the toy stopped dead.

Nicholas picked it up. "I hope that isn't an omen," he said.

Beth found that as soon as they returned to Belcraven House she was expected to drive in the park with the duchess. She had done this a few times before her marriage. It was, apparently, essential to see and be seen again now she was the marchioness.

Only she and the duchess were in the carriage which rolled slowly through the fashionable throng, and this was generally the case. The gentlemen rode, drove themselves in curricles and broughams, or strolled nearby, quizzing the beauties. The

Belcraven carriage was frequently stopped for pleasant exchanges, and Beth recognized some of the people from the days before her wedding. She was warmly welcomed back to Town. She was beginning to feel just a little less of an outsider, and she couldn't help but realize that as the Marchioness of Arden she was now a person of importance.

She wished she felt it. She knew she would be happier with the simple, chaotic lifestyle of the Delaneys.

"How on earth do you remember who is who, Duchess?"

The duchess waved a hand and bowed at a rotund gentleman. "Sometimes one pretends. That was Sefton, by the way. People of significance tend to impress themselves on one's mind. Do you know," said the duchess, between more inclinations of the head and slight waves of the hand, "I think you should call me *Maman* as Lucien does."

Beth found the conventional notion disturbing. She had never had a mother, in any real sense. But then she realized she could think of the duchess as her mother with no trouble at all.

"I would be pleased to, *Maman*." she said, and the two women shared a warm smile. Then she saw Clarissa and her mother, accompanied by Lord Deveril. Clarissa waved to Beth like a drowning person, but the duchess gave the carriage only her slightest acknowledgement in passing.

"Is that young lady a friend?" she asked mildly.

"She was a pupil at Miss Mallory's. She called on me yesterday."

"I see. I do not much care for her family or the company she keeps, but I will not try to restrict your acquaintance. I would advise you, however, to have nothing to do with Lord Deveril."

"Willingly, *Maman*. Poor Clarissa, however, is going to have to marry him."

The duchess paused a moment. "That is unfortunate," she said.

"Very. I wish I could do something to help her." Beth hoped for some guidance or expression of support.

The duchess looked seriously at her. "Such marriages are

not uncommon," she said with meaning. "Any family can experience difficulties, but in the case of the Greystones, the
evil, I believe, is gaming. Without that so many people would
not be brought low."

Beth discovered later that she had neatly been deflected from
Clarissa's problem to the larger problems of Society.

Beth was inexorably drawn back into the mad social whirl
and wondered when she would have the opportunity to visit
the Delaneys again. She supposed Lucien went there, for the
rigorous socializing seemed largely to be a female occupation.
If he didn't, then perhaps he was spending all his time with
the White Dove. Beth certainly saw little of him.

Two days after their visit to the Delaneys, Beth found herself
alone with her husband as he was about to escort her and the
duchess to a rout. He placed a finger under her chin, the better
to study her face. "You are finding this hard, Beth," he said
kindly. "This society life does not suit you at all. Just a few
more weeks, then I promise you need never come to London
unless you choose."

"And you, Lucien? Will you not come to Town again?"

He looked puzzled. "But I enjoy it, Beth."

"I suppose you do," she said.

She had thought perhaps this evening would be an opportunity to grow closer, but now she lost the urge to try. It would
doubtless suit him very well to have her in the country bearing
children while he conducted his debauches in Town with the
White Dove. If, she thought bitterly, they ever progressed to
the stage where bearing children became a possibility.

He frowned and looked as if he would question her, but
then the duchess joined them and he changed the subject, re-
lating an amusing anecdote. Beth couldn't help laughing. He
could always make her laugh, but it never lessened the bitterness inside.

Over the evening, the chill in her manner eroded his good
humor, and he spent less time with her, tried less to amuse
her. Beth felt the loss like an aching void but could not change

her behavior. It was amazing, she thought, how two people could have such a thorough falling-out without a word spoken in anger.

When she rose from her bed the next morning determined to turn a new leaf and try to win him back, he was, as usual, already out.

To distract herself from her unhappiness, Beth concentrated on Clarissa's problem. She tried to think of solutions but got nowhere. If she had money she could send the girl to a distant town or even to the Americas, if she would go. Did Clarissa have that kind of character?

If she had money she could offer it to the Greystones as a dowry, but that would solve nothing. They did not simply wish to marry Clarissa off; they wished to get the fee offered by Deveril. If they were paid to forego that marriage they would find another similar.

Besides, Beth had virtually no money. She had the guineas Miss Mallory had given her, and Lucien had arranged pin money for her. But all the accounts for the house, her clothes, and such like were settled by the de Vaux man of business.

If nothing better occurred, Beth could help Clarissa to return to Miss Mallory's, but that would be the first place her parents would look. Beth was not even sure Miss Mallory would conceal the girl from them. Aunt Emma always had to balance her principles against business sense.

As she was sitting in her boudoir that afternoon, taking tea and worrying about the problem, Lucien came to join her. It was so unusual an event these days that she felt panicked and quite unable to take advantage of the situation. She rushed straight at the subject on her mind.

"Did I tell you one of the girls from Miss Mallory's visited me last week?" she chattered. "Clarissa Greystone. Her parents are selling her to an unpleasant husband. She expects an offer any day."

The marquess raised a brow. "With anticipation?" he queried, obviously not outraged by the affair.

"No. With trepidation."

"If he is not to her taste, she would be well-advised to reject her suitor unless she puts money before other considerations."

"Her parents do."

"Yes, I hear Greystone's rolled up," he said off-handedly.

Beth wondered why he had come, if it was of significance. An awkward silence was growing, and so she picked up the topic, hoping for some worldly wisdom. "It seems a shame for the girl to be sacrificed for her family's sake."

He shrugged. "For her sake, too, surely. If the money's all gone, she'll end up as a governess if she's lucky. Marriage is preferable to that."

This was pragmatic and possibly true. It irritated Beth. "There should be some better way. No woman should be so forced—"

She broke off as he rose angrily to his feet. "I wondered why you were so obsessed by this silly chit. I am sorry, my lady, I have no mind to sit and have guilt heaped on my head again."

With that he walked sway out of the room.

Beth sat stunned.

Was that what he thought? That she was cold to him because she still harbored a grievance about her marriage? In one sense it was true—she would never feel comfortable with the way she had been forced to act against her will. But any tendency to blame Lucien had died weeks ago.

She saw how destructive her present behavior was. Nothing was less likely to detach the marquess from his mistress than being refused his wife's marriage bed and given only cold words. Her thought processes were even more tangled than poor Laura Montreville's. Laura at least had a clear line of thought, no matter how unrealistic. Beth could not persuade herself that she had been operating on logic at all, which was very galling for someone who prided herself upon her intellect. Looked at objectively, her husband had been kind and considerate throughout. If he could not love her, there was no blame in that. He was willing to be as loving as was in his power.

She forced herself to acknowledge that she had been motivated by that base emotion, jealousy. Jealousy because she wanted more than kindness, more than friendship. She wanted him to return her love.

She loved him.

Beth took a deep steadying breath. How foolish, how very foolish to have succumbed, and how useless to expect him to reciprocate. What on earth was she to do?

If she were free, Beth would have put herself as far away from the marquess as possible. What other sane course was there for a woman besotted by a man who merely found her bearable? That choice was not available. The only other thing to do was to fight. Impossible as it might seem she must gamble that she could one day gain his love, and undoubtedly the first step to that was the consummation of the marriage. The unnaturalness of their lives and her own anxiety and longings hung like the sword of Damocles over them.

Being a logical woman, Beth resolved to sort this all out in the straightforward way, in writing.

It was not quite as easy as she had hoped. One problem was that she felt it necessary to be discreet in case the note should be read by a third party. Another was deciding quite how much she was willing to say. She could not even think how to start it. My lord? My Lord Marquess? Lucien?

Eventually she wrote, *My dear husband*. That at least addressed the point in question.

At your convenience, she wrote at last, *I would wish to speak to you in my bedroom on a matter of importance. Postponing matters in the hope of change in me seems unlikely to lead to success. Perhaps the elimination of anxiety in that respect would serve us better.*

There. That seemed clear enough, and if he were in any doubt, the word *bedroom* should eliminate it. She signed it, *Beth* folded it, and sealed it thoroughly, stamping the wax with the de Vaux arms.

Then she felt a strong urge to tear it into tiny pieces and dispose of it somewhere.

She would not let herself play the coward at this point, however. She left the note on his shaving stand in his dressing

room. It was only later she was informed he would not be in
for dinner that evening but was engaged with friends.

Friends? What friends? Beth fought and won a battle with
raging jealousy. There was no reason for him not to be at the
Delaneys. She pleaded tiredness and canceled all her own engagements so as to be at hand when he finally read the note.

She could not help but be disappointed that he was out of
the house indefinitely. Too late she knew she could have chosen her moment more carefully, but what was done was done.
She had no intention of trying to retrieve her letter.

She prepared for bed that night with care and in a state of
nervous anticipation, wishing she could ask Hughes whether
her husband had been in the house since the afternoon and
whether he had read the note.

Would he come?

How late would he be?

If she fell asleep would he just go away?

Despite her efforts, she fell asleep and had no way of knowing whether he had come or not.

When she woke the next morning she was the victim of
sick anxiety. How was she to stand another day of waiting?
Would he come to her to discuss the matter in broad daylight?
That seemed horrible to Beth, so detached and coldblooded,
when she wanted to regain the passion she had so briefly
known.

Beth had no need of pretense to appear to be under the
weather. She breakfasted in her room, waiting for the tap on
the door which might signal a visit from her husband. At mid-
day she discovered he had returned home in the early hours,
slept, breakfasted, and gone out. He must, at least, have got
her note by now. What, oh what, had been his reaction, and
what was she to read into the fact that he had not come to
speak with her?

Was it of such small significance to him?

Perhaps, Beth thought bitterly, she should not have said, "At
your convenience."

She had to escape from the house, and so she went for a
long walk accompanied by her maid. She attempted once or

twice to strike up a conversation with the woman, but Redcliff, though obviously fond of her mistress, was determined to keep to her place and never encouraged familiarities.

They were nearly home again when a young man hurried over to them. 'Your ladyship," he said.

Redcliff moved forward as if to drive him off but, with astonishment, Beth recognized Clarissa in boy's clothing and stopped the maid.

"What is it, Charles?" she asked, hoping the girl had the wits to go along.

Clarissa looked at the end of her tether, but she tried. "I need to speak to you," she whispered. "I have run away from home."

"Oh, lord," muttered Beth, "why now?" But Clarissa was so distraught it was unthinkable to abandon her. The only possibility was to take the maid into their confidence. Beth explained the situation in brief and asked the maid to keep the secret.

"Well, I never!" exclaimed Redcliff. "It isn't right, milady."

"Right or not, I intend to help Clarissa," said Beth firmly. The maid clucked in disapproval but reluctantly agreed to be an accomplice.

"We cannot stand in the street like this," said Beth. "The question is, Redcliff, can we get Miss Greystone into the house without her being seen? Her parents will soon set up a hue and cry."

The maid's face was set in lines of rigid disapproval, but she said, "There is a side door, my lady, for the coal deliveries, and a back stairs up from there. If it is unlocked we could probably get to your rooms without being seen."

"Very well," said Beth. "Lead on."

Belcraven House stood detached from the other nearby houses, but there was only a narrow passage down the side, wide enough for a cart. Along that passage was the doorway. It proved to be unlocked.

The door and floor were sooty, and all three ladies eased their way carefully through the small hall and up the narrow, bare-wood staircase. Eventually, the maid led them through a green baize door into the sudden opulence of the corridor off which the bedrooms opened. Beth wondered how many of those bleak little staircases there were to enable the servants to care for the house without intruding in the lives of their employers.

Once in the boudoir Clarissa pulled off the old-fashioned tricorne she wore and tossed it into a corner. She was pale and close to hysterics. "Oh Beth! Lord Deveril came today to offer for me!"

"Well, really, Clarissa," said Beth impatiently, for she knew they were in a pickle, "could you have not appeared to comply? I haven't had time to make any plans."

"I did," wailed the girl, bursting into tears. She pulled at her loose cravat and used the ends to wipe her eyes. "And then . . . And then my mother *left* us! He . . . he *kissed* me!"

Beth looked at the girl with appalled commiseration.

"I threw up my breakfast over him," added Clarissa, not without a touch of satisfaction.

"You didn't!" Beth gasped and began to laugh. "Oh Clarissa. What happened then?"

"Everyone was dreadfully angry," the girl sniffed, though there was an echo of Beth's amusement in her eyes. "My mother tried to say I was unwell but . . . but he looked at me so hatefully." She was making a mangled wreck of her neckcloth. "Then when he'd gone she . . . she beat me and locked me in my brother's room. My room doesn't have a lock."

"She beat you!"

"She said she would beat me harder if I did such a thing again, but truly I couldn't help it!" The girl's twisting had worked the neckcloth free and now she pulled at it with her whitened fingers. "His mouth tastes like the midden, and he terrifies me!"

Beth gathered the girl into her arms. "I can believe that, my dear. But how did you escape? Did your brother help you?"

"Simon?" said Clarissa incredulously. "No, he's off at Oxford, and anyway, he thinks it a famous thing just as long as his comfort is not disturbed. I took some of his old clothes and climbed out of the window."

Beth looked at the girl with new respect. "Good heavens. Was that not very dangerous?"

Clarissa shrugged. She looked down with distaste at the damp and tortured rag in her hand and dropped it on a chair. "It was only the first floor, and there's a high wall by his window. I got onto that and sort of wriggled my way along to a shed, then to the ground. But you can see I couldn't have done it in a gown," she said with a blush. It was obvious that the girl felt her boy's clothes were the most heinous aspect of it all.

"You must change straightaway," said Beth and led her into the dressing room. There Redcliff produced a shift and one of Beth's old gowns, a plain blue muslin. Clarissa changed with alacrity. The gown was a trifle long but otherwise an adequate fit.

"That feels so much better," said Clarissa with a wan smile. "You have no idea how horrible it was to be standing in the square waiting for you. I was certain everyone knew I was a woman and was looking at my legs."

"But what are we to do?" asked Beth. "Your parents will hunt for you. They will be concerned."

"No, they won't," said Clarissa stonily. "Except about Lord Deveril's money."

"I can't keep you here, Clarissa. The servants will be sure to find out. Do you have any friends who would hide you?"

Clarissa shook her head, beginning to look frightened again. "Are you going to send me back?"

Beth hugged the poor girl. "Never. But I may not be able to prevent them taking you."

"Could I not hide here?" asked Clarissa desperately. "No one except your maid saw us come in. It's a very large house."

Beth had little choice. She simply could not throw Clarissa out. "Perhaps for a little while," she said.

She turned to the maid, who was still the picture of disapproval. "Where could Miss Greystone hide and not be detected by the servants, Redcliff?"

"It's not proper, milady," protested the older woman.

"Never mind that. Where? The attics? The cellars?"

"No, milady. The servants rooms are up under the roof, some of them. And the walls are thin. If she made a move it'd be heard. And the cellars have the stores in them. There's people in and out every minute."

"Well, where then? As Clarissa says, it's an enormous house. There must be somewhere."

Redcliff's mouth became even tighter, but she answered in the end. "She'll have to go in one of the spare bedrooms, if anywhere. The one next door to your boudoir is empty."

For some reason, hiding Clarissa in a guest room seemed much more shocking than concealing her in the cellars, but the maid was doubtless correct.

"Very well," said Beth. She took Clarissa to the bedroom which housed her court dress. With a grin, she twitched aside the covers. Clarissa gasped. "It's beautiful."

"I suppose so, but I'm not looking forward to wearing it."

"I haven't been presented," said Clarissa wistfully. "I'd like it, I think."

"Do you really have a taste for such things, Clarissa?"

The girl smiled. "I don't think I have a noble mind, Beth, like you. I like fine clothes, and balls and flirting with young men. I like fireworks and illuminations and masquerades. Now, I suppose the best I can hope for is to be a governess or a schoolmistress. I *loathe* Lord Deveril," she said bitterly. "This is all his fault."

Beth could have retorted that it was the fault of Clarissa's father's addiction to gaming, but there seemed no point and she had no objection to Deveril receiving all the opprobrium. She left Clarissa with *Self-Control* to pass the time and strict instructions not to make any noise. As she returned to her apartments, however, Beth couldn't help reflecting on the difference in their tastes. What a shame Clarissa hadn't been the duke's daughter.

The very thought made her hands clench. She wouldn't go back to Miss Mallory's now for all the tea in China. Never see Lucien again? Truly, she feared she would die.

Back in her dressing room, she gathered up the clothing

Clarissa had taken off. "What are we to do with this, Red-cliff?" she asked.

"Give it to me, my lady," said the older woman with resignation. "I'll stash it somewhere below stairs. I don't know what the marquess will have to say when he finds out."

"You are not to tell him," said Beth sharply.

"I know that," said the woman, "but you better do so, mi-lady. He can't harbor a fugitive in his father's house without knowing of it."

When she left with the bundle under her cloak, neither of them remembered the tricorne and the crumpled cravat still lying in the boudoir.

Chapter Eighteen

Afraid to leave Clarissa in the house alone, Beth pleaded a headache and kept to her rooms. She even took her dinner there, sharing it with the girl. She desperately tried to think of a place Clarissa could find safety, but the only possibility was the Delaneys. Though they seemed so warm and welcoming, the acquaintance was too slight to boldly ask them to be her accomplices in an illegality. If necessary she would do so, however, rather than meekly hand Clarissa back.

Beth lent the girl a nightgown and saw her tucked up in the bed. At least it was warm weather so the unaired sheets were not too cold. All they needed was for Clarissa to take sick.

Then, seeing no need to put off the matter, she prepared for bed herself and gave Redcliff the evening off. Sitting curled up on the sofa in her boudoir, fretting uselessly hour after hour over her problem, she had completely forgotten about Lucien until he walked into the room carrying a decanter and two glasses. Red wine, just like on their wedding night.

His blue eyes were bright, his beautiful mouth curled in a happy smile. "Dutch courage," he said lightly, "though I'm not sure which of us will need it most."

Beth could not hope to conceal her shock and alarm. Her principal thought was that Clarissa was in the very next room and might walk in at any moment.

Lucien's expression dimmed. "You perhaps?" he said and

poured her a glass. This time her hand did not shake very much, and she gratefully gulped the encouraging claret.

He studied her before he spoke. "I thought your note was unambiguous, my dear, but I'm beginning to wonder. Would you prefer that I leave?"

There was a great temptation to say yes, but Beth did not *want* him to leave and quailed to think what such an answer might do to their fragile relationship.

"Of course not," she said, holding out a hand to him. "I . . . I just did not expect you so early. You have been out late these last few nights."

He relaxed and smiled again as he came to sit beside her. "Am I to be under the cat's paw? I might like it, I think. Truly, I thought you needed a break from my company."

He seemed so honest. She wished she could believe him. "Of course I didn't," she said. "I've missed you."

He didn't move. There was no significant change in his expression and yet something altered. Something took her breath away. He gently took the empty glass from her hand. "Have you? You may be right, then, about eliminating our anxiety. I thought you'd taken me in dislike again."

Beth felt her heart hammering in her chest, a warmth spreading through her body. He raised her hand and kissed it, his lips soft and warm against her fingers. She watched his lowered head breathlessly as he turned her hand and pressed a kiss into her sensitive palm.

"Oh."

It was a meaningless little exhalation on her part. She had to breathe sooner or later. He looked up, and she had the impression fire danced in his eyes. His cheeks were beautifully touched with color.

He pulled her gently and she swayed into his arms. "I should have seduced you that morning, shouldn't I have, my little radical?" he said softly.

Beth remembered. "Yes, I think you should."

He buried his face in her curls and she felt his lips at her neck. Her hands sought him but found, unsatisfactorily, the fabric of his jacket.

"Lucien," she said. "You have too many clothes on."

He choked with helpless laughter against her shoulder and then pushed back slightly to look at her "Of course I have. It would have been a trifle brash, though to have come in my night robe, wouldn't it?"

"Would it? You weren't ashamed of your banjan before."

"But then," he said, "I was fairly sure I wouldn't be your lover. Now, my wonderful angel-light, I'm fairly sure I will."

There was the slightest question in the last phrase and, by way of answer, Beth raised a hand to touch his face. So that quotation hadn't been an insult. "I am not quite sure I see the logic in that, my lord," she said lightly, over the staccato of her heartbeats and the singing of her nerves.

He turned his head to kiss her palm again. "In my state, you expect logic, *ma chère?*"

"Oh." She understood what he meant. She seemed to be reduced to incoherence herself.

"I think," he said, smiling, "I will see how many times I can make you say, 'oh.'"

She expected to be kissed, but he traced her lips with a delicate finger, leaving them tingling, hungry.

Then he licked his finger and traced them again.

"Ohhh."

He smiled as he slowly unbuttoned her nightgown and slipped his fingers to nestle between her breasts. She waited for his hand to move over a breast, rub a nipple as he had that evening; waited in shuddering expectation for that deep, stirring excitement, welcome now.

He leaned forward and sucked softly on her earlobe.

"Ohhhh." It was a long-drawn-out moan.

Then she became aware that his hand had moved and was rubbing butterfly soft over her nipple through the silk of her nightgown. A dizzy hunger surged in her, and she turned her head to meet him in a desperate kiss. His arms around her, pressed to him, she wanted only to eliminate all their clothing and be skin to skin, and more.

When the kiss died and his hot lips trailed down her throat,

Beth said, "Oh and oh and oh. *Please* will you take some clothes off?"

He laughed again, so hard he had to stop kissing her. "You're adorable! What a terrible amount of time we've wasted."

Running a wondering hand through his curls, she asked. "Why did you not seduce me that morning? I was more than half willing."

He captured her hand. "I have never forced a woman," he said softly. "You had so little choice in events that I feared I would have been forcing you then." With a teasing smile he asked, "How willing are you now, my courageous one? Still more than half? Three-quarters? Four-fifths?"

Beth pretended to give the matter deep thought. "Ninety-nine one hundredths," she said at last.

He drew her back into his arms. "I'll have to work on that fragment of doubt, my enchanting schoolmistress . . ."

Like an icy shock, remembrance of Clarissa, so close, stiffened Beth's muscles.

He frowned in perplexity. "Beth, there's no need to hurry into this," he said, drawing back. "I'm sorry if you feel I've been neglecting you, but I require no price for my presence."

If he left her now, Beth thought, she'd tear the room apart. "Lucien," she said, "stop being so noble, damn you!"

He burst out laughing. "Oh Beth, I do love you."

That shocked her into a semblance of sobriety. "You do?"

He met her eyes calmly. "Yes, I really do. I think I fell in love with you at Hartwell. I've missed our time together these last few days. I've missed your challenging way of looking at things and your wit. You always catch my jokes first time, and often cap them. Do you mind very much being loved by your enslaver, my darling houri?"

Mind? She felt as if she could float away with happiness. "How could I mind? I've been trying to persuade myself for weeks that I don't love you. And failing."

As he took her in his arms again she murmured, "Do you think we can keep it from the duke, though?"

His lips were against hers as he said, "Why?"

"He'll be so pleased with himself."

He laughed even as his mouth came down on hers and the magic started again. With playful hands and velvet lips, he teased and tantalized her into delight but always, a barrier to ecstasy, was the knowledge of Clarissa.

Then Beth had an inspiration. "Lucien!"

"Yes, my darling," he said against her breast.

"Lucien. I want you to make love to me in *your* bed."

He looked up into her blushing face, his eyes bright with delight. "You are a box of wonders, my angel. What strange fancy do we have here, and where did you find the courage to demand it?"

Beth could only think that in his bedroom they would be four doors away from Clarissa. "Am I not a flaming radical, my dear baboon?"

He laughed and swept her up in his arms, twirling her round and round on the way to the door. "What do you expect, I wonder? It's a perfectly ordinary room, exactly like your own." He stopped with her high in his arms and lowered his head to gently torment one swollen nipple with his teeth. Beth arched and gasped as an aching need filled her.

When he looked at her, she knew her eyes spoke for her, though she was beyond speech. She knew her eyes said, "I need you. Now." His breathing became ragged and his eyes were strangely dark with passion.

They were at the door to her bedroom. He hesitated as he considered the situation. "Do you know, delicious wanton, I will either have to put you down or ask you to manage the knob. I prefer the latter." He bent slightly and twisted so she could reach it. His lips took the opportunity to brush again across her breasts so that her fingers trembled as they tried to grasp the knob.

As she twisted to reach it, she felt him stiffen.

"What—"

He put her down so abruptly it came close to a drop. Shocked, senses adrift, left leaning against the wall, Beth watched him walk over and pick up a man's tricorne. He turned with it in his hand and stared at her. God knew what he saw in her face, but it was doubtless guilt. It bleached his fine skin.

"Lucien—"

"No." It was quietly violent.

He walked a few paces, stiffly as if in pain, and picked a crumpled cravat from a chair. When he turned to face her, he had regained a kind of control, brittle and terrible to see. "Part of your new habit, perhaps?" he queried, his eyes like chips of blue glass.

"You know it isn't." She tried a smile, but fear was icing through her, surely without cause. She would have to tell him about Clarissa. He wouldn't be pleased, but he wouldn't be too angry. Despite reason, instinct was screaming, *Danger!*

"Of course I know it isn't," he said quite casually, turning and turning the hat in his hands. "Has it all been acting? What a fool you've made of me. It would have worked, too, if it hadn't been for this sluttish piece of carelessness. I would never have noticed tonight if your cries were false, if the bladder of blood had been employed." On the last measured, almost judicial, words, his eyes blazed fury and he hurled the hat viciously from him.

"Lucien," cried Beth, too frightened to think straight. "I don't know what you mean."

He strode over to her and grabbed her arms bruisingly. "Stop! Never again. We'll deal together if we must, but there'll be no more lies!" He punctuated the last three words with violent shakes.

"You're hurting me! I haven't lied to you!"

"You are a lie, damn you," he shouted and thrust her from him so that she staggered. He gestured towards the hat and the cravat. "Who owned that archaic piece, that rag? A groom, perhaps? Tell me your tastes, madam. I need to know if I'm to serve you as well as he did!"

Revelation flashed upon Beth. She ran forward. "No, Lucien, no! It's not that. I've never loved anyone but you!"

He backhanded her. She was thrown bruisingly against the wall, her brief cry silenced by shock.

After a blank, disbelieving moment he turned sharply away, his hands to his face.

Into the tomblike silence Clarissa burst, wild-eyed, with a candlestick in her hand. She saw Beth on the floor, hand to her throbbing cheek. She screamed, "You beast! You swine!" and went for the marquess swinging.

He was clearly disorientated by shock himself. She landed a crashing blow to his temple before he grabbed the weapon from her and wrapped her in a grip that prevented further assault.

By that time, Beth had struggled up and run over. "Clarissa, stop it! This doesn't help. Lucien, let her go."

He did so cautiously, and Clarissa fled to Beth's side, partly comforting and partly seeking solace. "I couldn't help but hear, Beth. He *hit* you!"

"Yes."

Beth and Lucien stared at each other in bleak silence. Could life ever be the same after that explosion of violence? How could she have been so dense not to immediately see what interpretation he was putting on things? Those careless words of so long ago were still coming back to destroy.

He turned away from them, moving slowly as if exhausted, and drained the long-forgotten wine.

"I think some rational conversation is called for," he said at last in a flat voice. "Are you willing to attempt it?"

"Of course," said Beth and seated Clarissa firmly in the straight-backed chair. She herself took a seat on the sofa and wondered if he would join her. She could have wept, and not because of the blow. Where had all that beautiful passion gone? Exploded in a brutal moment.

He preferred to stand. He was white-faced and rigid. He took up her towel and absently dabbed at the trickle of blood on his face.

"Who is she?" he asked. "And whose is the hat?"

"This is Clarissa Greystone, Lucien. She came disguised as a boy. I'm giving her refuge from her parents."

He closed his eyes and sucked in a deep breath. When he

opened them again, it was to look at Clarissa with dislike. "Oh God."

Clarissa scowled back at him fiercely.

He turned back to Beth. "Can you forgive me? That was an unpardonable thing to do even if you were—I have no excuse except disordered emotions."

"You have every excuse," said Beth clearly, still rubbing at her throbbing face. She could taste blood where her teeth had cut the inside of her cheek. "If I found evidence you had the White Dove in your bedroom, I would have enjoyed doing much the same thing."

He straightened and frowned. "How did you . . . ? No, let's not be distracted. I have to point out it is not the same thing, Beth. Women have a traditional right to express their grievance on a man's face. For one thing," he said, with a trace of bleak humor, "they can rarely land more than a feeble swat. You are likely to have a bruise there."

"I must practice my technique then," she said pensively, "against the time I need it."

He laughed briefly and looked a little more like himself. He soaked her washcloth in the water bowl and came to look at her face, turning her jaw with gentle fingers. He placed a gentle kiss where it throbbed the worst, then held the cloth over it. "I love you more for your gallantry," he said softly, "but I will never forgive myself for this to my dying day."

Beth took the cloth and held it. It was true she understood and forgave, but she was not sure she could ever feel quite the same about him. The next time he was angry, would she have to fear blows?

"So I would hope," broke in Clarissa shrilly. "Beth, don't let him cajole you. He *hit* you."

"We know that, Clarissa," said Beth in her best Miss Mallory voice. "I understand your feelings, but I have to point out that you do not understand ours."

Having quelled the girl, Beth filled in the details of Clarissa's situation. By the time she had finished, the marquess had a look of disbelief on his face.

"Beth, there's nothing you can do. Her parents have all the

rights. Marriages like this are made every day. People learn to make the best of it."

"That is merely a sign of all that is wrong in the world," said Beth firmly. "Clarissa is not going to marry Lord Deveril against her will."

"Deveril!" he exclaimed, and Beth realized this was the first time she'd identified Clarissa's rich suitor. "That changes matters."

"How?"

"He certainly cannot be allowed to marry any gently born woman. Any woman at all, if it comes to that."

"Then you'll help her?"

He thought. "It's still not easy. We could probably keep her out of Deveril's hands, but there is no way in law of freeing her of her parents. It'll be another beating and another Deveril."

"No one can be as loathsome as Lord Deveril," said Clarissa with a shudder.

"There," said the marquess, "I admit you have a point."

"And if Clarissa escapes," Beth said, "Lord Deveril will merely seek out another victim."

The marquess shook his head. "Am I to spend the rest of my life rescuing innocents from villains? There's a never-ending supply of both."

Beth smiled at him, despite the twinge of pain it cost her. "I will try to learn to ignore some of the troubles of the world, Lucien, but I cannot step over the victim in my path. At the moment, however, our main requirement is a safe haven for Clarissa. You know London. There must be hundreds of places she can hide."

"Not in the London I know," he said.

"I did wonder about the Delaneys," Beth said hesitantly.

"They'd be willing to help," he said, "but there are reasons it would be better not to involve them in anything to do with Deveril at the moment." He grew thoughtful. "You mentioned the White Dove. What do you know?"

Beth could feel her color rising. "She's the actress at Drury Lane. She's beautiful, and she's your mistress."

"Was. How did you know?"

"Was?" Beth echoed, a little glow starting within. She knew he wouldn't lie to her. He nodded. "Lord Deveril told me," she said.

The marquess's eyes flashed. "Did he, by God? It strikes me the simplest way out of this coil is to kill him."

"You can't do that!" Beth protested. Violence again. Was that his solution to everything?

"He is a bit old for a challenge," agreed the marquess thoughtfully. "I wonder if I can get him to challenge me."

Beth was horrified. "Lucien, it would be murder."

"Call it an execution," he said, and she saw, with dismay, that he was perfectly serious. Before she could marshal all the arguments against the evils of dueling, he spoke again.

"To return to the point," he said, seemingly much refreshed by the prospect of killing someone, "if you know about Blanche, she may provide the help we need."

"How?" asked Beth, finding this turn in the conversation no better. He might have given up the actress, but that was no proof he had given up his feelings for her.

"No one would connect Blanche with Clarissa, and Blanche would give her refuge."

"A Cyprian?" gasped Clarissa.

"An actress," corrected the marquess coldly. "And a remarkable lady. It's the only refuge you're likely to find. If your parents know you've visited Beth, they'll be on the doorstep tomorrow."

Clarissa looked to Beth for guidance.

"I think you should accept this help," said Beth. "It seems safe, and it's a trifle late for us to be fretting about your reputation, Clarissa. I truly don't know what's to become of you, but as you said, anything will be better than marriage to Lord Deveril."

The girl nodded. "Very well. What should I do?"

"Go and dress," said Beth.

When Clarissa had left the room, Beth asked, "Can she go to this place now? Or will Madam Blanche need warning?"

"How very discreet. I don't believe Blanche has a new protector, but I should send a message. She will be at the theater now, anyway. We'll have to wait an hour or two I think. A messenger . . . Ah yes, the little bird."

He turned to go but then looked back. "Can you forgive me?" he asked seriously.

She smiled. "I already have. It all began anyway when I convinced you I had known a dozen lovers. You were right—words have a life of their own once spoken."

He came and held her, a gentle hold of cherishing. "I stole it from Horace," he confessed. " *'Semel emissum volat irrevocabile verbum.'* Let's cap him with Virgil. *'Omnia vincit amor.'* I love you, Beth. Even if you were debauched, God help me, I would still love you. That was what drove me mad. I thought you a whore, but I still hungered for you."

Beth tightened her arms around him and completed his quotation, " *'Nos cedamus amori.'* " Let us surrender to love.

"I know you to be virtuous," he continued. "I know you to be a virgin." With a hint of humor, he added, "Unfortunately."

Beth laughed and looked up at him. "And I love you, though you're a barbarian." Shyly she added, "I, too, think it unfortunate."

But what she thought unfortunate was that the moment of delirious pleasure had been destroyed. She could not imagine how they were to recapture it.

He moved out of her arms. "I am not a barbarian," he said. "A barbarian would throw Clarissa out of the window and carry you to his bed. I'm a baboon in its milieu. I will act according to my code."

"Will you ever let me forget that?" she demanded.

"Never," he said with a grin. "It is the most wonderfully rude thing anyone has ever said to me."

"What *is* the code of a baboon?" Beth asked.

"I thought you knew. Must I lose my faith in you?"

"A baboon," said Beth, inventing quickly, "is always indulgent of its mate. It unfailingly helps the weak of its society, especially young females, and never seeks to kill except in the extremes of self-defense. It is also," she added pointedly, "totally monogamous."

"Hmm. In any primitive environment, baboons would be extinct."

"But this is London, the most civilized city in the world," declared Beth.

He raised a brow. "Remind me not to allow you out of the door unescorted, my naive blue stocking. I have to go and make arrangements." She could sense in him, as in herself, a simple disinclination to part, even for a moment.

"You must dress," he said. "I'm not handling Clarissa alone, and I want you to meet Blanche." He smiled. "I can't imagine any other wife in the world I could say that to."

"Is that a compliment?" Beth queried.

"The greatest I can offer," he replied, and his look was a caress.

Chapter Nineteen

Hours later Beth and Clarissa crept down the servants' staircase to the side door and out onto the street. Lucien had arranged to pick them up nearby.

The waiting time had not been pleasant. Lucien had returned to her room only briefly with instructions, and Beth knew it was not Clarissa's presence which constrained him. He could not bear the sight of her face, already beginning to discolor. When she put on her outer clothes she chose a close-fitting bonnet which shadowed her cheek.

Soon he drew up in a hired coach and handed them in. "I thought it best not to involve the servants except Robin. He carried the message to Blanche, and he's waiting at her house."

"You sent a child out into the streets of London at this time of night?" Beth protested.

"He's doubtless better equipped to survive there than I am," said the marquess dryly and passed the journey telling them how he had first become acquainted with Robin Babson.

"There must be so many children like him," mused Beth.

"No," said the marquess firmly.

Beth flashed him her first deliberately appealing look. "A school, perhaps? To train them for a trade?"

He sighed, but his lips twitched. "Perhaps."

She grinned in triumph, and he shook his head.

The coach drew up in front of a row of houses and the marquess handed the ladies out and paid off the driver. As soon as the vehicle rolled away, a slight figure slipped out of the shadows.

"All's right, milord," said Robin proudly. "The mort's in and waitin'."

"Well done. You go and wait in the kitchen then." Lucien went forward to apply the knocker. In a moment Blanche herself opened the door and let them in.

It was a pleasant house, Beth thought, well-proportioned and furnished with taste. Not, as she had imagined, the home of a lady of easy virtue. Feeling stiff and awkward, she looked at the White Dove. Seen up close she was as beautiful as on the stage. Her milky skin was touched with roses, her large eyes fringed by tawny lashes, and there was no sign of cosmetics that Beth could detect. Her plain white gown was the simplest of muslins trimmed only with a little lace, and yet it seemed to enhance a long slender neck, full high breasts, and a very graceful carriage. The woman's long silvery hair was gathered on her crown in a simple knot. Beth felt like a mill pony next to a thoroughbred.

Worse, in a sense, was that Blanche looked both kind and intelligent. Mary Wollstonecraft might have railed against women who were trained for nothing but pleasing men, but what was one to say of a woman so gifted by God who had apparently still retained the powers of her brain?

Having closed the door, Blanche showed her intelligence by standing back to allow Lucien to handle this unusual situation.

He turned. "Beth, may I present Blanche Hardcastle?" Instead of the formal words, it was an honest question.

"Of course," said Beth and extended a hand to the woman. "I am very pleased to meet you, Mrs. Hardcastle, and very grateful."

Blanche shook the hand firmly and smiled warmly, but as her eyes caught the discoloration on Beth's face, they widened and she looked incredulously at the marquess.

"And this is Clarissa Greystone," he said quickly. "She is the one who needs your help."

Clarissa was clearly at a loss. After a moment, she dropped a little curtsy.

"Let's all sit down," said Blanche, leading the way into her parlor. "Tell me exactly what's to do, and I'll help in any way I can."

Lucien quickly outlined the story. Somewhat to Beth's surprise, Blanche was totally on Clarissa's side. "Lord Deveril is a wart," she said. "If half the stories I hear of him are true, he shouldn't be allowed to touch the toughest binter, never mind a young lady. I'll gladly have you here, Miss Greystone, but it can only be a temporary measure. You'll have to think what you intend to do in the future."

"I know," said Clarissa, looking pale and exhausted. "But I can't seem to think at the moment. This has been the most awful day of my life!" She burst into tears.

Beth immediately went over to her. "If you please, Mrs. Hardcastle, I think we should get her to her bed. Tomorrow will be soon enough to make plans."

Blanche took them upstairs to a small, comfortable room and saw that Clarissa had everything she needed. She left her there with Beth and descended the stairs thoughtfully. She found Lucien sprawled in his favorite chair, knocking back a brandy.

"I like your wife," Blanche said. "Am I allowed to say that?"

"Say what you damn well please. Having broken just about every rule of polite society, I'm in no mood to quibble."

Blanche wasn't sure what was making him so disgruntled, but she let out the laughter that was bubbling inside her. "You are in a mess, aren't you, love?"

He sat up a bit and looked ruefully at her. "Do you mind me bringing the chit here?"

"No. I'm a bit surprised you bothered, though. I'd not thought you the philanthropic type."

"My marriage sees me a reformed man," he said dryly.

"Then why does your wife have a bruise growing?" asked Blanche quietly.

He straightened and glared at her, a de Vaux through and through. Blanche faced him unflinchingly. A clock ticked. They could hear, faintly, voices from the upper floor.

"I hit her," he said at last and swallowed the last of the brandy in a gulp.

Blanche picked up the decanter and refilled his glass. "Because she was helping the girl?"

"No." Lucien could not bring himself to tell her the sordid tale, but he waited for Blanche's judgment. Though he knew he deserved only disgust, he felt Blanche was the one person who might make sense of everything. She'd seen the worst of life.

"You'll feel better in a while," she said at last.

He stared at her. "I? I'm not the one in pain."

"Are you not, my dear?"

He looked thoughtfully away. "Yes, Blanche, I am. But what of Beth? Don't you feel for her?"

"I can see in her eyes you've made amends, though I suspect you have a way to go yet to wipe the record clean. I hope so. It doesn't do for women to be too forgiving. If you lay a hand on her again, I hope she wraps a poker round your head."

"Is that what you'd have done?"

"It's what I have done, and worse," said Blanche straightly. "My father knocked my mother about all the time. I promised then no man would raise a hand to me and get away with it."

They heard the door open above.

"Thank God," said the marquess dryly, "I never gave in to the temptation to beat you."

"Why didn't you?" asked Blanche. "We had our fights and you've certainly got a temper, but I'll go odds you've never hit a woman before in your life."

He looked down at the amber liquid in his glass. He hadn't drunk from it since she'd refilled it. "Do you really want to know?"

"Yes, I think I do."

"I've never loved a woman before in my life," he said, adding almost angrily, "It's not all it's cracked up to be, either."

Coming down the stairs, Beth heard this and stopped. She couldn't help a glow of warmth at the admission of love, but she'd rather not have heard the rider.

"And what's that supposed to mean?" Blanche asked, with laughter in her voice.

"I've never been so miserable in my life as these last few weeks. I don't remember when I last had a good night's sleep."

"Well . . ."

"Not for that reason, damn it!"

"Oh." There was a wealth of meaning in Blanche's voice, and Beth could feel herself color up. She knew she should go down and join them, but embarrassment and curiosity kept her fixed where she was.

"Well," said Blanche, "even with a guest, I've a spare bed here. If I were you, I'd just get on with it. You'll both feel a great deal better."

The marquess laughed out loud. Beth felt herself burn with embarrassment. And longing. She remembered how she'd felt not that long ago, before it had all broken into disaster.

"Straight to the point," said Lucien, humor still in his voice. "I'm doubtless a fool, but I feel there should be some decorum to the whole thing."

"A total fool. What's decorum got to do with it?"

"Heaven knows. I've got to get out of here before you corrupt me, woman."

Beth knew he had risen, and she pulled herself together and began to descend the stairs so that when he came into the hall she met him there.

"How long have you been listening?" he asked tolerantly.

"A while."

"Shall we take one of Blanche's beds then?"

Beth looked away and shook her head. Though there was a hunger in her, the flames had died, the moment passed. She couldn't contemplate stirring them up so cold-bloodedly. Especially not here. She turned to Blanche.

"Thank you again, Mrs. Hardcastle. For everything." She saw Blanche understand as she smiled. Beth realized with surprise that she liked this woman. Perhaps just due to the extraordinary situation, Blanche felt more like a friend than Miss Mallory or any other woman.

Beth and the marquess left the house and stood on the pavement.

"What now?" asked Beth.

Lucien laughed. "My wits are scrambled. We have no carriage, do we?"

At that moment Robin came dashing up from the basement, a half-eaten bun in his hand.

"What's the chance of getting a cab hereabouts this time of night, Robin?"

"Not much, milord."

They set off to walk back to Marlborough Square, Robin a discreet distance behind.

"I could have left you at Blanche's and sent for a carriage," he said after a while.

"Why didn't you?" asked Beth, though she was enjoying this stroll. The streets were largely deserted. The theaters had emptied some time ago, and the grand balls were still in full swing. With Lucien beside her she felt no fear of footpads.

"I'm not leaving you alone with her," he said. "She's full of dangerous ideas."

"So am I," Beth remarked. "Don't forget I am a follower of Mary Wollstonecraft."

"Then you don't need any encouragement."

She looked at him. "Have you ever read any of her writings? I fail to see how an intelligent person can fault them."

"Yes, I have. Some of what she says does make sense, but I think she's intolerant of human nature in both men and women. Not all men are heartless brutes, nor are all women given over to a feeble-minded delight in trivialities. I actually wonder how much she liked women, apart from the few who fit her narrow pattern of what a woman should be."

Beth was shocked. "Can you support that?"

He smiled. "I prepared a quotation in anticipation of this discussion. 'As a sex,' the earnest lady wrote, 'women are habitually indolent.' "

"But she meant because of their poor education and their enforced subservience."

"Perhaps, but she didn't qualify it in the context, and I

gained the impression she regarded most of the human race, of both sexes, as children to be taught better by herself. Her comments on the aristocracy are equally biased."

"Well, you would think that," Beth retorted, enjoying this meeting of minds very much.

"True enough. But you can hardly expect me to be in favor of doing away with the aristocracy altogether."

"I must confess," said Beth, "that having become better acquainted with the species I find there are many who are responsible and industrious and certainly fulfilling their potential. Do you not agree, however, that expecting women to slavishly obey men, even when they are obviously wrong, is ridiculous? Look at poor Clarissa's situation."

She thought he might make a flippant reply, but he answered her seriously. "Yes, I do think it ridiculous. But I don't think I've ever expected that. My mother doesn't strike me as slavish and my sisters never cowered before me. In fact, they could pin me to the ground until I was thirteen, and frequently did. I suppose they slavishly obeyed the duke but then so, by God, did I."

"Yet you threatened to beat me. Twice." She didn't mention it, but the blow which marked her face hovered between them.

They walked a little way in silence before he responded. "I suppose I consider force appropriate on occasions, but I have no excuse or justification for what happened tonight." Thoughtfully he added, "It worries me considerably." After a moment he continued, "As for my threats, I threatened to beat you—though I don't know whether I could do such a thing—when you seemed about to bring scandal into the family. If it helps, I'd threaten to beat a man in the same situation and be more likely to do it. Does that make you more equal, or less?"

"I don't know," said Beth frowning. "It's late and I'm tired. That must be why you can justify violence to me. It can't actually make sense."

He stopped and wrapped his arms around her. Right there in the street. Beth's eyes felt gritty and her head was not very clear. She leaned against him gratefully. "Hitting you tonight made no sense," he said softly. "That was pure barbarian, and out of control as well. Nothing like that will ever happen again, I promise. Even if you take a thousand lovers—Beth!"

She realized she had drifted off to sleep. She looked up and shook her head to gather her wits. He lifted her into his arms.

"You can't carry me all the way home," she protested.

"We're three doors away, you goose," he said.

"Are we just going to walk in the front door?" she asked. "There's a little side door where they deliver the coal."

"I'll be damned if I'll sneak into my own house," he said as he put her down carefully. "It would be better if you walk in, though. Otherwise, the footman will probably think you're drunk. Robin," he said to the hovering boy. "Off you go. I'll tell Dooley to let you sleep in."

Lucien put his arm around Beth and encouraged her up to the big, carved doors. "What will the footman think?" she asked.

"One of the advantages of our position, my love, is that we don't have to care." Beth had proof that she wasn't yet fully a member of the highest aristocracy when she felt her cheeks color in the face of the young footman's astonishment.

He was obviously startled by their appearance, on foot in the dead hours of the night, particularly as no one had been aware of the marchioness leaving the house. Of course he said nothing other than a polite, "Good morning, milord, milady."

Beth made it to her bed. Just. She was three-quarters asleep by the time Lucien had taken off her gown and shoes. Sadly she remembered the events of the previous evening.

"I meant what I said in that note," she said sleepily.

"Don't worry," he replied as he gently stroked her hair back from her face. "Tomorrow night nothing is going to prevent us from eliminating our anxiety, I promise you, my darling."

Beth awoke the next morning when Redcliff drew back the curtains to let in bright sunlight. The maid bustled over with the tea tray and stopped, staring.

Beth realized she was in her petticoat, and she dreaded to

think what her face looked like by now. What on earth should she say, particularly since the staff must know she and the marquess had returned to the house in the small hours of the morning?

"We went to take Miss Greystone somewhere, Redcliff, and I fell. Bring me a mirror, please."

One look was enough. There was a distinct purpling of her right cheekbone. "I think I will keep to my rooms today, Redcliff," said Beth, trying to ignore the maid's disbelief at her explanation. She wished she had the true arrogance of a de Vaux and didn't give a damn. "Perhaps you can try to keep visitors away, too."

"Very well, milady. But it's a shame you didn't put something on that sooner."

Beth found she experienced only a slight twinge at eating her toast, so the damage could not be very serious. "Is there anything that would help now, Redcliff?"

"Well, some say vinegar and others witch hazel. I'd say the cosmetic pot would be your best chance, milady." The maid was stiff with disapproval. Beth wondered if it would be obvious to everyone she met that she'd been hit. It increased her resolve to keep to her rooms.

"Let's try witch hazel," she said. "I don't much care to smell of vinegar all day. Then you can buy me some face paint in case I have to go out later."

When the maid had gone, Beth recalled Lucien's parting words. They were going to eliminate their anxiety. She experienced the mix of trepidation and anticipation she had lived with for days, weeks even, but now anticipation was definitely in the ascendant. She knew, however, the sight of her bruise was going to upset him. He deserved to be upset, but she didn't want it to spoil the night. When Redcliff returned, she applied the witch hazel compresses conscientiously.

Beth was sitting at her desk reading, her cheek propped upon the pad in her hand when Lucien came into her boudoir. She hastily dropped the moist cloth and smiled at him, keeping her face turned slightly away. It did little good. He came straight over and took her chin to angle her cheek to the light. His lips tightened. He did not look well-rested.

"It would serve me right if you never wanted to be alone with me again," he said.

"How ridiculous," Beth said. "And most improper, too."

It at least elicited a twitch of humor. "Shy, are we?"

"I can't speak for you, but I would at least consider myself modest."

" 'Ways without reproach, unadorned simplicity and blushing modesty,' " he quoted with a smile.

Beth knew she was making his words true by blushing even as she looked a question. She did not recognize the quotation.

"Ovid," he said with a triumphant grin. "The *Amores*. I rather suspected Miss Mallory wouldn't go quite that far in your liberal education."

"I'm surprised Harrow went that far in yours," Beth responded.

"Cambridge. There's absolutely no limit to what one can learn at Cambridge. Isn't it wise they don't allow ladies there?"

Beth had opened her mouth to plunge into this argument when she saw the teasing look in his. "Picking a fight, My Lord Marquess?" she asked sweetly.

He perched on the edge of her desk and took her hand. "It did cross my mind that if we had a flaming row and I didn't raise a finger it might restore your confidence."

"Do I appear nervous?" she responded and raised his hand to kiss it. "Forget it, Lucien, please. I know it will never happen again. Hopefully those circumstances will never occur again."

"But you have feared me from the first," he said, standing up and drawing her into his arms. "And see how right you were."

"No," she said, snuggling comfortably against him. "This has reassured me. Pushed to your worst you've hardly hurt me and you're so very unhappy about it."

His lips came down in a sudden, ardent kiss that spoke of contrition and caring. And desire. Beth was beginning to think of morning love when the door opened and Redcliff breezed right in.

"I got it, milady—Excuse me!"

The maid disappeared, but Lucien reluctantly drew back. "I actually came to excuse myself for most of the day, Beth. I'm supposed to be racing Viking against Stephenham's Major Grey over at Richmond. I'd much rather stay here with you, but all the arrangements are made and bets have been laid. Do you mind?"

"Of course not, Lucien," Beth lied. "But what about Clarissa?"

"There's no urgency," he said carelessly. "She's safe enough. Give it time."

"But what if her parents don't believe that I haven't seen her? What if they try to make trouble?"

He was all de Vaux. "Here?" he said in amazement. "They wouldn't dare. Have a peaceful, restful day, my love." He dropped a kiss on her lips. There was a wicked twinkle in his eye. "Have a long, restful nap in preparation for the night."

Beth's heart speeded. "While you gallop around on Viking all day?" she queried.

"Practice," he said blithely and made a quick exit.

Beth burst into laughter though she knew her cheeks must be flaming. Thoughts of the night wound around her, making her hot, nervy, and restless.

Her contentment with being secluded in her room evaporated. She needed action and fresh air. Still, she was reluctant to show her face in Society. When Redclfff returned, they experimented with the cosmetic cream, which did disguise the worst of the darkening. The maid then dressed Beth's hair with side curls. It was not a style she favored, but it helped with the concealment. The addition of a Pamela bonnet with a large bow at the side completed the effect. Turning from side to side in front of the mirror, Beth was sure her bruise was unnoticeable.

But where to go?

She flicked through her invitations and found none of interest. Then she went through the listings Lucien had given

her. A talk by Professor Richards on his travels to China, a
musicale at Lady Rossiter's, a reception for Mrs. Edgeworth. . . . She had intended to go to that as she much admired
the author of *Castle Rackrent* and *Tales of Fashionable Life*.
She looked at the mantel clock. There was still time. Beth
sighed. Today she could not do justice to such an interesting
speaker.

She was interrupted by the duchess, who stared to find Beth
sitting at her desk *en deshabillé*, yet with a bonnet on.

"Redcliff and I were just trying the effect of a new coiffure,"
explained Beth with a straight face.

"Ah," said the duchess, studying the effect. "I'm not sure
it is flattering though, Elizabeth. It makes your face look rather
round."

"I was of much the same opinion myself, *Maman*. Is there
some way in which I can assist you?"

"A tedious matter. Sir Peter Greystone was here asking for
his daughter. Marleigh dealt with him, but he reported to me.
It seems the silly girl has run away and they thought she might
have come here."

Beth hoped her practice in dissimulation would hold up un-
der the duchess's carelessly shrewd eyes. "Here?" she said.
"They thought Clarissa was here? I can assure you she is not,
Maman."

"I did not see how she could be, and she did not visit here
yesterday, even."

"But has she truly run away?" asked Beth.

The duchess gave a very Gallic shrug. "That is what they
say, and one cannot imagine a reason for them to make such
scandal over nothing."

"Well, I am very glad," said Beth, feeling she must stay in
character. "No young girl should be forced to marry Lord Deveril."

"You are right, of course," said the duchess with a moue
of distaste. "A horrible man. He called here, too, but Marleigh
soon dismissed him."

For once, Beth thought, the army of servants had its advantages.

"Do you have engagements?" asked the duchess, glancing at the pile of cards in front of Beth. "I am to visit Lord Taberley's to see his collection of medieval jewelry. One of the best in the world, they say. Do you care to come, Elizabeth?"

"Thank you, but no, *Maman*. I am a little tired and will have a quiet day."

The duchess looked at her with concern. "Are you sure you are well, *ma cherè?* You seem so easily tired. Perhaps—"

"Oh, I doubt it," said Beth, reading the woman's mind.

"One never knows," said the duchess. "I gave birth to Maria nine months after our wedding."

"Er . . . I feel that is unlikely in our case."

"Oh," said the duchess. "I see. In fact, that is as well. You have plenty of time and once the babies come life changes." The duchess gave Beth a warm, perfumed kiss on the cheek—Beth was careful to turn her left cheek—before leaving.

Beth immediately pulled off the bonnet and undid the silly hairstyle. She then tried to settle to peaceful solitude. The day's edition of the *Times,* which she usually read with relish, could not hold her interest. Just more speculation about Napoleon's whereabouts and troop movements, all four or five days old. A fascinating article in the *Quarterly Review* on the Hapsburgs had no appeal. She looked at the clock a dozen times and the hands had hardly moved at all.

She picked over her luncheon, plagued by tantalizing questions. When would he be back? He hadn't said. Would he be home for dinner? There seemed a vast wasteland of time to be got over before even then. Would it be very bold if she were to order a quiet dinner to be served in her room for them both? Very bold or not, it was too bold for Beth.

The only thing to do, she decided in the end, was to go somewhere. She was not a prisoner, after all. She could visit the fashionable emporiums. The idea held little appeal, for she was still most uncomfortable with spending large amounts of money on fripperies.

She could visit the Delaneys. But they were such perceptive people, and today she felt transparent as glass.

What she needed was a long walk to dissipate some of her

nervous energy. Decided at last, Beth summoned Redcliff and dressed in a pale blue figured lawn gown and blue twill spencer which matched the high Pamela bonnet. She submitted once more to the curls down the sides of her face and the tower of white straw on top.

Looking in the mirror, she sighed. "This is ridiculous. In this bonnet I must be quite six feet tall!"

"It's all the thing, milady. And it's not as if you have to watch such matters with his lordship. He'd still be able to give you some inches."

Beth glanced at the clock again. Hardly half the afternoon had passed. How could she yearn for him so much? It wasn't lust even, just a simple longing for his presence, his mischievous grin, his quick and salty wit, his comfortable embrace.

"Is something the matter, milady?"

"No," said Beth, gathering her wits. "We are going for a long, brisk walk, Redcliff."

The maid's face fell. "Where to, milady?"

"I don't know," said Beth cheerfully.

"To Green Park, perhaps, milady?" offered Redcliff.

"Good heavens, no. That's no distance at all. Perhaps to the Tower of London."

"What!" exclaimed the maid. "But that's miles, milady. And through some not very nice areas. You must take the carriage for sure."

"I don't want a carriage ride, Redcliff," said Beth tightly. Perhaps this house was a prison after all. What would happen if she just walked out of the front doors? She imagined striding around the square with a bleating train of anxious servants behind. Her sense of humor returned and she smiled. But what was she to do? It would be no pleasure to drag an unwilling maid around London, and the woman was probably correct about the dangers. Beth knew little of London other than the circumscribed area of Mayfair.

"I know," she said suddenly. "We'll visit Clarissa. I need to talk to her anyway."

"Miss Greystone? Where did you take her, milady?"

Beth could feel herself freeze in the face of this new problem. Would Redcliff know the name? Blanche, along with other popular actresses, was often featured in the prints displayed in shop windows.

"To a Mrs. Hardcastle," she said carelessly.

No reaction, thank heavens. "Do you want the carriage then, milady?" asked the maid with the clear implication that the answer should be "yes."

"No, I don't think so." Apart from her desire for exercise, Beth did not want more servants aware of her scandalous association with Blanche Hardcastle. "It is not so very far—" she said and then broke off. "Goodness, I don't know the address. How foolish."

Redcliff looked relieved, but Beth was not to be so easily deflected. This outing was assuming the nature of a major challenge.

"The boy," she said triumphantly. "The stable boy called Robin. He knows. Send for him."

"A stable boy!" exclaimed the maid. "Here?"

"Very well, Redcliff," countered Beth firmly. "We will go there."

"To the mews, milady?"

"Yes."

The maid obviously recognized that her mistress's patience was at an end. They exited the mansion by the majestic front doors and then made their way around to talk to Granger, the head groom in Town.

Dooley was apparently off with the marquess and Viking, but Robin Babson was around. The wiry, sallow-faced man was considerably astonished that anyone wanted to speak with him.

"That varmint," he muttered. "He's here right enough, for all the use he is. And the marquess saying he should sleep in. No right being out at night, that's what I say—"

He broke off because Beth had had enough of contrary servants. For the first time she used a de Vaux look. His grumbles died.

"Right away, milady," he said hurriedly. "Oy! Sparra! Come out here!"

Robin came dashing out, a rough apron over his shirt and breeches. He had a piece of leather strap in one hand and a polishing rag in the other.

"Yes, Mr. Granger?"

"The marchioness wants to speak with you."

The boy turned and gave Beth a cocky grin. "Yes, your ladyship?"

Beth drew him away from the listening groom. "Where did we go last night, Robin?"

"What?"

"The address. I want to visit the young lady there."

"Oh, number 8, Scarborough Lane. But how you going to find it, milady?"

"Won't Redcliff know?" asked Beth, amused by the direction she could see the conversation taking.

"Nah," said the boy positively. "It's a small street and quite new."

Beth looked at him and smiled. "You think perhaps you should be our guide?"

"Might be best, milady," said Robin innocently.

Beth turned to the man. "Mr. Granger, would you mind if I took Robin away from his duties for a while? He can guide me to where I wish to go."

The man frowned. "The coachman's available, milady. He knows London like the back of his hand."

"I wish to walk," said Beth with amiable firmness.

"One of the footmen would be more suitable than Sparra, milady."

Beth raised her chin and stared at the man again. "I prefer to take Robin, Granger. The marquess also wishes the boy to be addressed by his proper name."

"Yes, milady," said the man quickly, and in a few minutes they were on their way with Robin, as smart as possible in a sturdy woolen jacket, walking a few paces behind.

Once they were in the street and heading in the right direction, Beth said, "I don't see how you can lead us from the rear, Robin. Why don't you walk ahead."

Robin was very willing to do this and sauntered along whistling while Beth and Redcliff walked composedly behind. None of them noticed a sharp-featured individual who gave up supporting the iron railings around the center of the square and began to follow them.

This time a sensible-looking young maid opened the door of number 8, Scarborough Lane. Her eyes opened wide, however, when Beth gave her card, and it almost seemed as if she would shut the door in their faces. Perhaps the de Vaux look was becoming a part of her, thought Beth, for the maid gave in and admitted them, directing them to the parlor, before tottering away, muttering. With a wink, Robin followed her.

In a few moments the White Dove entered. "You've given poor Agnes a turn, my lady." She glanced at Redcliff who had finally put two and two together and looked outraged. "And your maid, too, I'll go odds. Why don't you send her to the kitchen where she and Agnes can support one another over hot, sweet tea."

Beth agreed, and it was clear Redclfff was only too pleased to escape the presence of such a notorious creature.

As the two women took seats, Blanche said, "I should offer you refreshment, Lady Arden, but to be honest, I'm not sure anything potable will come out of the kitchen for the next little while. This is a somewhat unusual situation," she added with a twinkle.

"Scandalous," agreed Beth amiably. "You should have seen the trouble I had getting out of Belcraven House and to here without turning everyone on their ear."

"Lucien often found the same thing," said Blanche, and then stopped, looking conscious.

Though the words did give her a slight pang, Beth said, "I don't suppose we'll get anywhere if we ban his name from conversation, will we, Mrs. Hardcastle? I must make it clear, however," she added amiably, "that if I find you still have designs on my husband, I'm likely to put a bullet through your heart."

Blanche grinned. "Good for you! Is it possible you'll go so

far as to call me Blanche, your ladyship? My real name's Maggie Duggins, you know, and I should tell you I'm a butcher's daughter from one of the less desirable parts of Manchester." She paused for a moment to give Beth the opportunity for comment. When none came, she smiled and continued, "I'm well-used to Blanche by now, but Mrs. Hardcastle never sounds like me at all."

"I will," said Beth, "as long as you don't 'your ladyship' me. I find that equally strange. In private, please call me Beth."

"I doubt we're ever likely to meet in public, Beth," said Blanche wryly. "You've come to see Miss Greystone?"

Beth nodded.

"She's in her room, and I'll call her in a minute. I'd like to talk to you first, though. That girl is in a very awkward situation. Do you have any plan for her?"

"No. I wanted to talk to her again and see if she has any ideas. I also wanted to warn her and you that her parents and Lord Deveril have started a full-scale search. I had hopes they would be more discreet for fear of scandal."

"Money on one side and lust on the other leaves little room for discretion," remarked Blanche. "Miss Greystone did ask if I could train her for the theater, but aside from the fact that it would be improper it's hardly a place to hide."

"She could become a teacher or governess, though I'm not sure she is really suited to the profession," said Beth thoughtfully, "but how it would be achieved, I don't know."

"Perhaps you could fake references for her," said Blanche casually.

"What?" asked Beth in horror.

Blanche shrugged. "If she went after some provincial position with references from the Marchioness of Arden, it would doubtless work."

"Oh, I couldn't," said Beth.

"If you're going to be squeamish, you'll have her married to Deveril," said Blanche plainly. "She can't stay hidden here too long without word getting out, particularly if they post bills and a reward. She needs to be well away with a new identity and some form of employment. Someone will have to forge something."

Beth felt as if she had suddenly found herself at the edge of a precipice. "So if I behave correctly I will fail a girl in dire need," she murmured.

" 'Rules to regulate behavior,' " quoted Blanche quietly, " 'and to preserve reputation, too frequently supersede moral obligations.' "

Beth stared at her. "Mary Wollstonecraft!"

Blanche smiled. "You seem like a woman who would have studied her. Surely she would say, 'Help Clarissa and be damned to Society.' After all, Miss Greystone's position can't help but remind me of her Maria in *The Wrongs of Woman*," she said, referring to Mary Wollstonecraft's novel.

"Indeed. I wouldn't put it past Lord Deveril to consign Clarissa to an insane asylum if it suited his purpose. But it's not just reputation, Blanche. It's the law."

The two women immediately plunged into a penetrating debate on right and wrong. Only the rapping of the door knocker broke their absorption. As Agnes passed through the hall on her way to answer it, they looked at one another and smiled.

"Oh," said Beth, slightly appalled at the situation in which she found herself "but this is likely to be a tortuous friendship."

"It'll give Lucien giddy fits," said Blanche, laughing.

"Indeed," said a sneering voice. "A more improper association is hard to imagine."

Both women turned sharply to see Lord Deveril standing in the doorway with a pistol in his hand. Two unpleasant-looking men were behind him, one dark and bearded, one sandy with piggy eyes. Pig-eyes was holding Agnes. His fat hand was clamped over the maid's mouth and above it her pale eyes bulged with terror.

"I think it my duty to remove my bride from such a den of iniquity," said Lord Deveril.

Chapter Twenty

He was as horrible as Beth remembered—gaunt but with a brutish strength in his jaw and hands; sallow with shadows almost black around his bloodshot eyes. The vile smell of him was already oozing across the room.

Beth looked at Blanche and saw she was almost exploding with rage at this invasion. She spoke quickly before the other woman could make the situation worse. "Clarissa is not here."

"No?" remarked Deveril. "You consort with your husband's whore of your own accord? No wonder he chose you for his bride. So compliant. Do you perhaps enjoy the *lit à trois?*" He turned his disgusting gaze on Blanche. "Do you allow voyeurs Mistress Blanche? I would gladly pay for such a spectacle."

"You bloody grubshite," said Blanche between clenched teeth. "If you aren't out of here—"

The room reverberated with the explosion of the pistol. The delicate crystal chandelier plunged from the ceiling to lie shattered on the crimson and gold carpet. Agnes fainted, and her captor let her fall to the floor.

While Beth and Blanche were still frozen with shock, Lord Deveril handed the smoking pistol to the bearded man and pulled another from the pocket of his greatcoat. "The next ball will go into you, Mistress Soiled Dove. What's one trollop more or less?"

Beth forced herself to her feet. "I hardly think you dare kill me, however, Lord Deveril."

Before he could respond, Redcliff came running and was immediately grabbed by the other man. "Take both the maids to the kitchen," said the viscount. "Tie them and gag them. If everyone is sensible, it shouldn't be necessary to kill them." He looked at Blanche. "Do you have other servants?"

Blanche seemed to have trouble speaking, but eventually said tightly, "A cook. It's her day off."

Deveril studied her for a moment, then nodded. "Get on with it," he said to his men. "Then go upstairs and find Miss Greystone."

Beth wondered about Robin. If he hadn't come running up with Redcliff, surely he would have gone for help.

Deveril showed his brown and rotting teeth as he smiled at Beth. "I have come here for my bride-to-be, Lady Arden, with the full force of the law behind me. If I have to kill all of you, I will. I'm sure the ever-proud de Vaux family will pay richly to hide the fact that you met your untimely end in this house."

Beth feared he was only too correct, but she was mainly thinking about Robin. If he had the sense to run for help, where would he go? As Deveril said, he had the law on his side. The person needed was the marquess, but he was in Richmond. Beth wondered if the duke would help in such an unlawful situation.

Whatever was to happen, it would be wise to play for time. Beth sat down again and pulled Blanche down beside her. She saw that the actress was almost frozen with pure rage. Her hands had formed little claws and her eyes were feral as she stared at Deveril. He seemed totally unaware of his danger.

"Very wise, Lady Arden," sneered Deveril. He looked Blanche over. "You refused my offer of protection once," he said. "I never forget an affront like that."

"Such an offer is a gross insult," hissed Blanche with a sneer to match his own.

Beth wished the fiery beauty would be more careful until the situation turned in their favor but suspected caution was not in the woman's nature. Beth wondered if she could make some move while it was two against one. She slowly reached out towards a china figurine on a table. Lord Deveril turned such a baleful look on her that she quickly gave up the notion.

She heard the men leave the kitchen and clatter up the stairs. In a moment they were back, pushing a pale and trembling Clarissa ahead of them. The girl let out a cry when she saw Lord Deveril.

"Fear not, my little chicken," he said, with a parody of fondness. "See, I have come to rescue you and return you to the bosom of your family."

Clarissa clutched the newel post but was dragged forward by the bearded man to face her husband-to-be. Lord Deveril put out a bony finger to stroke the girl's cheek. Clarissa flinched away.

Unable to bear this tormenting, Beth leapt to her feet. "Stop that, you vile man! How can you marry someone who hates you so?" Ignoring the pistol, she ran over and grabbed Clarissa, pulling her away.

Lord Deveril's eyes narrowed, but he did nothing to prevent the act. "But hate, Lady Arden, is the finest spice for the bedroom," he said, showing too many of his rotten teeth. "I myself am an enthusiast for it. I seek it out. If necessary, I create it."

"Hardly necessary at all, I assure you." Blanche rose stiffly to her feet. "You're loathed the length and breadth of London, you chancrous scab. Even if you manage to take that girl from this house, do you think we'll leave her in your hands?"

"Oh," said Lord Deveril, "I think I can persuade her to be a biddable wife." Beth felt shivers run down her back.

"If you live to wed her," said Blanche.

Holding the trembling Clarissa, Beth desperately wished to gag the White Dove. She was going to get them all killed.

Lord Deveril, however, seemed to find amusement in the situation. "As you have so clearly stated, Mistress Blanche, I have plenty of enemies and yet I survive. I am well protected. Even," he added dismissively, "from an angry dove."

Blanche's lips turned up in what could have been a smile if her eyes had not been filled with hate. "You have not yet had an enemy like me, my lord," she said. She seemed to relax slightly and even rearranged the folds of her white-on-white figured skirt. A shrug of her shoulder made the neckline slip a little.

Beth carefully eased Clarissa back to a seat on the sofa, willing Blanche to stop before she provoked the man. If only he would go, even if he took Clarissa, there were still many opportunities to do something. If Blanche drove him to violence, none of them would survive.

It was too late. In chilling silence Lord Deveril gave Pigeyes his pistol and took the one he had fired. Without haste he took out his powder-box and loaded the second weapon. Beth watched in numb horror, wondering if this was the preparation for their deaths. Surely he wouldn't kill Clarissa, but she was convinced he could keep the girl so confined and terrorized that she would never tell what had occurred. But Lucien would know.

She spoke up quickly. "Arden brought Clarissa here. If anything happens to us, he will know the cause."

Lord Deveril looked at her with the flat malevolence of a snake. "Then I will have to kill him, too, won't I? Even a strong and healthy young man will fall before a pistol ball."

"You imagine you can call him out and win?"

"I am an excellent shot," remarked Lord Deveril, "but I don't think I would put myself to such inconvenience. A few guineas and any number of rogues would do the job from behind some bushes."

Beth felt as if her heart would stop. More than her own death, she could not endure the thought of Lucien's. Casually disposed of, dishonorably, from out of the shadows. She surprised in herself the sudden conviction that Lord Deveril *must* die. She, who had always despised violence, would shoot the man now, in cold blood, if she had the means.

Lord Deveril gave the newly loaded pistol to the other man.

"You are to guard those two," he said, indicating Beth and Clarissa. "If they cause any trouble, kill Lady Arden. Shoot my dear little Clarissa in the leg. Mistress Blanche, you will come with me."

"What are you going to do?" asked Beth.

"As the White Dove pointed out, I have never *had* an enemy like her. She is going to entertain me, with her hate to spice the pleasure. If she serves me well, you will all live. If she does not, you, Lady Arden, will die with her, and dear Clarissa will have yet more to bear to make up for my disappointment."

Clarissa gave a moan and Beth wrapped her arms around the girl. Blanche seemed little affected by all this, though Beth could no longer see her face. Lord Deveril jerked his thumb at the stairs and Blanche walked towards them. He spoke to his men. "I would let you watch if I didn't need you here. Never fear, I will find some suitable recompense." With that he followed the White Dove up to the bedroom.

Beth couldn't believe there was nothing she could do. God only knew what was going to happen upstairs, though she suspected that Blanche understood. And even if Lord Deveril left with Clarissa, leaving the rest of them alive, he would shoot down Lucien in cold blood. No, he couldn't let Beth live, for she would warn Lucien or report all to the duke. She had only lived so far as a weapon against Blanche.

Did the White Dove know it? Almost certainly. The maids too would die, leaving only poor Clarissa as witness to the whole. Once married she would not be able to testify, and her future life did not bear contemplation. Lord Deveril was surely mad, but it was a cunning madness backed by wealth, and Beth feared he would accomplish his plan.

Had Robin got away? Surely the bullies would have mentioned it if they had found an extra person in the house. Would he bring help? Even the officers of the law would be welcome now.

Beth looked at their two guards. They were bored but not unalert. "I feel faint," she said. "May I pour a glass of brandy for myself and Miss Greystone?"

The two men looked at each other, then Pig-eyes shrugged. "If you want. But don't try any tricks. I don't mind shooting you."

It was said with convincing callousness.

Beth walked to the sideboard wondering what a pistol ball felt like as it tore into flesh. Did it kill immediately or slowly?

She splashed spirits into two glasses with a shaking hand. She didn't want to die, fast or slow. She looked for anything she could use to any purpose. Short of hurling the decanter at one of the men, which would hardly have good effect, she could think of nothing.

"Would you gentlemen like some?" she asked, wondering if she could get them drunk.

"We'll have our pleasure later," said the bearded man with a grin unpleasantly reminiscent of his master. Beth shuddered. Perhaps death was the least of the evils she faced.

As she walked back towards the sofa with the glasses, there was a sharp, high-pitched cry from upstairs. She froze, looking up as if she could see through the plaster. The sound was not repeated.

"Ah, I wish I could see this one," muttered Pig-eyes, and the other sniggered.

"So proud and white," sneered Black-beard, "She won't be so white after he's had his way with her. Black and blue and bloody, too." They both grinned at their wit.

Beth sat down abruptly and thrust one of the glasses into Clarissa's hand. "Drink it. It's vile-tasting, but it helps. Drink."

She herself took a deep swallow and grimaced as it burned down. She thought she caught a movement outside the window. By great force of will she did not look. After a few seconds, she turned to place her glass upon a table. Through the lace curtains she saw the edge of Robin's face and a thumbs-up sign. She hastily looked away.

Her heart speeded. She had to struggle not to show the up-surge of hope. Who had Robin found? She didn't care. Their situation could not possibly be worse.

Though the men never stopped watching the two women, their other senses were clearly directed to catching traces of the events in the bedroom. Another cry came, this time more guttural and despairing. It almost sounded like a cry of death. Surely the deranged man wouldn't kill Blanche for his pleasure. Why not? They were all to die anyway.

Oh hurry, whoever you are!

There was a crash from above and a heavy thud. Clarissa gasped and spilled her untouched brandy.

The pig-eyed guard licked his moist lips and nudged the other man. "If we're going to kill the fancy one anyway," he said, giving up any pretense otherwise, "do you think he'll let us have her first? I need a woman bad."

"There's a chance," agreed the bearded one. "There's the maids, too."

"That's right," said Pig-eyes with enthusiasm. "I forgot the maids. One of 'em's a bit scraggy, but the other'd do. Gor, I wish I could go now. I hurt something bad."

"You'll hurt worse if he finds you've left your post."

Beth concentrated on keeping her face blank as she sensed movement in the hall behind the men. She wasn't sure she was breathing, but her mind seemed clear. Someone was there, and whoever it was was their hope of survival. She reached for her glass. As soon as she saw a figure, she knocked the crystal onto the floor. It shattered into a hundred pieces. Both men jumped.

Black-beard took a step forward. "Watch it—" He stopped speaking.

"You have a pistol against the back of your head," said the marquess, "and your friend is similarly favored. We can't possibly miss. Give us your weapons."

Beth saw Black-beard consider shooting her anyway—Lord Deveril must be a fearsome employer—but then he gave up his weapon with a curse into Lucien's hand. It was Robin who took the other pistol, for the man holding the gun to Pig-eyes's head was the one-armed Mr. Beaumont.

"Robin," said the marquess, "go and find something to tie these two." The boy dashed off.

"Lucien," said Beth, leaping to her feet. "You must help Blanche. He has her upstairs . . ."

The marquess looked at the two men and his one-armed friend, then beckoned Beth. When she had carefully moved next to him, he gave her the pistol. "Hold it so, pressed against the bone. If he twitches, just squeeze the trigger."

He gave her a quick kiss and then raced for the stairs. To stop.

Beth glanced up, then turned to look, forgetting the man at the end of her pistol. Blanche was descending the stairs with a long, wicked knife held loosely in her hand. Her gown was torn from her breasts and she was streaked with blood—a macabre study in red and white except for her eyes which were dilated black with horror.

" 'The sleeping and the dead are but as pictures,' " the actress quoted dreamily. Beth recognized the words of Lady Macbeth " 'Tis the eye of childhood that fears the painted devil. . . . Who would have thought the old man to have had so much blood in him.' "

"Blanche," said Lucien, rooted at the base of the stairs.

Hal Beaumont shook him and gave him his pistol. "Look to the men. They are more likely to require two hands."

Beaumont then went quickly up the stairs. He removed the knife from Blanche's relaxed grip and dropped it. Then he took her firmly in his one arm, despite the blood. "Did you kill him?" he said in a calm voice. "Good for you."

Beth remembered Hal had been a professional soldier, no stranger to gore. His matter-of-fact tone was just what was needed. The White Dove burst into body-shaking sobs.

Beth tightened her grip on the pistol and quickly looked back at her target, but both the bullies stood frozen. "She can't have killed him," Pig-eyes said. "She can't have."

"Whether she has or not," Lucien said coldly, "your part is over."

Robin scampered up from the basement with a length of rope and the men were securely bound, hand and foot. When Robin explained he'd got the rope by untying one of the maids, who'd promptly had hysterics, he was sent back with instructions to untie the other but keep the two women down there until further notice.

Then Lucien carefully relieved Beth of the weapon she still clutched in her hand and uncocked it before taking her in his arms. "Are you unhurt, sweetheart?"

It felt wonderful to be safe. "Oh yes, Lucien, but it's been horrible. The man is mad. Quite mad." She was trembling with reaction and fighting hard not to burst into tears herself. His hand gently stroked her neck.

"Was, I suspect. I don't think Blanche would mistake such a thing." He turned with Beth still cradled in his arms to look at the White Dove, protected by Mr. Beaumont's one strong arm.

The two of them had made their way down the stairs and Blanche's tears had ceased, though they could still be seen on her cheeks. Her gown had been rearranged to cover her and was fastened by what looked like a man's cravat pin.

"He is dead, Blanche?" Lucien asked.

"Oh yes," she replied with a calm which was a clear indication of shock. "I gutted him like a pig."

"I wanted to kill him," said Lucien in mock outrage.

"You'd have to stand in line," said Hal.

"He was mine," said Blanche with such a look in her eyes that the men gave up the flippant debate. "He was mine," she repeated and then took a deep shuddering breath and assumed a light manner. "I have always wanted to do *Macbeth,*" she remarked. "I think I will next season."

"God, Blanche . . ." Then Lucien just shook his head and went to pour four glasses of brandy. Everyone drank them to steady their nerves. Beth replaced Clarissa's scarce-touched glass in her hand and once again said, "Drink."

"She really killed him?" asked the girl faintly.

"I believe so."

"I'm glad really, but—"

"I know. Don't think about it. We don't need a scene, Clarissa."

The girl finally took a shuddering sip from her glass.

"I always keep a knife down the side of the bed," explained Blanche, who was a little more normal after the spirits, and consequently rather shaky. "I got into the habit quite early in life." She knocked off the last of her brandy. Her hand was visibly shaking. She looked down at herself and grimaced. "I must go and wash. The White Dove never wears colors . . . In the kitchen, I think."

"No," said Hal, looking at Blanche like a man seeing the Holy Grail. "Think of the poor maids. Go to one of the spare rooms and I'll bring you water. Just let me check on Deveril first. It's always possible he still lives."

He went upstairs and returned in a few moments, considerably paler. "You are rather thorough, aren't you?"

"He wanted to enjoy my hate in bed," said Blanche flatly. "I obliged him."

Clearly this was enough to startle even a soldier, but then a blissful smile spread over Hal's face and he tenderly escorted Blanche upstairs. In a few moments he came down for the water.

"I gather Blanche has a new protector," said Lucien dryly to his dazed friend.

"Protection? She doesn't need it," Hal said with a smile. "Isn't she magnificent? Anyway, I'm going to marry her." He shrugged and gave a slight smile. "Somehow. She isn't taken with the notion at the moment. I must admit, it's not the best time to have offered. But think of the magnificent offspring that hellcat would produce." He then hurried off on his errand.

Beth started to laugh. Once started, she could not stop until the hysteria dissolved into painful tears. She clung to Lucien and he gently drew her down to sit on his lap.

She heard his awkward, concerned murmurs. "There, there. Don't cry, love. You're safe. I'll never let anyone hurt you . . ."

"He—he was going to have you *killed*."

"Me? Why?"

Beth pulled herself together and sat up a little. Her bonnet was askew and the silly curls were plastered by tears to her cheek. "I must look a sight . . . Because you would revenge me. He was utterly mad."

"What I want to know," asked Lucien with an attempt to severity, "is how you came into his hands. How you came here at all."

"I came to check on Clarissa," said Beth.

"You had no business coming anywhere near this house."

"You brought me here last night!"

"An unfortunate necessity. You will not come here again. It's the outside of enough—"

Beth leapt to her feet and stood facing him. "You will not rule me, Lucien de Vaux. Husband or no husband, marquess, duke, or king!"

After a stunned moment, Lucien burst into laughter. "Oh, Beth. How could I survive without you? Don't tell me. You and Blanche are bosom-bows."

"Precisely."

"Beth, you can't . . ." He shook his head. "Oh, to hell with it. You probably can. Hal's mad enough to marry her, too, if he can get her to agree. I suppose it's no worse than John Lade marrying Sixteen-String Jack's leavings."

"Who?"

"You've probably never met Letty Lade. Doesn't exactly move in my mother's circles. Sir John's coaching mad and so's his wife. Own their own rig and drive like maniacs. Letty's an innkeeper's daughter from East Cheap and she took up with a highwayman, Sixteen-String Jack. When he was hanged, she married Sir John, but she's still a foul-mouthed trull at heart. Blanche is another type entirely."

"She certainly—"

"Oh!" They were interrupted by Clarissa, huddled forgotten in a corner of the sofa. "How *can* you? Beth, I thought you were a lady. A person of sensibility. These people are all mad. Everyone's mad. That woman is a . . . a . . ." She glared at them and forced the word out. "A whore! She's just killed someone. Up there." She looked at the molded ceiling with dilated eyes. "I keep expecting blood to seep down. Did you see all the blood?"

Beth quickly picked up the girl's glass. "Clarissa, drink this!" She forced the liquid into the shaking girl's mouth. Clarissa spluttered and started to choke. Beth thumped her firmly on the back, and the girl started to cry.

Beth took her shoulders in a firm grip. "Clarissa, stop that, and listen to me. All this has happened because of you. I won't say it was your fault, but this has come about because of people trying to help you."

Clarissa stopped crying and stared at Beth, looking much younger than eighteen.

"Mrs. Hardcastle has been kind to you. She did what she did to save us all, me from death and you from Lord Deveril. It is not for you to judge her morals."

"But—"

"No."

Clarissa subsided.

Beth let the girl go. "I am not sure what we're going to do now, but you are to tell no one, no one at all, about what has happened here today. Do you understand?"

Clarissa nodded. "But what is to become of me?"

"Well, at least," drawled the marquess, "you won't have to marry Deveril. Pity you weren't already hitched, though. You'd be a rich widow."

Beth had an inspiration but schooled her features. She wasn't sure it was one she wanted to share with Lucien just yet.

There was a knock at the door, a significant pattern of raps. Lucien hurried to open it. Nicholas Delaney came in with Lord Middlethorpe. His quick gold-flecked eyes took in the bound men, glass on the floor, the streaks of blood on the banister, and the gory knife. "Francis, we've missed the action."

Lord Middlethorpe pocketed the pistol in his hand. "Is everyone all right, Luce?" he asked. "We just got an incoherent message from your man Dooley."

"Everyone except Deveril," Lucien said with a meaningful glance at the knife.

"I rejoice," said Nicholas with a smile. "Who gets the reward?"

"Blanche," said Lucien.

Nicholas's smile widened. "One can always rely on a good woman." He looked around. "It seems to me we can do our bit by tidying up. Get rid of the body and all that. I think you should take these ladies away. Who's with the heroine?"

"Hal," said Lucien and shrugged. "He says he's going to marry her."

Beth could tell Lucien was relieved to have reinforcements,

particularly Nicholas Delaney. Beth shared the feeling. Nicholas just gave the impression that everything would turn out well.

"I approve," Nicholas said. "We need more viragos in our circle. For one thing, a woman could probably fix that toy grenadier. None of us can." He stepped carefully around the glass on the floor and shepherded Beth and a very dazed Clarissa towards the hall.

He wrapped an arm about Clarissa and gave her a brotherly, but very firm, hug. Beth realized that while she had been hugged and comforted by Lucien, and Blanche by Hal, no one had looked after Clarissa until now. "I'm Nicholas Delaney," he said to the girl. "You must be Clarissa Greystone. Don't worry about anything. I think it's all going to work out."

Clarissa clung to him and mumbled something incoherent.

Beth saw his hand come up to rub firmly at the back of the girl's head. "Yes, I know. But the worst is over. The best thing for now may be for you to go back to your family."

"No!" protested Clarissa, pulling away from him.

"They have been most cruel to her," Beth protested.

"If you take her home," Nicholas said, "and she pretends to be repentant and willing, I don't think they'll be too angry. Make it clear she has the support and friendship of the de Vaux. The Greystones will hesitate before offending you."

He looked at Clarissa. "You won't have to be enthusiastic about marrying Deveril, that would be uncalled for. Just act cowed. If we're clever, his body won't be found and identified for days. When his death is discovered you will have some time before your parents can come up with another such. By then matters may well be different anyway."

"How can things change?" Clarissa asked, but it was clear his tone of calm confidence was giving her courage.

"In all kinds of ways. For one thing, somewhere in Belgium the great battle is over."

"There's news?" Beth and Lucien demanded in unison.

"Only the vaguest. Nathan Rothschild knows something. He sold heavily and now he's buying at low prices. They say he uses pigeons while the government relies on riders. As well, a man called Sutton who captains a packet out of Ostend has brought word that the battle was well under way some days since and wounded were already arriving in Brussels and Ghent. There's little firm news." After a moment he added, "I spoke to him. He says the 42nd were hit hard."

"Con's regiment," said Lucien.

"Yes." Nicholas gave a movement of frustration. "It's all happened, of course. Somewhere in this same world the living are rejoicing, the dead are dead, the wounded are suffering under the knife. . . . And maybe tomorrow or the next day we'll find out about it."

"Is it a victory, though?" asked Lucien.

"It's always a victory for somebody," Nicholas said wryly. Then he snapped out of his philosophical mood. "The indications are yes, but the Stock Exchange is hesitant after Rothschild's little foray. The odds are, however, that definite news will break at any minute and London will be in turmoil for the next few days. Excellent conditions for concealing our nefarious plans. Take the ladies away, Luce, and let us clean up."

"That reminds me," said Lucien. "There's a lad of mine, Beth's maid, and Blanche's housemaid downstairs."

"Will they keep their mouths shut?"

"Blanche's Agnes will keep mum. She saved her from the workhouse. Robin can be trusted, I think." He turned to Beth. "What about your abigail?"

"I think Redcliff will hold her tongue. It would be as well, though, if she didn't realize the full extent of what has occurred."

Lucien thought for a moment. "Why don't you and Clarissa leave by the back way. You can pick up Redcliff and Robin. I'll take the curricle and meet you at the end of the lane." He drew Beth into the warm comfort of his arms, kissed her gently, then left.

Feeling wonderfully strengthened, Beth shepherded Clarissa down into the cozy kitchen. There they found the two maids and Robin. Both the maids leapt up and began to gabble at once, but Beth quelled them.

"Silence! Agnes, your mistress is unhurt but she does not

wish to be disturbed at the moment. You are not to go upstairs until you are summoned. Redcliff and Robin, we are leaving."

"Yes, milady."

As soon as they were out of the door and walking through the small garden to the back lane, Beth said, "Neither of you is to breathe a word about anything that happened here today. Do you understand?"

A bright-eyed Robin said, "Yes, milady."

Redcliff, obviously much shaken, said, "I'm sure I wouldn't know what to say if asked, milady! Tied up. And that man touched my—Well, I really don't know. That Agnes said there were three men, and guns. Was it a robbery?"

"An attempt at one," said Beth. "Nothing was taken." She suddenly realized how to handle the maid. "But you must see, Redcliff, that it would be disastrous for anyone to discover I visited this house."

"Indeed I do," said the maid sternly.

Beth adopted a repentant attitude. "I didn't quite realize," she said. "It was only when the marquess arrived that I saw how wrong it was. No one must suspect."

"My lips are sealed, milady," said the maid with resolute kindness.

"Thank you Redcliff," said Beth meekly and caught up to Clarissa.

Redcliff and Robin were sent to walk home while Beth and Lucien drove a nervous Clarissa to her parent's hired house. Beth assured the girl there would be no more beatings and just hoped that was true.

Clarissa's parents were too relieved at having their hope of solvency returned to them to rage, and were quite overwhelmed by the exalted company their daughter was keeping. They didn't even question the story that Clarissa had taken refuge with an unnamed school friend where Beth had discovered her.

Beth made much of Clarissa in her farewells. Lucien dealt out the de Vaux arrogance with a heavy hand. By the time they left they could be fairly sure the girl would receive no more than a scold.

"Though I suppose we'll have all this to go through again

when the next husband's lined up," said Lucien as they drove toward Marlborough Square.

Not necessarily, thought Beth, but she said nothing. She had to think through her plan and decide whether her husband would be for or against it.

By the time they entered Belcraven House it was close to dinner time, but the thought of eating in state deprived Beth of any appetite. As they entered the house she said, "I think I would like to have a quiet meal in my room."

"My thought entirely," said Lucien with a smile. Beth became aware of their situation again and promises that had been made. She stared at him nervously. It was not even dark yet, and after the events of the afternoon . . .

"Don't worry," he said gently. "Go and change into something more comfortable and rest. I'll arrange everything and be up in a little while."

Chapter Twenty-one

"I'll arrange everything." Beth was filled with a warm trust which eased away her anxieties. She returned his smile and climbed the stairs.

She did not quite feel it appropriate to put on her nightwear, however, and changed her walking gown for a soft muslin with simple drawstrings at neck and waist. She had Redcliff brush her hair into its natural style. She didn't even bother with the cosmetics to hide the bruise. *Without honesty there is nothing.*

Finally she gave Redcliff the evening off and lay on the chaise in her boudoir. The events of the afternoon had already become like a dream. Had she really been held at gunpoint in danger of her life? She remembered the threat to Lucien's life, however, with crystal clarity. Her heart started pounding even at the thought. Oh, it was frightening to love like this. What had this to do with *Self-Control?*

There was no place in her heart for rationalization, no place for moral judgment. She remembered him saying, "Even if you were debauched, I would still love you." She felt exactly the same. Love was a madness, a tyrant.

It was wonderful.

When he walked in she smiled and held out her hand. He came over and sat on the edge of the chaise. He had discarded his jacket, his waistcoat, and his cravat. In the open-necked lawn shirt and buff pantaloons he looked relaxed and . . . and accessible.

Jo Beverley

She raised a hand and touched the skin of his chest at the base of his throat.

"How can you look so bright-eyed?" he asked as he covered her hand with his. He felt hot to her fingers.

"Because I'm in love," she replied softly.

His smile widened. "So am I. Remarkable, isn't it?"

"Convenient, at least," she teased. "You were worried once, I remember, about me falling in love with someone else."

He shook his head and drew her into a warm embrace. "Don't. I don't ever want to think about the things that have happened, the things we have said. Let's put everything behind us."

She rubbed her cheek slowly against his chest. The fine weave of his shirt was silky soft, but his flesh beneath seemed to burn. She could sense the pounding of his heart and each breath brought the warm and musky scent that was his alone. "I don't want to forget anything," she said. "Everything that is you, I will cherish to my dying day."

His fingers gently traced her discolored cheek. "Even this?"

"Even that," she said, looking up at his troubled face. "Because I know it will never happen again. The circumstances were a little strange, after all."

It was most extraordinary. All he was doing was holding her and yet her mouth was dry and her heart was pounding. A faint, aching need was growing in her that was driving her. Demanding. She reached up and took his face between her hands.

"Kiss me, Lucien."

His mouth settled on hers, slick and hot, assuaging some of her hunger. Her hands slipped into the crisp silk of his hair to hold him close and she opened to taste the sweetness of him. His tongue played against hers, and her whole world concentrated into that point of contact. Then she collapsed back and his solid warmth settled over her so that the delight extended the length of her body, every part in contact with him.

It was not nearly enough.

She felt his hand at her breast through the soft muslin, a thumb rubbing softly at her nipple. When the kiss ended, his mouth trailed down to play at the same spot, and a shudder passed through her like a wave.

He deftly changed their positions so she was lying in his lap. Clever fingers made short work of the drawstring at the neckline of her gown. Beth made a brief, instinctive move of denial but then relaxed. She was his. He smoothed the creamy material back from her breasts.

"Ah, my darling," he breathed softly as one long finger slowly circled first one nipple then the other. Watching her with a loving smile he played with her. Beth was trapped by his passionate eyes as her body was caught in delicious, spiraling magic. Then his mouth came down, warm and moist to tease her.

Beth released a shuddering sigh. "Oh heavens. Oh, Venus and Mars," she whispered.

"What?" he asked, laughing.

"I'll tell you sometime. Not now. Don't stop."

"Oh, I won't, my love," he said huskily, his fingers returning to their magic game. "Just promise me there's no surprise guest next door. No secrets lurking."

Beth shook her head, hot and dizzy. "Nothing." She feasted her eyes on his beauty. The long muscles of his neck begged to be stroked, and she raised her hand to them. Then she boldly slid her hand inside the neckline of his shirt to feel the rippling muscles of his shoulder.

He caught his breath and she hesitated. "Am I allowed to do this?" she asked.

He stripped off his shirt. "You can do anything, Beth. Touch me anywhere. Ask anything of me."

Beth looked at his beautiful torso and licked her lips. It was finely muscled and tawny from some type of masculine outdoor exercise. She wondered what, and if she might have the chance to watch. There was a line of golden curls down the center of his chest, and she reached up to tangle her finger in them.

"You are very beautiful, my husband."

"And so are you, my dearest wife."

Beth moved to plant little kisses over his warm and silky

skin and found this brought her naked breasts against his chest, where they found a new delicious pleasure. She heard his breathing become ragged and delighted in it. Perhaps Venus could take part as well as Mars. She let her tongue begin to trace moist patterns working towards his small, flat nipples. He stood suddenly with her in his arms.

"My room, you requested, madam?"

"That was only because of Clarissa," Beth mumbled, continuing her delicious work.

"Never mind," he said unsteadily and twirled her around and around across the room.

At the door he bent slightly and Beth turned the knob. They progressed through the sequence of rooms somewhat unsteadily, but finally arrived at his bedroom.

Beth had never been here before. It was, as he had said, very much like her own save that the colors were greens and golds, not blues. The bed was larger and had a canopy over it with curtains hanging down which tied back against the wall. When he laid her down on the silken cover, she saw the underside of the canopy was decorated with his coat of arms.

Beth chuckled. "For the glory and honor of the de Vaux!" she declared, opening her arms.

He fell beside her on the bed so that the whole solid frame shuddered. "Indeed yes. Lots and lots of little de Vaux. Don't mind the escutcheon," he said, laying a flat possessive hand on her abdomen. "It was commissioned by my grandmother for my father. She didn't think he was sufficiently aware of his dignity."

"The duke?" Beth queried in surprise. Her mind seemed to be neatly divided—one half in passion, aware of his hand as a fire which burnt its way into her, the other still capable of rational conversation. She decided to try fingers on his nipples. Then, gently, her nails.

Lucien sucked in a sharp breath. "He was . . . less starchy in his youth, I gather. Beth!" He captured her hand and kissed each fingertip moistly. Then he began to suck on them. He rolled onto his back and carried her with him so she lay on top of him. "Don't worry," he said as his fingers loosened the waist-tie at her back, "I've been sleeping under the thing since I left the nursery and it hasn't stiffened me yet." The drawstring fell loose, and her dress was held in place by nothing at all.

Lucien's fingers played messages on her bare back. "But speaking of stiffening . . ." he said softly.

Positioned as she was, Beth was perfectly, and nervously, aware of his stiffening. All unconsciously, she wriggled, and he caught his breath and held her still. With a wicked smile, Beth fought his hold and wriggled again. She had never realized what fun it could be to stir a response.

"God save me," he muttered and rolled her off him. "Listen, you delicious wanton, you can seduce me and drive me to incoherent delight as often as you want after the first time, but I'd rather have some hold on my senses just now."

"Why?"

"Because I don't want to hurt you, my love," he said seriously, cradling her head, "and believe it or not, I've never taken virginity before."

"That's ridiculous."

"Why?" he asked as his hand slipped down the front of her body and came to rest at the cleft of her thighs. "I can't see that it adds to the pleasure. Look what it's doing to us now. I could be lying helpless under your delectable, wriggling body." He leaned down and brushed his lips softly over hers. "Let me love you, Beth, and carry you to delight. This time, just let me love you . . ."

It hardly needed the touch of his lips to spin her beyond thought, beyond control, beyond everything except pure sensation. His hands worked tantalizingly up her body beneath her loosened gown. It was up and over her head and she was naked. She hardly noticed, except that it was better to have her skin against his. She wrapped her arms around his chest and filled her mouth with his flesh. It was a hunger she felt. A driving need to engulf and possess.

He left her briefly and returned. Now the contact was complete, head to toe. He parted her legs and moved between. Suddenly, the hunger, the need, the ache, all centered there.

"Lucien," she moaned.

"I know, love," he said unevenly. "I know."

He began to slide slowly, tentatively, into her. Beth's need coalesced into driving hunger. This. This was what she wanted. She rose to meet him and the brief pain was nothing. She wrapped her legs around him in fierce delight.

She lay in the dim evening light, resting her head on his shoulder, playing gently with the sweat-damp curls on his chest. "That was remarkable," she said.

"Thank you," he replied. His chest shook slightly with a chuckle.

"Oh. Was it just you, then?" she asked with an assumption of innocence. "Would it not be like that with anyone?"

"Beth," he warned.

She turned on her front and looked up at him. "No free love?"

He tried to look stern. "Only with me."

Beth began to feel breathless again just looking at him. A Greek god. She'd thought that when she'd first seen him, and it had terrified her. Now it excited her. His hair was in disarray and darkened by sweat along his brow. His color was heightened, and his eyes seemed a brighter blue than ever. His magnificent body was stretched beside her, smooth and muscular. Hers. Hers to touch, to taste, to take within her.

"And you?" she asked. "Will there be free love for you?"

He gathered her into a fierce embrace. "Impossible. I can't imagine wanting any other woman, my pearl. You radicals do have a way of taming the aristocracy, don't you?"

"We'll do anything for the cause," said Beth contentedly.

It was a considerable time later that they ordered a meal. It was already dusk and the candles had to be lit. They were hungry by then, but that didn't stop them feeding one another tidbits and stopping often for a kiss. They talked of their time together and the time before they had been together. For the first time they shared the hidden parts—the hurts and disappointments of their lives, the hopes and the dreams.

Beth tentatively raised the question of social issues and found that in his own way, he was not indifferent. One of the reasons there were so many servants in the de Vaux houses, he told her, was to give employment. It was family policy to buy local products as much as possible and they were careful of the needs of their tenants.

Beth's instinct might say that it was not enough when the family continued to live in such rich state and yet she had learned to balance two very different realities. Little purpose would be served by the de Vaux family going off to live in a cottage on dark bread and stew. It was enough for the moment to know that her beloved did not look on hardship with callous indifference.

The clocks were striking midnight when they extinguished the guttering candles and climbed into the big bed to snuggle together. Beth let her hands stroke over the beloved contours of his back, but he captured them.

"Oh no, you don't, you enchantress. I'll go odds you'll be sore enough tomorrow as it is. And I'm only a mortal man, you know."

But Beth was a clever student and would not be restrained. *"Hoc volo, sic iubio, sit pro ratione voluntas,"* she said with a grin as she slid on top of him and wriggled. "I refuse to be reasonable. What I want, I get. And I want to seduce you to incoherent delight."

She saw his eyes darken, but he grabbed her to try and hold her still. "Back to the schoolroom for you, my girl," he said huskily. "That is not a good translation."

Beth nibbled on the nearest tasty object, which happened to be his earlobe. His grip relaxed. "At a time like this, Lucien," she muttered, "you expect a good translation?"

"I've lost faith in the classics entirely," he said unsteadily as she moved to one side and her hand wandered down past his navel. "God, Beth . . ."

She found the hot, velvety firmness of him. "And what have the classics to do with this?" she asked softly.

"Juvenal," he said like a groan. " *'Nemo repente fuit terpissimus.'* 'No one becomes depraved in a moment.' The man was a fool, or he just didn't know anyone like you."

Softly in the dark he added, "Poor man."

Chapter Twenty-two

The next day Beth had considerable trouble getting rid of her husband. She knew how he felt. She could hardly bear to be out of his company for a moment and yet it was necessary for her plan. She wasn't at all sure he would approve.

Military matters helped. They breakfasted together sharing a copy of the *Times* and reading the Duke of Wellington's dispatch. As yet there was no news of casualties except for the death of the Duke of Brunswick.

"It was clearly a terrible battle," Beth said at last.

"But a great victory. See what it says, 'A complete overthrow of the enemy.' Wellington's not one for hollow boasts. Napoleon's done for at last."

"But at what cost?" She was thinking of all the soldiers, but chiefly of the ones she knew, Amleigh and Debenham. It was unthinkable that those merry, vibrant young men, no older than Lucien, be dead, and yet it could be so. There had been that report that said Amleigh's regiment had suffered.

She saw the look in Lucien's eyes. She didn't really understand this group of friends he had, Nicholas and the rest, but it was clearly a deep relationship. It would hurt him bitterly if any of them suffered. Hurt them all.

She laid her hand over his. "When will the lists be out?"

"At any time," he said. "They may put out a special edition of the paper."

Beth sighed. "There's so much grief just waiting to be unleashed. I'm thinking what it would be like if you were there."

His hand tightened on hers. "And we're just hoping the people we care for aren't on the list."

There was no ulterior motive when Beth said, "Why don't you go to your club or to the Delaneys'. There may be more to discover."

"You don't mind? Or you could come with me to Nicholas's"

"No, I'd rather stay here for now."

He left her with a kiss. Beth knew he shared her guilt at being so happy, so fulfilled, when the happiness of others was all at an end. It was always so with war, she supposed. Today London would echo with the cheers of victory while many, many people wept.

Eventually she got a grip on herself and put her plan into action. She claimed she was going back to bed and did not want to be disturbed. As soon as Redcliff had gone away, however, Beth got up again and dressed. She carefully applied the concealing cosmetics to her face though she couldn't persuade herself that they would fool careful scrutiny. Blanche knew the worst anyway. Then Beth chose the old clothes she had brought from Miss Mallory's and her most concealing bonnet. Inconspicuous, she hoped, she crept down the servants' staircase and out of the coal-room door.

She needed to contact Robin, for she still wasn't certain of the way to Blanche's house, and she needed to speak to him without alerting anyone to her "escape" from Belcraven House. She bit her lip and chuckled as she glanced up at the massive mansion. It was ridiculous to be creeping out like this when no one could actually stop her if she chose to walk out of the front door.

She'd probably drive Lucien to contemplate violence again, once he found out what she was up to. That she felt no tremor of fear told her she really did trust him. She knew she had a foolish smile on her face as she slipped down towards the mews.

What excuse could she make for her visit, and how could she speak to Robin alone? For excuse she could say she was visiting Stella. The poor beast had been given little enough exercise since Hartwell—only two trots in the park. Privacy with Robin was more of a problem. Granger or Dooley would appear like a shot when the marchioness visited the mews.

She was rubbing Stella's soft, velvety nose when Granger appeared.

"Good morning, milady. Can I help you?"

"No thank you, Granger. I just wanted to visit Stella. I hope he is being exercised."

"Never fear, ma'am. Robin takes him out. The only horse he's much good for," the man grumbled. "And, begging your pardon, it does the scamp no good to be taken away from his work and given privileges. Getting above himself for sure."

"Oh," said Beth, concealing a smile as she saw her excuse. "That is unfortunate. Perhaps I should speak to him about it."

"Well, there's no need—"

Beth gave him a de Vaux look.

In a few moments she was talking to Robin in Stella's stall. The boy eyed the horse nervously all the time.

"Really, Robin," said Beth, "you can't possibly be scared of Stella. He has the sweetest nature."

Robin just looked down sullenly.

"I do think it would be better if you let us find some other position for you," she said gently. "Is there nothing you'd rather do?"

The boy wriggled around and scuffed up some wisps of hay. "Don't mind as long as I serve him," he muttered.

Beth smiled as she understood at last. Pure hero worship. "I'll think about it, Robin. Now, I want you to take me to Mrs. Hardcastle's. Without telling anyone."

The boy looked up, wide-eyed. "I can't, milady. Old Granger'll have me hide. Honest he will."

"Robin. If I give you a task, it is nothing to do with Granger."

Robin fidgeted some more. "The marquess told me not to," he muttered at last, looking down.

"The marquess! When?"

"This mornin'. Said if you asked, I weren't to."

Well, the cunning rogue, thought Beth, not unhappy to be

back in a battle of wits with her husband. She bit her lip as she thought.

"Can you tell me how to get there, Robin?" she asked at last.

He looked up. "You'd never go by yerself, milady!"

"Why not? It didn't seem a very dangerous route."

"Ladies just don't," he said with a masculine assertiveness which made her eyes twinkle.

"This lady does as she pleases," said Beth firmly. "If you don't tell me I'll just try to remember the way and ask for directions if I become lost."

This clearly alarmed the boy even more. After a few more protests he gave in. "They'll be standing in line to leather me after this one," he muttered morosely.

He gave the directions clearly enough, however, and Beth slipped him a crown as she left.

For the first little while she felt an itching between her shoulder blades and expected pursuit. Then she settled and began to enjoy the walk. It was a fresh June day and the streets were a-bustle with people. The excitement of the news of the victorious engagement was fizzing about London like champagne. Every now and then some man would call out, "Three cheers for Wellington!" and everyone would huzzah.

The mood was so good, however, that Beth felt in no danger. As there was little chance of recognition in her dowdy clothes and wearing a concealing bonnet, she was enjoying being one of the people again instead of isolated in the ranks of the high aristocracy. She decided there were changes to be made in her life. She grinned at the thought of the battles to come over it.

Soon she left the busier thoroughfares behind and did experience some nervousness as the streets became quieter. Then she took herself to task. These were hardly notorious warrens, full of beggars and criminals, but quietly genteel residential streets. She had walked through such areas in Cheltenham all her life. Just because she was the Marchioness of Arden she would not be deprived of her freedom.

When she was close to Blanche's house, however, she acted

on a cautious impulse and went down the back lane instead of knocking at the front door.

Agnes, the maid, gawked when Beth walked into the kitchen. There was another person there, a wizened older woman who was obviously the cook.

Agnes dropped a bemused curtsy. The cook put her hands on her hips. "And who might you be?"

"Hush, Lily. It's . . . it be the march'ness. You know."

The cook gaped, too. "Lord love us. What is the world coming to? You ought to be ashamed of yourself," she said to Beth.

"Well, I'm not," said Beth, holding back amusement. "Is Blanche in?"

Agnes rubbed her hands on her apron. "I'll go ask. Please to take a seat . . ." She looked helplessly at the two plain chairs. "Oh, I don't know," she wailed as she left the room.

"Now see what you've done," said Lily. "And I'd just got her calmed down after all that business yesterday! We all get along a deal better when your sort keeps to yourselves in your fancy houses."

Beth sat in one of the chairs. "Are you an admirer of Mary Wollstonecraft, too?" she asked in a friendly manner.

"Who? Not if she's one of the nobs."

"Well," said Beth thoughtfully, "I suppose in a way she was." She was quite prepared for an enjoyable philosophical discussion when Agnes returned with a surprised Blanche.

"Beth, I have the feeling you shouldn't be here," said the White Dove.

"More than likely," replied Beth.

"More than likely," echoed the cook. "You watch yourself, Maggie. Her sort's no good for you."

"Hush, Lily," said Blanche in a comfortable way. "I know what I'm about. Agnes, we'll have tea, please."

With that she escorted her guest to the parlor. Beth noticed the bloodstains had been removed from the stairs and there was no sign of the previous day's events except for the absence of the chandelier.

"You have interesting servants," she said as she took a seat.

"They serve me well," said Blanche. "As you may have

guessed, I choose unfortunates. I admit it's partly because it
would be hard for one such as myself to find good staff who
wouldn't be insolent, but it's also because I've known poverty
and despair. Agnes I picked from the workhouse. Her whole
family was sent there when her father died. I trained her, thinking she'd move on, but she chooses to stay. Lily, now Lily
helped me when I was young, when I first ran away from
home. She's been more a mother to me than my own mother,
but she won't play the lady. Doesn't hold with it. I hope she
wasn't rude. She has no reason to love the higher orders."

"I like her. Perhaps in time she'll come to accept me."

"You really plan to make a friendship of this, then?" said
Blanche. "Lucien won't like it you know. Men don't like their
lives muddied."

"We all have to make adjustments," said Beth. "And when
you're married to his best friend—"

"Which will be never," said Blanche firmly, though Beth
was interested to see that she blushed. "The man's wits have
gone begging. I've told him I'll consider an . . . an arrangement."

Beth let the matter pass though if she'd been a gambling
woman she would lay odds the White Dove's days of freedom
were numbered. "Has everything been sorted out?" she asked,
not able to bring herself to refer directly to the body.

"Yes," said Blanche. "That Nicholas Delaney is a remarkably efficient gentleman. With some interesting accomplices.
I didn't ask too many questions, but I gather the hired bullies
have been press-ganged and the body, with identification removed, has been left in the warrens of St. Giles. He'll be found
in a day or two, I suppose. In that quarter, no one's going to
ask too many questions. Even Bow Street only goes there in
numbers. Deveril had been known to haunt those parts looking
for something to slake his tastes, so I don't suppose there'll
be great surprise."

Beth shuddered. "He was more horrible than I imagined. It
is incredible that men such as he be tolerated merely because
they have inherited a title. Inherited privilege is very wrong."

"Perhaps," said Blanche with a smile. "But take my advice

and fight the skirmishes, Beth, don't take on the war. There's plenty for good-hearted people to do without destroying themselves and those they love."

Beth considered her newfound friend seriously. "You mean Lucien?"

Blanche nodded. "He's making great progress, but you'll never turn him into a William Godwin or a Wilberforce. He's a damn-your-eyes de Vaux and always will be."

"I know it. And," said Beth with a rueful smile, "apologies to Mary Wollstonecraft, I wouldn't want him any other way. Which reminds me, I had better get on with my reason for coming here and return to Marlborough Square before he realizes I'm gone."

She paused a moment while Agnes brought the tea tray and Blanche poured. She sipped the tea, finding it a little hard to broach the subject. "Blanche, how do you feel about forgery? And, I suppose, burglary."

Blanche put down her cup. "They're hanging matters, Beth."

Beth licked her lips. "I know. But I doubt it would come to that anyway, with the power of the de Vaux family involved. Isn't that terrible?" she remarked. "I'm just as bad as they are."

"Beth," said Blanche. "Say what you have in mind."

Beth took a deep breath. "If what he told me is true, Deveril has no heir. The title and fortune will revert to the Crown. What if Clarissa was his heir?"

Blanche sat up straighter. "A will?"

Beth nodded. "It would have to be found in his house," she said. "I think that's the most dangerous part."

"We'd need a sample of his writing anyway . . ."

Beth sat with her hands gripped together. She must be mad. This was definitely against the law. Inexcusable. Except, of course, that it would solve so many problems. "Deveril was reputed to be very rich," she said out loud. "When the will is found, Lucien's solicitor could make sure at least some of the money was tied up for Clarissa. Her family would take the rest, no doubt. It should keep them out of the Fleet for a while."

"And, little as I like the sound of them, they will make better use of it than Deveril ever did," said Blanche.

"And why should it go into the bottomless pit of the government? The Regent would only buy another gold trinket or two."

They looked at each other, both slightly awed by the plan.

"Can it be done?" Beth asked.

Blanche nodded. "Will you tell Lucien?"

"I don't know," said Beth.

There was a sharp rap of the knocker. Agnes came hurrying across the hall. Blanche said, "I have a feeling . . ."

Beth said, "So do I." She felt her nerves begin to twitch.

Lucien walked in. "You," he said to Beth, "need to be locked up."

Despite the words, he couldn't help but smile, and she couldn't help but echo it. It was nearly two hours since they'd parted, after all.

He sat down beside her and took her hand. "Tell me what you're up to. The whole truth."

Despite the smile, Beth knew the demand was serious. Wishing her heart wasn't doing a nervous dance in the back of her throat, she gave him a speedy outline of her idea.

"My God, woman!" he exploded. "I'm revising all my notions of wife-beating."

"Ha!" she snapped back. "As soon as you're crossed—"

"Crossed! You're looking to me to save you from the noose! Peers of the realm have been hanged before now, you know. And having it done with a silken rope can't be much consolation."

Beth just looked at him. After a moment his lips twitched. "It is a rather clever plan," he said more moderately. "Better than Nicholas's, in fact."

"Nicholas's?" both women said.

"I've just come from there. Via Marlborough Square," he said with a mock frown, "where I discovered my poor exhausted wife had recovered her energy."

Beth just gave him a saucy smile. "What is this about a plan of Nicholas's? What interest has he in Clarissa?"

"None, but he has his own reasons for wanting to deprive Deveril of his money. Since it's all sitting there in his house in steel-banded chests, we had pretty well decided to go in and take it."

"House-breaking!" exclaimed Blanche. "You're all mad."

"Not really. We have a peer of the realm, a de Vaux, and a member of parliament on board, not to mention the disorder at Deveril's place because of his disappearance and the growing chaos in the streets because of the celebrations. Which reminds me," he said to Beth with exasperation, "of all the days to choose to walk about unescorted, why pick today?"

"Because today is today," she retorted. "And, I should point out, I've been walking the streets unescorted all my life. And," she said, rolling over his attempt to speak, "it occurs to me to wonder how long you overgrown schoolboys have been hatching your plan and why you never said a word to me."

"Overgrown schoolboys!" He swallowed that and continued, "It was nothing to do with you, Beth. It was old, unfinished business."

"It was to do with me when I expressed concern about Clarissa being forced to marry the man. You just stormed out, thinking I was complaining about our affairs."

He frowned in puzzlement. "Oh, that time. But you never mentioned who the husband was to be. It was only the other night that I realized Deveril was involved. It was only then I developed any sympathy for the girl. I thought she was just being miss-ish."

Blanche, who had been the fascinated audience of this squabble, cleared her throat. "We were discussing burglary, forgery, and a number of other criminal offenses," she reminded them.

"So we were," said Lucien. He turned to Beth. "I think what we ought to do is go over to Lauriston Street and put your idea to Nicholas, but I don't think we should involve Blanche any more than necessary."

Beth rose. "Of course not. I only came here because I hadn't the faintest idea how to bring about anything illegal and I thought Blanche might." She turned to the actress. "Do you?"

"Not from first-hand experience, no," said the actress dryly. "But I have a few disreputable friends. Including, it would appear, Lucien de Vaux."

He grinned unrepentantly. "And Hal Beaumont. He's at Nicholas's." He winked. "Why don't you come with us?"

Blanche blushed again. "I have lines to learn for tonight."

"Coward," teased Lucien.

Blanche glared at him.

Beth stood and shook hands with the White Dove. "I'll see you again soon, my friend."

"No, you won't," said Lucien.

"When you're Mrs. Beaumont," said Beth firmly.

"Which will be never," retorted Blanche.

Beth simply laughed at both of them.

When they arrived at Lauriston Street, the house was crowded as usual. Eleanor rolled her eyes at Beth. "Have you heard? They're all quite mad. I expect to live to see them strung up in a row."

"I think we have a slightly less dangerous plan to offer," Beth said. As she took off her bonnet, she watched Eleanor, but if she noticed the bruise she gave no sign.

When they were settled in the drawing room Lucien gave Beth the floor to explain her plan. Despite her belief in equality, she felt rather nervous to be addressing a large group of men—six members of the Company of Rogues, Peter Lavering, and a rotund little man called Tom Holloway.

When she'd explained, however, everyone approved.

"I like it," said Nicholas. "It has subtlety and I do like subtlety. Apart from planting the will in Deveril's house, there's no real danger. I know an excellent forger I can trust."

Tom Holloway said, "We'll need a sample of his writing, Nick, and it has to be done quickly. If the will's found in his desk as soon as the body's discovered, it's less likely to be questioned than if it suddenly turns up after the event."

"I wonder if Clarissa has anything he wrote," said Lucien. Beth gave a little gasp. "Probably not, but I have!"

"What?" he asked.

"When Clarissa first came to see me she brought a letter he'd written her. It was more like a list of rules for his wife. A horrible thing. She left it and I forgot all about it. It's between the leaves of *Self-Control*."

"Remarkably inappropriate," said Lucien. "We'll send it over and trust Nicholas to handle the rest of it. If you don't mind, Nicholas."

"Not at all," he replied. "There's little to connect me to Deveril."

"And what's more," said Beth, "once this succeeds, it should make sure Clarissa keeps the secret. To let it out would lose her the fortune."

Lucien looked at her and shook his head. "You seem to have lost all moral scruples," he said. "A case of galloping depravity if ever I saw one."

Beth couldn't help but smile at the memories his words evoked, and she saw him take a sudden breath. "Having settled this unholy pact, Beth," he said quickly, "we're leaving." To Nicholas he said, "We'll send over the handwriting."

Nicholas and Eleanor walked them to the door. "Mad adventures suit you both," Nicholas said and yet Beth was sure he had seen the mark on her face and interpreted it truly. In dismissing it, of course, he was quite correct. It was a mischance along the way, nothing more.

"On the whole," said Lucien, "I think I prefer a quiet life. I died a hundred deaths yesterday after seeing Beth sitting there with a pistol trained on her."

"Love can be the very devil, can't it?" Nicholas said, wrapping an arm around his wife.

"But on the whole, it's all it's cracked up to be," said Lucien, drawing Beth to him, "once one's got the knots worked out, that is."

"Have I been such a tangle for you, Lucien?" Beth inquired solicitously.

"I have been thoroughly entangled," he said with a warm look.

There was a sharp rap at the door.

Nicholas opened it and a lad shoved a paper at him. "There you are, guv." The boy ran off to make his other ordered deliveries of the special edition.

They were all abruptly sobered. Nicholas looked at the paper then up at Beth and Lucien. "Do you want to know?"

"Of course," said Lucien.

They went back into the drawing room. Silence fell. Nicholas opened the paper and scanned the page. "God, what a list," he muttered. "And the damned thing is it can't be complete . . ." He ran his eyes over the fine print then stopped, as if he couldn't quite believe his eyes.

Then, "Dare," he said.

He passed the paper over to Hal Beaumont and went to stare out the window. Eleanor joined him and after a moment he drew her to him, and she rested her head on his shoulder.

Beth looked at Lucien, a very sober Lucien. She reached out and took his hand. She'd only known the lighthearted young man slightly. He'd been the one who had once tried to build a champagne fountain. She remembered dancing with him at her betrothal ball. "I'm sorry," she said softly. It was inadequate, but it was all she could think to say.

He squeezed her hand. "Another sacrifice. He wanted so much to be part of it . . ." He looked at Hal. "Are there any more?"

"Many, many more," said Hal, grim faced. "I'm sorry. I know too many of these fellows. I don't see Con." He passed the paper blindly to Stephen Ball and hid his face in his hand. After a moment he looked up. "Do you think . . . Would Blanche turn me from the door?"

"No," said Lucien.

Hal walked out.

Stephen said, "I don't think Con's name is here. Or Leander. Simon's in Canada anyway. As Nicholas said, the list can't be complete but there's hope." He passed the paper on to Miles Cavanagh.

Nicholas came back and poured wine for all, making it clear he was about to propose a toast. Everyone stood. "The Company of Rogues is now nine," he said soberly. He raised his glass. "To all the fallen: may they be young forever in heaven. To all the wounded: may they have strength and heal. To all the bereaved: may they feel joy again. And please God," he added quietly, "may there one day be an end to war."

He drained his glass and sent it smashing into the empty fireplace. Everyone followed suit, even Beth, though she was shocked by the moment.

Soon after she and Lucien slipped out of the house to walk home. The streets were still vibrant with the delirium of victory but every now and then Beth saw a face as sober as theirs.

"It may not be the end of war," she said tentatively, "but it surely is the end of this war."

"I should have been there," Lucien said and quoted again the words from Henry V. " 'And gentlemen in England now abed / Shall think themselves accursed they were not here, / And hold their manhoods cheap . . .' Not for glory," he said with a sigh. "I don't know if there was any glory. It's just that I should have been there. And to hell with the pride of the de Vaux."

Beth felt helpless in the face of this grief, felt almost as if he was shutting her out. Acting on instinct, as soon as they were in Belcraven House she said, "Let's go to my rooms."

Once there she sat on the sofa and drew him down beside her. "Tell me about him."

And so he did. Eyes closed, resting in her arms, he recalled for her the whole story of the Company of Rogues. How Nicholas Delaney, already a leader at thirteen, had gathered together some boys to be a mutual protection society with vague overtones of the Knights of the Round Table, which was why they'd stopped at twelve members.

"We wanted to call ourselves the Golden Knights, I think," Lucien said with a smile, "but Nick said we weren't there to protect the weak and innocent but to protect ourselves. And so we became the Company of Rogues. Which was pretty apt. The tricks we used to get up to . . ."

He went on to describe their tricks—some acts of revenge for cruelty done to one of the members but many just very inventive mischief. "We had a rule—I'm sure it was Nick's doing—that we couldn't use the Company to evade just punishment. I seem to remember him saying it was necessary to learn not to get caught, but if we were caught we had to take our medicine. God, when I think of some of the floggings. . . . Do you think it toughens us into mighty warriors?"

Beth stroked his hair. "I don't know, love."

"Dare," he said. "Dare could take the worst beating with a smile. Afterwards he'd howl, but at the time he'd keep this silly smile on his face. It used to drive the masters wild. I suppose he smiled . . ." After a moment he went on. "There's nine of us now, assuming Con's all right. Allan Ingram followed his father into the Navy straight from Harrow. He was killed three years ago. A fight with a Yankee ship. Roger Merryhew died of wounds he received at Corunna. Leander—he's Lord Haybridge—he's with the guards. He must have been at this battle of Waterloo."

"His name wasn't on the list," Beth reminded him.

"The lists aren't complete, and they give scarcely any of the wounded. He could have lost a limb, been blinded . . ."

They lapsed into silence. Beth found herself pondering the business of the toy soldier. Eleanor had reported Nicholas's comment that there was no reason his daughter shouldn't grow up to be a soldier. It was clear that Nicholas Delaney had no fondness for war, so why would he say such a thing? Because it was a consequence of the equality of the sexes he obviously believed in. Beth found herself chilled by that implication which had never been addressed by Mary Wollstonecraft.

Lucien sat up and buried his head in his hands. "I'm sorry, Beth, I think I want to go back to Lauriston Street. Apart from anything else, there's still this Deveril business to be taken care of. Do you mind?"

"Of course not." She understood the Company's need to be together. She went and found Deveril's letter and gave it to him. But then she found she didn't want to be left behind. Somewhat hesitantly she asked, "May I come with you?"

"Of course. You're a member by marriage, and it is your plan."

They found the Delaney household returned to normal, a rather sober normal, but normal all the same. Eleanor was nowhere to be seen. Nicholas, Francis, Miles, Stephen, and Peter were around the dining table discussing their plans. Nicholas smiled when they came in. Beth thought it was significant that he had a sleeping baby in his arms. She thought Arabel was the magic key in this house.

"You have the letter? Excellent. I'll take it to my clever friend shortly, then all we have to do is fight over who gets the fun of breaking and entering."

It was Miles Cavanagh, the gingery Irishman, who said, "I think we should rule out married men for a start."

Peter Lavering eyed him. "I think we should rule out foreigners."

The Irishman's eyes flashed. "Ah, if only Ireland were a foreign land."

"No politics today, please," said Stephen Ball. "I get enough of the Irish Question on the floor."

Nicholas spoke up. "With Amy due to have the baby any day, Peter, we can't involve you in anything. Besides which," he added, "you aren't a member."

Peter looked belligerently uncomfortable. "It ain't my fault my family always goes to Winchester."

Nicholas smiled apologetically. "I'm sorry. You are, of course, a full honorary member. But you're still not getting involved in this. I missed Arabel's birth, and I have strong feelings on the subject. Stephen, you're not coming either. If anything goes wrong we may need your influence—"

Eleanor popped into the room. " 'Ware servants!"

A few moments later Hollygirt and a maid came in to lay out a cold collation, tea, and ale. When the servants had left and the food was being passed around, they continued the discussion.

"If I'm proscribed," said Sir Stephen, "then I think Francis should be, too. He's a member of the Lords though he rarely takes advantage of it."

Lord Middlethorpe said, "Stubble it, Steve."

Nicholas shook his head. "We only need one to plant the will. The rest will be to guard and distract—" He broke off at the sound of the knocker.

In a moment the door opened and Hal ushered Blanche into the room. A rather tense and uneasy Blanche. "He would insist that I come," she said.

Eleanor came forward. "You must be Mrs. Hardcastle. You're very welcome."

Nicholas said, "Yes, indeed. Come join us at the table."

Hal and the bemused White Dove were soon seated in the circle. Blanche looked at Nicholas with a slight frown. "We met before last night," she said. "About a year ago." There was clearly some significance to this. Almost a challenge.

"Yes, I know," Nicholas said easily. "I was with Thérèse Bellaire."

Blanche glanced at Eleanor, and Eleanor smiled. "It's all right, Mrs. Hardcastle, I know all about it."

Blanche's brows rose. Nicholas said dryly, "Not quite all about it." Eleanor looked startled. "Go on," said Nicholas.

Beth looked between the two of them, wondering what was going on.

Hal said to the company as a whole, "She was fermenting all these strange ideas, so I thought she'd better come and get them off her chest. Anyway, she may be able to help us."

Blanche flushed but faced Nicholas resolutely, "You were also there with Deveril."

It was Beth's turn to stare at Nicholas. A more unbelievable acquaintanceship was impossible to imagine.

"Not quite," said Nicholas. "He was there with Thérèse as was I. I was definitely not with him."

"Strange company all the same."

"You were there, too."

"A mistake. I left quickly."

"And I stayed there all night." There was something distinctly bleak in his voice but then he looked down at the baby and gently smoothed her fuzzy hair. "You think my past makes me unsuited to take this business in hand?" he queried, looking up again. "On the contrary."

Blanche studied him thoughtfully for a moment and then nodded. "I see. Very well. How can I help?"

Beth hadn't the faintest notion what that had all been about and after a glance at Lucien's wooden face suspected she was never going to find out. This time last year, however, Eleanor must have been pregnant with Arabel. It seemed unbelievable that Nicholas Delaney had been consorting with a whore at that time, particularly one who counted Lord Deveril as an intimate.

Eleanor did not seem disturbed, and Nicholas picked up their planning. "Are you on stage tonight?" he asked Blanche.

"No."

"You said you had lines to learn for tonight," Lucien interrupted with a teasing smile.

"I lied," said Blanche pertly, then turned back to Nicholas. "What can I do?"

He grinned. "Do you think you could play the part of a common whore?"

Blanche grinned back. "Difficult," she said, "but I am an actress, after all. What do I do?"

"Distract."

She chuckled. "I think I can manage that."

Beth took her courage in both hands. "I want to play a part, too," she said. "Surely two whores will be better than one."

"Over my dead body!" Lucien exploded.

"That can be arranged," Beth retorted.

Lucien opened his mouth and took a deep breath. "It's out of the question, Beth," he said more moderately. "You're not an actress."

"I was always very competent in theatricals."

"That is hardly the same thing."

Beth fixed him with a cold eye. "Lucien de Vaux, either you are implying I am too delicate a creature to take part in this adventure, or you think that Blanche is too coarse to care about. Which?"

Random seating had placed him between Beth and Blanche,

and he looked between them and sunk his head in his hands. "I don't believe this is happening."

There was a wave of laughter, but Beth could see some of the men were scandalized by her behavior. Nicholas, however, said, "If you want to come, Beth, you're welcome. Eleanor?"

Eleanor's eyes widened. "Will you think me very tame if I say no?"

"Of course not." He looked at Blanche and Beth. "If the will is not to be questioned there must be no hint of strange goings-on at Deveril's house, but there may still be a couple of his men there. If we're lucky they'll have taken his absence as a chance to go out and join the fun, but he was a hard master who paid well for obedience, so we can't depend on it. Deveril was in the habit of bringing in women for himself and his men. You will turn up in that guise and keep them occupied. It should only be for a matter of minutes."

"How do we get out without raising suspicion?" Blanche asked.

"Your protectors will turn up and drag you out. You see, you have arranged this little bit of business for yourself and deprived them of their cut."

Lucien looked up sternly. "In that case, I am one of them."

"Of course. And Miles."

Beth raised a problem. "Won't this little foray be seen as suspicious if the will is questioned?"

"Unlikely. The scenario's not unlikely and with luck the men will be off as soon as Deveril's death is discovered. The beauty of your plan, Beth, is that no one has a pressing cause to investigate anything. Besides, if questions are asked, the doxies will never have penetrated into the upper floors of the house. All we're trying to avoid here is bodies or an obvious break-in."

Nicholas looked at Francis and Hal. "You two have the boring job of hanging about in the street as your normal selves ready to help if need be."

They didn't look too happy at being cut out of the action but agreed.

Nicholas addressed Lucien and Miles. "We're all dressing

as the great unwashed. I'll get the clothes. We'll meet at Tom Holloway's to change, but try to turn up there inconspicuously. You, in particular, Luce, tend to glitter."

"How can you say that," Lucien demanded, "when you think of my low tastes?" He cast a baleful look at both his mistress and his wife.

Beth giggled.

"What time?" Miles asked.

"We'll meet at nine. It'll be growing dark and the streets should be lively with impromptu celebrations." He looked at Beth and Blanche. "Make sure you can't be recognized. I don't want to have to kill the men if I can help it."

Beth was startled at how easily she believed him capable of killing when required. She was beginning to wish she'd not, volunteered, but it was too late now.

Blanche nodded. "I'll get wigs from the theater and paint. Anything else we're likely to need?"

Throughout the following discussion, Beth was aware of Lucien's silence. If he was *that* angry, why had he not made a stronger objection? What would she have done if he had made a stronger objection?

Soon Beth and Lucien were walking back to Marlborough Square. He didn't speak, and Beth didn't try to make conversation. However, he followed her into her boudoir.

Beth looked at him nervously. He wasn't in a rage but neither was he happy. He ran a hand through his hair. "I would like to be allowed to keep you safe," he said.

Beth faced up to him. "I can't live in a gilded cage, Lucien."

"There is a lot of ground between a gilded cage and the gutter," he said angrily, "and that is where you're going tonight. You remember Deveril's henchmen. What if something goes wrong? What if it takes time for us to intervene?"

Beth hadn't really thought it through that far, and she swallowed even as she stuck to her guns. "It is not right that Blanche be asked to do things I am not asked to do."

"For God's sake, Blanche is a whore!" he exploded. "She's a gem and I love her—in a platonic way these days, of course—but she worked her way to London on her back and bought her way into the theater the same way. Now she depends on her acting for her livelihood, but she's seen and done things you can't even imagine!"

"With you, no doubt," Beth snapped.

"Yes, sometimes!"

"I'm sure I'm a very boring lover compared to her! I'm sure you'd rather go off tonight and adventure with her and leave me safe here at home to ply my needle!"

"Yes, I would!"

Beth decided *she'd* like to hit *him* and clenched her fists. "Well, I won't."

He glared at her. "Fine. Just remember I warned you!" With that he slammed out of the room with a reverberating crash.

Chapter Twenty-three

Beth put a horrified hand over her mouth. He'd wanted them to have a flaming row, and they certainly had. And he'd never shown any sign of hitting her. But, Lord, he was angry and very frightened for her. Was she being an utter fool?

But she didn't see why Blanche should be exposed to risk while she was protected. And, she admitted, she wanted a part in the working out of her plan. She trusted Nicholas Delaney.

Then she remembered Nicholas's wife had declined the adventure and that brought to mind that strange confrontation between Blanche and Nicholas. He had once been an intimate of Deveril's . . .

Oh Lord, she had tangled herself in a mess, but it was impossible to back down now.

Beth went down to dinner with the duke and duchess that evening, for the first time in days, and found Lucien there, too. He treated her in the same reserved manner that had marked the days before their marriage.

The duke and duchess did not seem to notice. "You are looking so much better, Elizabeth," the duchess declared. "But surely that is a bruise upon your face?"

"I fell against a table, *Maman*," said Beth. "It is nothing."

"You must be more careful, *ma chère*. And is it not good news about the battle? Perhaps my poor France can finally know peace."

Talk over the meal was all of the battle. Lucien joined in

amiably and said nothing of Lord Darius or his other friends. Beth decided she hated this cool-headed courtesy of his.

Afterwards the duke and duchess had a number of separate engagements. Lucien and Beth said they were spending the evening at home. The duchess clearly thought this very romantic.

Lucien accompanied Beth to her rooms. "Dress simply and I'll escort you."

Beth frowned at his cold manner but went into her dressing room and dressed again in her darkest old clothes. When she was ready she walked through into his dressing room with only the briefest of knocks. He was bare-chested and just about to pull on a shirt. Beth looked wistfully at his splendid torso and thought how they could be spending the evening. But no, he would still be going out.

"How would you like it if I just walked in on you?" he asked as he pulled the shirt over his head.

"I wouldn't mind."

Something warm flashed in his eyes, but then he concealed it. Beth was heartened, though. He wasn't as cold as he was pretending. She went to hand him his jacket. "It's rather fine though, isn't it?"

"Unlike you," he said, "I don't possess any plebeian clothes. We'll just have to hope anyone who sees us thinks me a swell out slumming with the upstairs maid."

"Lucien," said Beth, "this really isn't fair."

He looked at her. "I beg your pardon?"

"You may not be hitting me, but you're punishing me all the same for not doing exactly as you wish."

He turned away to arrange his cravat. "I'm supposed to turn a blind eye to any foolishness that enters your overeducated head?"

"There, see," snapped Beth, sinking into anger again. "How can any human being be overeducated?"

He turned to look at her. "Very well, then. Undereducated. Which is doubtless going to be corrected tonight."

Beth sighed. "I have a right to make my own mistakes, my dear."

"Do you?" he asked coldly, facing the mirror again and finishing an elegant knot with a few deft movements. "You might have a thought to those affected by them. I didn't join the army, because my death would be the end of our line, in law if not in fact. Your death would be just as disastrous."

"I hardly think our lives are at risk. And if they are you're risking yours tonight. You just don't want me involved in anything unpleasant."

He sighed and looked at her, then pulled her roughly against him. "Right. I don't want you involved in anything unpleasant. I don't want any other man mauling you, even for a moment. Don't do this, Beth."

Beth snuggled against him. Marriage was a funny business. Endless compromises. "I want to come," she said at last. "But if Blanche can handle the men on her own, I'll let her."

He pushed her back to study her. "You promise?"

"I promise."

He smiled. "Thank you. I confess, I wouldn't have wanted to miss this either." He gave her a steamy, ravaging kiss. "I must admit, too, I'm quite curious to see what you look like as a whore."

Later, when she looked at herself in the mirror in Blanche's temporary dressing room at Tom Holloway's rooms, Beth wondered what Lucien would think. She was sure he'd blow up again. Certainly Aunt Emma would have a fit of the vapors if she saw Beth now.

A brassy blond wig flowed over her shoulders and her face was so vividly painted there was no question of anyone seeing her bruise. Her skirts were halfway up her calves and her bodice was so low it barely skimmed her nipples.

"Lord above," she muttered.

Blanche, who was still in a wrap and beginning to apply her own makeup, grinned. "Getting stage fright?"

"A little."

"You don't have to come. I can manage."

Remembering Deveril, Beth had no doubt of that. "I have to go through with it."

Blanche smiled her understanding.

"Blanche," said Beth, "what was all that about with Nicholas Delaney?"

Blanche looked over with heavily darkened lashes and brows which made her look vulgar but very enticing. "I don't know."

"But did you really meet him with a whore?"

"Yes." Blanche enlarged her lips with scarlet.

"He must have been married then."

"I suppose so.

"Am I giving in to vulgar curiosity?" Beth asked.

Blanche grinned. "Yes. Irresistible vice, isn't it?"

Beth couldn't resist a few more questions. "Just tell me, was Lucien there, and why did you leave?"

Blanche considered her face and then skillfully applied a little more rouge. "No, Lucien wasn't there. He was out of town. I thought it was just a social evening among the demimonde. It was a ballum runcum."

"What on earth is that?"

"A naked ball," said Blanche prosaically. "At least, the women are naked. Most of the men keep their clothes on most of the time."

Beth stared at Blanche, having difficulty even imagining such a thing. "You're on Lucien's side, aren't you? You don't think I should be here."

Blanche turned to face her. "I think you have every right to make your own choice, but if you enter this world, Beth, even for an evening, don't think it's a game."

Beth looked at herself in the mirror and thought back with disbelief to the days when she'd fought battles as to whether to wear a cap or not. But she was going through with it. It would, she supposed, be a valuable extension of her education.

When she turned resolutely towards the door, Blanche said, "Good for you."

At the sight of her, Lucien briefly covered his eyes but then he grabbed her and pulled her into his lap. "How much for an evening's tumble, Molly?" His eyes were laughing, not angry. When she pushed at him, he said, "Come on, I think you should get into your part."

"Charge 'im at least ten guineas, ducks," said Blanche in a heavy accent. Beth looked over at the White Dove and gasped. The actress had obviously been easy on her.

The high dressed dark wig and vivid face-paint were vulgar but it was Blanche's gown which was outrageous. Stays pushed her full breasts up outlandishly high and her bodice was all but transparent. Beneath it, her nipples were rouged scarlet. She looked nothing like the ethereal White Dove.

Hal Beaumont took a deep breath and stepped over to the actress. "Is that your price too, you shameless hussy?"

Blanche placed a hand on her hip and somehow managed to thrust her breasts a little higher. "I'll give a discount to a wounded soldier, luv."

"Done," he said and grasped her chin to kiss her.

Beth hid her face in Lucien's jacket. "Will it set a terrible precedent if I admit you have been right."

He held her tight. "I promise not to crow. Do you want to go home?"

Beth got her courage back. "No. But if I cling to you, don't blame me."

Lucien, Nicholas, Miles, and Tom Holloway were all dressed in grimy frieze and cheap finery, their faces dirtied. They'd greased their hair, too, and Lucien, who didn't seem to lose his aristocratic elegance no matter what they did, also wore a battered, low-brimmed hat to shade his face.

They were all in fine fettle, bubbling with excitement. Overgrown schoolboys, Beth thought, but she couldn't help catch their enthusiasm. Once out on the street she began to feel her part as if she was an actress walking onto a stage. "I think this comes easier than playing the marchioness," she said saucily to Lucien.

"Just remember this isn't your true calling."

"Swing your hips a bit more," Blanche said quietly. "You're walking like a nun."

Beth studied Blanche and then began the same kind of swaying walk, hand on hip, light on the feet, moving her shoulders to greatest effect.

"Hey, lovely!" called a roughly dressed passerby. "Want better company than you've got there?"

Beth winked at the man over her shoulder. Lucien dragged her against his side. "Gerout of it!" he snarled at the man, showing a fist. The man hurried on his way.

Nicholas was almost helpless with laughter. "We are supposed to be on serious business, my friends. Beth, you can come out and play harlot another night." He took Beth's other arm and hurried them along. Blanche had Miles and Tom Holloway to escort her as Hal had reluctantly split to do his duty with Francis at the front of Deveril's Grosvenor Square house.

As they had expected, the streets were already filling with merry crowds celebrating the victory. All the buildings bore extra lights though they hadn't had time to mount proper festive illuminations. Drink was flowing but the mood had not yet turned wild.

Beth had never been involved in such an atmosphere in her life and, safe between Nicholas and Lucien, she loved it. When the crowd began to sing "God Save the King," she joined in lustily.

She laughed up at Lucien. He grinned at her, swung her out of Nicholas's grasp, and into a thorough kiss. The crowd shouted and whistled its approval. Beth was left feeling dizzy and very much that she wished they were in a more private place.

The crowds thinned as they got closer to Grosvenor Square. There had been riots here earlier in the year over the unpopular Corn Laws but the mob had no reason for anger tonight, no reason to seek out the homes of unpopular ministers and break the windows.

Such a disreputable group as they were gained a few funny looks in Mayfair, but the pavement was still supposed to be free to anyone, and so they strolled along without interference.

Near Deveril's house they passed Hal and Francis, every inch the gentlemen and apparently chatting while waiting for a friend or a carriage. Francis held up two fingers as they passed. He thought there were two men in the dark house.

They continued to Upper Brook Street, where Miles actually had his rooms, then slipped down the alley to Blackman's Mews, which ran behind Deveril's house. It was dark and slimy underfoot.

Nicholas seemed to have a mental map, for he stopped by a path leading up to a house. "All right," he said. "You go up first, Blanche, and get in there. They'll be cautious about opening the door—Deveril was a tough master and they don't know he's dead—but they'll open for you quickly enough. Keep them distracted and make a lot of noise. I'll climb on the roof of the scullery and in the upstairs window. It shouldn't take more than a minute or two to do the job. Lucien and Miles will watch near the kitchen, and Tom will watch back here with Beth. All right?"

Beth grasped her courage and pulled away from Lucien. "I think I should go, too." She carried on over his protests. "Two on two will be so much easier, and it's only for a few minutes. Please, Lucien?"

After a moment Lucien sighed. "You're determined to have your piece of the glory, aren't you? Go on then."

Beth recognized the extent of his sacrifice and gave him a hug. Then she followed Blanche up to the back door while Lucien and Miles slipped along behind them.

Lucien whispered, "Scream for help if you need it. Either of you." Then he and Miles moved off to the side to conceal themselves.

Blanche and Beth could see through a lighted sunken window into the kitchen. Two men were sitting at a table playing with greasy cards and drinking what looked to be a good wine.

"While the cat's away . . ." Blanche muttered. "At least there's no sign of a gun. Ready?"

The men were rough and dirty and reminded Beth of the two men who had accompanied Deveril, but she nodded firmly. "Ready."

Blanche went down the steps and knocked. They heard a bolt drawn back then the door was opened cautiously by a bearded man with a pistol in his hand. He hadn't been one of the card players. There were three.

"Yeah?" he grunted.

"Well," said Blanche in a heavy accent, "is that any welcome for a lady? I've a mind to share that bottle of wine, luv."

The man relaxed and opened the door a little more but also looked carefully out behind them. "Where did you fall from, me angel?"

"Heaven, of course," said Blanche. "Your master, he ordered us up for your supper, 'andsome."

The man's eyes sharpened. "His lordship? You've seen him?"

"Yesterday, luv. Look," Blanche added with a pout, "are you goin' to let us in? There's other fish in the sea tonight, you know. In fact, I think we should all go out and join the fun."

"Can't, me honey," the man said, adding with a grin, "but you'll certainly make a dull time brighter." He opened the door wide. "Come on in. Hey, lads, come see what his lordship's sent for us!"

The two men threw down their cards. "Bleeding sight for sore eyes," said one who was largely without teeth. His eyes seemed to strip the clothes off both of them.

"Too soddin' right," said the other, flashing a great many very yellow teeth.

Beth found herself frozen.

Blanche sauntered over to the table, and the two card players stared at her, mesmerized. "Wot a lucky girl I am, then," she purred, "to have such fine fellows smilin' at me."

Beth gathered her wits and quickly entered the kitchen and shut the door. The third man turned and leered at her, putting down his gun. As she'd hoped, he didn't remember to shoot the bolt again. Lucien could get in if things turned bad.

She smiled at the bearded man, though she feared it came out a bit sickly. "Hello, sweetheart."

He reached out to grab her, but she sidestepped him. "Don't I get some wine, 'andsome?"

He grabbed her anyway. "Pay a kiss for it," he said.

His mouth was slack and wet and sour. Beth was sure he wasn't as foul as Lord Deveril, but she could quite see how Clarissa had thrown up her breakfast. She commanded her rebellious stomach to be still and writhed about as if she were enjoying it. She hoped Lucien couldn't see this, or he'd be fit to kill.

When the man's mouth freed hers, he chuckled. "You're a proper spicy dish, aren't yer me little molisher? Come on, Pepper, and have your wine. There's plenty more where that came from." He wrapped an arm around her and pulled her to the table where Blanche was skillfully playing one man off against the other with much shrieking and banging about.

Was Nicholas inside? Just to do her bit, Beth staggered and knocked over a stool.

Her escort pulled her straight. "You're well on the go already, ain't yer?" He thrust the bottle at her. "Have some more."

They needed to play for time. "Well," said Beth with false refinement, "hi ham more haccustomed to drink from hay glass, sir."

Blanche shrieked with laughter. "Right spark, she is. We call her 'the duchess!' "

All the men roared, and the black bearded one casually tweaked one of Beth's nipples. Fortunately he took Beth's outraged squeal as part of her act. "Right away, Yer Grace. The best crystal, do yer?" To Beth's horror he went out of the room to get it. Was he going upstairs? Nicholas was up there somewhere. She ran after him.

The man turned, then grinned knowingly. "So that's yer game, Duchess. Yer a smart one and no mistake. Fancy a nice comfy bedroom, do yer? Come on, then."

Beth glanced around frantically. They were at the bottom of the stairs leading up to the ground floor, and the wall was lined with shelves holding bowls and pots. The noise from the kitchen was deadened by the closed door. She could hear nothing from above. Nicholas must surely be in, which was the noisy part. If necessary she'd break some pottery.

"I think I'd better go back to me sister" she said coyly. "She'll get awful jealous."

"Let her, Pepper. Perhaps I'll give her a turn upstairs, too. Come on." He grabbed her wrist in a beefy paw.

"Let go!" Beth squealed. She suddenly remembered that they weren't supposed to go upstairs and dug in her heels.

"Wot the hell's up wiv you?" the man growled. "Don't you play off your airs and graces wiv Tom Cross, Duchess." He yanked her to him, turned her over his knee, and landed two stinging blows on her behind, which her flimsy skirts did little to cushion. Beth saw red.

"You disgusting man!" she shrieked as soon as she was upright. She grabbed at the shelves. The first thing that came to hand was a small iron skillet. She crowned him with it with all her might. His eyes crossed, and he collapsed down at the base of the stairs.

"Bravo!" declared Nicholas from the top of the stairs. "I was beginning to think you'd need rescuing."

"I rescued myself," said Beth, aware of a flicker of pride. She rubbed her behind and rearranged her bodice. "Are you finished?"

"Yes. I'll give Lucien the signal and you can get out of here."

"What about him?" asked Beth, pointing to her victim. "Won't he spoil the plan?"

"No, he won't be surprised to find you crowned him. But he won't keep long either. Get on your way." He disappeared back to the upper reaches.

Beth put on a brazen face and sauntered back into the kitchen. Blanche was on the toothy man's knee, feeding him wine from the bottle. The other man was hovering impatiently. He turned quickly. "Where's Tom?" He wasn't so much suspicious as wary of poaching on the other man's property.

"Gone to get me a glass, of course," said Beth saucily. The man came at her. Beth backed up. She really couldn't take another mauling kiss. She looked around for a weapon—

Lucien and Miles burst in. "Wot the hell you doing, Molly?" Lucien roared, grabbing Beth.

Blanche leapt off the toothy man's knee with an impressive squeal of fear. "Help!" she cried. She tried to hide behind the toothless one, but he didn't look keen to fight.

"Who're these then?" he asked.

"We're the ones wot say where they go and who they go with, that's who," snarled Lucien. He dragged Beth towards the door. "I'll give you wot for when I get you home!"

Beth started to wail. Miles grabbed Blanche without hindrance from either of her would-be swains. As they got to the door, Beth saw the pistol Tom had put down and grabbed it. Then they were out.

As they ran through the back yard towards the mews, there was a roared obscenity. "No little drap's going to do fer me!"

"Tom!" Beth gasped and thrust the pistol into Lucien's hands.

"What have you been up to?" he drawled as he quickly checked it. A glance back showed the three guards in the doorway.

"Come on!" whispered Nicholas.

They all ran into the mews, heading for the exit into Upper Brook Street where Tom Holloway was waiting with a carriage in case they needed a quick escape. A carriage entered the mews from that direction.

"Hell," muttered Nicholas.

They looked back. Deveril's bullies were coming into the mews and at least one had a pistol. With a curse, Nicholas flattened himself against the wall out of sight. Lucien waved the pistol, and the men hesitated.

It seemed an age they were frozen there. Would the men raise an alarm? Or were they too disreputable to call attention to themselves? Would the coachman try to stop them if they ran past him?

"Scylla and Charybdis," murmured Lucien lightly. "Can we take them?"

"Psst!"

They all looked in astonishment at the nearest carriage house. A small figure appeared and beckoned urgently.

"Robin!" Beth gasped.

"Come on!" the boy whispered and beckoned again.

After a moment they ran towards him, Nicholas carefully moving behind them.

"Stop them!" bellowed Tom. "Thievery!"

"Oy there!" yelled the coachman. "Stop!"

They were in the coachhouse. "Follow me," said Robin and darted through the vehicles towards the back.

Without question, they obeyed. He led them out an unglazed window and into a narrow gap between the coach house and the wall of a nearby house. It was clogged with weeds, but they trampled along it after the boy. He stopped and disappeared through the wooden wall into another building of the mews. When Beth got there she found two planks were missing, allowing enough space for a person to squeeze by.

They were in a stable with three horses standing in stalls. The beasts shifted lazily. In the distance they could here the bangs and voices of their pursuers.

Robin silently pointed to a ladder. They crept over and climbed up to find themselves in unused sleeping quarters, dusty and almost pitch dark. Robin moved the ladder over against a wall then reached up. Getting his meaning, Lucien leaned down, with Nicholas and Miles anchoring his legs, and hoisted the boy up.

They shut the hatch and collapsed in the dark to get their breath back. Beth could hear someone, probably Nicholas, trying not to laugh. They could hear faint voices but none nearby.

There were two windows. They were very dirty but they let in some light and gradually Beth's eyes adjusted so that she could see a little. She wriggled over into Lucien's arms.

"Exciting enough for you?" he murmured.

She laughed softly. "Truth to tell, I'm enjoying myself."

"So I gather. What did you do to poor Tom?"

"Knocked him out with a skillet. He was taking liberties."

He stifled his laughter against her shoulder.

"To what do we owe the pleasure of this rescue?" asked Nicholas of Robin.

"Oh, allow me to introduce you," said Lucien. "Nicholas Delaney, Robin Babson. What on earth are you doing here, Robin?"

"Looking after you," said Robin cockily. "Seemed too good of a night to be tucked up asleep, what with the battle and all, so I sneaked out to see some fun. When I saw you doing the same, I reckoned there was something up. You could have knocked me down wiv a feather when I saw you all togged up like that." He looked at Beth and rolled his eyes. She giggled.

"I were behind you all the way here, and you never knew a thing. I knew you'd end up needing help. I heard a bit of your plan, and while you were striking the dub I sneaked around this place."

"Well done indeed, said Nicholas. "Wellington couldn't have done better. We shall see you rewarded. If, that is, you can be relied on to stand mum." There was an undeniable note of steel in his voice.

"You can depend on me, milord!"

"Plain Mr. Delaney. What do you want?"

"What?"

"What reward do you want?"

Robin looked blank. Beth quickly said, "I think he should be allowed to choose what profession he wants to train for."

"He's learning stable work," said Lucien with the clear meaning that there was no other job on earth worth having.

Beth could see that Robin was torn between a desire to be away from horses and a fear of being away from his idol. "Perhaps you'd prefer an inside job, Robin," she prompted gently.

"Perhaps," he muttered.

"I have a fancy to have a page. Of course, you'd have to spend a lot of time with me and wear a fancy livery . . ."

He glanced up, wary but bright-eyed. "Might not mind."

"And I'm afraid I would have to insist that you learn to read and write and all kinds of other things if you are truly to be of use to me."

"Do you think I could?" he asked uncertainly.

"I'm sure you could. After all, you can't stay a page forever. You may want to become a footman, or even a butler one day."

"Like old Morrisby?" he asked, as wide-eyed as if he'd been offered the crown of England.

"Exactly. So if you cared for such a change . . ."

"Yes, please," he said with careful good manners.

Lucien ruffled his hair. "Ambitious little imp, aren't you?

Now, if you want this glorious future, you'd better get us all safe away from here or we'll be too busy picking hemp to assist you."

"Garn!" scoffed the boy, grinning at them. "Not but what you'd have been in a bumblebroth without me. Wait here."

He slithered over to the hatch and raised it a crack. Then he pushed it up carefully and swung himself down. Beth gasped at the drop, but they heard him scamper away.

In a few moments he was back. "All's bowman. Here's the jacob."

Within minutes they were all safely down and the hatch closed. Lucien replaced the ladder against the wall. "There's a back way out the mews," said the boy. "Follow me."

All went sweetly and soon they were on Park Street and working their way, a group out for a lark, to Grosvener Square to tell Hal and Francis all was done. They turned onto the square and froze.

Hal and Francis were there, talking to the First Minister of England and the Duke of Belcraven. Francis looked over and gave a wild look.

The duke caught it. He turned, curious. His eyes passed blankly over the ill-favored group, paused thoughtfully on Robin, then traveled back.

Beth felt herself color up and hoped her garish face paint hid it. She could sense Lucien fighting laughter. He got enough voice to say, "Evenin' guv. And a grand night for England!"

"Indeed it is," said the duke and looked at Robin. "Don't I know you, boy?"

"Who, me, guv? Nah." True to his part he walked boldly forward. "Got a sixpence, mister, to help toast the duke?"

Blanche, the other professional, swayed forward. "Give me a shilling and I'll sing a ditty."

At the sight of her, the Earl of Liverpool grew red in the face. "Begone with you, you shameless hussy!"

But the duke laid a hand on his arm. "They are only out rejoicing on this great day, Liverpool. He produced a dollar coin. "Let me see. . . . I wonder who is your leader."

Without hesitation, Lucien dragged Nicholas forward. "Here he is, milord."

"I might have known," murmured the duke and passed over the five-shilling piece. "Be sure everyone gets a bumper, my good man."

Nicholas groveled and touched his forelock. "Surely, Yer Honor. God bless your lordship. Long life to Your Grace . . ."

"Enough!" declared the duke, but he was clearly struggling to keep a straight face. "Be on your way." His gaze wandered over them again, pausing appreciatively on Blanche and even more so on Beth. Quite clearly, he winked. "After all," he said to the disapproving Lord Liverpool, "on such a night as this, are not all the people of England one big happy family?"

"This rabble is not family of mine," said the earl haughtily. "I doubt they are even voters."

"Don't be so harsh. Who knows how even a small change in fortune could transform them." He addressed the group once more. "Can I not depend upon it that you will improve yourselves rapidly, my good people?"

They all chorused their agreement.

"I do not think it beyond possibility, Liverpool, that one day soon these promising fellows could aspire even to a house in Grosvenor Square."

"You're mad!" said Liverpool. "Come along, Belcraven. The horses are standing."

With a smile, the duke followed.

Beth called after him. "No reason a lady can't aspire to live in Grosvenor Square too, Yer Honor!"

He turned back, laughing. "No reason at all. But you're a saucy piece, aren't you?"

Beth cocked her hip and ogled him. "I'm the apple of me father's eye."

"I don't doubt it," the duke said, and his glance encompassed both Beth and Lucien. "I don't doubt it at all."

Liverpool's carriage rolled away, and they all, including Hal and Francis made haste to Upper Brook Street, where an agitated Tom Holloway was waiting with a carriage. There were two. Eleanor waved out of the second.

Nicholas, Lucien, Beth, and Robin scrambled into Eleanor's hackney while Hal, Miles, Francis, and Blanche piled into the one driven by Tom Holloway. A glance back at Deveril's house showed it quiet and dark. The guards had doubtless decided, no harm having been done except to Tom's head, not to cause a commotion.

"What are you doing here?" Nicholas asked Eleanor as he drew her into his arms.

"I didn't want to miss all the fun. Did you carry it off?"

"Only just. We had to be rescued by this gallant fellow," he said, ruffling Robin's hair. He passed over the dollar. "I think you earned this."

"Thanks, sir!"

"But," said Lucien, "you are not going on the Town to spend it tonight. Promising young men need their sleep."

Robin glowered slightly but muttered, "All right."

"Think, Robin," said Lucien gently. "A change is a change. You're not the same boy. If you came up with any of your old friends now, they'd roll you naked and sell every scrap you owned."

"Reckon you're right, milord," said the boy, much struck. He gave a little sniff. "It's hard, givin' up what a person's used to."

Beth leaned over and put her hand over his. "It is hard, Robin. But life is change, if you want to make anything of it." She smiled at Lucien. "And it is definitely worth it in the end."

Nicholas smiled at his wife. "And here I've been persuaded to settle down."

Eleanor surveyed his rough appearance. "You call this settling down?"

"Tamest of the tame. But we have finished our business and, praise be, can return to Somerset."

They had arrived at Tom Holloway's and went quickly in. When Beth went to change, however, Lucien said, "You could just put your spencer over that dress, since we are going to have to smuggle you into the house anyway."

Beth looked down. She had long since forgotten to be conscious of her exposed state. "I could," she agreed.

Lucien counted out ten guineas and proffered them. Face burning, Beth grinned, took the coins and dropped them down her bodice. She grinned at Nicholas and Eleanor. "I reckon I got to ensure me independence one way or another, eh?"

Lucien bundled up his good clothing and they slipped away, passing Blanche and Hal on the stairs.

"Get the money up front, luv!" called Blanche.

Beth giggled. "Oh, I've certainly 'done that!"

Later, limp and content in Lucien's arms, Beth said, "Can we go back to Hartwell?"

"Yes," said Lucien. "After you've been presented." He caught the protest on her lips with his own. "I've let you play the whore, Beth, and I haven't even asked what Tom did to cause you to wrap a skillet round his head. Now it's time for you to play the marchioness."

Beth snuggled closer to his warm, hard body. "I don't think there's much difference between the two."

"I'll go odds the queen wouldn't agree. You could always borrow Blanche's dress for court and see."

Beth chuckled. "Do they throw the highest aristocracy out for lewd behavior?"

"I'm not at all sure."

Beth ran her hand along the fine contours of his arm. "What's the duke going to say?"

"Nothing, I suspect. You know, I've never seen him laugh like that. He's changed. It's as if we've all changed since you've came among us, Beth."

"For the better?" asked Beth.

"Indubitably. You've been like warm sun on frozen ground. My mother sings, my father laughs. And I . . . I delight in the wit and the strength and the spirit of my friend for life. More men should be as fortunate as I."

"Clever men," said Beth softly, "always will be. And clever women will appreciate a clever man when they meet one.

Celebrate Romance With Two of Today's Hottest Authors

Meagan McKinney

___In the Dark	$6.99US/$8.99CAN	0-8217-6341-5
___The Fortune Hunter	$6.50US/$8.00CAN	0-8217-6037-8
___Gentle from the Night	$5.99US/$7.50CAN	0-8217-5803-9
___A Man to Slay Dragons	$5.99US/$6.99CAN	0-8217-5345-2
___My Wicked Enchantress	$5.99US/$7.50CAN	0-8217-5661-3
___No Choice But Surrender	$5.99US/$7.50CAN	0-8217-5859-4

Meryl Sawyer

___Thunder Island	$6.99US/$8.99CAN	0-8217-6378-4
___Half Moon Bay	$6.50US/$8.00CAN	0-8217-6144-7
___The Hideaway	$5.99US/$7.50CAN	0-8217-5780-6
___Tempting Fate	$6.50US/$8.00CAN	0-8217-5858-6
___Unforgettable	$6.50US/$8.00CAN	0-8217-5564-1